BY THE SAME AUTHOR
published by Ballantine Books

THE HOLE

SOPHIE

A Clock
Without
Hands

A Clock Without Hands

A N O V E L

Guy Burt

BALLANTINE BOOKS
NEW YORK

A Ballantine Book
Published by The Random House Publishing Group

www.ballantinebooks.com

Library of Congress Cataloging-in-Publication Data is available from the publisher upon request.

ISBN 0-345-44656-9

Text design by Meryl Sussman Levavi

Manufactured in the United States of America

First American Edition: October 2004

9 8 7 6 5 4 3 2 1

For Chon

With thanks to:

Jozef Nyeste, for help with the Hungarian;

Dinah Weiner, for believing in me right from the start;

my family, for support of all kinds.

"What do you call a clock without hands?"
CHILDREN'S RIDDLE

clock: trivial name for the pappus of the
dandelion or similar composite flower.
[So called from the child's play of blowing away
the feathered seeds to find "what o'clock it is."]

A Clock
Without
Hands

*A*ltesa is in the rain, the rain starts as the bus rumbles down from the head of the valley towards the coast, fat drops spattering on the window against which I rest my face, and it is still falling when the bus pulls away, tyres hissing on the slick flagstones, leaving me standing on the north side of the square. It is a little after five in the afternoon, and the square is almost deserted. A young man is taking in chairs and tables under the awning of the café-bar across from me: he is the only person I can see. I stand in the partial shelter of a plane tree, the suitcase with the pictures propped against my leg. I see myself for a moment as part of the scene, in the way I sometimes do, and realize I look like someone lost—a middle-aged man who has fallen asleep on his bus and, waking in a panic, jumped off at the wrong stop. An out-of-season tourist who has lost his coach party.

Nothing much has changed. The few shops, the small church with its seventeen white steps. The few streets winding off—no signposts, but I know where each of them goes. The drinking-fountain with the lion's head that sits in the corner opposite the church: Lena's church. On the steps there, the water lies in sheets, not running away, and I remember Lena saying the terraces in the valley are like that. To keep the water. And I remember telling Jamie, to try to satisfy some of his questions about the valley, and I remember him accepting it, soaking the information away into himself, moving on to something different.

When it's sunny, the space around you here is white, all white, capped with blue, and the eye is drawn and caught by the bright scatter of water from the lion's mouth.

Some things are different, I notice. The café is no longer Toni's: the red, cursive script in the window reads *Café Co-Co*, and the chairs and tables now gathered in are plastic. Small details. They feel bright and brash on my eyes, intrusive.

Up close, I know that the lion's face is almost as big as mine; but from a distance he looks small, like a toy or a tame lion. His eyes are dark and sometimes I think he looks sad. The tumble of mane around his face is deep brown, sea-brown, the colour the metal he's made of goes after a long time. It's bronze, I know now; bronze like the sundial on the church wall, and some of the numbers on the gateposts. Like the dandelion clock, too.

"*Signore?*"

I blink. The young man, the waiter from across the square, is right beside me, staring at me with a look that is half amusement, half concern. I wonder for an instant how long he has been there.

"*Signore*, there is no other bus here for a long time. Where is it you want to go?"

He speaks in English, and again there is a little surge of petulance in me. But then I remember how I must look—more so now, with the shoulders of my pale jacket splotched with rainwater, and rain running over my face, standing as if frozen to the spot. I shake my head. "No. I'm not going anywhere. I was just—thinking. I'm all right."

He raises his eyebrows. "Your Italian is excellent," he says, switching languages.

"I used to live here," I say.

"In Italy?"

I can't help smiling a little. His accent gives him away; he comes from the city, not this little town. He is more an outsider than I am. "No," I say. "Here, in Altesa. I grew up here."

"Really?" he says, politely.

I nod. "Before your time, I should think."

"Ah," he says. "Well, come in for a drink some time, yes?"

I glance at the street which leads to the boarding house, and my eyes skip off it to the road leading up out towards the edge of town. "Yes," I say. "Yes, of course," though I doubt I'll have the time.

"And welcome home." He smiles again, and goes back across the square through the gradually thinning rain. When he reaches the awning, he turns, gives me one brief, curious glance before disappearing into the dark doorway of the bar. The square is silent again, except for the rainfall.

I heft the strap of my suitcase across my shoulder and wipe the rain from my face.

Welcome home.

I never meant to come back to Altesa. I thought I had no reason to. When I last left, twenty-six years ago, the place felt hollow: all that had once filled it was gone. I left sure that I could discard it.

Then, a fortnight ago, there's the phone call, and everything changes. Lena has died, a few weeks short of her eighty-fourth birthday. The house is empty now, and there are decisions to be made: whether to sell, to rent it out again, to have work done on it. I know at once that I have to come myself. Max wants me to do it all by phone—get a surveyor in, have the solicitors in Salerno handle everything; but I can't. It's my house, and I shall check it over in person. When I see he's genuinely worried about how much time this will take, I reassure him that there's nothing much to do. Just look things over, sign a few papers. Two or three days; that's all. Besides, I say, it will be good for me to have a break. The past few months have been exhausting. A chance to escape from London and all the endless preparations will do me good. In the end, he relents.

I think about it all on the plane to Naples, and on the train to Salerno, and on the bus all down the forty-mile stretch to the head of the valley: about how I've lied to Max. There's no point my coming here, not really. He's quite right that it could all be handled easily enough over the phone. It's not even that I'm keen to see Altesa again: it's hard to imagine that the hollowness has in any way ebbed over the past twenty-six years. It's none of that. In my suitcase, I have over a hundred and fifty eleven-by-fourteen photographs which are the real reason for this trip. But I can't tell Max that; he'd think I was mad.

I have come here to try to settle myself, and to try to understand. I have the photographs, and I have some time to myself; I hope that out of these two things will come some measure of calm, or comprehension. The house, Altesa, coming back to Italy—it's all really just an excuse to spend some time with the images which I have begun to realize trouble me so deeply.

I can't really explain it, even to myself. I just know it's important, and that I have to resolve it one way or another.

I leave the square behind me. My footsteps are muted by the rain as I walk, and I keep my eyes on the road until the valley starts to open up around me.

The valley is sharp, and Altesa extends about a quarter of the way up it from the sea. The buildings of the town are huddled together between shoulders of land that rise on either side. From the very top of the town, the coast is only an hour's walk away, if you're young. You can go the whole way in bare feet in that time. The beaches are rocky, and there are inlets and coves hidden away which can be reached only by the cliffs, or by scrambling around promontories. In summer, the sea from the cliffs is hugely blue, like deeply fired ceramic, but glittering with motion. Gentle Mediterranean currents guide the shoals of fishes, and underwater the rocks are furred with weed and patterned with constantly moving bands of cool light.

Above the town, the valley steepens, and the road to the north winds to and fro between cracked stone and concrete barriers, some hemming it in from sheer drops, others holding back from it the scree which tumbles from the crumbling sides of the valley. All along, old farming terraces, left now for many years untended, carve regular steps into the landscape—though sometimes wind and rain and weather have eroded them, so that from a distance the lines are blurred or smudged, as if the valley is a drawing in charcoal which has been handled carelessly. Dotted among the terraces are occasional structures: houses with no roofs, or fallen walls, or trees coming up through the empty windows. It looks as though the inhabitants of the valley, once spread throughout its area, have gradually drained down towards the sea over the centuries, leaving these abandoned shells behind them like the high-water marks of a receding tide.

The valley unfolds through the rain as I leave the last of the buildings of the real town behind me. Looking around me for a moment, I am suddenly struck by something—a sense of things scratching at the edges of my awareness, pulling, tugging at me—and I shiver slightly. But perhaps it is just the cold. Although at first the rain seems light and warm, my clothes feel chill now. The tarmac underfoot is stained with thin, watery ochre mud. My shoes too. I concentrate on them as I walk on, counting my steps to myself for a while, shifting the weight of my suitcase across my shoulder: little things to drive away the itchiness in my head. I am short of breath, but I increase my pace, slapping my feet down in the rain and mud until my sides hurt.

The town is behind me now. The only thing between where I am and the emptiness of the high part of the valley is the last straggle of buildings.

There are four of them, settled into a kind of ledge in the side of the valley: big old villas set back from the road a little way. A wall runs along the roadside there, and over it spill the branches of trees from the gardens. The driveways are closed off with wrought-iron gates.

The house I have come to see—the house I grew up in—is the nearest of the four. Its pale pink walls, mottled with shade and rain and age, are just visible from the place I've reached on the road, and I stop for a moment, uncertain. The rain has eased a little more as I've walked, and now it is only a fine drizzle which draws across the valley in gentle billows when caught by the breeze.

I feel a stab of doubt. Do I really want to do this? There isn't the time; I should turn myself around and get back to London at once, before I get—caught up here.

I stand on the road and let the feelings run their course. They are a kind of panic, but I reassure myself that there is nothing to panic about. While this is happening, the house hangs there in front of me in the drizzle as if suspended, until at last all my quick doubts and panics are swallowed up in watching it, seeing how it looks there through the slow gusts and curtains of vapour that drift from the tree branches. The little spasm of emotions is quenched, and I feel as if someone has taken my clenched fist and soothed it into compliance with cool, soft clay. I take a breath, and go on again. Before long I am at the gate.

In the rain, the garden is gloomy. The high walls and the overarching branches and deep shade of the dark trees there cast everything into shadows. It is a shock, this first sight of it—more of a shock than it would have been if there had been bright sunlight and sharp, fluttering coins of light between the leaves of the trees. The shock, I suppose, comes because this is always how I think of the place: a dark, secretive, heavy place, gloomy and withdrawn, kept from the thick and dusty sunlight of the rest of the valley by tall walls and gates.

I push the gate open. The driveway, under a canopy of branches, is sprinkled now with wild grasses and weeds. In the borders, the rosemary and lavender that my mother planted have run to huge, unkempt masses, thick with fallen twigs and debris from the trees. The scent of them, and of wet fir needles and soil and bark, is heavy in the air, like molasses or yeast. I blink at the strength of it.

Don't you remember these? she says. *They're rosemary. Here. Smell.*

It has rained in the night. Just before it becomes light—a thunderstorm. Everything seems to tremble as the thunder rolls up from the sea. There must be lightning too, but I don't look. I lie awake in my room at the top of the house with my eyes tightly shut. Maybe I can fool the storm into passing me by. And eventually it does, and I hear it grumbling its way on up the coast. I stay awake until it is time to get up.

Thunderstorms scare me.

Coming outside after breakfast, I find my mother on her knees at the side of the house. She has a trowel in one hand, and she's turning out small plants from a potting tray. She has spread an old sack on the ground to keep her knees dry, and it's scattered with loose earth. In the border in front of her the soil has been cleared for a space on either side of her, and in the gap there are holes, dug neatly.

"I'm going to get them in while the ground's wet," she says, looking up at me. "It's better for them that way." She is a little out of breath.

"What are they?" I ask.

"Don't you remember these? They're rosemary. We took them as cuttings from the big bush at the bottom of the drive."

My father has come round the side of the house now. He is wearing the clean, pale clothes he always seems to wear. Today they are: pale tan trousers, a white shirt with thin rusty-reddish lines running down it, and canvas-coloured braces over his shoulders. His shoes are a sandy colour, like his hair. "What's Mummy doing, Alex?" he asks. He is smiling.

"She's planting plants," I say, and they both smile, as if I've said something clever.

My mother says, "Here. Smell." She has pinched the tip from a leaf and is holding it out to me. I sniff it cautiously—a sharp, warm, peppery smell. "That's rosemary. And here—" She picks another fragment, and holds it. This one is sharp also, but colder, steely, clean-smelling, like a knife. "Lavender. They're different. See?"

"I like the rosemary best," I say.

"Ah," my father says. "Rosemary. 'That's for remembrance.' " He says the last words in a different voice, as if they are more important. "Do you know what that means, Alex?"

I think hard. I always think hard when my father asks me things, but I am usually slow. Today I am slow. I shake my head, and my father takes a breath.

"Well," he says, "it means that rosemary—this plant—is supposed to be especially good for helping people to *remember* things." A thought seems to strike him. "Perhaps it will help with your reading, eh?" he says, and his smile widens at the idea, and he brushes the top of my head lightly with his hand.

I am slow and also bad at reading.

"Should we stay and help Mummy?" I ask, because I know what is coming. My father looks briefly at my mother, surrounded by earth and roots and sprigs of green, with her gardening gloves on and her plastic sack, and then he looks even more briefly down at himself. He shakes his head.

"I don't think so," he says cheerily. "I think Mummy's doing just fine by herself, don't you? And besides, it's time for your story."

I have been able to tell for a long time that he thinks calling it a story makes it better, makes me like it more.

"Come on," he says. "Don't look like that. You can come out and play later."

I am about to follow him inside when a thought comes to me. I pick up one of the little plant fragments laid out by my mother's side.

"Can I take this?"

They look at each other, and I can see they're trying not to laugh; but I can see also that they're sad, the way they sometimes are when I say things. I don't understand how they can want to laugh and be sad at the same time.

"Of course, darling," my mother says. "Good luck."

So I go inside dutifully for that morning's story with a piece of rosemary clutched tightly in my hand.

It is just like any other day. My father's finger moves patiently along the lines of shapes and he says the letters out loud very clearly and they spin up off the page into my head, where they join the thousands of others left from each of these sessions, all whirling and echoing and leaping back and forth. I clutch at the eddying shapes at random, and they catapult me to a car journey to the hills (passing a van with *this shape* in black, big on its side), and to a boy in town with *this shape* on the front of his blue and red shirt, and back to the book where *this shape* is on the page of the story and I have a scab on my knee from a fall on the gravel. And sometimes the sound of my father's voice—endlessly patient, but never really rising or falling much in tone—makes me go numb, until I feel I am sinking down through my chair into one of the places I prefer to be—my room, or the kitchen with Lena, or sitting on the top of the wall at the end of the garden, looking up at the sides of the hills.

I am different from what my parents want, and it makes them sad. I am slow and bad at reading, but there are worse things than this. Now that I am slow, they are sad; but before, when I was a liar, they were angry, and that was worse.

"Where have you been, Alex?" My father's voice is tense, clipped. "Your mother and I have been looking everywhere for you."

"Sorry," I say at once.

"It's all very well being sorry, but where were you?"

"With Lena," I say. "We went down the road to town and bought sausage." The afternoon has been bright and sunny. Lena and I sing songs on our way, ones she has taught me. When Lena and I are together, we talk differently from the way we talk with my parents, and because I have been told, I am aware of the difference between *Italian* and *English*. Lena and I talk in Italian, and our songs are Italian, and the people of the town and the children who go to the school there all talk the same way. My father can talk like this, too, but his voice sounds funny—strange—when he does, as though he can't get the sound quite right. My mother is even worse. When my parents and I are alone, we talk the other way—the English way—which they prefer. It's a part of the way my life works which I sometimes find puzzling. It's to do with being foreign.

In the piglet shop—which Lena calls *il macellàio* to anyone else, but which between us we call the piglet shop, because of the three stuffed piglets which sit outside it in the sun, dark and bristly and wearing glasses—we buy a string of sausage and a whole ham. The ham will hang in the corner of the kitchen for a week, growing smaller and smaller as Lena shaves pieces off it. It is a good afternoon—one of my favourites.

I look at my parents, and I can see the displeasure grow tighter on their faces.

"Alex, you know this is Lena's day off," my mother says. "Tell the truth."

The words of Lena's song are still sounding in my mind, and my mother's words—English words—feel surprising and confusing, as if they've been dropped into the middle of a place they don't belong. I fumble around in my head for the right thing to say, but I can't.

"Alex," my father says, a sharp warning note in the word.

"With Lena," I blurt out, knowing it is the wrong thing to say, but not knowing how else to fill the silence. My father, who has been standing rigidly by the mantelpiece of the living room, suddenly strides towards me. His movements are jerky, like a clockwork toy whose mechanism has been wound too tight.

"Right," he says, in that same harsh voice. "You'll see what comes of lying, my boy."

"John," my mother says faintly, but she does not get up from her chair.

It happens a few more times, and each time I see the disappointment in their faces before the storm of anger actually breaks. After one row, my mother and I are alone. My father always seems upset afterwards, and disappears, as if he's feeling ill.

My mother says, "Why do you do it, Alex? Why do you lie to us?" She sounds very sad.

"I don't know," I say miserably. "I don't mean to. I don't know."

It is late, and I have been put to bed, but I creep down from my room to the kitchen for a glass of milk. I am allowed milk after I've done my teeth. In the passage at the foot of the stairs, I hear my parents' voices, quiet, from the living room. They are talking about me.

"I'm worried about him, John," my mother is saying, and I hear my father grunt a little in reply. There is the smell of my father's pipe in the air. She goes on, "I've been watching him. Have you noticed how he sits by himself? Sometimes for hours at a time, just sitting and staring into space. It's not normal."

"Maybe it's his age," my father says. He sounds bored.

"Well—maybe. But other children don't do that, do they? They're all running about and playing games and—*doing* things. Alex just sits and stares."

"That's not so hard to understand, though, is it? They're Italian and he's English. He'll settle in, given time."

"But he's had time," my mother says patiently. "He's had three years." There is a pause. "There's something else."

"What?" my father says, and I hear the faint *clink* as he lays his pipe down in the ashtray.

"These stories he tells."

"You mean when he lies," my father says, a little brutally.

"Yes. Well—on Sunday. You remember?"

My father grunts again. I stand in the passage, my body frozen against the wall there as I listen.

"He said that he'd been drawing a picture of the garden, and you asked to see it, and then—well, you remember."

"He didn't have it, because he hadn't been drawing at all."

"Well," my mother says, rather slowly, "it came to me afterwards that I saw him drawing something last week. He had his colouring pencils out and some paper Lena had given him, and he was sitting here—by the window—looking out. At the garden. And then later—Tuesday, maybe—I found it in the kitchen. It was just a scrawl—you know how children's pictures are—and he'd obviously forgotten all about it, so I threw it away. I think Lena sometimes pins them up for him on the walls, but she gets rid of them after a while."

She says this last part as if she's guilty about something. In the hall, I shake my head to myself; Lena doesn't get rid of my drawings. She keeps them in my special drawer in the kitchen. I can look at them there any time I want.

"What are you getting at?" my father asks.

"It was just scribble," my mother says, "but I suppose it could have been a picture of the garden, like he said. So maybe he just got muddled."

"How can you get muddled between 'this afternoon' and 'last week'?" my father demands. "That's absurd." My father likes this word. People talking on the radio are sometimes *absurd.* So are the political views of the left in the newspapers.

"Perhaps it's not absurd for Alex," my mother says. There is another pause, a longer one this time.

She goes on, "You know what he's like. The silences, staring at nothing. And learning to talk so late, too. Maybe he doesn't lie—not deliberately. Maybe he doesn't remember things properly; like when, exactly, he did something."

"He is sometimes a little—slow, I grant you," my father says, thoughtfully. "But he's a sound enough boy. You make him sound as though . . ."

His voice trails off. I press my hands against the plaster of the wall and wait.

Eventually my father says, "Maybe you're right. Maybe he doesn't mean it. But he has to learn, doesn't he? He won't get any better if he doesn't exercise what he's got." There is another muted *clink* as he takes his pipe up again.

Time passes, and there are changes in our house. My parents are trying to stimulate my mind. I know this because I hear my mother tell Lena one morning. Lena promises to try to stimulate my mind as well, but though I keep watching for it, she never seems to do anything different from the way she always does.

My parents do, though. They set me little puzzles, ask me questions, take more of an interest in me than they have before. It is difficult and awkward and it makes us all sad. My father takes it upon himself to teach me to read, because I am nearly six now and should know. Our stories happen almost every morning.

I am gradually realizing something, though: I have begun to understand how to talk to adults. When my father asks me "Where have you been?" now, I say, "Just around," and he tells me off for playing out of sight of the house and not coming in when he calls. But there are no more beatings for not telling the truth.

In the end I stop being a liar. Now I am just rather slow, dreamy, a bit of a loner. When my mother asks me what I've done all day and I say "Nothing," she ruffles my hair with her hand and says "Oh, Alex," to herself in a soft, sad way—but this is better than before.

A part of me rages at this—at the complete lack of understanding, the expanse of ground between us that we never quite manage to cover. It is a problem of world views. In my parents' world, you draw a picture once and once only. What happens last week is locked away somehow and can never come back. What you do each day is the same as someone watching you would say you did. I struggle through my childhood with none of these things holding true for me, and—not realizing—my parents drive me deeper into my own confusion. They stop me being a liar. They try to stimulate my mind, crowding it with even more whirling complexities. And with what seems, later, a painful irony, they tell me about rosemary and remembrance, so that on the day my mother is planting what will become huge bushes of rosemary, I sit inside with my father, clutching a sprig of it in my hand: to help me remember.

They never understand. But for years, nobody does—except Jamie, of course. Jamie tells me to keep the strangeness inside me a secret. Jamie orchestrates the miracle when I am six and a half. Jamie, who calls me "Mad Alex," but who loves me more than anyone else. Jamie—

But it's not him; and she turns, and I see her clearly—the kitten still playing in the dry grass—and her face—

Frozen in the doorway—not seeing for a long moment as our eyes accept the darkness—half-light—and the man she's holding in her arms—

Jamie—Anna—the hermit—all of them, all my childhood—

The rain has stopped. There is weak sunlight coming through the leaves—evening sunlight. I have no idea how long I have been standing here, in the driveway, staring at the house, seeing nothing but fragments of nothing: my mother planting rosemary and lavender.

It overwhelmed me in an instant. Something as intangible as the smell of the garden in the rain has swept me up with itself. For however long I have stood here, it has been as it always was back then, in my childhood: when I could spend an afternoon walking into town with Lena to buy sausage whenever I wanted, always the same, always as bright and real, no matter when or where I was.

But nothing like this has happened to me for—well, for nearly forty years. I had thought it had finished for ever. I had thought there was a distance between me and the past, the same as there is for anyone else.

My shoulder is stiff and painful where the strap of my suitcase is cutting into it, an old scar there burning dully. I take the thing off, carrying it awkwardly in my other hand. My neck is stiff, too; the cold, and the rain, seem to have set the tendons in place. I must have been standing absolutely motionless.

"Mad Alex," I mutter to myself, and the words come out in a croak.

I stand for a time, and it feels like I'm working up courage. Then, shuffling a little to get the sensation back into my legs, I am able to go on.

The lawn at the back of the house is matted and patchy. I glimpse a movement in the corner of the garden and, glancing with a start, see a slim grey cat jump up onto the wall, run along for a little way, and then jump down out of sight on the other side. I wonder which of us has been more startled by the other.

The little verandah which my mother insisted on having built is still standing, though the corners of it are thick with fallen leaves. At the far end, the little pot-bellied stove still squats comfortably. I go up to the French windows and, cupping my hands around my face, peer inside.

What happens next isn't intentional. It just happens: like everything that has brought me back to this place, it just happens. It's late and I should be getting back to find the guest house where I have a room—a little *soggiorno* in a side-street of the town—but now I think to myself that I will go inside, maybe look round, maybe change into dry clothes from my suitcase before the walk back. These are the only thoughts in my head as I unlock the door. It feels like such a simple thing to do.

I step inside, and the full realization strikes me. It is a physical sensation—a kind of vertigo—the moment I am in the house, and I have to struggle to overcome it. I feel for a second as though I could become lost, adrift in a flat sea of things not really here—becalmed, stranded. I have to battle it down. When at last I can look around me almost calmly, I tell myself it is just a reflex, like the sense of panic that gripped me from nowhere on the road; just the ghosts of things long gone. But then I think of what has happened in the garden—

No. It's a reflex, that's all. Seeing this room, this house, must have triggered some spasm of memory from long ago, and given me back for a moment something lost long ago, in childhood. It won't happen again. I won't let it. I have only a short time here, and so much to do that has nothing to do with my life back then: the pictures, the exhibition, things that are part of my adult life—my present. These little flashes of the past are distractions I will have to do without.

I tell myself I should leave, get to the boarding house, get some distance. I really try to do it—to walk back out as easily as I walked in. But I don't seem to be able to. The house draws me in. I can almost feel them—my parents and Lena, the hermit, Jamie, Anna—all of them here in this empty house, as if they have been waiting for me. As if the blank, implacable stare of the dandelion clock has caught me in its gaze and frozen me to the bare boards. After a while, I realize that there is nothing I can do.

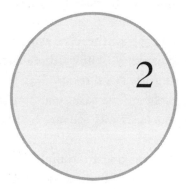

I go into Altesa early the next morning and call Max. The sky has cleared from the rainstorm, but the valley is still steeped in moisture that the sun hasn't yet parched away. Down beyond the clustered houses, wave-crests dance brightly in the shallow bay, but further out, the deeper waters of the Mediterranean glower green and brown, still sullen from the force of the wind and rain.

"It's Alex," I say.

"Alex. How's Italy?" His voice sounds very far away; a bad connection, perhaps.

"It's fine."

"And the house and so on? Everything sorted out all right?"

"Well—" I say. "Not yet. I mean, there's—"

"Is it legal stuff?" he breaks in. "You don't need to worry about that kind of thing. You've seen the attorney there?"

"Yes," I say. "I got the key from him yesterday. I was going to call in again on my way back. But it's not that. It's—the place is really run down, Max." I grope for a way to explain it to him. "I mean, it's a terrible mess. I don't think anyone would touch it the way it is at the moment."

"Oh," he says. "Yes. I see. Are there structural problems?"

"I don't know. I don't think so. I mean, the verandah—the one my mother had—well, that's all rotted at one end. And the chimney's broken loose. From the stove. I think a storm did that. I've hardly had a proper look—I'm going to do that today. There are bound to be other things as well. I mean, there's a window broken in the room where I slept, and the garden's—the garden's awful. It needs work doing on it, that's all. It's mostly small things."

"You slept there?" he says, sounding incredulous.

"Yes, of course. It was too late by the time I'd—when I'd finished looking round."

"Well, at least it doesn't sound like it's falling down," he says cautiously. "You'd expect a little work to be necessary after—how long has it been?"

"Eight years," I say.

"Well, quite." There's a pause. Then he says, "Oh, listen, Alex. There's something I meant to say to you before you left. You know Julia Connell?"

"Of course," I say.

"She's got this idea for the catalogue; a kind of overview of your work in conversation with the artist. She wants to meet up and talk to you about some of the paintings—hang on—I have it right here—"

"Max?" I say. "Max, can you hear me?"

There's a moment's pause, and then, "Yes," he says. "Have you got a bad line?"

"I don't know," I say. "You just sound—very distant."

"Oh. I'll try to speak up. Yes—it says here that she wants to cover themes in your work, and she's listed a few. She wanted me to ask you if you can think these over and come up with some ideas—you know, why they feature, what significance they have for you, symbolism, all that. Then she'll talk to you and turn it all into some kind of stream-of-consciousness thing. I think—yes, she says she wants to run it along the bottom third of some of the catalogue pages, with the pictures and the notes on them above. Can you visualize that? Alex?"

"Yes," I say. "It sounds fine."

"OK. There are a few things on this list, but the main ones—do you have a pen?"

"I'll remember," I say.

"All right. First—intersections of form and surface. That's a principal element, apparently. She also writes: transgressions of boundaries; crossing edges; intrusions of one form into another. Is this making sense to you?"

"Yes," I say, slowly. "Yes, I know what she means."

"Thank God for that. Then we've got group-of-three motifs: groupings of forms in arrangements of three; similar forms repeated three times, ungrouped but within the same work; trilaterally symmetrical forms or forms divided into three." He pauses. "Are you sure you can remember all this?"

"You have to concentrate, Alex," my father is saying. "How can you remember things if you don't concentrate?"

"I try," I say.

"Well, try trying a bit harder."

"Alex?"

"I'll remember," I say again.

"Well, it doesn't matter if you don't. I can give you a copy on Thursday. Did you know there were trilaterally symmetrical forms in your paintings?" I can tell he's joking.

"Yes," I say. "Fruit segments, sometimes. Some other stuff."

"Really? I didn't know that. Well well. And last of all—there are others, like I said, but these are the ones she's keenest to get you to talk about—starbursts and seedheads; dandelions particularly, apparently, and motifs with the same shape-patterns as dandelion seedheads. So. Think you can come up with something for her?"

In my head there is a ghost of a voice: my voice, lodged somewhere out of sight in a different time. *It's still a crap joke, Jamie,* I hear myself saying; and a moment later, there is the ghost of Jamie's voice also: *All the best ones are.*

I say, "I'll try."

"Good. I've been up to look over the gallery. Paul Horshot's in charge. It's going to be tremendous, Alex. There's advance publicity coming out right now. Deborah's working the press for us, and we'll probably do a preview showing the day before it opens—get the reviews out on the day, which should be good. And Alan Harper wants you to say something at a kind of drinks and vol-au-vents bash, which I know isn't your kind of thing, but would be very good for the momentum of it all. It's—wait a moment—it's two days before, on the twenty-second. It shouldn't be too difficult. Alex? Alex, are you there?"

"Yes," I say. "Look, Max—I'm not sure—"

"I can get you out of it if you're really not happy, but I think it would do us a lot of good. Get you some more sales. Get me some more commission. Please all of the people all of the time."

"I didn't mean the party. I meant—I was trying to say that I'm not sure I can be back tomorrow. It's got complicated this end. I may have to stay a while longer." I have no idea why I say it. The words are out of my mouth before I've even thought them through.

There is a sharp silence. At last he says, "Alex, how long are you talking about? The weekend?"

"Maybe," I say. "I don't know."

"Well, that's all right—just. But let's not cut things too close here. This is the big one, remember?"

"Sure," I say.

Suddenly he laughs. "You really hate all of this, don't you?" he says. "I wouldn't be surprised if the house was perfect and you were inventing rising damp so you can sit in the sun and keep out of my way."

"Actually, it's been raining," I tell him.

"Whatever. Look, enjoy yourself, all right? Have some beers in between fixing up builders and all that. When things are sorted out, give me a call. I suppose we'll all survive without you for a few more days."

"OK," I say.

"And don't forget to think over those ideas Julia came up with. They've got to go to press by the fourteenth at the latest, and she'll need some time before that to put it all together."

"I will. I'll call you, Max."

"Bye, Alex," he says, still sounding amused, and the line goes dead.

The valley is warm on the walk back from town, smelling of sage and greenery. The last of the puddles on the road are turning to dust now, though the leaves of the roadside asphodel and myrtle still have their newly washed crispness. Going over the conversation in my mind, I can't help feeling I haven't said what I meant to, that I have been some-how sidetracked. I seem to have bought myself time here, and I don't know quite why I should have wanted to do that. But it's done now. Per-haps I can call him later·in the week; perhaps things will be clearer by then.

I sit on the edge of the verandah to eat, and great blue-black bees zoom over the garden while I pile torn pieces of bread high with cheese and salami I've bought on the way back from town. I am very hungry. I had nothing to eat last night. Through my head go the things Max said, and especially the questions Julia Connell wants answered. I can't stop going over them. Why has she picked *these* things?

I can feel my mind floating through the questions, drifting. There is almost a physical sensation. I remember this. I remember it from very, very long ago, and I fight it, pushing it back from me.

Jamie says, "Oh, Alex is no good with things like that. If you leave him alone he goes dreamy. He's probably been sitting doing that half the time." He grins, and his eyes sparkle for a moment in the afternoon sun. "He's mad," he adds.

There is a broken pane of glass in the French windows next to me, cracked where a stone has struck it. I stare at it: the central star-like contact point, the silver-edged cracks radiating from it like ribbons of metal. I force Jamie's voice from my head and concentrate instead on this broken pane, staring at it with a kind of foolish fixation, as though it will keep from me these ghost voices. The little fused nebula of dense, almost white craquelure around the hole—a starburst, a sudden splash in flat-calm water, like gossamer—

Anna's hands reaching above me, her neatness, her precision, and a deep blue that is almost black—set with stars—

I shiver, rub my eyes. I am back where I should be.

It is gone now; I looked last night, before going to sleep. So much has changed. In all the time that has passed, I suppose it would be strange if it hadn't.

The hall and the kitchen and the front room have been repainted.

The colours are all wrong. As an artist I know this. The colours aren't right for the rooms, or for the house. The kitchen: the kitchen has always been white. Now it is a pale russet which, in yesterday's evening light, makes it look like an abattoir. The front room, which my mother had painted herself—a kind of smoky umber which made it very cosy and comforting—is now a light, airy blue, cavernous and sterile. They are errors of judgement, all of them, and I imagine—as with the window—people getting an unconscious sense of something amiss, something not right, from the colours. It frustrates me.

Upstairs, the walls are the wrong colours. And the ceiling of my room—Anna's ceiling of stars—has been painted over.

That is the worst thing.

She had said it was like the night sky when the sun has died, but the real night hasn't yet come. I can see her reaching up to paint in the last details: careful, always accurate, until at last the ceiling is set with glittering silver against an expanse of blue-black that pulls your eye in and in for ever.

There is the sound of running water from the shower; the faint sound of traffic from the main street, a long way away; the occasional agitated burring of a Vespa in the little side-street over which the window opens. Florence is warm and easy and the spring air fills the room. I am lying on my bed, shoes off, staring at the plaster on the wall opposite, listening to the sounds. On the floor beside me are my things: a case with clothes, another with sketch pads and boards, inks, pens and pencils, charcoal, Conté, tubes of acrylic and watercolour and oils, brushes, linseed oil and turpentine and white spirit, rags and nibs and craft knives. More than I'll need, I am sure, but I find it difficult to decide what not to take: some part of me hates the decision, and I always end up carrying too much.

On the other bed are Anna's bags and cases. I glance at them, and the way the sun is falling across them from the open window makes me think for a moment that they would be good to draw—even if only a quick thumbnail sketch. But I am too lazy and tired. I let my eyes go back to the plaster of the wall, which is traced with patterns of age like maps.

The room is very tall and light, with a high doorway and high, shuttered windows, the shutters now hooked back to let in the afternoon.

There is a second door through to the bathroom, and from this comes the sound of water hissing on tiles, sometimes constant, sometimes shifting its pitch. I realize after listening for a while that the changes must be Anna moving about under the flow, blocking it more and less from moment to moment with her body.

The moment I realize this, I am imagining seeing her: the water on her skin, her head back, hair drenched and clinging, the slenderness of her neck and body. It is as if the wall has dissolved for a second and I can see through it. I feel something clench in the pit of my stomach at the sight of her, and then I force the image from my mind. I actually make myself shake my head and smile ruefully, as if someone might be watching me and checking my reaction—is he her lover or her friend?—and I have to be seen to do the right thing.

But it is difficult to get her out of my head.

She has changed a lot in the five years since I last saw her. I see it the moment I catch sight of her in the airport in Pisa—a difference about her I would never have guessed at. It's the same when we embrace: something that has altered, something I can feel for the short time I'm holding her, before she pulls away and grins and we start to talk. I keep looking. I can't help it. Even on the train I keep stealing glances at her, hoping she won't realize. And I keep trying to find what the things are that have changed; and I keep failing. She has her hair shorter now, to the nape of her neck rather than to her shoulders. But I've seen that before: it's the hairstyle she had when I first knew her. And she is five years older. But the physical changes are, when I isolate them, so slight, and I still see that she has changed a lot, and I don't understand.

We drag our cases up the staircase of the sixteenth-century *palazzo* hidden away in the backstreets near the Duomo and sign in. The proprietor glances approvingly at Anna and nods to me as he shows us to our room. Inside, she goes straight to the windows, opens them to let in the sound and light of the city afternoon.

"Well, we got here," she says.

"We did."

She slings her cases on the bed and looks around. "Huge room. How can it be this big and still be so cheap?"

"It's out of season," I say, shrugging. "And we have to eat out."

"Suits me. God, I'm stiff. My feet are killing me." She's kicking off her shoes as she speaks. "There's time for a shower, isn't there? You don't want to rush off and do anything right away?"

"No. Fine by me."

"Good. I'm going to soak myself. I feel all shrivelled up, like a prune."

I make a face, and she laughs.

"I do. It's flying. I hate flying. Excellent—they've given us towels." She's going round the room inspecting things. "And a writing-desk. That's nice. I had the *most* awful flight. You should have seen who I had to sit next to."

I think briefly. "Not—an old woman who fell asleep and kept blowing bubbles?"

She stops in her pacing of the room, looking at me quizzically. "No. You say the weirdest things sometimes." As she talks she goes round to her bed, sits down, pulling off her trousers. "No—it was this business-man type, maybe forty. *Such* a letch. I thought I was going to get groped for sure."

"Did you?"

"No. Spineless. I kept the second half of my Coke ready, though, so I could chuck it over him when he did. That's probably why I'm so dehydrated."

She stands up and pulls her shirt off over her head. I look quickly away, pretending I haven't noticed. I know she doesn't care—wouldn't mind me seeing her standing there in her underwear—but I'm not sure I can carry off the pretence that *I* don't care. It's easier to look away. She says, "Not a bad view either. There's a little square down there, and a tree. I think that's a church. You know all this stuff better than I do. You'll have to tell me about it later."

"It's a deal," I say, looking fixedly at the writing-desk in the corner. I hear her walk over to where the towels are laid out, bare feet padding on the stone.

"I'd say I won't be long, but I probably will be," she says, a smile in her voice. I risk looking up. She has a towel wrapped around her, and I am able to pretend that, as far as I'm aware, this is how it's always been.

"There's no hurry," I say. "Take as long as you like."

"Thanks. I'll see you in a bit."

She closes the door after her and, a few moments later, there comes the first hiss of water from the shower, and somewhere far off the rumble and clang of air through the plumbing of the old building. I am left lying on my bed, staring at the wall, trying to keep the thought of her out of my head.

I look again at her luggage. Bags and suitcases. There is still something about them that draws my attention, but now it doesn't feel as if they're a good composition for a sketch; it's something else which I can't readily identify. I stare at them, and can feel myself frowning. Something is—I don't know what. Not right? What can be not right about suitcases? But something—

I look back to the wall, try another rueful smile, and this one works better. In the next room Anna is naked, and that is what's bothering me. Because I shouldn't be thinking of her like that. Because she's Anna. The suitcases—the suitcases are square and prosaic and dull and incredibly unerotic. *That* is why they keep nagging at me, tugging at the corners of my mind. In a way, it all makes perfect sense.

I almost laugh at the convolutions of it all. Alone in a room, trying not to laugh, not allowing myself to think of the girl showering just behind the wall, filling my head with her casually piled suitcases instead. *Mad Alex,* Jamie would have said.

I like him the moment I see him: the way he is staring at the distance, the way he is alone in the garden, the way his face seems to be looking out and at the same time lost in something inside him.

Physically we are quite different. Jamie is a year older than me, and taller. While I have my father's straight fair hair, Jamie's hair is dark and a little wavy. He is shaped differently, too: where I am rather stocky, he is slender, and he is never as clumsy or awkward as I am. Even before he sees me, and speaks to me, I like him.

In my childhood, all is confusion for a time, and then out of this confusion I begin to make sense of my world. Jamie helps me with this, sees things I don't, asks the questions I can't, until between us— eventually—we manage to piece together the whole picture. The focus shifts and sharpens and sense and understanding happen.

But most of that is still to come. I am six, and Jamie's parents move into the house at the other end of the row from ours.

The house at the end has been empty for a time. Next door to us live Signora Bartolomeo Cassi and Lucia. The *signora* is well into her eighties, my mother says, and Lucia doesn't look all that much younger. Adults say that Lucia is the *signora*'s maid, that she's been with her ever since she was a young woman of nineteen. The children of Altesa are not taken in, though, and know Lucia to be a witch, and they keep an eye open for her on Fridays, when she comes into town shopping. There is a sign to make to ward off her spells when she looks at you in a certain way. For the rest of the week, both she and the *signora* stay mostly out of sight.

Beyond them live Signor and Signora Brunelli, who have twin two-year-old girls. I think my mother likes the babies; she and Signora Brunelli sometimes have coffee in our front room and watch the twins crawl and toddle round the floor. The twins will both learn to talk very early, and their parents will be proud to have such intelligent babies.

The house at the end is the largest of the four. The new occupants are already talked about in the town before they arrive; the father is English, and though the mother is Italian, she comes from the north, from the city. In Altesa's small-town world, this makes them as much foreigners as my family. There is a boy, too, I hear. The thought of another boy who is a foreigner intrigues me. In my head, I start to think what kind of boy he will be: whether he'll be like me, slow and bad at reading; whether his father will work in the English bank in the city like mine; whether he will get in trouble sometimes like I do.

There have been vans and cars coming and going all day at the other end of the road, and I have seen men carrying boxes and furniture in through the gates of the house there. But I am told not to get in the way, and by early evening the vans are gone again. I can't get rid of my curiosity. At the bottom of our garden is a tree whose branches are low enough for me to scramble up into, and it is easy from there to climb onto the garden wall and drop down behind it.

Back here, the level of the ground is higher than it is in our garden, and it makes the wall seem lower. It's a strange thing and I don't understand why it should be so, but it is. I know this little patch of waste ground well. Sometimes I spend hours out here sitting or lying among the rocks, watching lizards skittering around in the sunlight. When they first come out, in the early morning, they are slow and sleepy, but by midday they have heated up and are like brown bullets ricocheting off the stones. Once I see one with two tails, lighter than the rest of its body; it lives somewhere near where the wall adjoins Signora

Cassi's house, and I wonder if it has been caught in the kitchen by Lucia.

Sometimes, too, I sit here, out of sight of anyone, and do the thing my mother calls *staring into space* and my father calls *lying*.

I go along to the end of the wall, and laboriously find footholds and handholds to help me clamber up. I peer over the top, and for a moment I don't see him, he is standing so still.

The garden here is, again, larger than ours, and sunnier as well. There aren't so many trees, and some angle of the valley side seems to have positioned the lawn so that it catches the evening sun straight-on. The doors and windows of the house, all around the ground floor, are open, and I can hear voices—a man and a woman—inside. There are some of the boxes that came from the van, standing on the edge of the grass, waiting to be taken in.

I let my attention wander around the garden, and it is now that I see him: in the shade of a tall purple bush in the border, standing with his hands in his pockets, looking upwards towards where the valley crest reaches the skyline. For a second I think he is looking right at me, but then I see the faraway expression on his face, and know he hasn't seen me. We stay like that for some time more, he staring at the horizon, I staring at him, like children frozen in a fairy tale. Then my foot slips a little, and the sound reaches him, and he shivers and sees me. He looks at once wary, but almost as quickly the wariness vanishes and is replaced by curiosity. He glances towards the house, once, then runs across the garden until he's standing below me.

"Hello," he says. "Who're you?"

A quick flood of warmth comes with the words: he speaks like Lena—Italian. "I'm Alex," I say. "Hello."

"I'm Jamie. Pleased to meet you," he adds, formally. Then he says, "How did you get up there?"

"It's not as high this side."

"What's back there?"

"Rocks," I say. "And lizards."

"Really?" I can see him looking at the wall, which must be almost hidden from him by bushes and flowers, looking for a way up.

"My garden has a tree," I explain. "You climb that, then you climb the wall."

"There's nothing here," he says, sounding frustrated. Then, "Wait— I know." He looks up at me again. "You'll stay there?"

"OK."

"Won't be long." He turns and runs away across the lawn to the side of the house, and disappears from sight there.

I cling on where I am, wondering what he is going to do. It is like a puzzle, like one of the ones my father gives me to stimulate my mind.

"Imagine, Alex," he says, "that you have three pieces of string."

I try my best, and nod.

"The first one is as long as two fingers. The second is as long as three fingers, and the third is as long as six fingers. Do you think if you put the first and second end-to-end, they'd be as long as the third?"

I stare at the table, but the words muddle me. String and fingers dance in my head: Lena shows me how to make a cat's-cradle and pass it from person to person; I stretch string tight and twang it, feeling the quick-dying vibrations in my hands; I coil string tightly around my thumb and leave a red spiral mark when I take it off, neat grooves running all the way up.

This problem is easier, though. The boy—Jamie—*Pleased to meet you*— wants to get over the wall, but there's no tree like the one I have. I think it through, and am pleased to realize he has gone to get a ladder, when there is a scuffling sound off to my left, on my side of the wall. I look round, and to my surprise see Jamie coming round the end of the wall. I drop down from where I'm hanging and go to meet him.

"How'd you do that?" I ask, impressed.

"I went round," he says. "I ran. It *is* higher back here, isn't it?"

After a second or two, I start to see what he means. If you go out of the front gate of his house, and followed the wall to your left, and went through the fence that runs beside the road, and kept following the wall round the next corner—you would be here, at the back. The idea is amazing. In another couple of seconds, I see that I can do the same from *my* front gate, turning right instead of left. It has never occurred to me before that this might be possible. You get to the rocks and the lizards by going up the tree and over, that is how it has always worked. I have never imagined—

"What is it?" he says.

"Nothing."

"You looked weird."

"I was just thinking," I say.

"Oh." He is quiet for a moment. "How old are you?"

"Six."

"I'm seven," he says. "So. Where are these lizards?"

I look around me. "They're not here any more," I say. "They go away when it's evening."

"Oh," he says, sounding disappointed. "But you said they were here."

"They'll be here tomorrow," I say. "If you could come tomorrow, I could show you some."

"Yeah? OK."

At that, we both hear a woman's voice calling, "Jamie!"

"That's my mum," he says. "I've got to go. I'll see you tomorrow. Bye, Alex."

"Bye," I call after him, as he runs off around the end of the wall. He runs quickly and easily, his feet sure on the uneven ground, almost as if he is floating. I trudge back to my end of the wall, but rather than climb over, I go around the end, and find to my astonishment that what I have worked out is right: after getting through the fence, I am outside my own front gate. The discovery makes me smile as I go inside, and the smile is made wider by the thought that tomorrow, Jamie and I are going to look for lizards together.

I am staring at the window, still. The more I look at it, the more I can't bear it being broken. It's as if some important part of the house's warmth and security is gone. It speaks of neglect, too, and there's something peculiarly upsetting about that. I shall have to—

I stop myself abruptly. I am supposed to be concentrating on the paintings, not on fixing window panes. They're still in the suitcase; I haven't even got them out yet. I have spent a whole evening and most of this morning doing—what?

Doing something I haven't been able to do since I was twelve.

I want to shake my head, clear it of these distractions so I can focus on the things that are supposed to be important. But it's more difficult than I have thought. How can I concentrate on the pictures when, all around me, small signs of change and neglect are needling in at me, whispering their presence? It will be impossible.

Perhaps I could mend some things, fix some things; get the house a little way back to how it should be. It wouldn't take too much effort. Just some very basic repairs would perhaps be enough to give me the peace of mind to concentrate properly.

I can make a start with the window. I have to start somewhere, after all. I tell myself that I will think about the exhibition, and the paintings, while I work; and this sounds so convincing to me that I almost start to believe it.

3

I do get to the paintings eventually. In the afternoon, I buy what I need to mend the broken pane, and more besides; heavy bags of tools and materials for which I am bound to find a hundred uses. I buy house paint, too: emulsion for the walls, to get them back the way they were—the way they should be. I set out all I have bought on the sitting-room floor, and go to work to fix the window. All through the afternoon, in the easy rhythm of working with my hands, the past comes, floating up around me and threatening to engulf me; and I fight it back, trying to stay in the here and now, trying to gain control. Sometimes—most of the time—I manage it.

I can't understand why this is happening to me now; and why so strongly, so—insistently.

Jamie and Anna. I tell myself that it must be inevitable that being back here again would stir up memories of them. It's natural; this was their place, of course, as well as mine. It's no surprise that they're here in my thoughts so much.

But it has been so long since I've thought of them, and these aren't just *memories*—these are fragments of reality, snatched from the past and creeping up around me in the present. It's something I've learnt to live without all my adult life, and now it's here, it's back, and I can't even control it. I might have expected to think of Jamie and Anna once or twice while I was here—but not this, not this.

In the evening, I try to lose myself in the pictures. I open the case and spread them out on the floor of the sitting room, covering the boards with rectangles of colour. From them, faces look out at me, their features fractured and then regathered, as if seen through a thousand cracked lenses at once. I remember how the critics first called this style of mine a bastardization of cubism; and how later they found in it a fusion of styles that they were pleased to decide broke down the barriers between formal movements in painting; and how finally it became so accepted that now there are younger artists who make their own fusions from it, and find in it new barriers to be broken down. Sometimes it makes me laugh, and sometimes it makes me angry. Right now, I find I hardly care: they all seem so very far away.

I try to arrange them vaguely as they will be in the gallery. It's to be a chronology, from my earliest work through to the present day. A retrospective. I deal out the photographs like a fortune-teller arranging the cards, spreading them out on the boards, first to last in a wide arc. Gradually the sense of them starts to become apparent: the shifts of style and focus that have happened over the years. I sit in their centre, staring, puzzling, trying to see what it is that feels so wrong—so *incomplete*—about them. There must be something. It's strong enough to have made it impossible for me to stay any longer in London; and yet at the same time it's so slight that I can't get hold of it, can't lay my hand on it. All I know for sure is that something is missing. Even that shred of understanding is new to me, has come only with this business of the exhibition, and the gathering together of the pictures that it's involved. Individually, the paintings are whole. Seen together, they are—

I can't understand.

I stare at them, frowning, and the colours shift under the intensity of my gaze: change for a moment and are darker, as if a cloud has come over the sky and cut out all the light of the sun—

Darkness but the light of stars—

*   *   *

It's dark; the shadows of the rocks and cliffs are very deep. It is night-time, and the cliffs and the vegetation that straggles along their top are leached of colour. Somewhere close by is the sea: the sound of it, slowly rhythmic; the interlocking patterns of the waves discernible by moon-light, some blue-black here between the pearlescent ribbons of light that blur across the low crests. Off to one side are three rocks breaking out of the water, and to the other is a little promontory of land that curves out into the water, defining a naturally calm place sheltered from the greater expanse of the sea beyond. The shadow of the rock where it hits the water kills the moonlight, and makes a dark, impenetrable hol-low by the curving underside of the promontory.

Standing on the curve of land—

With a quick gasp and shudder the pictures are around me again. I stare at them blankly for one long, uncertain moment when the floor feels not quite solid and I am not sure whether I can keep my grip here or not. Then everything is hard and real again. With clumsy hands I sweep the photographs together into a pile, fumbling them together, pushing them away from me.

What was that? Where did that come from?

I look around the room and everything is how it was.

I need to do something. I need simple work that will—steady me. Hold me together.

By the wall are tins of paint. I remember: the room is the wrong colour. All the rooms are wrong. I have to change them back. Moving quickly—eagerly—I leave the paintings in the middle of the room and turn my back to them, getting brushes, a screwdriver, levering the lids from the cans of emulsion. I look at the empty expanse of the wall, ready for new paint, and take a deep breath.

The Art rooms smell of turpentine and oils—chalk, charcoal—white spirit—

The picture I have made is the still life we are supposed to draw, but there is something else—a face breaking through the surface of the pic-ture, half submerged there—his face—Jamie's face—

*   *   *

As soon as I can, I scramble over the wall to wait for Jamie. I have endured the morning's story with my father and am free now until lunch. It is hot back here already; the sun rises at the head of the valley and sets down over the water, and though this side catches it a little more fully, the whole of Altesa is bathed in light from mid-morning through to sunset. The stones of the waste ground here soak up the heat and hold it, and even after dusk will be warm to the touch, as though alive. Jamie is nowhere to be seen. After a few minutes of walking back and forth, I settle down to wait, finding a comfortable place to sit and raking together a pile of pebbles to throw at the larger rocks.

It is warm and I feel lazy and happy.

Lena and I go for a walk up the valley. Sometimes we do this, though not often; more usually our walks take us down, to the shops and the central square and the piglets and the drinking-fountain. I like the drinking-fountain a lot. The bronze lion's head, with its snarlingly open mouth and constant stream of bright water, entrances me. Even when we are sitting at Toni's waiting for ice-creams and Cokes, I keep my eye on it.

This afternoon, though, we go further along the road, and then, once we are quite far from the town, down a side-track that Lena says once led to one of the outlying farms. Lena is telling me stories, too—some of which I've heard before and know almost by heart—and keeping her eyes open for wild herbs growing by the track: sage, sorrel and thyme, to pick and use in the kitchen. A bunch of wild myrtle hung at the window will keep the flies away. I go happily along with her, sometimes running ahead and waiting for her to catch me up, sometimes carrying her basket for her.

We walk for a long time, further than I have ever been before; I can't see our house any longer, and the countryside around us is full of the sounds of crickets and the quieter, daytime cicadas. We pass a few derelict buildings, and two which clearly still have people living in them: in the fenced-in yard of one, a big brown dog raises his head gently from where he is lying in the shade, but doesn't seem able to work up the enthusiasm to bark at us. At last, just as Lena is saying that maybe we should be heading back, I see a bridge ahead of us in the dirt road.

"Lena—a bridge!"

She smiles. "Go on, then."

I dash on to reach it. The sides of the bridge are higher than they have looked, and as I wait for Lena I haul myself up to lean over the edge. Below me, though, there isn't a river, as I'd hoped; the ground is dry, sandy, though there are what look like waves and ripples in the sand. The sand—or dust; some of it looked more that way—is reddish, like all the earth around Altesa, but much finer, and smooth. Where rocks stand up in its surface, the sand seems to have flowed round them, making strange, fluid shapes. In several places there are matted thatches of dead sticks and twigs and rubbish and leaves, turned brown and dry by the sun.

Lena stands beside me and looks over also.

"There's no water," I say.

"No," she agrees.

"But it looks like a river. And there's a bridge."

"Sometimes there's water in it," she says. "When the storms come. But most of the time it's dry. It's not really a river, you see, it's just a place where the water runs when it rains in the hills."

"Oh," I say. I am slightly disappointed that there's no water, but the not-a-river is peculiar and a little magical. I let my gaze travel up along its length, tracing the course back up through the valley. It twists and meanders from side to side a bit, but I can make out its paler route among the dark earth and grey-green grasses and scrub right up towards the foothills of the valley's end. Just at the point where it fades from sight, I can see a little building: white walls and rust-coloured roof, standing alone in the middle of nowhere.

"What's that?"

"Where?" she asks. I point, and she bends her head down to follow the line of my arm.

"That. The little house."

"Oh," she says. "That's not a house. That's a church." She pauses for a moment. "Well, rightly it's more like a chapel. That's a small church. It's not used now. You know the church in the town?"

"Yes."

"People go there. The chapel—well, it's a ruin now. Not many people live up that end of the valley any more."

"Mm," I say.

"There's a story about that place," she says after a second.

"Tell me!" Lena's stories are always good. It's Lena who tells me about the people in the town, and the things that happened when she was young; and about the strange white house high up on the far side of the valley, where Signor Ferucci lives, and hardly ever comes out.

"Well—maybe on the way back home. Now have a good look, and fix it in your mind so you can picture it when I tell you."

I do so, staring at the distant building, frowning with concentration. Lena smiles.

"Right, that's enough. Let's go."

I jump down from the bridge and trot along beside her. "What's the story?" I say.

She clears her throat the way she does when she's going to tell me something. "Well now. Like I told you, the chapel there isn't used any more. I don't know when they built it—maybe hundreds of years ago, for all I know—but now it's a ruin. And it was a ruin thirty years ago, when I was a girl." We walk on in silence for a few yards, while she orders her thoughts.

"But for a long time, back then, it wasn't quite deserted. There was a hermit, you see, who lived there."

"What's that?"

"A hermit?"

"Mm."

"He's a man who lives all alone. They're supposed to be monks, though I don't know if this one was. Maybe he was just a tramp, or a gypsy; but because he lived in the chapel people began to think of him as if he was a holy man. He lived there for—oh, many years."

"What was he like?"

"I don't know. I never saw him. My parents used to tell us to keep out of his way."

"What happened to him?"

"One day he packed up his things—he could carry everything he owned on his back—and he went off into the hills over there." She points. "And he was never seen again."

"Where did he go?" I ask, impressed.

"Nobody knows."

"Maybe he went off to find a different chapel," I say.

"Maybe. Or a cave. Hermits are supposed to live in caves, too."

"In caves?"

"That's right."

"That would be fun," I say.

"You know, I used to think the same thing when I was little. But now I'm not so sure. It might be a bit cold, don't you think? And damp."

"And smelly."

"Probably."

"Lena?"

"Yes?"

"Do you think Signor Ferucci's a hermit?"

Lena shakes her head. "No. Just someone who keeps themself to themself."

"Oh. All right."

We walk on in companionable silence and, in my head, impressions of the hermit whirl, becoming confused with details Lena has mentioned until the church in which the man crouches has an interior like a cave, with rock walls and stalactites and bones, while at the entrance blazes a bonfire, sending up a column of smoke that alarms the distant townsfolk.

"Alex?" comes a voice out of nowhere, sounding somehow bigger than the valley around me, and—

And the afternoon tumbles away from me and—

"Alex?" Jamie says.

I blink. "Hello," I say.

He is crouched next to me. "Are you OK?"

"Yes," I say. "I didn't hear you."

"You were like you were asleep," he says, "but your eyes were open. I could see them. I kept calling you but you didn't move."

"I was thinking," I say. Saying this, I have found, usually works.

"It was weird."

I shrug. "I was just thinking," I say again.

After a moment's hesitation, he sits down on the flat rock beside me. "What were you thinking about?"

Now it is my turn to hesitate. I have become used to what to say to my parents, but perhaps this is not the right thing to say to Jamie. I look at him, and his brown eyes are interested, not suspicious. I say, "I was thinking with Lena."

"Who's Lena?"

"She's our cook. And she looks after me, sometimes." He nods, and I am encouraged by the way he accepts what I've told him. "We're going for a walk up that way, and we see a bridge, and a chapel where a man used to live. A hermit," I add. "He went away, though, into the hills."

Jamie is frowning. "When?"

"When what?"

"When do you go on the walk?"

I am thrown into confusion. I don't want Jamie to know that I used to be a liar, but the conversation is becoming like the ones I used to have—back then, when I was a liar—with my parents. I don't know what to say. But Jamie is still looking at me, his face open and waiting for me to say something, and in the end I just say it. "Just now."

"This morning?"

"Just now. Before you came." Suddenly I want him very much to understand. "That was what I was doing. Staring into space."

"You mean you were imagining it?"

"No . . ."

"What, then?"

It is the tone of his voice that makes the difference: not impatient, just curious. I try to find the words. "You know when—you go somewhere—"

He nods.

"And then you come back."

Now he is looking puzzled. "What, like a walk?"

"Yes," I say. "Like that. *That's* what I was doing."

He is quiet for a time, then he says, "So you'd gone with Lena and then you came back and then you came here and I found you?"

"No," I say, surprised he doesn't understand. "I was with Lena and then you called me and I came back. I heard you say my name."

"But I saw you. You were right here." He isn't laughing at me and he isn't angry with me. His voice is steady and serious, as though he has found something that must be examined until it makes sense. He doesn't sound like he cares if it takes him all day.

"I was with Lena too," I say.

"You mean like a dream?"

"No." Dreams are all fuzzy, blurred, strange; they aren't real. "When you *go* somewhere. Like up the valley with Lena."

"You make it up?"

"No. Like now, like I'm here with you."

"I don't understand," he says.

I can't think of anything else to say to make it clearer.

He sits there, still frowning slightly, thinking it all through. Then he says, "Can you go anywhere?"

"Sure."

"Like the moon?" He sounds suddenly excited.

"Oh. No. Just—places in the valley. With Lena, or the town, or the garden."

"Oh." Another pause. "Anywhere in the valley, though?"

"Just places I know," I say, and at that there is a sudden sense that something heavy has shifted—just a little—in my head, moving reluctantly, trying to accommodate what I've just said. The questions Jamie is asking aren't ones anyone's ever asked me before. I haven't asked them to myself either. They feel like they're prodding at me, searching, trying to find me out.

"Just places you've *been?*" he says, his eyes bright.

"I—I suppose."

"So you're *remembering* them," he says triumphantly. "You know— remembering, like when you remember what you did on Saturday. That's all." He looks pleased at having pieced the puzzle back together, and I am pleased too. But then a look of vague disquiet crosses his face. "Only—you really looked strange. Your eyes were open, but you didn't see me, and you didn't hear me."

"Yes I did," I say, surprised. "That's why I came back."

We look at the rocks, and the side of the valley beyond them, together.

"You're weird," he says eventually. I blink. But then he says, "I like you, though." And my heart skips once, and feels as if it is grinning inside me.

"I like you too," I say.

"And wouldn't it be great if you *could* go anywhere, just in your head—the moon or Mars, or different planets?"

I have never thought about this either. "I suppose," I say.

"I'd love that." He looks entranced with the possibility. "Do you like comics?"

"I don't know."

"I've got some great ones. They're in English, though," he adds, doubtfully.

"But I speak English," I say, surprised. It takes me a moment to remember that Jamie is a foreigner, like me. Astonished, I switch from the way we have been talking—the way I talk with Lena—to the other way I talk, when I'm with my parents. "Can you speak like this?"

Jamie looks just as astonished, but he answers the same way. "Yes. My father's English."

"Mine too," I say. "And Mummy," I add, remembering.

Suddenly he begins to laugh—a little at first that quickly grows into a great uncontrollable peal that rings against the side of the valley. He points at me, helplessly, and then at himself, and I understand immediately what he means—*We're such idiots!*—and the funny side of it strikes me, too. I can't help it; I join him, laughing harder and harder until my sides hurt and there are tears in my eyes. I can't think of a time when I've laughed harder.

At last we quieten down. Occasionally we look sideways at each other and giggles overwhelm us again; but in the end we are too tired to laugh any more. We sit side by side with big, idiot grins on our faces.

Jamie rubs his eyes with his sleeve and says, "You're mad, you know? You're mad. Mad Alex." In the laughter, the realization of English has left us as suddenly as it arrived, and Jamie's words are in comfortable Italian once more.

"I'm not," I say. "You're mad."

"I'm not as mad as you, though," he says.

"You are."

"Mad Alex." He grins at me. "If you show me your lizards I'll show you my comics. They're brilliant. Is it a deal?"

"Yes," I say at once. He sticks his hand out, and I shake it. His hand around mine is strong and warm, like a stone in the sun.

When we go to look for the lizards, though, there are none to be found. Our laughing has scared them all away.

Jamie is my first friend; I have never had a real friend before.

For Jamie, everything is a question waiting to be asked. He wants to know why the lizards we watch blink in the sun, but snakes never do. We try not to blink until our eyes are hot and dry and gritty with the effort, but we can't manage it forever, like the snakes. He wants to know why, when we have lemonade, the *outside* of the cold glasses becomes wet—how does the water get from inside the glass to the outside without our seeing? If water can get through the glass, why doesn't the glass empty? We stare at our glasses until they are warm in the sun, and not so nice to drink, but we can't find out the answer; in the end, the little beads of liquid vanish as mysteriously as they arrive. He wants to know why the rock in the sides of the valley is arranged in layers like a stack of sandwiches, even where the farmers haven't cut terraces. Lena has told me about terraces—that they are to hold the rain for the olive trees—and shows me how water runs down the sloping street next to the church but gathers in puddles on the church steps, an idea I grasp quickly. But she has never told me about the hidden sandwiching of the rocks, and when I ask her, she only shrugs and says that is just the way they're made.

Jamie wants to know everything about Altesa. He quizzes me on everything he notices or can think of: about things, and places and people. I tell him all about me, and what I like and don't like. I tell him about my family—things which I don't really know myself but have in turn been told—like when we used to live in a different place. London. My parents still talk about it sometimes. He makes me tell him about the people—the figures he's seen around town, the other children, our neighbours. I pour out all of Lena's patchwork history of the town while he sits, attentive, soaking it up again. And I tell him the things Lena doesn't know, or doesn't like to mention: like Lucia being a witch. Like Signor Ferucci.

"Up there on the side of the valley," I say, pointing out the window. "Well, you can't really see it from here. But there's a big white house, and it's got a wall all round, high up, and gates. For miles. And he lives in there and he never comes out. Well, hardly ever."

"Have you ever seen him?" Jamie asks.

"Well, sometimes. In town. He's got a beard and he looks a bit scary. He's really tall."

"Is it a mad beard—like, all wild?"

"No," I say, slightly surprised. "No, it's neat."

"Oh."

"Nobody knows what he does in there," I add. "Lena says—"

There's a pause. I concentrate very hard on not going away from Jamie. He doesn't always mind it when I do, but sometimes I sense that he is a little worried. Lena's word comes drifting back to me.

"Lena says he's—recluse," I say.

"What's that?"

"Someone—someone who doesn't like to come out."

"Why?"

"I don't know."

"Maybe he's a vampire," Jamie says.

"Yeah." I think for a moment, and something else comes back to me. "I think he used to be that other thing," I say vaguely. The word hits. "Politician."

Jamie says, "I've got a whole story about vampires from a haunted tomb in one of these." He indicates the several stacks of comics that are lined up against the wall of his room.

Jamie's bedroom isn't anything like mine. My room is quite small, with a ceiling that slopes down from the door to the window. Under my window is the gentle pitch of the kitchen roof; if I crane my head far out to the left, I can see the end of my mother's verandah roof at the back of the house, where the iron stove-pipe of the little fat stove comes up through it. My bed is against one wall, and a wardrobe stands by the door that leads through to the back bedroom that is sometimes Lena's. I have a little cupboard of toys, too, and some big picture-books which I still love and look at, though I know my father doesn't like them. Apart from these things, my room is quite bare: the walls are pale, the ceiling white, the surround of the window dark wood. The best thing is the view: right along the row of our neighbours' houses and up the valley.

Jamie's room is much larger. Although there is more space, it all seems to be filled: with books and magazines and comics, with bed-clothes, with packing cases and boxes both empty and half-full and un-opened, with posters—rolled up and piled untidily in a corner. Near the window is a little red telescope on a tripod, pointing out, and by it on the wall is pinned, carefully, a large piece of card which looks as if it might be a map of something, though the scattered mass of little dots and larger dots and numbers and words makes no sense to me at all. On one of the bookshelves is a small black case, lined with worn red velvet, in which Jamie keeps his clarinet. He's played it to me several times. Once school starts, his parents are going to find him a new teacher here, and he'll learn new pieces, and play those to me as well.

"Here. This is the Silver Surfer. You'll like him. And here's Spider-man. You know him, of course."

I nod, unable to confess that I don't—that I have never before seen the red and blue masked figure that leaps towards me from the page Jamie is holding open. He tells me how Spider-Man was normal until he was bitten by a radioactive spider; he points things out, tells me who each of the characters is, passes me other comics to compare. I sit, entranced, while the bright colours and vivid panels of the cartoons accumulate around me, until I am like an island in a pool of brilliantly hued pages.

"You can borrow them, if you like," he says. "Take them home to read."

"Thanks!" I say, but then I realize something.

"What is it?" he asks.

"I—nothing."

"Tell me."

"I can't read the words," I say.

"I can help you with the long ones," he says.

"No—I mean, I—"

"Can't you read at all?" he asks. He sounds shocked, but I know he won't laugh at me or be unkind; he is just amazed that I can live without this essential ability. In a flash of understanding, I look around me at the room and see why he might think this.

"My dad's teaching me," I say.

"Oh," he says. For a moment he seems at a loss. Then he says, "I suppose what you do—you know, the going places in your head—that's like reading stories, isn't it?"

I know what he means. This is the second time he's called it something like that: *going places in your head*. Again, I can feel heavy structures grating and moving laboriously in me, as I try to fit the words into place. Very, very tentatively, I begin to see that the difference between *going somewhere* and *going somewhere in your head* might be what Jamie has been struggling with. *In your head* is the key. And I know in that moment that Jamie has already understood me better than my parents and everyone else ever have. I meet his eyes with a surge of gratitude pushing up inside me. I want to say something, but I can't imagine what.

"Hey," he says. "I know." His eyes are suddenly bright with inspiration. "Ask if I can come over to your house this weekend. To stay, I mean. There's an annual in one of the boxes with whole stories in it—fourteen episodes, one after the other, so you don't have to wait a week or find the next issue. I could read it to you, if you want." He says this last almost shyly, as if he's afraid I might say no.

"That would be great!" I say. "I really like them."

"Yeah," he says. "Me too."

Downstairs I hear the sounds of people moving about—his parents, I suppose. He glances towards the door and sighs.

"It's time for lunch," he says. "I'd better go."

"Oh. And me," I say.

"But I'll see you later."

"Yeah."

"Don't forget to ask about the weekend," he says. "Ask if I can stay the night."

"I will," I promise.

In the darkness, there is the shape of a figure: pale, outlined against the shadows.

For a moment it is all confusion, and then the room clears and I know where I am.

Night has come down around me and outside it is dark. The darkness in front of me is a wall, deep in shadow. Somehow my hand, holding the broad, thick-bristled brush I have bought in town, has made marks on the shadow. They are fragmented, hesitant; little uncertain sweeps and arcs of paint which have run and dripped, pale against the darker wall.

I blink. The marks coalesce, and for a second I see it: the pale shape of a figure there.

Christ, I think, *what's happening to me?*

The distant echo of laughter rings through the house: childish laughter, but too bright, forced; laughter at a joke that isn't funny, but which *has* to be funny.

I was too young, I think to myself, rather wildly; *I was too young to understand. He should have known that.*

The image on the wall is back again now: a pale body, taut, tensed somehow, as if caught in the instant of time between intention and act. The slender curve of it is white, like moonlight.

I press my hands to my eyes to blot it out; but it still floats behind closed eyelids, the pale, stretched body now alone in an infinity of darkness. I press harder, trying to drive it away from me into the black, until the figure shifts and blurs and separates, until it looks as if it might be three figures and not one, and until phosphenes shimmer and burst across the range of my vision like fireworks, or seedheads.

4

*I*n bare feet I light some of the candles I have placed around the room, and the cheerful light they cast drives away some of the shadows that have been tugging at me. I don't feel ready to sleep yet. I want to think of something to push the uneasy memory of these fragments away, to give me something else to concentrate on as I lie in bed. Some part of me is aware that the old childhood fear could so easily come back to life now; the fear that I will wake, in a moment, to find myself old and dying, my life already spent. I can't face that again. So I take one of the candles and wander the house with it, eventually finding my way up-stairs. Once I am in my old bedroom, it seems the most obvious thing in the world to open the window there, and to sit on the sill, looking up the valley at night.

I know this view to the last detail. The darkness obscures many of the small changes that are doubtless there, and would be clamouring their presence to me were it daylight. Now, though, I am only conscious that the branches of the tree that cut off the left-hand part of the horizon are longer by some small amount, and that the sound of the World Service radio is missing from downstairs. Above, the stars are unchanged;

I look for Orion, and find him almost at once, a small smile of acknowledgement twitching the corner of my mouth. There are a few clouds low on the line of hills, but leaning out of the window I can see that the sky overhead is clear.

I find myself searching the darkness at the head of the valley for the winking green light that is my signal, but I am more than forty years too late. There is nothing there, and yet I still can't get rid of it: the suspicion that I might catch it out of the corner of my eye—the three blinks of green from up by the dandelion clock that mean it is time to set off.

I shake my head. There is no hermit any more. There never was a hermit; not a real one.

I look up at the sky again. It's not the time of year for the shooting stars yet; a few months must pass before the Perseids wash through the Earth's orbit and burn briefly through the high atmosphere. Jamie tells me all about them. We watch them together.

"There's one—over there."

I turn my head a fraction and catch the last dying trace of light as the star burns out. "That's fourteen," I say.

"They're great, aren't they?"

"Yeah."

"People say you should wish when you see one."

"We should do that."

"OK. On the next one."

"We could have had fourteen wishes by now," I say.

"Do you believe in all that?"

"All what?"

"Wishes and stuff."

I think about it. "I don't think so," I say at last.

"Me neither." I can hear the grin in his voice as he adds, "But let's do it anyway."

We wait until the next star cuts across the sky.

"What did you wish for?" I ask.

"It's a secret," he says. "You have to keep them a secret if you want them to come true."

"Oh."

"They aren't really stars, you know," he says. He speaks quietly, almost dreamily. "They're pieces of rock. Meteors. They drift through space, and once a year this big sort of cloud of them—it's called a swarm—comes. They go round the sun, you see, like us, only we only catch up with them once a year. And then they burn up."

"Why do they burn up?"

"Because of the air."

"Rocks don't burn," I say.

"Yes they do. Look at volcanoes. That's rock."

"Oh, yeah," I say. He's right. "Why does the air make them burn?"

"There's another."

"I see it. Sixteen."

Jamie stretches his arms behind his head and cradles it in his hands. "They move really fast. Much faster than anything else—cars or jets or anything. So fast that when they rub against the air it makes them hot. Like when you rub your hands together it makes *them* hot, you know?"

"Air makes you cold," I say.

"Not when you're going as fast as a shooting star," he says.

We are lying on our backs on the gentle slope of the roof outside my window. The terracotta tiles under us are still slightly warm from the sunlight they've soaked up during the day, and though it is half-past eleven, the air is easy and fragrant with the scents of pine and rock. It is August. We have waited until the sounds of my parents going to bed have ceased and the house is silent, before climbing out.

"How do you know all this stuff?" I say.

"I read it. I've got lots of books."

"I know," I say.

"Everyone thinks I'm pretty clever, but I just read a lot."

"I wonder why they don't teach us anything like this at school?" I say.

"Maybe they will later. There's another."

"Seventeen."

Two years pass from the time Jamie and I first meet. For a short while, I catch him up: I'm eight, and for the next couple of weeks, so is he. It is the same the previous summer, this short time when our ages overlap: and then his birthday will come and he'll jump ahead of me again. But even though he's older, it never seems to distance him from me. We are firm friends now—best friends—and after school, and in the holidays, we are hardly ever apart. Around Altesa, we are recognized as a pair, a duo; like the superheroes in Jamie's comics, I sometimes tell myself.

It is the comics, and Jamie, which are responsible for what my mother calls "the miracle."

It happens soon after we have met. Jamie's father comes to our house one evening, and he and my parents sit out on the verandah and talk, and drink gin and tonic and fresh lemonade which Lena takes out to them. I have to go and say hello: Jamie's father is *Mr. Anderson* and he also says *Pleased to meet you,* though it sounds different to the way Jamie says it; almost as if he's amused at something. They are out there for a long time; I peep round the sitting-room door to see them out there, their backs to me.

At last, Mr. Anderson goes. My father walks him to the gate, and they're talking as they go. They seem to be getting on pretty well, I think. My mother comes inside.

"He was very nice," she says. "Do you know, Alex, he used to live in London too, before he came to Italy?"

London is a vague impression of green carpets, and a little wooden train; long, green curtains; and cold. I know, because I have been told, that we lived there when I was three, but to me it feels like that must have been another Alex; I remember hardly anything of it. London really does feel like a dream. I say, "Oh."

"And Mrs. Anderson comes from Italy. You'll meet her at the weekend—they're coming for dinner."

My father comes back a few minutes later. He seems pleased with himself. "Fancy that," he says. "It's a small world all right."

"I can't help feeling we're becoming like a little colonial outpost," my mother says. "The Brits, at the head of the valley."

"Nonsense," my father says, but I think from the way he says it that the idea doesn't strike him as entirely unwelcome. "Anyway, Alex seems to have been successful in his diplomatic overtures."

I look up at the mention of my name, and they both smile at me. "Daddy means you were lucky to make friends so quickly," my mother says.

"It'll be nice for him," my father says thoughtfully, as if I am not in the room. "Having someone his own age close by. We're too far from the town up here. It'll help keep his English up, too." My father doesn't know that when Jamie and I are alone, we never talk in English. He looks back to me. "We don't want you going native on us, do we?" he says with a smile. I don't know how to answer that, so I keep quiet.

When the weekend comes and Jamie's family arrives, my mother welcomes them all into the drawing room. Jamie and I exchange brief, rather shy smiles while the adults talk, and then Lena appears and rescues us. We say good night to everyone and go upstairs to my room, Jamie clutching a carrier bag that I can see is padded thick with comics.

"I brought all the best ones," he says as we go up.

I show him around. "This is my room. That's Lena's room. That's the bathroom. That's my parents' room." We are briefly overcome by a kind of formality, but it soon passes.

"OK," he says. "Do you want to see what we've got?"

"Yes," I say. "Put them there."

He unloads his bag and spreads the comics and annuals—which are hardbacked—on the mattress on the floor. At the bottom of the bag are some pyjamas, a toothbrush and a parcel which he unwraps. "Sandwiches and biscuits," he says, setting them on one side.

"*Ottimo!*"

"Right," he says, once the bag is empty. "Which one do you want?"

I am not sure. I look over the covers carefully before making my choice. "That one."

"OK. I like this one," he adds. "It's a bit scary."

"I don't mind," I say. I keep my slight doubts—how scary?—a secret.

We sit on my bed as if it is a sofa, with our backs to the wall and our feet sticking out over the side. Jamie turns the pages as he reads the story for me. Comic-book conventions are new to me and it is a struggle at first to understand how the story follows through the different images, and what is meant by the differently shaped panels of writing that break through them. But as Jamie reads, and changes his voice to suit what is happening, I begin to see that some panels—rectangular ones—tell more of the story, or describe things, while others—rounder ones with tails—are what people are saying. The tails always point the way to the mouth of the person speaking, as if their words have frozen as they say them, and become visible in the air, like breath on a cold morning.

He doesn't trace the lines of writing like my father, but he does keep one finger under each panel of the story while he reads it to me, so I can keep track of where on the page we are. As the story unfolds, I become mesmerized by it: the plot holds me captivated, while the intensity of the little coloured squares is wonderful to look at. I realize now why Jamie has whole boxes of these things.

We read until Lena knocks on the door and brings us food. "I won't disturb you," she promises as she sets the tray down on the floor. "Don't forget to do your teeth. You can bring the plates down in the morning."

"Thanks," I say.

She glances at the comic and looks amused. "Don't give yourself bad dreams," she says.

"We won't," Jamie says seriously.

"We won't," I echo.

"*Buonanotte,*" she says, and closes the door quietly behind her.

Jamie sets the comic down on the bed while we eat. Looking at it, I can see that we've read almost a third of the way through. Time seems to have passed without touching us. I can't wait to start reading again.

"Lena's nice," Jamie says.

"Yes. I like her."

"We haven't got anyone yet," he says. "Perhaps we will soon."

I munch away happily.

Jamie says, "Next week I'm going to school."

"Where?"

"In the town. We went and saw it yesterday. It's quite a long walk. The playground's quite big."

"I don't go to school yet," I say, a little uncertainly.

"That's because I'm older than you."

"Do you want to go?"

"Yes," he says. "It's going to be fun. It looks nicer than my last school. Mummy says it's much smaller, too, and I'll make friends more easily."

I feel a stab of something cold inside me at that. Perhaps if Jamie meets other people at school—people older than me—he will stop being my friend. I say, "Oh."

"I have to walk there every day. We looked at things on the way back so I know where to go—like landmarks."

"That's clever," I say. A thought comes to me. "I could walk with you—if you like. I know the way."

"Yeah?" he says, sounding pleased and a little relieved. "That would be great. I think I remember where to go—but it would be nicer if you came as well."

The coldness fades away when he says this, is replaced by warm happiness: I can be useful, and Jamie wants my company.

He is looking around my room. "What are your hobbies?" he asks.

"I don't know."

"Mine are comics and astronomy," he says. "Well, you already know about the comics."

"What's the other thing?"

"Astronomy's watching the stars," he says. "That's what my telescope's for. And I have a chart, too, with all the constellations marked on it, so you can look for them."

On the wall by the window is a strange map, pinned there beside the telescope, marked with strange groupings of different-sized dots. Constellations? This is a *chart*.

"What's a constellation?" I ask.

"It's a collection of stars. They make shapes. There's one that looks like a big saucepan—there's a little saucepan, too—and a man with a belt, and lots more. Orion—that's the man—his belt's made of three really bright stars in a row. That one's easy to spot."

"Do you know them all?" I ask.

"I know almost all of them by heart," he says. "But there are lots and lots."

"I wish I had a hobby," I say, looking around my bedroom. Now that Lena has tidied it, it looks strangely empty.

"Perhaps lizards are your hobby," he says.

"I don't think they are."

"Or perhaps visiting places in your head," he adds.

"Maybe," I say, brightening a little.

"Do you want to go on?" he asks, picking up the comic.

"Yeah!"

So we read on. Jamie's voice is steady and precise. Sometimes the longer words make him pause for a second, but he rarely stumbles. Always I can see by the position of his finger where on the page we are, and the way the images tie in with the story itself—are part of it—is wonderful. I feel as if I am being pulled into the world of the story, through the surface of the paper.

And now something begins to happen. As Jamie keeps reading, and I keep watching the images on the turning pages, a kind of buzzing starts to seep into my head. Through the buzzing I can still hear Jamie's voice and still see the pictures, but everything else seems to slip and slide away from me. The little boxes and speech bubbles swim and blur on the page, as if they are struggling to break free of it, and their contents— the neat black shapes of the words that Jamie is saying aloud—writhe and twist. Whenever I stare hard at them, they freeze back into immobility; but as my eyes drift, they tremble and shudder at the edge of my vision.

The colours are more intense now than before, and as I stare, I begin to see them with an amazing clarity. The pictures glow larger in front of my eyes until I can see tiny rosettes of coloured dots; red, and blue, and yellow, all intersecting and forming other colours, oranges and greens and purples and browns. All the colours are made of these little wheels of dots; all the pictures are dots; an illusion of dots. The only solid colour—*real* colour—is the black of the writing, which is clean and clear and unbroken. I trace in my mind the shape of the next word—

Streetlight

and the solidity of it is like cast iron, massive and permanent amid a whirl of coloured confetti.

Then the picture pulls back from me and I can once again see the image itself, and not just the tiny pieces of which it is composed. In it, a man in a raincoat is standing under a streetlight—*Streetlight*—on the corner of a city street; behind him, a tall building on which stands a masked figure.

Jamie is still reading. ". . . behind the windows. Beneath the street-light there, he can see the man he has been searching for."

My breathing catches and hesitates, and I must tense, because Jamie stops suddenly and looks at me.

"Alex—are you all right?"

"I think so," I say. My head is normal again; there is nothing of the shimmering and whirling that was there a minute ago. Everything is the same again.

"You looked strange there for a moment," he says, sounding cautiously worried, as though he is becoming used to the idea of my looking strange.

"I'm OK," I say, and add, "I think I can read."

"What do you mean?"

"I think I learnt to read," I say. I point to the next frame. "The man at the desk says, 'What happened out there?' "

"Yeah," Jamie says slowly. "That's right. 'What happened out there?' But—then you must have been able to read before."

"I don't think so," I say.

"Well, why did you learn now?"

"I don't know."

"That's really strange. You *must* have been able to read before. Just a little, perhaps."

"I don't think so," I say again.

"Well. I mean—it's good, but it usually takes longer than that, I think."

"How long did it take you?"

"I don't really remember," he says, looking puzzled. "I remember reading with Mummy when I was small. But sometimes she was reading, not me." He thinks for a while. "And at school. Other people at school used to have to learn to read. And sometimes it took them a long time."

"My daddy's been teaching me," I say. "But I never worked it out. Until now."

"Oh," he says, sounding relieved. "Oh, well, that's why, then. If you've been learning, then it's normal, I think."

I smile uncertainly. "Oh, right."

"Still . . ." He sits for a moment, staring at the wall opposite, apparently lost in thought. It occurs to me that Jamie is *staring into space*—that this is how I must sometimes look. The thought is very peculiar. Then he turns back to me. "Do you want to read for a bit?"

"Well—OK. But you do the voices really well."

"Just for a bit, then. You can do to the end of this episode."

I prop the book up on my lap. " 'It's a bit hard to ex—' "

"Explain."

" '—explain.'—'Start at the beginning, then.' "

Later, when we have reached the end of the section and Jamie has taken over again—I am secretly pleased, because I like it much more when he reads—I find myself thinking briefly how happy my father will be now that we won't have to do any more stories together. And later still, it occurs to me that perhaps, now that I can read, my parents will let me go to school with Jamie.

"There's one," I say.

"That was a big one."

"Yeah."

"Some of them get through," he says, sounding lazy and happy. "All the way, and hit the ground. Space rocks."

"Yeah?"

"Mm. All the way through."

My mother says my learning to read is a miracle. My father is, I think, almost suspicious at first—as though he begins to think I have known how to read for months, and have been concealing the ability from him. When the suspicion fades, it is replaced by puzzlement. I am left embarrassed and self-conscious about the whole episode, and keep wishing I had learnt to read normally, instead of in this obviously improper fashion. I am also, secretly, afraid that I might stop being able to read as suddenly and spontaneously as I started. When I tell Jamie this, he laughs, and says it doesn't go away once you know how; but when I tell him a little more about how it felt when I learnt, he becomes quiet and thoughtful, and in the end says that he doesn't think I should tell my parents about *that*. I am well aware of how important it is not to tell my parents everything. I can still remember too vividly how bad things were when I was a liar.

My mother asks me what I think of the idea of going to school. It is a relief; it saves me from having to ask her the same thing. The only sad thing is that I am in the year below Jamie—he's eight, but I'm still seven—and so I can only see him at break-times and after class. It's not enough.

School is strange to start with, but not so bad after a while. I have always been an outsider with the children of the town, a foreigner; sometimes weird; a bit slow. I realize that I have expected the children to think the same way about Jamie, but they don't: Jamie is a person it is impossible not to like. He is open and friendly to everyone, and brave and good-looking and clever without being *too* clever. I think in school he is sometimes a little lazy in his lessons, but his teachers can forgive him anything. At break-time he keeps mostly away from the games of football that are so central a part of the playground culture; but sometimes he will join in, called to by the players. The fluidity of his movement when he does makes the other boys look as awkward and monolithic beside him as I always feel. He isn't interested in soccer, though. His ability to run—to set his feet surely and certainly on any terrain, to co-ordinate his whole body to the rhythm of his footfalls, to seem suspended half an inch above the ground itself—is something he takes for granted, like the colour of his hair or eyes. He is inevitably popular. He puts me back in the centre of things, too: I gain an acceptance simply by being near him.

Nobody thinks of Jamie as being an outsider.

But then things start to go wrong. Although my first year is fun, after that my lessons start to become more and more of a struggle. The more structured the subjects are, the more overwhelmed I am by confusion. Having thought I was starting to make sense of my world, it now seems to be coming apart around me once again.

The concepts of mathematics are impenetrable to me. I stare at the symbols and numbers on the board of our classroom with increasing desperation, while around me the other children copy down the sums and work out the answers. It is learning to read all over again; endless hours of tedious incomprehension, broken into only by the unintentional travels my mind takes. *Going places in your head.* To begin with I am a joke that even the teachers find a bit amusing—dreamy Alex. Vacant Alex. Then I am a nuisance, an irritation. Lazy. Finally I am a serious concern, and my parents are called in.

Miserably, I sit at home with Lena waiting for them to return. Lena tries to cheer me up, but it's no good.

"I try to understand," I say. "I try really hard. But nothing happens."

"Don't be sad, little Alex," she says. "It will come, you'll see."

"Can you do maths, Lena?"

"Yes. I can add up the groceries faster than the girl in the *supermercato*," she says with a smile. "For all she's got a machine to help her." I try to smile; the *supermercato* is in Salerno, and we sometimes go there to buy things we can't get in town, like the English gin my father likes. Lena's scathing opinion of the place and its employees is well known to me. But it is difficult to fall into the old jokes.

She goes on, "People learn things at different speeds, you know. It doesn't mean you're stupid."

"Maybe I *am* stupid," I say.

"No you aren't. You're—thoughtful, that's what. You think about things." She laughs gently. "Perhaps sometimes you're thinking about things too much to learn, eh?"

But I know this isn't true; it is Jamie who thinks about things, not me.

A while after my parents go into school, my mother takes me to see a doctor—a specialist. I am excused classes for a day to make the trip to Salerno. We go in the car, my mother out of her element and driving with an air of terrible focus and constant apprehension. The further we go from the dusty valley of Altesa into the stark, industrialized landscape of the city, the more apprehensive I become.

In Dr. Ribecci's office I stare at coloured lights, and flashing lights. There is a little drum with black and white lines on it which he spins round for me to look at, and a little torch he shines in my eyes. I have to read numbers and letters from a board—I am pleased to be able to do this. I don't like Dr. Ribecci much. My mother sits all the while twisting the cuff of her blouse. I am very careful all the time not to go away, because Jamie has told me to keep the going places thing a secret. He says that doctors might not understand it. It is comforting, as I watch the flashing lights and read the numbers and letters, to know that Jamie, at least, *does* understand.

At the end of all the tests, I can tell Dr. Ribecci is a little puzzled and a little irritated. I am not any of the things that he has thought I might be. I can see well, and hear well, and look at flashing lights and spinning drums with no trouble at all.

In the car on the way home, my mother seems preoccupied. I watch her for a while, and then say, "At least I'm not putty-mal."

"What, darling?"

"What the doctor said." I think briefly. " 'There are no primary indications of putty-mal.' That's good, isn't it?"

My mother blinks, frowning. "Yes," she says. "Yes, darling, that's good." She doesn't sound quite sure, though.

When we get home, my father isn't sure either. I can hear his voice raised from where I am, at the top of the stairs. "*Nothing?* He can't find anything wrong at all?" There is an angry silence; then, "Well, that settles it. I've thought all along he was just being idle. He learns fast enough when the mood takes him, doesn't he?"

There is the sound of my mother's voice, protesting, the words not discernible.

"Well, perhaps that's the whole problem. You're soft on him. Lena's soft on him, too. And he spends too much time with that Anderson boy. If he made the same effort with his schoolwork that he makes with those—damned comic books, he wouldn't be so far behind."

Again there are the quieter sounds of my mother, trying to smooth things over. She must manage it, because the row never makes it up to the first floor of the house, remaining instead lodged in the living room, where it eventually burns itself out into mutterings.

The next day, though, before school, my father takes me on one side.

"You have to concentrate, Alex," he says, seriously. "How can you remember things if you don't concentrate?"

"I try," I say, looking at my shoes.

"Well, try trying a bit harder."

I can tell from his tone that he's not angry, exactly; he's trying to *jolly me along.* I nod. "I will," I say.

"Good man. That's all we want." He pauses, then tips my chin up so I have to look at him. "You know you can manage it when you try. Just look at your reading. That happened in the end, didn't it?"

"Yes," I say.

"And that was because you worked at it," he says. "It wasn't always easy, but you got there in the end. That's what you have to do at school."

"OK."

I am left with the strangest feeling that the history of the past year is changing around me; that the details of the "miracle" are no longer quite so miraculous. In a flash of rare insight, I wonder whether by the end of another year, anyone will remember anything unusual about the way I learned to read.

I go to wait for Jamie before school on Friday, eager to tell him all about my visit, and all the tests. I have only been there for a minute or two when Mr. Anderson comes out. He has his hands deep in his trouser pockets and he looks, I think, uncomfortable.

"Buongiorno," I say politely.

"Hello, Alex," Mr. Anderson says. His Italian is much better than my father's—he doesn't have that strange, awkward accent that my father has—but he talks to me today in English. "Ah—Jamie won't be coming to school today, I'm afraid. You'll have to walk in on your own."

This is the first time something like this has happened. "Is he all right?" I say. "Is he ill?"

"No," says Mr. Anderson, shortly. "He's in trouble."

"Oh."

"You'd better get along now, or you'll be late." And he turns and goes back inside the house.

It's my fault Jamie's in trouble. I have to piece it together bit by bit over the course of the day, from things overheard, from gossip in the playground, but that's what it comes down to: it's my fault. If I hadn't gone to the doctor, nothing would have happened.

On Thursday, when I am not at school, there is the normal interest in where I've gone. Someone—Jamie says later that he suspects Signorina Martelli, our Maths teacher—lets it be known that I am away because I have to see a doctor in Salerno. A *special* doctor. The school quickly makes the connection between special doctors and my occasional strangenesses in class. A girl in Jamie's year comes forward with the impressive assertion that her cousin has been to see a special doctor, and that he is no longer allowed to go to disco parties or even to watch television, because these things make him weird. The special doctor makes clear and official what is wrong with the English boy: he is weird in the head, probably insane. Word in the playground quickly determines that I may never come back; that sometimes they lock people like that up.

By the lunchtime break, everyone is in on the story. In a group by the painted goalposts of the soccer pitch, one boy is explaining what happens to people like the English boy once they've been locked up. Quite a little crowd has gathered to hear his ideas. Because of the crowd, he isn't able to see Jamie attach himself to the edge of it. Before anyone knows quite what has happened, Jamie has heard what the boy is saying, has pushed through the crowd to its centre, and has knocked the boy down.

The boy is older and heavier than Jamie: a tough-looking lad who, on his back in the dust and holding the lip that's been split across his teeth, looks dazed with pain but also stunned with surprise. The crowd instinctively pulls back, makes a ring around the two boys. From around the playground, others join. Someone starts a chant of "Fight! Fight!"

The older boy gets to his feet, shaking his head. Jamie waits until he's standing, and then hits him a second time: a hard, straight punch to the face which knocks him over again. Something about the way he does it—the clinical neatness of the punch, the lack of bravado, no threats or posturing or hesitation—gets through to the crowd. The chant of "Fight!" dies abruptly, and an uneasy silence takes its place. The older boy's nose is bleeding and there is blood in the dust. The fight should be over, but the tautness of Jamie's body says it isn't. His hands are loose, unclenched, but not hanging by his sides; they're slightly elevated, ready, his shoulders ready, his eyes waiting.

When he sees that the boy isn't going to get up again, Jamie says, "Don't say things like that about my friend."

Everyone hears it. He turns, then, looks at the ring of children that has gathered, and in his eyes each of them sees that he's ready to fight anyone there: they see the way his hands are ready, and the circle spreads wider, as if his gaze is pushing them back. "Don't *any* of you say things like that."

His face is white, but his voice is very even. One of the younger girls starts suddenly to cry.

Jamie and the other boy are sent home and told not to come back until after the weekend. Nothing like this has ever happened before, and for a week or more Jamie and I are the centre of all the attention of the school. But embarrassing and awkward though this is, at least my fears of reprisals prove unfounded. Nobody picks on me. After a while, I realize that nobody ever will: they're scared. I start to understand how good it is to have a friend like Jamie.

"There's another," I say. "How many's that?"

"I don't know. I lost count."

We stare up at the night sky, sated with shooting stars, full of sleepy contentment. Jamie says, "It'll be my birthday soon."

"I know. What're you going to do?"

"There'll be a party," he says. "I'm going to invite some people from school."

"And me."

"Mm—all right, you can come."

I giggle and punch his arm gently. "Anyone else?"

"Anna's coming," he says.

"Who's Anna?"

"She's my cousin."

"What's she like?"

"I don't know her all that well. I think she was at a wedding I was at once. She's OK. She's just moved to Italy this year. Mummy said it would be nice to invite her because maybe she doesn't have many friends here yet."

"I s'pose."

He says, "I asked for a torch with different colours. There's one that has blue and red and green as well as white."

"That's a good present."

"I thought we could signal to each other. You know, at night."

"Your window doesn't face the right way."

"I know. But the spare room does. It's just across the hall from mine. My parents never notice what I do anyway."

"We could have a code."

"Or learn Morse code."

"Yeah."

There is a zip of light across the darkness, but neither of us bother to point it out to the other.

"It'll be a good party," Jamie says. "I can't wait."

"Me neither."

It is late when the last image of the stars fades and the dark valley takes their place. The candle I have taken up has burnt down to a third of its original length, and the night air coming through the window is starting to be cooler. I rub my eyes, unstick the candle from its little pool of hardened wax, and go slowly downstairs.

Jamie's party. His ninth birthday. It should have been nothing much, just a lot of kids having fun, balloons and birthday cake and presents. And it was all of these things, of course, but there was one thing also—one thing in particular.

But perhaps it's not right to say that it was the party that was the fulcrum of change, because it is two days before that, on the road out of Altesa as I am coming back from buying sweets in the town, that I first see her. She is sitting under one of the lemon trees in the patch of scrub land opposite our house. Anna. This is my first image of her. Her face is turned away from me, a skinny ten-year-old girl, her jeans and T-shirt dusty from the earth on which she's sitting.

She is plummeting like a stone towards water that is too far below her, and the air is frozen and on fire in my lungs as I watch her fall, unaware—or at least unafraid—

She is tying a bandage tight with hands dark with blood in the dusty afternoon light of an abandoned chapel, dust motes swirling in the air around her like a halo—a *pietà*—

She is naked by the open window, neon light from the street shaping her breasts and her hair, not caring—enjoying it—

* * *

She is sitting under a lemon tree, turned from me, watching a cat that is hardly more than a kitten play in the dry grass there. Her jeans are dusty with the red dust of the valley, and her T-shirt and her shoes too. I see her from the road. She sits oblivious to my presence, looking away from me, not yet even knowing that I exist in her world, or she in mine.

5

*E*ngland: a dark green carpet, a wooden train that I play with. The windows are tall and the curtains that hang from them come all the way down to the floor. Outside, behind the window, rain is coming down; the light is grey, and it feels cold.

England is still cold and grey when I am thirteen. The September air is dank and misty in the mornings, and it seems to rain constantly. It's not even the fast, hard rain of the coastal storms back in Altesa, but a slow, penetrating, steady rain that looks like it will never let up. The weather is as grey and bleak as I feel in this place.

I tell myself, before I arrive, that because Jamie will be here with me, everything will be all right again; that somehow the strange distance that has come over us in the past year will be flushed clean away. It's not true. We have left it too long. If only we had seen each other at Christmas and Easter, I keep saying to myself, Christmas and Easter and the summer before—then maybe it wouldn't be so bad. But it is.

So much has changed. I see Jamie—he's there in the corridors, at meal times, at chapel in the morning. He doesn't meet my eyes. He's different now. Different on the outside: taller again, and his already dark hair has darkened further, and hangs in a kind of swatch over one eye. Different in other ways, too. When I go up to him on my first day here—try to talk to him—it's like he doesn't know me. His eyes are blank, and he hardly looks at me. Confused and upset, I let him be; and as I go, I hear one of the boys passing say, "Who's that?"

"Carlisle," Jamie says. "I used to know him."

I used to know him. The words follow me all day, and wrap me in a cocoon of loneliness and incomprehension. So: this is England. This is the next five years.

My room, on the first floor of the house, is small and bare. I have unpacked my clothes and the few books and other things I have brought, but even though the room is small, they don't seem to have made any impression on it. The walls are cream-coloured and spotted with the marks left by blu-tack from old posters. Jamie's room is on the second floor with the other fourteen year olds: fourth-formers. I am a third-former. Sixth-form boys look like adults to me: except for their clothes, it's difficult to tell them apart from the teachers. On my second day, reporting for a squash trial, I call the man in charge "sir," and everyone laughs. He is not a man; he's a sixth-form boy. I still can't see a difference.

The week passes me by in a frantic haze of disjointed images and half-comprehended instructions. I am issued with books and paper and files, with timetables and a calendar and a fountain pen. The lessons are hard to follow, and people expect me to know things I don't. I want to ask someone, but I don't know anyone here. Not even Jamie.

When the weekend comes I am exhausted, but there are more lessons on Saturday morning. Before lunch is a double: an hour and a half which, my timetable tells me, is Art. At least I know where to go. I have seen boys coming out of this building with paint on their hands or streaks of clay on their trousers; it's easy to work it out. When I arrive, I am slightly early.

It is a big building, with tall windows. The expanse of floor is divided up into areas with screens, and in each area is a clutter of easels and stools and tables with brushes and jars and palettes on them. The whole place smells of paint and paper and glue and ink and a thousand other unidentifiable things. There are a few older boys working in some of the areas, and also a man arranging wooden stools in a big, open part of the room. I approach, hesitantly, and he looks up.

"Hi. You're a bit early," he says. "Do you want to give me a hand? I'm just putting these into rows."

"OK," I say. I am surprised how normally he speaks to me. Most of the teachers seem far more remote. He is wearing a painting smock, spattered and daubed with different colours. He is, I realize, the first teacher I have seen not wearing a suit.

"I'm Mr. Dalton. What's your name?" he says, as I carry stools into place.

"Carlisle."

"What about your first name?"

"Alex." It is the first time a teacher has asked me that.

"Do you like Art?"

I have to think for a moment. I have never done Art before—not properly. Something comes to me of drawing pictures for Lena, and her keeping them for me, and of designing rockets with Jamie some time long, long before. I say, "Yes."

"Good. You'll find things are a little different in here. We tend to be a bit less formal. Now. Which do you think—the boots or the bottles?" He is pointing to a pair of old leather boots and a cluster of differently coloured bottles on a table.

"What for?"

"You're going to draw them."

"The boots," I say.

"OK. Why?" While we are talking, he arranges them on a pedestal in front of the rows of stools.

"I don't know. They look more interesting, I suppose."

"How come?"

"The colours," I say slowly. "All browns and greys. And the way they're all creased up."

He smiles. "Fair enough. We'll see how you get on."

Other boys are filing into the room by now, and taking up seats in front of the boots I've chosen. When the whole class is there, Mr. Dalton gives out wooden boards to rest on, and paper, and thick black pencils.

"Just see what you make of them," he says. "Try to catch the way the light from the window creates these shadows here. And here's a tip—if you just draw the shadows, and ignore the highlights, they'll take care of themselves. And you'll at least end up with a picture that *says* something rather than one which is just grey all over. Give it a go, and we'll see what you come up with in forty minutes or so, and then we'll have a crack at something else."

I have drawn castles and spaceships and copied cartoon figures from the comic books with Jamie and Anna, but I can't remember drawing something real that is in front of me. It is a difficult idea. I realize I have to use my eyes as a kind of camera, to put what I can see in front of me onto the paper. All around me, I can hear the scratching sound of pencils working diligently, but I am still struggling to understand how to begin. I find I daren't make a mark on the paper; it will be wrong, and I won't know what to do next. I can see why Mr. Dalton has chosen this for us: it is a kind of test to start us off, to see whether we can draw at all. And I have said I like Art. Panic builds in me as I wonder whether I will finish the session with a blank piece of paper in front of me.

A memory flickers in me of the wonder that just paint and brushes can make something so beautiful; so huge. In a strange way, the thought gives me courage.

I am staring at the paper, trying to will it to receive the image I know should be on it, when very gradually the boots on their pedestal, and the boys' heads between me and them, and the windows and the table with the bottles and everything, all start to float up through the whiteness of the paper. I blink, shocked, and they are gone at once.

But I have the idea now. I try again, harder, and it is an effort because of the dim awareness of people breathing and shuffling and drawing and moving all around me, and because it has *all* become so much more difficult now. But I am able to manage something. The image trembles in and out of my vision for a while, and then I am able to hold it steady. Mr. Dalton says to draw the shadows and so I start doing that, carefully shading in where the dark parts of the image are. It is disconcerting at first to see the pencil break the surface of the room and dip under it, and more disconcerting still to find that there is paper, hard against a board, just under what I see. For an instant everything wavers and threatens to fall away again. But I hold it there, forcing myself not to let it go. And gradually—very gradually—a second room starts to take shape underneath the one in front of me: a monochrome room with deep shadows and vague, uncertain highlights. The heads of the boys in the rows in front of me are dark, and then there is a slab of rainy brightness where the pedestal is, and the convoluted surfaces of the leather, and the darkness under the table and in the long curtains off at one side. The pencils we've been given are soft, and the blocks of shade I make with mine are pleasantly deep.

For the first time all week I actually feel calm. Through the whirlpooling confusion that has tugged me this way and that, I have been constantly aware that everyone else seems to fit in here more than I do. I don't even know anything about England—can't remember anything much of the first three years of my life that I've been told were spent here.

I do remember dreaming of the start of a term when Jamie and I would go to England together, instead of saying goodbye to each other at the bus-stop in the square. But so much has changed since then, and the dream doesn't feel anything like the same any more.

Jamie. I see his face now, in front of me: his eyes and mouth and features. But it's not the face I know; it's changed. Somehow, there is someone different there. I don't know what it is. I wish I understood what has happened to us.

"Alex?"

It doesn't make sense to me for a moment, and then things shift subtly.

I am in the Art room. The stools in front of me are empty, though; the other boys are leaving. I can hear footsteps and voices as the big double doors that lead into the room swing closed.

"Alex?" Mr. Dalton says. His hand is on my shoulder. He smiles. "You were pretty engrossed there," he says. "Everyone else has learnt a bit about lino cuts. I thought you looked as if you'd like to keep going on your own."

"Oh," I say. "Thanks."

"Lunchtime in five minutes," he says. "Don't worry, you won't be late. Let's have a look at what you've done."

He takes my picture and props it on the table. He looks at it for a long time, looking once or twice over to where the boots still sit.

"Not bad at all," he says at last. "Have you done much Art before?"

"No," I say. "We didn't do much at school."

"Well, that shows," he says slowly. "There's a lot you can learn about technique. But the representation—that's impressive." He pauses again. "What about this?" he asks, pointing.

It takes me by surprise, almost. On the left hand side of the picture, where there is a big unbroken area of shadow cast in the angle of the wall and a curtained-off part of the window, my pencil has changed what is really there—added to it. I have made it look as if features—a nose, an eye, the corner of a mouth—are visible, coming through the shadow.

"Don't I recognize him?" Mr. Dalton says.

"It's a friend," I say. "Jamie. James Anderson, I mean."

"That's it—knew I knew him. Musician, isn't he?"

"Yes."

"Not bad," he says quietly, peering closely at the picture. "He looks younger here, though." Then he straightens up. "Why did you add him into the picture?"

"I don't really know," I say. "I just wanted to put something there. I was just—daydreaming, I suppose."

"Well, it's the best work I've seen from a third-former in a very long time," he says. I blink at the praise. He adds, "The department's open in the afternoons and evenings. I expect they've got tons of junior sports and stuff lined up for you, but if you're free—if you'd like—come in some time. This afternoon, if you can. There's always someone here. I'd like to see how you get on with paints, too." He stops, smiles again. "You'd better cut along if you want to get to lunch. But perhaps I'll see you later?"

"OK," I say at once. "Yeah."

I leave the building with a wonderful and strange buzzing feeling inside me. I can do this; I can fit in here. If anyone asks me where I'm going this afternoon, I can say, *To the Art department. I'm going to do some painting*—and everyone will understand. Everyone knows what that means. Even the thing that has been lost, buried in some strange avalanche in my head, has left behind it this ability to see the drawing through the paper, and to capture it there: something I can use. It is as if, in an instant, I have made sense of myself.

"What are your hobbies?" he asks.

"I don't know."

"Perhaps lizards are your hobby."

"I don't think they are."

"Or perhaps visiting places in your head."

Running down the path towards the dining hall, I wish I could go back and tell that Jamie—the Jamie who was still my best friend—that I've at last found the answer.

I have spent two weeks' worth of pocket money on liquorice and boiled sweets in the early afternoon. Lena says it is not long to wait until Jamie's party, but to me—and to Jamie—it feels like an age. The sweets are supposed to wait for Saturday, but our resolve isn't strong enough. It feels good to have no resolve, and, walking back from town with the pleasingly heavy paper bag clutched in one hand, I almost skip along the dusty tarmac.

Nearly home, a movement catches my eye. On my right, on the side of the road across from our houses, is a little patch of land in which old lemon trees are arranged in rows. It is overgrown, thick with weeds and the brown debris of past summers, too small a field to compete economically with the great expanses of lemons cultivated north of us. Someone owned it once, but now it is common property. In season, all the lemons for Lena's delicious lemonade come from here, picked by Jamie and me in amounts dictated by Lena, our labour repaid in lemonade later in the day. A low whitewashed concrete wall divides the field from the road.

I see what has moved: away in the middle of the trees, a young cat is playing—running to and fro, pouncing at nothing, catching glimpses of its own tail which prompt it to frenzies. I am about to pass on by when I catch sight of Jamie, sitting under a tree closer to the road. He is clearly watching the cat, too, hugging his knees, not realizing I am there. I could call to him, but an inspiration comes to sneak up on him instead, to surprise him. I clamber over the little wall and, putting my feet down with care so as not to make any sound, I creep closer and closer to where he is sitting.

He has his back almost completely to me. I can see only his left shoulder and part of his head past the trunk of the lemon tree, his dark hair stirred every so often by the slight breeze that is making the leaves whisper drily. In front of us, a little way off, the cat is scratching at a stump, bending the whole of its body with the luxurious effort of it.

I am a few yards behind Jamie now—nearly ready to shout *Surprise!* and run at him—when something makes me stop. Something is wrong— different. I stare at the back of his head: his lightly curling hair moves enough for me to see every now and again the pale curve of his ear. He is wearing a rust-coloured T-shirt, almost the same colour as the earth round here, which I haven't seen him wear before, and jeans. One foot is splayed out to the side a bit, and I can see his shoes are different, too; not trainers, but canvas shoes, battered-looking. I have never seen him wear canvas shoes either.

So I don't yell. Instead I call, more quietly, "Jamie?"

And she turns round. She is a girl—not Jamie at all. I can see her face now, as she stares at me, and I am seeing him there as well— though she doesn't look so much like him; maybe just the colour of her hair, and her eyes, and something in her expression. But it is him too.

Then the confusion passes, and she is just a girl with short hair. I have made a mistake, that's all.

"Who're you?" she says.

"I'm Alex," I say. "Who're you?"

"Alex?" she says, without answering. "Jamie's friend?"

"Yes."

"Jamie said about you. I'm his cousin. I'm here for the party."

"It's not till Saturday," I say stupidly.

"I know that," she says, getting up. The cat suddenly becomes aware of us, and after staring for a moment, frozen, takes off into the scrub, bounding swiftly out of sight.

"I thought—" I say.

She walks over. She is about Jamie's height and build, too, though the way she speaks makes her sound a bit older to me. She says, "My name's Anna." She looks around at the valley. "I got here this morning. There's not much to do here, is there?"

"I don't know," I say, not sure what to make of this.

"Let's go and find Jamie," she says. "He's in his room with his books, I think. He's got a lot of books. How old are you?"

"Eight," I say.

"I'm ten," she says, her voice becoming a little more distant as she says the words. "Come on."

She leads the way to Jamie's house. I follow on behind her, still hug- ging my bag of sweets. I have bought two of all the good ones, like I always do; but now there are three people, and they will never go round properly.

Later, it will be clear to me how different Anna is from Jamie and me. Jamie's dreams are dreams of the imagination, fuelled by his comics and his always-questioning mind: dreams of the surface of the moon, and of what it would be like to fly, and why the sky changes colour at dusk and dawn. My dreams are dreams of my own past; I am enmeshed in afternoons with Lena and first meetings with a boy called Jamie so hopelessly that it is sometimes difficult to know what is reality and what is a slipping-away into what has gone before. But Anna inhabits the here and now, the moment, the world of impression and action and sensation. Jamie's books and comics don't interest her; they are fiction, not real. The world around her is enough of a story for her, and she makes it her own. Jamie looks beyond what he sees because he senses that there is more to know, more to discover and find out. It is curiosity which pulls him in. Anna looks beyond what she sees because she wants to feel more, to experience more, to flood herself with life until she can hold no more—and then turn to something new and start again. It is a need which drives her. It is not of her own will, even; it goes beyond that. She can't help it. It is what she is. But I am eight years old, and I know nothing of this part of her.

We take Anna to the little cove that afternoon. Nobody comes here but us. The walk takes you along the cliff and around a rocky spur, and then a treacherous little path leads the way over a spit of land. On the far side of this is a way down to the shore, and then, following the coast around still further, you come abruptly on the cove itself: a neat scoop out of the line of the cliffs, protected in part by a rocky promontory which keeps the larger sea-waves out of the deep, gentle water there. The beach is shingle and large, flat rocks, extending about a third of the way round before it straggles off into huge boulders and fallen debris, and the base of the cliffs has been eaten into a little so that where the water comes right up to them they overhang the sea. The day is hot and still and the water is moving only a little, lazily, against the stones. We are breathless and sticky after the walk and the climb down.

"What do you think?" Jamie says.

"It's nice," Anna says, and there's approval in her voice. "Does anyone else come here?"

"No. Well, hardly ever."

"What do you do here?"

"Swim," he says. "The water's really clear, and if you keep your eyes open you can see the fishes. And dive, too. There's a place on the rock there that's good to dive from."

"Out there?" she says, pointing to the promontory.

"Yeah."

Anna stares for a second. "We should do it," she says. "I'm really hot."

"Can you dive?" I ask.

"Yeah," she says. "Can you?"

"Well, yes," I say. "But if you curl up in a ball you make a big splash. I like that better."

"You can't, can you?"

"Yes I can."

"Bet you can't. Come on, then." Anna sets out along the promontory, picking her way carefully on the rock, which has sharp places like craters. Jamie and I follow until we're out to the right place, the deep water of the cove on our right, the open Mediterranean on our left. We turn our backs to the sea and all we can see is water and cliff and sky.

Anna shrugs off her T-shirt and jeans, and after a second's hesitation Jamie does the same. I am overcome by a sudden and surprising shyness. When Jamie and I come here on our own, we often go swimming, and aren't embarrassed by being naked. With Anna here, though, I feel awkward; there is a vague, self-conscious unease about undressing in front of a girl. I fumble with my shirt, blushing, and then the problem is resolved for me. Anna sets her socks on top of her pile of clothes and stands there for a second in her pants; Jamie is the same. Then she turns and shouts, "Race you!"

Jamie is caught by surprise and hesitates; Anna has dived the moment the words are out. Her body breaks the water before he's realized what she's said, and then he grabs a breath and throws himself after her. I watch them, palely visible under the water, until they break back up through the surface further out. Now that I know we're keeping our pants on, all the shyness has left me, and I'm only aware that I'm missing out on the fun. I struggle to get my trousers off and hop on one leg while pulling off my socks. When I look up again, Anna has reached one of the three big rocks that stand out of the water, and is waving one arm over her head. I can hear her shouting in triumph. Jamie is treading water a little way from her, and I can hear his breathless shouts also: "Not fair!"

"Wait for me!" I call, and then launch myself into the water along with them, curling up like a depth-charge and squeezing my eyes shut for the impact. When I surface, the water around me effervescent with tiny bubbles from the splash, they are swimming back towards me, Anna grinning, Jamie looking irritated but not angry.

"We'll do it again, if you like," she says. "Proper start. Alex can judge."

"Well—all right," Jamie says. Then he grins too. "You're pretty fast for a girl."

"I know."

"I'll judge," I say.

Jamie says, "All right, then. Let's do it right, if we're going to do it. Alex, you say three, two, one, go. OK?"

"OK," I say.

"And get over near the rock so you can see the finish properly."

He and Anna scramble out of the water while I scull my way towards the finish post. I haven't seen much of girls except at school, and I squint at Anna's figure as she and Jamie stand ready to dive. Side by side, their bodies are a lot alike; something I register with a vague sense of approval.

"Three, two, one, go!"

We swim for over an hour, making regular trips to the promontory to jump in. The water is cool enough to take the heat of the walk from us, but warm enough that we're never cold, even standing dripping on the beach. After a time we gather together on one of the big flat rocks of the shore, getting our breath back and letting the sun dry the salt on our skin.

I notice Anna looking up at the cliff where it hangs out over the water. "What is it?"

"I was just looking," she says. "See there?"

"What?"

She points. "There's a ledge," she says. "Like a little shelf. See it?"

I'm not sure. "I think so," I say.

Jamie is looking too. "Yeah, I think so," he says. "What about it?"

"I think I could get up there," Anna says. "Wouldn't it be great to dive from?"

"You couldn't get up there," Jamie says uncertainly.

"Yes I could. It's not so hard. There's plenty of places to hold on."

"Isn't it too high?" I ask, worried.

Jamie is looking harder, now. His brow is furrowed with thought, and I know he is working things out, imagining how he would make the climb, running through it all in his head. I wait and let him finish.

"Maybe you're right," he says slowly. "I think I can see a way."

"Told you."

"But isn't it too high?" I ask again.

Jamie shakes his head slowly. "No, I don't think so. It's like the big diving board in Salerno, maybe. And the sea's that deep, isn't it?"

"What are you so worried about?" Anna says impatiently.

"You've got to be careful," I say importantly. "Someone at school dived into the shallow end of a swimming pool by mistake. He broke his nose and broke out all his front teeth. And he got—that thing. Concussion. He could've drowned."

"Well, the water's a lot deeper here," she says. "Come on. Let's do it."

Jamie says, "Alex is right. We've got to be careful. I'll go first and see. Then if it's safe you can go."

"Of course it's safe," she says.

"Well, I'll go first anyway. To make sure." Jamie stands, and picks his way carefully across the jumbled pile of rocks at the base of the cliff. Anna and I follow him a little way. When he reaches the junction of rockfall and cliff, he turns back for a moment and waves. Then he turns his body and his attention to the cliff surface. He moves carefully but quite quickly, choosing where he puts his feet and hands with his easy precision, pulling himself up the rock until he can get one foot onto a horizontal lip which follows one of the sandwiched layers running through the cliff. He shuffles patiently along this while we follow his progress from the beach. At last he is able to lower himself the eighteen inches or so down to the ledge. Once there, he turns round and waves again.

I wave back, and turn to see if Anna is doing the same. She is frowning, though, staring at Jamie.

"What?" I say.

"That's not where I meant," she says, sounding cross.

Jamie puts his arms up and bends his knees and casts himself into the air. He is in shadow on the ledge, but halfway through the downward arc of the dive his body is caught by the sunlight, suddenly startlingly bright before it slices into the surface of the water. Three long seconds pass, and he surfaces ten yards away, grinning, his hair plastered down over his head.

"It's really great!" he shouts.

Anna waits until he's swum back to shore. "That's not where I meant," she says.

Jamie looks puzzled. "That's the only place there is."

"No. Up *there.*" She is pointing again. Jamie moves close to her to follow the line of her arm, and he frowns sharply. I am trying to see also, and at last I do: another ledge, higher and much smaller than the one Jamie has reached.

"That's far too high," he says after a moment. "I mean, that'd kill you."

"Wouldn't, I bet."

"The bottom here's all rock, not sand," he says. "And it's not so far down right by the cliff. It's deeper in the middle there, but not at the cliff." His tone is patient.

"I bet I could get up there," she says.

"Well, probably you could get up there," he says. "But you couldn't dive. It's too high. It's twice as far up as the other place."

Anna looks from one part of the cliff to the other, and gradually acceptance comes into her face.

"You're right," she says at last. "OK. But it was good from that one?"

Jamie grins again. "Yeah. You got to try it. You, too, Alex."

"Yeah!"

"Me first," Anna says. We watch as she climbs over the rocks and follows the path Jamie has taken. The way she moves is different to Jamie, I realize. When I watch Jamie I always feel safe; know that everything he does has been thought through carefully and will be all right. Anna's movements are easy, casual like Jamie's, but they make me tense watching her: as she makes her way up the cliff, I am always afraid she will fall. But she never does; not navigating the change from scree to cliff; not when edging along the little lip of rock; not when letting herself down into place. All the time I am watching, it is as if she is on the edge of falling, but she never does.

She turns and waves and waits a second. Then she kicks away from the rock and drops cleanly to the water. It is a good dive, almost as good as Jamie's. A few moments later she surfaces, gasping and laughing.

"It's good!" I hear her call.

"Me now!"

"Go on," Jamie says. "I'll tell you where to go."

We climb the cliff, and dive, and climb again, until we're exhausted. The beach is bakingly hot, the rocks painful to touch at first, and it isn't long before we're dried off. Jamie looks at his watch regretfully.

"We ought to go back soon," he says.

We get dressed, brushing the grit from between our toes before we put our socks back on, and start along the little path that leads back to the harbour.

"I like this place," Anna says.

"It's great," I agree. "We come here lots."

She's staring around her as she walks, taking in the cliffs and the sea and the sky as if it is all completely foreign to her—as if she's never seen sunlight or water before. "Yes," she says quietly.

Seawater has made me thirsty. "I want a drink," I say. "We could buy Cokes."

Jamie searches his pockets. "I've enough," he says. He has the change from our sandwiches. "But the store shuts soon."

"We could go to Toni's," I say.

"It costs more there. We don't have enough for that."

"Oh."

He looks at his watch. "I could run there," he says. "And wait for you."

Anna and I glance at one another. "Yeah, OK," she says.

"I'll wait for you by the signpost tree."

"OK," I say. I know where he means: a big old tree by a roundabout on the edge of the town with signs nailed up on its trunk, pointing the distances and directions of five or six little villages.

Jamie takes off at once, quite slowly at first, but then quickening his pace in long, even strides. He can run much faster than I can ever hope to. It isn't long before he's out of sight around the curve of the land.

"He's fast," Anna says, sounding impressed.

"Yeah," I say. I wish, suddenly, that I have something I can do as well as that, which would impress her as well. Then she stops, frowning, her hands going to her pockets.

"Oh no."

"What?" I say.

"My watch. I haven't got it. It must be back on the beach." She hesitates, glancing first in the direction Jamie has gone, then back towards the cove. "It was a present. I've got to get it."

"OK," I say.

"Look, I know the way back. You go on and tell Jamie I'll be late. I won't be long. Well, not very. I might have to look for it."

"I can help," I say.

"No, it's OK. I know where it should be. He'll worry if we're too long, but if you tell him, it'll be OK."

"Oh. Yeah. All right," I say.

"Thanks," she says with a quick smile. "See you in a bit." She turns, and half-runs away down the path the way we've come.

I stand there feeling suddenly lonely, and then start to trudge on towards town. I go slowly, thinking vaguely to myself that she may catch me up and keep me company if I'm not too quick. But as I walk, a doubt comes over me. Anna has said that she's left her watch on the beach; and there's something about that which is wrong.

I can remember her watch—can remember how it looks when she tilts her arm to check the time earlier in the afternoon. *It's half-past three,* she says. *There's ages.* In my head I see the sun glitter on the watch face against the pale brown of her arm, the tiny hairs there bleached straw-blond by the sun.

There is a glitter in the corner of my eye as we walk back towards Altesa. I am thirsty; the thought comes to me that we could buy Cokes. Jamie has money, I know; what's left from the sandwiches. Anna is walking on Jamie's other side, her arms swinging slightly. Almost out of my vision in the bright afternoon light comes an intermittent glitter, a sparkling of light on metal.

"I'm thirsty," I say.

She hasn't left the watch back at the beach; she has been wearing it further back along this path. I've seen it on her wrist.

*   *   *

Even now, it doesn't cross my mind for a moment that she might have deliberately deceived me, that she might have slipped the watch off and pocketed it in the same motion which I have taken to be her checking her jeans for it. I just think that it must have come off her arm some way back along the path, and that now, searching for it on the beach, she'll never find it. I have to go back and tell her.

I trot back, keeping alert in case I spot the thing on the way, but the path is bare. At last I reach the corner that leads to the beach, and something here makes me pause. I can see the beach where we have been, but Anna isn't there. I frown. Suddenly I feel apprehensive, as if maybe I shouldn't have come back after all.

I shuffle around the shoulder of sandstone, keeping in close to the protective shadow of the cliff for some reason I can't quite explain to myself. There is a dash of colour on one of the massive stones at the foot of the cliff. Anna's clothes.

I look at once to the diving ledge we've discovered, and sure enough, she is there beside it, pressed against the cliff face, feeling with one foot for a hold. She obviously wants one more dive before going back home. I wonder briefly why she hasn't just said so.

Two things about her strike me at the same time. The first is that this time she has taken all her clothes off. Her body looks much paler against the cliff, in shadow, than it does in the sun. The second thing is that she is climbing the wrong way—past the point where she should be easing her way along, ready to drop down to the ledge. Instead she is climbing upwards and to one side. Her movements are determined, focused, and I know now that she is aiming for the higher ledge, the one she had seen at first, but which Jamie has said will kill us.

I find I have gripped hold of the rocky surface beside me with both hands, as if perhaps my grip will help to hold her as well. I want to scream at her, to yell *Come down!*—but I can't. The air is on fire in my lungs, but it is frozen there, too. There is nothing I can do.

She makes it to the ledge. I see her straighten and glance quickly around the cove. She pauses for a minute—getting her breath back after the climb. She looks very small at this distance, diminished by the vast presence of the cliff, and for a long moment I am sure she is going to edge her way back down again. She has to; it's the only way.

Then she throws herself off, hands pointed, doubled up for a moment before straightening. She seems to hang in the air for one interminable, vertiginous second, as if suspended. The sun catches her as it has caught Jamie, but for longer—infinitely longer. My stomach has contracted into a fierce knot of tension. And then she breaks the surface of the sea and vanishes.

The knot in me becomes an awful slackness, as if everything in my belly has turned to lukewarm water in an instant. My eyes are fixed on the surface of the sea, unmoving, unable to blink. Seconds go by and the waves lap slowly at the pebbles of the shore. Somewhere far off, a sea bird calls and another answers it.

Then her head comes up, and after a second I hear a shrill cry. I think *She's hurt—she's hurt herself*—and then she shouts again, a long whoop of exhilaration and release. For a minute or more she floats there on the calm surface of the water, shouting at the top of her voice at the echoing cliffs of the empty cove, and laughing, and shouting again. At last, she swims slowly to the shore and walks up the beach.

I am still holding the rock, though I find I can breathe again. It is only with difficulty I can make my hands open. The palms are impressed with little grains of sand and the shapes of the strata they've held. I pull myself further back into shadow, but I can't stop watching her. She turns slow circles on the beach, her hands out from her sides, letting the sun and the air dry her. She must have known that waiting for clothing to dry would take much longer—too long—might give her away; that is why she's made the climb naked. Gradually, the terrible anticipation of watching her climb too far up the cliff is wearing off, and my stomach is starting to feel more normal. From my hidden place by the rock I watch Anna turning round and round, her face lifted towards the sun. I stare at those parts of her which were covered before, and I see that in one place at least, her body is very different to Jamie's.

Then she begins to draw her clothes on, and with a slight lurch I realize that she will be where I'm standing in a matter of minutes. I have to go.

Forcing my legs into an unsteady obedience, I run awkwardly and irregularly back along the path, running to get as far away as possible before she catches me up. Whatever it was that made her go back, she clearly meant it to be a secret; this, coupled with a nebulous fear that I can't pin down, spurs me on. I want very much to preserve the myth that she has gone back for her watch, and that I have walked on along the path. Admitting to anything else feels somehow dangerous, like playing with something you don't understand. I keep running until I'm out of breath and have a stitch and have to slow down; but by this time, I'm a long way along the path.

She catches me up just outside the town, and we meet Jamie together.

"Where have you been?" he says. "You were ages."

"I forgot my watch," Anna says. "I had to go back. Alex was supposed to come and tell you." She glances at me. "What took you so long?"

"I—don't know," I say. "I just walked."

Jamie says, "Oh, Alex is no good with things like that. If you leave him alone he goes dreamy. He's probably been sitting doing that half the time." He grins. "He's mad," he adds.

Anna looks at me curiously. "Really?"

"Well, a bit," Jamie says.

"Yeah," she says. "Why not. Do you have the Cokes?"

Jamie has kept them in the shade, and they're still cool. We drink them thirstily as we head home.

Jamie's party is great fun, with a little crowd of children from school—mainly his year, of course—and also some other relatives of his. There are decorations and ice-cream and games in the garden which we all enjoy until we feel tired and happy and slightly sick. I don't see much of Anna at the party. I have the vague impression that she keeps away from the crowds much of the time, and towards the end she vanishes from view. Jamie's torch is silver, and twisting a ring set into its handle cycles through the colours. It comes in a neat cardboard box and there are several sets of extra batteries. I give him a little pocket-knife that I've saved for, with a black handle and two blades. I test how sharp it is before I wrap it, and cut my finger badly enough to need a plaster.

The day after the party, when all that's left of it are a few damp paper streamers in the garden, Jamie comes to find me.

"What is it?"

"It's Anna," he says.

"What about her?"

He's quiet for a moment. "Do you like her?" he says.

I think for a second. "She's OK," I say. "You know. For a girl."

"Yeah," Jamie says. "I s'pose."

"Why? Don't you?"

"Well, yes."

"So what is it?"

He says, "She wants to stay for longer. She says she doesn't want to go home."

"Oh," I say, surprised. "Why not?"

"She says she likes it here."

"What do your parents say?"

"We haven't told them yet. She asked me first."

"Would they mind, do you think?"

"I don't know. I don't think so. What about you, though? I mean, she'd be here all summer. Would you mind?"

I know what he means. With Anna here, there will be three of us. The things Jamie and I do—the comfortable way we are together, almost knowing what the other is thinking sometimes—that will all change. It might be weird. We might not want to play together. We might argue. Anna might turn out to be bossy or boring or clingy or irritating. It could ruin the whole summer. And besides, she's a girl.

All of this goes through my head, but I hardly hesitate at all. "I think it would be good," I say.

Jamie shrugs. "OK," he says. "I mean, I don't mind. I think she's all right. You're sure?"

"Yeah," I say. "I like her."

He looks at me, slightly curiously, as if he's intrigued that I'm so certain. "All right," he says. "We can go and tell her, then. And we can ask my parents. They'll have to phone and ask her parents, too."

"Her parents," I say, half to myself. Jamie has explained about how cousins work: Anna's mother is the sister of Jamie's mother. Anna lives up in the north, where—I remember—Jamie's mother comes from. I have tentatively put together in my head that Anna's mother must have stayed when Jamie's mother left to come south. Sometimes I keep all this straight, and sometimes there seem to be too many mothers involved, and it gets confusing. I think for a moment. "Will they let her stay?" I ask Jamie, a little anxiously.

Again Jamie looks at me for a second before he replies. "Yeah, sure. Course they will. Come on, then."

Part of me feels that I ought to try to explain it to him, but I hardly understand it myself. It's something about seeing her up there, high in the shadow of the cliff: and the expression of fulfilment as she stares at the sky at the end. The smoothness of her body in the sunlight gives me a warm feeling inside—warm enough almost to forget the climb or the horrible hesitancy of her body in free fall. It's something to do with all this; but I can't explain it properly even to myself, and so I say nothing to Jamie. Together, we go to find Anna, to tell her that we'll be spending the summer together.

I snuff the last of the candles I've lit in the living room, and feel my way to the bed. Lying in the darkness, staring at a ceiling which I can't see, I can imagine I'm in my bedroom upstairs, glimpsing by moonlight the glimmers of a ceiling strewn with stars.

At the time, it is impossible for me to understand. The way she climbs the cliff face—the eager, almost greedy way she seizes the chance to put herself on the edge of a danger that would have numbed me, frozen me to the rock—I can't reconcile it with the calm, frail figure turning slowly in the sunlight of the beach when it's all over. It is beyond my ability to make sense of what she does—of who she is.

I should have known, though. I should still have known.

Jamie is under the lemon tree, and there is a cat playing in the tinder-dry grass a little way off. The afternoon buzzes with crickets and cicadas as I creep up on him. I am ready to run—ready to shout—when something stops me. Something is wrong; something has changed; is different.

Alone on the path, I walk slowly towards town, hoping Anna will catch me up; and I think of her searching the beach for her watch, and something makes me stop. It is as if imagining her makes something glitter in the back of my mind. I frown to myself; something here is wrong. I struggle to see what it is.

The sounds of the shower in the bathroom come and go at the edge of my mind, and I stare around the room. Anna's things are on her bed: old suitcases and a shoulder bag and other bits of luggage. Her clothes are there, too; jeans and a loose shirt by the pillow. Her bra. I look away.

There is something about her suitcases which feels—strange. As if something is not right. As if something has changed; is wrong.

And I laugh at myself, thinking all the while that my mind is playing tricks on me, distracting me from what is *really* bothering me.

6

"*M*ax? It's Me."

"Alex."

"How are things?"

"Things are fine—except we don't have an artist." He laughs, but it sounds forced, and I'm sure he hears it as well as I do.

"I'm sorry, Max. I'm having some—complications at this end. It may take some time to sort out."

"You might have to leave it, you know. Deal with it once the show's over."

"Well—it's not that easy." I wonder what I can say to him that will make it clearer for him. "There's just—so much—to be done. I mean, I'm thinking about what you said—about what Julia asked. It's fascinating, Max. She's right. There are themes in the work like—like strata in rocks, and the critics have only found the first few. I hardly realized it myself. But—groups of three, I mean, that's an obvious one, isn't it? How come people didn't notice?" I stop myself, afraid I am saying too much, babbling.

"Alex. Is everything all right?"

"I'm fine," I say.

"I've been trying to call you."

"Oh. I'm—I'm still staying up at the house. There isn't a phone. I never really—got to the place I was supposed to be staying."

There is a long pause. "Alex. What is it that you're *doing* up there?"

I blink. "Well, it's—I can't explain now. I'm low on money. But—Max. You know the exhibition?"

"Yes." His voice is obviously patient.

"The hanging order. It's chronological, isn't it?"

"Yes, Alex. It's a retrospective exhibition—an overview. Of course it's chronological."

"It's just—"

"Alex. What is it?"

"The hanging order. I mean, I know it makes sense, I know it's *logical*, I just can't help thinking maybe we're—I don't know, looking for the logic in the wrong place. Like maybe the paintings won't make sense like that. Don't you ever get the feeling that there's something—*missing*? Like something's been left out, and we haven't noticed?"

There's a long silence. Then, "When are you going to be back?"

The display clicks down to the last few lire on the card. "Shit, Max, I'm out of money. I don't know. Look, I'll call you—"

But he isn't there any more.

"Shit."

The call hasn't gone the way I planned it. I stare at the phone for a time, running his words and mine back. I've made a mess of this. I start to walk back, wondering what I could have said differently, how better I could have explained things. But how could Max ever understand about Anna and Jamie and me? I was trying to communicate without a language. Even trying to tell him about the paintings—about my doubts—was no good.

I'm bound to be finished here before the exhibition opens. Bound to be. Max will just have to hold on as best he can.

In the living room, the scrawl of paint on the wall is framed in morning light. Sometimes it just looks like a scrawl, and sometimes it looks like something quite different: like the start of something. I hesitate to look at it square-on, and so it catches me at the periphery of my vision, in glimpses.

*   *   *

Mr. Dalton lets me come into the Art department whenever I want. It isn't long before I am spending every free hour there. There are more still lives to be copied down—mushrooms and toadstools one day, with their big vari-coloured caps splayed open and cracking at the edges, gills the colour of cream and liver and wine. And another day flowers, and another, pieces of moss-encrusted bark stripped from a dead tree. Gradually I come to understand how the different materials work together: how to use the grain of the paper against a pastel or a stick of Conté, how to soften an edge, to sponge back a wash of ink or watercolour, to use a putty rubber to draw out a highlight. The process of it all enthrals me, grips my brain tight. I love the smell of the linseed and turpentine, but also of printing ink and chalk dust and fresh watercolour paper. I learn how to draw at speed: how to catch the impression of something in a few lines put down almost casually. I feel there is a lifetime of learning to cram into these grey afternoons, with the rain coming down outside the brightly lit building.

After the still lives there comes life drawing: an old man in a dark suit one week, a woman with long hair and a parasol, like something from a nineteenth-century French painting, the next. We each have a big portfolio in a rack with our name stencilled on it. Mine swells and thickens and is soon too full to fit in its place, and the drawings and paintings spill out of the department and into my study. Here, they fill up the blank cream-coloured walls, taking the places of those posters whose memory is still blu-tacked in place. But the pictures that come back here, to my room, aren't still lives or life drawings or exercises in acrylic or oil. They are pictures of home; they are my memory made real and put up all around me.

I can't do it any more, of course: can't slip away like I used to. The avalanche in my head has finished all that. The past has receded from me, gained a distance, and though with an effort of will I can force it down onto paper and hold it there, I can't let myself fall into it the way I once did. It is as if a heavy curtain has come down between me and that time before—between me and Altesa—and I can only glimpse what happens on the other side of it by screwing my face up, squinting, straining my eyes.

But the effort is worth it. I hold the images long enough to commit them to paper, and before long my room is a jumble of the past. The cream paint of my walls is covered and all there is now is Red Ochre and Raw Umber and Burnt Sienna for the earth and the pan-tiles, and Flake White and China White for the walls, and Cerulean Blue in the skies, and sea colours, and the colours of olive groves and lemon trees and big, dark cypresses and stone pines by the coast.

Also in the pictures come faces—sometimes almost by accident, like that first time, and sometimes deliberately. Lena is there, making pasta and sweet rolls at the big table in the kitchen; and Anna is there too. I don't draw Jamie, not after that first time, and I keep the picture with his face in it hidden away. I am afraid he would not understand. So Anna and Lena keep me company; but it is only Anna that the other boys ask about, when they come, intrigued, to look at the room without posters.

"Who is she?"

"She your girlfriend?"

I say, "No. She's just a girl I knew."

"How old is she?"

"Fourteen, there. She's sixteen now."

"Christ. I wouldn't mind meeting her. How about it, Alex? Ask her round."

"She doesn't live here."

"Shit. Cos she's not bad. Not bad at all."

I am embarrassed, watching them watching her; it feels wrong. I want to tell them to stop looking at her, but I can't.

And then someone says, "You can really draw, can't you?"

And there is a little chorus of, "Yeah, you can, you know. These are brilliant."

"Thanks," I say.

And when they're gone again, one boy hesitates, hangs around until he's left back from the rest.

"What's she like?" he says. Out of the company of the group, he doesn't sound the same; the conventional lust has been replaced by something like wistfulness.

"What do you mean?"

"I mean—what's she like? Is she nice?"

I think about that. "Yeah."

"She looks nice," he says, and then hurriedly he goes as well, head down, as if ashamed of letting something slip.

I stare at Anna's face on the wall, and run through what the boys have said, and what the boy has said. In this picture she is smiling a little, and her eyes looking back at me from the paper seem to be amused at what she sees. I keep her picture in front of me when I write to her; and I console myself by staring at it in the spreading silence when she doesn't write back.

"What shall we do, then?"

It's agreed now. Anna's staying for the summer. I'm pleased, and a little surprised, at how easy it's been to arrange: Mrs. Anderson calls Anna's home, and talks for twenty minutes or so, and it's all settled.

"We could go to the beach," Jamie says.

"Or to the rock pools," I remind him.

"Where's that?"

"The other way from the cove. We were going to explore that way," I say, remembering all the plans Jamie and I have made for the summer. "And we were going to build a tree house, too."

"Really?" Her eyes light with interest. "Where?"

"We're not sure yet," Jamie says. "We're still looking. Somewhere up the valley, perhaps. People don't go there so much. We need to find the right kind of tree."

"Of course," she says, seriously. "Let's do that, then—look for a place, I mean."

"I've got some toffees," Jamie says. "I'll get them."

So it is then, ten minutes later, we have left the four houses that my mother has called *a little colonial outpost* behind us, and are walking down one of the farm tracks that Lena and I sometimes visit. There is the smell of early summer in the air. It is not yet the thick, heavy heat of August, but you can still tell that that is just a few weeks away. Hunting-wasps weave delicately in and out of the grasses growing by the roadside wall, and there is the constant, sharp scritching of crickets. Unless you concentrate you hardly notice the cicadas: the sound is a constant backdrop to everything, and our ears have long since learnt to filter them out. Once in a while, one stops suddenly as we come close to it, and the unexpected cessation of sound is like a hole opening up in the air.

"How long are you staying?" Jamie asks.

"I don't know. Mummy says I can stay as long as you'll let me."

"*Bene,*" I say.

"Won't you get homesick?" Jamie asks.

Anna skips on a few paces and then, without turning round, says, "Shouldn't think so."

We walk further and further from the edge of the town. The trees we pass are all wrong; cypresses and green oaks and trees too small to be suitable. A half-hour passes.

"Where are we anyway?" Jamie says. "I don't recognize this bit."

"Are we lost?" Anna says. "I thought you knew all the valley."

"Well—not all of it," Jamie says. "A lot. Mostly down that way." He indicates the coast.

"But there's loads of stuff further up," Anna says. "Aren't you allowed up there?"

I feel at once that the question is barbed. Jamie glances at her. "Of course we are. We're allowed anywhere."

"But you don't go there."

"We do. Sometimes. We've been all over."

This isn't true. The emptiness of the valley is sometimes a bit frightening, even if you're with someone else, and Jamie and I tend to stick to the beach and the places we know. The network of little tracks up here is disorienting, and I have had an apprehension in the past that you could walk for days without seeing anyone, or recognizing a landmark, or finding your way home.

But the valley is our valley, and Anna is our guest and a newcomer. None of these truths can be admitted, and both Jamie and I know this.

Anna says, "Well how far *have* you been, then?"

"I told you. All over." I can see Jamie becoming more and more uncomfortable.

Anna says, "I bet you haven't. Tell me one place you've been that's further on than here."

As she's saying this, I see something up ahead in the road that sparks an idea off the edge of another, different, afternoon. Before Jamie can answer, I say, "We've been all the way up to the end. There's a chapel there. We've been all the way to it." I pause. Jamie is looking at me with surprise—and, perhaps, a little admiration. I go on, more confidently, "A hermit used to live there, once."

"Balls," Anna says; and then, "Really?"

"Really," I say, nodding. "There's a river in front of us there and you can walk on it all the way to the end of the valley." I am amazed by my sudden eloquence. I find I am half believing what I am saying.

"You can't walk on a river," Anna says. "On the banks, you mean."

"No," I say. "It's a special river. You'll see."

I am right—to my huge relief. The bridge I have spotted ahead of us in the path isn't the one Lena and I have stopped at, but my guess that the dust river under it will be the same turns out to be correct. Anna runs across the bridge, searching for a way down. Jamie and I stand looking up the valley. Jamie keeps looking at me. At last he says, "I didn't know you came here."

I say, "Only before you were here. With Lena. She told me about the hermit. It was—ages ago. I've never actually been to the chapel," I confess. "I just saw it."

"It sounds like fun," Jamie says. "Maybe we could get to it—like you said."

"I think we could." I stare up the valley, but from some fold of land or stand of trees the chapel itself is hidden from view. I blink, and let my eyes go steady on what I can see.

Lena is beside me as I focus on the tiny, distant building. I follow the track of the river up the valley, and I can see—just see—how close it comes to that little white-and-rust structure. It passes right beside it. In a moment Lena will tell me the story she's promised, about the hermit. But I can't stay for that; I have to let it go.

Jamie says, "Were you—doing it? Just then?"

"Yeah," I say. I am getting better at just dipping into the places in my head without becoming stranded in them for hours. "It looks like it's right up close to the river. I bet we could get to it."

"How long would it take?"

"I don't know. Quite a long time."

Jamie shakes his head, smiling. "You're weird," he says.

Anna's voice calls from somewhere below us. "I've got down! Come on!"

"We're coming!" I call. I am about to run after her—I can't wait to find out how the dust river feels under my feet—when Jamie catches me by the arm.

"Alex."

"Yeah?"

"Maybe you shouldn't tell Anna about—you know. What you do."

"OK. Why not?"

"Well—she might not understand. Maybe later, when we know her better, OK?"

I shrug. "OK." And with that, we round the far end of the bridge and scramble down a slope thick with dry grass and loose earth to the flat, smooth dust of the dry watercourse. Anna is standing in the centre, looking straight up the valley.

"Isn't it strange?" she says. "The sand still looks like water. It's like you're walking on something—I don't know."

"Yeah," I say quietly. I can feel again how I feel the first time I see it, from Lena's bridge.

"How far away is this church of yours?" she says, echoing Jamie's question. "I can't see it."

"Of course you can't see it from *here*," Jamie says. He glances at me, and we both struggle not to giggle at the audacity of his bluff. "It's a long walk."

"We'd better get going, then," she says. "Come on."

Anna leads the way, and kicks up dust with her feet so that it billows around us. Jamie and I are forced to run after her and catch her up, just so we can breathe properly. She grins at us. "This is great. I never get to do anything like this at home."

A question surfaces. "Where do you live, then?" I say.

"Vicenza, now," she says. "But we keep moving. We're always moving."

I think to myself that my family has never moved; but on the heels of the thought comes the quick, surprising recollection that we must have; that before here, there was London, even if that hardly seems real at all. I say, "What's it like?"

"Moving?"

"No. Vicenza."

"Oh, it's all right," she says vaguely. Then, "You're English, aren't you?"

"Sort of," I say.

"Uncle Robert says both your parents are, so you must be."

"I suppose I am, then."

"Say something in English."

"What?"

"I don't know. Something. Say—good morning."

I do so. She grins.

"Say—a cup of tea and some toast, please."

I do. She laughs—a delighted peal of laughter that rings in the still air. "That sounded *very* English," she grins.

"Can't you speak English, then?"

"No." She glances up at the far side of the valley. "What's that?"

"The big house?"

"Yeah."

"That's Signor Ferucci's house," Jamie says.

"Who's he?"

"He's strange," Jamie says.

"Yeah," I say. "Sometimes he comes down into town, but hardly ever. You see the wall?"

Anna squints, following the twisting line of the white wall across the slopes of the hills. "Yeah."

"All that's his. All that land. Lena says it was all a big estate once, with vines and stuff, and that now it's all gone wild. He lives in the big white house, and hardly ever comes out. Lena says he's . . ." I hesitate, remembering the word. "Recluse," I say.

"Hey. Weird."

"Yeah. He's a bit scary, I think. Cos you don't know what he does in there. Jamie says maybe he's a vampire or something."

"Does he look like a vampire?"

"No," I admit.

"You've seen him, then?"

"Once. With Lena, in town."

Jamie says, "My dad says he just keeps himself to himself. He's quite rich, I think."

"Oh." Anna's quiet for a bit, digesting all this. Then she says, "Are you two best friends?"

I look at Jamie. He says, "Yeah, I suppose."

"Yeah," I say.

Jamie says, "Do you have a best friend?"

Anna glances at a bird that darts across the empty river. "Oh, lots," she says.

Around us, the air hums with insects, and behind us the dust we kick up drifts slowly, turning the leaves of the myrtle bushes terracotta and ochre. Jamie fishes in his pocket and brings out toffees for us. I find before long that I am chewing in the same rhythm as I'm walking. I look surreptitiously at the others, and am delighted to see that they are doing the same. It looks peculiarly funny, and I snort with laughter.

"What is it?" Anna says, so I have to tell them. She says, "You notice the strangest things, you know."

"Alex is like that," Jamie says, shifting his toffee to inside one cheek to talk. "He's strange. You have to watch out for him."

"I'm not," I say, feeling a little rush of self-consciousness.

"He is, though," Jamie says with mock-seriousness. "Really *weird*."

Anna says, "You said that before. What's so weird about him?"

"Oh, everything," Jamie says casually. "Everything."

Anna looks at me, and I shake my head.

"I think you're both weird," she says. "Strange little kids."

"I'm not a little kid," Jamie says, nettled.

"You're younger than me."

"Not much. You're only ten," he says.

"That's still older than both of you."

"You're a kid, too, though."

She shrugs. "Maybe."

We round a bend in the riverbed and I catch a glimpse of something white, far ahead. "There!" I say, pointing. "That's the chapel."

They squint at it, shading their eyes from the sun.

"It's still a long way off," Jamie says uncertainly.

"We can make it," Anna says. "I'm sure we can."

"I don't know," he says. "I don't want my parents to be cross. This is your first day."

"Oh come *on*," she says. "It's not far. Half an hour, maybe."

I try to judge the distance to the building; it looks longer than that to me.

"We shouldn't be late," Jamie says, frowning. "We could come back tomorrow."

"Please, Jamie," she says. "I really think we can do it." She hesitates, watching him. "If we're late, I'll say it was my fault—that I ran on ahead for a joke. Promise."

I wait. At last Jamie says, "All right. But let's be quick."

"Thanks," she says. She smiles quickly at him. "We'll be OK, you'll see."

A few minutes pass, and then she says, "I'm sorry I called you a kid. You're not really."

"It's OK."

I say, "I'm not a kid either."

Anna shakes her head as if exasperated, though I can tell she's not really. "OK, OK. Nobody's a kid. And nobody's weird, either."

"Right," I say.

"So. Tell me about this chapel of yours."

I have sawdust in my hair and clothes from work that has been done. Small parts of the house are starting to be fixed around me, but I have hardly noticed it happening. My hands must have been working; tools are scattered about the place. But I have not been here. I have been all the time somewhere I thought I couldn't go any more.

The valley and the chapel have invaded the house, until the smell of the hot air and the dust of the dry watercourse are everywhere. Somewhere in that caked, crusted heat and tinder-dryness the house itself has faded away. It has been the strangest thing. I have not felt anything like this for—for most of my life. Since I was twelve. I am like a ghost pulled between different bodies, bodies lodged in different times.

Jamie's old riddle is going round in my head. *What do you call a clock without hands?*

I can't make it stop.

I pack the tools up slowly, feeling the weariness in my arms and back that says I have been working all day. There is the tiredness of the muscles, and the memory of exertion in the low throb of the scar in my shoulder, and there are the finished tasks—a straightened newel post, a fixed bannister—but there is so little left of how this happened. Some fractions of remembering do come to me: running my thumb along a straight-edge; marking a length on wood; sawing. But these are faint, like underpainting coming through something half-finished.

I have kept clear of the living room all day. In there is something not even half-finished; not even properly begun. A brief, haphazard swirl of paint on a discoloured wall, suggesting form and movement and a pale figure poised at the edge of something. I know I can't ignore it for ever.

*   *   *

"We don't call it a clock because we tell the time by it. We tell the time by it because we call it a clock. Do you see?"

"It's still a crap joke, Jamie."
     "All the best ones are."

Altesa has changed. I have changed. I gave this place up—moved on. But here, in the house, what has been changed can be put back, made right again. Even though it can only work for wood and glass and paint and metal, it's perhaps enough of a start. I can make things right again. I can wind back the changes and everything will be as it should have been—before it all shifts, and we grow up, and grow apart. Before it's too late, and the chance to say things, to tell the truth, is gone. Before they sit me down in that dark, musty study and tell me how Jamie is dead: how he's drowned; that they're sorry.

In the sitting room the pictures lie half forgotten, an autumnal drift of coloured rectangles. They're part of something that now seems irrevocably distant. London is a faint blur of memory. Jamie and Anna are right here—with me right now—and I can't leave things like this.

I stand in the scatter of photographs and stare at what I have begun on the wall, and I can start to see what has to be added to make sense of this: a mesh of moonlight across low wave-crests, and a dark shadow of land, and a hollow place under the curve of the foreground where the moonlight can't get and the waves are black.

A shiver runs through me like rain.

The air smells like there may be thunder on the way. I go round and make sure all the windows are closed and fastened in the upstairs rooms. I don't want any storm damage to add to what already needs to be done.

7

*W*e clamber out of the dry riverbed and through a tangle of scrub bushes and dusty grass. A little way in front of us is a ragged fence of iron railings, woven through with dark blue convolvulus and rusted almost apart in some places. It isn't too high. We help each other over it. The chapel itself stands beyond, in the middle of a bare patch of ground which is broken up only by a big pile of timber and some scattered collections of masonry. Weeds have grown up through the piles of wood and stone.

On the side where we are, the chapel's whitewashed walls are shaded by two big stone pines, and the hard-packed earth under them is padded with a layer of old needles and twigs. With the sun cutting through onto them, we can smell the faint tang of resin in the still afternoon heat. We stand looking about us for a few seconds, as if fixing this first proper look at the place in our heads. The chapel is rectangular, its roof overhanging the walls enough to make a deep block of shadow up there. At the near end, there is a stubby white tower, neatly capped off with its own little roof. Through the four narrow arches at its top I can catch a glimpse of a bell in silhouette. Then Jamie says, "Come on. Let's see if there's a way in."

We skirt the building. There is a big double-door at the end, but when we go up to it, it is locked shut. Round on the far side, though, is a small door set in close to the other end of the building. Bushes have grown up here, screening off the view down the valley to the sea. There is a grimy padlock on this door, but when Jamie pulls at it, the hasp through which it is linked comes right out of the old wood of the door jamb, cascading little flakes and splinters of dusty wood debris from its screwholes. We glance at each other—a kind of shared excitement makes us tense for a moment—and then Jamie pushes the door open and leads the way inside.

The interior of the chapel is surprisingly cool after our long trek up the valley in sunlight and heat. The air here is dry and smells old—of stone and fabric and, very faintly, of wood polish, and of the faintest ghost of old incense. All the smells are faded, rubbed back by time, and there is none of the heavy pungency of the chapel in town. The sounds of the crickets and cicadas from outside are muted to the barest whisper.

Gradually our eyes get used to the gloomy half-light inside. The room is a muddle of dimly lit shapes. At one end—the altar end—there is a big stained-glass window of a Madonna and Child. The bottom part of the window has been covered up with sheets of dark board, but a panel has fallen away from the top part and the Madonna's face, and her arms holding the baby, are alight and glowing. The orange and gold and blue from this window is all the light there is; all the other windows are blacked out.

Below the window is a wooden table, and down at the other end of the room—just visible—are wooden pews, shorter than the ones I've seen in town, and all pushed together as if to clear the floor for something. There are some sacks leaning against the wall by the door. When I look inside, they are full of brick dust and rubble.

"How long do you think it's been since anyone's been here?" Jamie says quietly.

"I don't know. Ages, probably."

Anna says, "I thought you came here all the time." Jamie doesn't reply; he's too busy looking around at the murky limits of the chamber.

Anna walks away from us through the gloom, towards the darker end of the building, where most of the rubbish has been stacked.

"It's good, don't you think?" Jamie says.

"Yeah."

Anna's voice suddenly rings out. "Hey! What's that?" We both jump a little; something about the place has had us keeping our voices low. We hurry after her.

"What is it?" Jamie says; then, "Wow."

I peer past his shoulder and shiver with surprise. For a moment, it looks as though there is a man lying against the wall of the chapel, somehow propped there on his side: I can see his face, pale in the shadows, and a hand reaching up towards the ceiling as if trying to clutch something. His body is hidden from view by the jumble of pews. My breath catches for a second, and then I see what it really is: a huge wooden crucifix, the Christ on it carved in wood and then painted to look real. It must be three times as high as me—the figure lifesize or even bigger. I can see from Jamie's face that he has been as startled as I. The cross has been leant against the chapel wall. Getting closer, I see the bottom part of it is covered with a sheet.

"It's huge," I say.

"Yeah. I wonder where it comes from?" We all look around the chapel trying to spot where such a huge cross might hang.

"Usually they go over the altar," Jamie says, a little uncertainly.

"But there's a window there."

"I know."

I say, "He's almost bigger than a real man."

Anna reaches out across some of the pews that are pushed up against the crucifix and, stretching, touches lightly the figure's hand, tracing the shape of the fingers. It is the hand I had thought was reaching up for something, except now I can see the darker bar of the crosspiece behind it.

"Wow," Jamie says again.

Anna's hand lingers a moment longer, and then she shivers as if pinched. She turns away from the crucifix. "Let's see what else there is. This is fun."

She heads further into the shadow at the end of the building. Jamie follows, and after a moment so do I; the depth of the gloom there frightens me a little, but I don't want them to know this. Although the air is cool—almost chilly—it also feels thick in my lungs, like water. The further back into the chapel we go, the thicker it feels.

There are three stone arches here, and, through them, we can make out the bulk of the big double-doors we have seen but found to be locked.

"This was where people came in," Jamie says.

"Look here," Anna says. Off to one side is a little door set back into the stone, slightly ajar. "What do you think it is?"

"I wish I'd brought my torch," Jamie says.

"You should, next time," I say.

Anna pushes the door wider. Our eyes are getting used to the heavy orange and blue half-light now, and I can just see the regular shapes of steps, curving round and up into black.

"I'm going up," she says.

"Really?"

"Of course."

She doesn't sound at all apprehensive. Jamie and I glance at each other. Now we have to go as well.

The stairs spiral round to the right, and we grope our way tentatively upwards. I keep one hand on the wall and one hand clutching the back of Jamie's shirt; I have become suddenly scared that, once we are halfway up and the darkness is absolute, Jamie and Anna will somehow vanish and leave me stranded here, unable to escape. But he doesn't vanish; and after a time, the darkness actually starts to lighten again. Little by little we progress, until I hear Anna, ahead of Jamie, say, "Hey! It's like a little balcony!"

The top of the stairway brings us through another little arch, and we emerge in a kind of gallery, spanning the width of the chapel. We haven't noticed it from the ground; it has been lost in the dark. We are high up now, with only a little stone balustrade between us and the big, empty volume of the chapel's main chamber. The late afternoon sunlight is coming straight up the valley from over the sea, and cuts through the stained-glass Mary and Jesus; from our new vantage point the window blazes with colour. I blink and have to look away; it hurts my eyes now that they're used to the twilight.

"What d'you suppose this was?" Anna says.

Jamie looks round the little area carefully. "There's something been taken out there," he says, pointing. He's right; there's a place in the boards where the wood is lighter in colour, and there are some ragged holes also, as if things have been ripped out. A paler patch on the stone of the wall marks where something large, like a wardrobe, has stood for a long time, but is now gone.

"It's the organ!" I shout, delighted one second by my sudden understanding, and then cowed the next when my voice shudders and echoes through the building. Much more quietly, I add, "That's where the organ went. That's where it is in town, in Father Antonio's church."

"Yeah," Anna says. "Yeah, I think you're right."

The window is casting big blurry panels of colour onto the wall up here. As Anna and Jamie walk slowly along the gallery their faces are caught and lit and changed: Jamie a deep blue like the blue of the sea on a still day, Anna blazing gold like fire. The blue seems to pool up in Jamie's eyes and in the shadow of his mouth, which is slightly open as he stares around him. Anna's hair, as she turns away from me, is rimmed with gold like a halo. Dust, disturbed by our feet, shifts and eddies around her, catching the light, glittering like stars.

Then she passes out of the light. "There's another door here," she calls from the far end of the balcony.

"Where?"

Jamie and I hurry along. The door Anna has found is another small, recessed one, like the one that brought us up here to begin with.

"Go on, then," Jamie says.

Anna pushes the door open, and there is a rush of light and noise. Anna jumps and gives a little shriek; Jamie and I start with fright and surprise. Then suddenly, Anna is laughing, holding her hand to her mouth as if guilty about something.

"What is it? What is it?" Jamie says.

"Sorry," Anna says, through the laughter. "God. Sorry."

She pushes the door fully wide and light—daylight—spills through. We troop through into the little room that is revealed. There is at once more of the heat of the valley in here; I can feel it pouring down onto me in languid waves. The room is small, half the size of my bedroom back home. The light and heat are coming in from open arches high above us. There is a wooden platform up there, too, and a little set of stairs—hardly more than a ladder, really—leading up to it. The floor is wooden boards, and the part not sheltered from above by the platform is scattered with bird shit and feathers and, in one or two places, fragments of eggshell. A few feathers drift lazily in the air as we stand staring, and I suddenly understand what the rush of noise that so startled us must have been.

"You know what this is?" Jamie says.

"What?" I say.

"It's the belltower. Look." In the middle of the little room hangs a thick, heavy-looking rope.

"*Accidenti!*" Anna exclaims, delighted. She grabs the rope and tugs down on it. Jamie clutches her arm.

"No! Stop it. Someone'll hear." There's no noise, but a drift of dust and more feathers sifts down onto us from somewhere above. Jamie says, "We'd get into trouble. Really."

Reluctantly, Anna nods. "Yeah."

I say, "Is the bell up there?"

"Let's have a look," Anna says.

"I hope it's safe," Jamie says, looking uncertainly at the wooden steps.

"Of course it is." Again, it is Anna who leads the way, and we file cautiously up the stairway to the little wooden platform.

"This is great!"

I stand, amazed, looking round. The bell—huge and dark—is hung in the middle of the tower here, the rope leading off from a long wooden arm. But it isn't the bell that grabs us deep in our stomachs: it is what we can see from the four arches that open out onto the valley. Enthralled, we huddle in close to fit ourselves at one of the apertures.

"We're really high up," Jamie says, with wonder in his voice.

"Yeah," I say.

The whole of the valley is spread out below us, from the patchwork of fields and farm tracks up here near the chapel right down to the cluster of buildings that is Altesa. The sea twinkles and shimmers in the afternoon light, and I can see boats out from the shore. A string of birds turns in the sky away to one side of us, and finally settles in a stand of trees there; I wonder if they are the same birds we have frightened off from their roost here. We are entranced, seeing this place that we know so well in a way we have never seen it before.

Jamie says, "Alex—is that our houses?"

He points to the side of the valley, just outside the limits of the town.

Anna says, "Yeah, I think so."

"Yeah," I say. "There's the wall. And you can see the trees. And Signora Bartolomeo Cassi's laundry is out."

"This is brilliant," Jamie says. "You can see everything from here."

"We can spy on people." A wonderful idea comes to me. "You could bring your telescope!"

Jamie's eyes go wide. "Yeah."

Anna says, "Better than a tree house."

I haven't thought of that. I say, "Yeah."

"Yeah," Jamie says.

"Nobody else knows about this?" Anna asks.

"Well—lots of people know about it," Jamie says. "But no-one comes here. I mean, you saw how it was all locked up."

"Yeah," Anna says. "Nobody's been here for years and years, I bet. Just birds."

"And us," I say.

"Yeah."

We stare down the valley at the little white-and-ochre buildings and the curve of the bay and the openness of the sea.

"We should come again tomorrow," I say.

This seems to remind Jamie of something. "We ought to be getting back," he says. "Really. It's late."

He's right; the sun is low in the sky over the water. Far away, down in the town, comes the faint sound of a bell ringing.

"But we'll come back?" Anna says, not moving.

"Yeah, sure. Now we know where it is."

She grins a little. "But you guys come here all the time," she says.

"Well—"

She shakes her head. "It's OK. I was only teasing. You're right, we'd better go."

Still, she waits a moment longer, staring down the valley, arms resting on the hot tile that forms the sill of the arch. Then she seems satisfied, and we climb down the ladder, and go across to the little door, along the balcony with its great panels of coloured light still stretched on the wall, and make our way carefully down into the dense darkness of the chapel. We stumble a little in the gloom, and I hear Anna giggle as she trips and grabs Jamie for support. I steal one last look at the figure of Christ where he is leant against the wall, and then we are out into the sunlight. After the cool of the air in the chapel, and the still, silent darkness, the valley feels like an oven—and full of sound.

Jamie makes a decent attempt at putting the lock back the way it was. Anna says, "There's no need. No-one ever comes here." Jamie just shrugs.

As we are leaving the little churchyard, heading back the way we came towards the uneven line of the fence, Anna stops.

"Look."

We follow where she is pointing. On the end wall of the chapel, high up, there is a clockface—a dark colour which I think might be the same metal as the lion's head in the square. We can make out the old-fashioned Roman numerals embossed around its edge.

"That's weird," Jamie says. "It hasn't got any hands."

"Maybe they took them off when they shut the place up."

"Why?"

"Well, there wouldn't be anyone to wind it, would there? Maybe they thought it would look strange if it only showed one time."

"It looks stranger like it is," Jamie says. I don't say anything, but I agree with him: there is something spooky about the way the clock looks. It makes me want to shiver, even with the hot afternoon sun on my face.

"Come on," I say, and we leave the chapel with its fallen Christ and blank clockface behind us.

On the walk back down the empty river, I am pleased to see that the footsteps we made in the dust on our way up are still there: crisp little indentations patterned with the treads of our shoes. Jamie is telling stories and jokes and I am only half listening, because I've heard most of them before. At the back of my mind is a vague disappointment that the interior of the chapel hadn't been anything like how I'd imagined it with Lena; there have been no stalactites or phosphorescent pools of water, no piles of bones or animal skins. At the same time, though, I am relieved. The reality of the chapel hasn't been as exciting as my fantasy, but it hasn't been as frightening either.

"Hey, Alex," Jamie says.

"What?"

"You want to hear a joke?"

"Yeah."

"What do you call a clock without hands?" he asks.

"What did you say?" Anna says, and after a moment I realize Jamie has asked the question in English.

"Tell it in Italian," I say. "So Anna can hear."

He frowns. "It doesn't work in Italian," he says. "I tried. Listen. What do you call a clock with no hands?"

"I don't know."

"A dandelion clock." He grins.

"I don't get it."

"You know dandelion clocks, right?" he says, reverting to Italian.

"I don't think so."

"You know dandelion seeds?"

I nod.

"Well, they're called clocks in English."

"Why?" Anna asks.

"You blow them to find out the time," Jamie says.

"You have to see how many times you blow it before all the seeds are gone, and the number of times you blow is the hours o'clock it is."

Anna and I look at him, puzzled.

"Don't you know that?" he asks.

"I don't think so," I say again.

"Does it work?" Anna says.

"Sometimes. Usually," Jamie says. "If we find one, I'll show you."

We keep a lookout for the next hundred yards, but it is the wrong time of year, and there aren't any seed-heads like the kind we need. After a while, I say, "That's a weird joke."

"No it's not. You just have to know what a dandelion clock is, that's all."

"Dandelion clocks and chapel clocks," I say to myself. "Clocks without hands."

"That's why I thought of it," Jamie says.

Later that night, when I've done my teeth and it's dark outside, I am sitting reading in bed when I catch a glimpse of something out of the corner of my eye. Going to the window, I can make out by the dim light of the night sky the outline of Jamie's house. Suddenly, a little point of green light winks on and off in one of the windows. I am startled for a moment, until I remember Jamie's torch with the different colours. A second later, the light winks again, red this time. I grin and wave, but can't tell if they can see me from that far away. Then an inspiration strikes, and I run to the doorway and flick the room lights on and off and on and off. Dashing back to the window, I can see the torch—green again—flickering on and off in response. Then it stops. I grin again, feeling warm inside that they've remembered me. For a moment I feel a pang of sadness that I am alone in my room while Jamie and Anna are in rooms right across from one another; they will probably stay up playing and talking and reading comics for as long as they want. But at least they've thought of me.

I curl up in bed with the smile still on my face, and fall asleep wondering what the three of us will do tomorrow.

There are so many possibilities. Jamie and I could have gone looking for trees for tree houses, and rock pools, and never seen the church. Anna could have come to stay another year, and we might still have become friends, might still have ended up in Florence together in the spring, though a different Florence, and a different spring. We could have been children, reading comics and playing on the beaches and telling stupid jokes.

And the truth of it is that we were those things as well.

Time goes past. The heat lies like lead in the valley, pressing down the grass by the roadsides and making the earth among the lemon trees shrink until it cracks. It looks like all of Altesa is on the beaches, except for the waiters keeping out of the sun under their awnings and surveying their collections of pavement tables. The three of us are almost constantly in each other's company. We are earning our parents the reputation of having let us run wild.

Time goes past. The days blur by in a haze of heat and red dust from the fields.

We keep returning to the chapel. The first few times, we just explore the building, and invent games to play in the seclusion of its cool half-light. We watch the valley from the belltower. We play hide-and-seek until we know all the hiding places, and then we make things up. We are a secret society—the Band of Three—and this is our meeting-place.

It is Anna's idea never to speak of the chapel by name. Jamie is worried that, if anyone finds out where we have been going, we might be forbidden from playing there. Although we are sure the building is safe, adults are bound to think of reasons why it might not be; and perhaps there is something inherently wrong with running and shouting in a church, even an old and forgotten one.

So from then on, we talk only of going to the dandelion clock, until the phrase is so worn into our minds that the reason for it—Jamie's original joke—is almost forgotten. The clock itself is always there, of course, staring blindly from its vantage point on the wall, but we hardly notice it.

It is an afternoon in early August. Anna has been with us for just over a month, and our lives have settled into an easy, happy pattern. Everything feels safe and comfortable.

Jamie and I come back from getting shopping for Lena and sweets for ourselves to find Anna gone. We look in all the rooms for her before spotting the note she's left:

Gone to the dandelion clock. Got an idea to make a theatre so I've taken a sheet. Come and meet me.

"What does she mean, a theatre?" I ask.

Jamie shakes his head. "I don't know. Perhaps she means she's going to use the sheet as a curtain."

"That's not bad," I say. "We could hang it from the bit where the organ was."

"Yeah," Jamie says, starting to see how it can be done. "And use the place in front of the doors like a stage. That's cool. We could put on plays."

"Batman," I say.

"Yeah. Or anything."

"We'd better hurry and catch her up," I say, struck with the terrible sense that I might be missing out on something fun.

We make it up the valley in record time, sometimes running until I am out of breath and then breaking back into a walk. Our footprints are still in the dust from several days before; it is only after a long time that the breeze rubs them out. Once or twice a lizard skitters out of our way, but otherwise the valley seems deserted. The riverbed marks its lowest point throughout its length, and looking up you can catch a glimpse from the corners of your eyes of hills, almost all around, like a bowl. Only behind us, where the sea is, does the sky remain unbroken.

We climb the fence and skirt the building as we have so many times before. Something makes me look up at the clockface as we pass it: it is still the same, still eerily incomplete. I wink at it, as if trying to make it wink back, but of course it doesn't.

"Anna!" Jamie calls as we round the corner of the chapel. The side door is slightly ajar, the hasp of the lock hanging loose. There is no reply.

"Maybe she's hiding," I say. Jamie pulls the door open and takes a step into the gloom before he freezes. I almost run into him, it's so sudden.

He blocks my view of the altar end of the chapel, but it isn't there that he is looking. I follow his gaze into the shadows down towards the organ-loft, and for a moment I can't understand exactly what it is that I'm seeing. The only adult figure we've ever seen in the chapel is the big wooden Christ; but he's still there on his cross in the shadows. The man Jamie's looking at—the man Anna is holding—is someone else. He is lying in the dusty half-dark back there among the pews, propped up slightly against the end of one of them, and Anna is kneeling beside him.

She looks up, staring as though seeing us for the first time. "Come in and shut the door," she says. There is something funny in her voice when she speaks.

Jamie says, "Who is it?" His voice sounds strange, too.

"I don't know. He's hurt."

I look again at the figure at Anna's side. In a flash I know who it is, and why he's here.

"It's the hermit," I say. "He came back."

8

*I*t's a tentative movement—cautious—exploring. I reach out with the brush and run a thin line down the slightly uneven plaster of the wall, and the faint, half-understood image that is forming there is reinforced in some way. I see it more clearly now: the underside of an arm, raised above the head; the shallow inward curve of the belly; some hint of a leg bending a little at the knee, tension running through the muscles, the whole figure caught in the moment of preparation.

Touching the brush to the wall, it feels like the plaster might give way in front of me and leave me—stranded somewhere. I don't know. It's moonlight, and the shapes of waves low under the curve of the land. The house around me—its walls and boards and joists—feels terribly fragile, like a soap bubble. The coarse bristles of this ungainly brush might punch right through it, puncture the illusion.

Where am I?

I do it again: a hesitant lining-in of the form which is hardly there at all, but which I've nevertheless *seen* as being there. I'm starting to wonder now whether it was my imagination all along: whether the scrawl of marks on the wall was just that—a random scrawling; whether what I've told myself was there was not just something—imagined. In my head.

Going places in your head.

It's too late now anyway. The new marks I've made define things: they mark boundaries, areas of space, distinctions between one thing and another. There is no longer the darker wall and the paler paint. Now there is a boy in moonlight. I let the hand that carries the brush drop to my side, and stare at what I've done as if at a dream.

We huddle together at one end of the chapel, talking in whispers.

"We should tell someone."

"What's he doing here? I thought you said nobody came here any more."

"I *told* you there was a hermit."

"He's too young to be the hermit, Alex. He looks much younger than my father."

"He must be the hermit."

"How did he get hurt?"

"I don't know. There's blood on his clothes. I think it's his leg, or something."

"You've got blood on your arm," Jamie says suddenly. "Look."

We stare at Anna's arm; there is a narrow streak of something dark there. She drags the arm awkwardly against her T-shirt, leaving a smeary stain.

"I moved him a bit. He was all leant over and his breathing was funny. I thought he ought to sit up."

"Is he unconscious?"

"I think so. He's been like that since I found him."

"We should call an ambulance," Jamie says.

Slowly, Anna nods. "Yes. We'd better. Where from?"

"Home, of course."

"Isn't there somewhere nearer?"

I frown. "Lena says we shouldn't talk to strangers," I say.

"OK, then. We'll go home."

There is a sound from where the man is lying, and a groan. All three of us jump a little, eyes wide.

"Come on," Jamie says. "We should hurry."

We have reached the door when the man shifts again. I glance back. His eyes are open for the first time, and he is looking around the chapel, but his expression is dazed, as though he isn't quite sure what he's seeing.

"Come *on*," Jamie says, louder, pushing my back.

The man blinks at the sound of the voice, and turns his head. He seems to focus on the three of us, bunched up against the chapel door. He opens his mouth and says something—or, at least, a sound comes out, almost a croak. But it isn't proper words, just noises.

Jamie is tugging at my arm, but Anna stops dead. We are so close together that I can actually feel her body go rigid for a moment.

"Wait," she says. Jamie lets go of me and turns to her.

"What is it?" he says. Anna takes a step back into the room.

"He doesn't want us to go," she says. Her voice has changed again; instead of the tension that had been there before, there is now a kind of wonder in it—surprise and recognition muddled together.

"What?" Jamie says.

"How can you tell?" I asked.

She doesn't answer. Jamie and I look quickly at each other, and then back to where Anna has taken another step towards the hermit.

"It's OK," she says. "We won't be gone long. We're going to get an ambulance."

The man shakes his head. When he speaks again, he seems to have regained command of his voice, and I understand him easily enough. His voice is low, and his breathing is still coming to him with difficulty, but I think he sounds nice.

"Don't do that, please," he says. "There really isn't any need. I'm not—I'm not so badly hurt."

"You look pretty bad," Jamie says, following Anna a little way but still keeping his distance from the man.

"I'm not. Just my leg, really." He smiles at us, and his smile is friendly and rueful at the same time, as if he is embarrassed at all the fuss. "I've had a bit of an accident—well, you can see that, of course."

"What happened?" Anna asks.

"I can tell you, if you like." He pauses. "Do you want to sit down?"

"I don't think we should," Jamie says, trying to keep his voice low enough that only we will hear. The man hears him, though, and nods.

"You're sensible," he says. "That's good. You have to be careful these days. You stay there, if you want. But I promise I'm not crazy or anything." He looks at himself for a second. "I'm a mess," he says, simply. "I hope I didn't startle you."

"Not really," Jamie says, and I can tell he is less nervous than he was a moment before.

"There's blood on your leg," I say.

"I see it. It hurts a bit, but like I said, it's not too bad. I think I cut it a little in the crash."

"There was a crash?" Anna says. "Where?"

"On the road into town," the man says. "Last night. I think I must have fallen asleep at the wheel, and then—" He stops, and looks at the three of us standing there watching him. Another smile crosses his face briefly. "Listen," he says. "I think I need your help. I understand if you don't want to get involved"—he says this looking straight at Jamie— "but I'd be grateful if you'd hear me out. Then you can make a decision."

"All right," Jamie says slowly. "Tell us."

"Of course we'll help," Anna says. She goes over and sits herself on the floor right next to the hermit, and then glares at Jamie as if daring him to say anything. I watch as Jamie struggles with what to do, and then he gives in and goes across as well. I follow, and the three of us sit there, Jamie and I a little warily, Anna as if nothing unusual is going on at all.

"Thank you," the man says quietly. "It was getting difficult shouting across the room like that."

"How did you hurt your leg?" I ask.

He looks at me; his eyes are brown and calm-looking. "What's your name?"

"Alex," I say. Jamie shoots a glance at me as if to warn me against something, but it is too late.

"Well, Alex, it was like this. I was coming to town to see my grandmother. She lives down by the sea here; she's very old now and she doesn't get to see me so often. I had a few weeks' holiday from work and I thought I'd drive down and surprise her." The hermit pauses, takes a breath. "That's why I don't want you to call an ambulance. If I have to go to hospital, they'll call her, and she'll think it's worse than it is. I don't want to worry her. At her age—well, you understand," he says. Anna nods, and, after a second, so does Jamie.

"And the crash?"

"That was last night. It was late and, like I said, I think I fell asleep for a moment. I'd been driving for quite a while, you see. The car went off the road and into one of the stream gullies up that way." He nods sideways, indicating the top end of the valley. "I woke up and suddenly the world was upside down. The car was completely smashed, but I was OK. It must still be up there."

"The road into town?" Jamie says, incredulously. "There's like a cliff there. It's really steep."

"No, not that road." The man nods gravely. "You're right; I'd never have survived that. But there are barriers there to stop you coming off, yes?"

"Oh," Jamie says. "Yeah. There are."

"The road I was on—it's more of a farm road. It comes down very steeply from the main road, and then it winds down to where the fields are. It passes very close to here. That's where the crash happened."

"You were lucky the car didn't explode," I say.

"Maybe. But I think that happens more in films than in real life, yes?"

Anna says, "You were still lucky to get out."

"Yes. The door was thrown open. If it hadn't been—well, I suppose I might still be there. But it was quite easy to get out. And then the only building I could see was this one, so I headed for it. You should have seen me last night when I got here," he says, shaking his head and smiling a little. "I'd got a stick to help me walk—there, you can see it." He nods again, and we turn to see a length of tree branch to one side of the door. None of us have noticed it before. "I was leaning on that, and lurching along like a pirate, and then I couldn't get the doors open—"

He breaks off, laughing softly. I find I am laughing too at the description.

"I remember saying some very rude things then. But in the end I found the side door. It was such a relief to be able to lie down; I think I fell asleep again. And that's how I got here."

"So what should we do now?" Jamie says. "If you don't want us to call an ambulance, I mean."

"Well . . ." The hermit is lost in thought for a moment. Then his face clears. "Of course. I should have thought of it earlier. Do you know Signor Ferucci?"

We glance at each other. Anna says, "In the big house on the hillside?"

"Yes."

Jamie says, "Not really. Nobody really knows him. But we know where he lives."

"Perfect. Well, I know him, too. He's a good friend of mine. I was going to pay him a visit while I was here anyway. Maybe if you told him, he could bring his car and come and get me. Then I could stay at his house until I'm well enough to go and see my grandmother without scaring her. What do you think?"

"You want us to go and tell Signor Ferucci that you're here?" Jamie says.

"That's all, yes. But please—nobody else. You know how people gossip in little towns. If you tell other people, my grandmother might hear. I'd never forgive myself."

"OK," Anna says. "Jamie?"

"Yeah, OK."

"Alex?"

"Yeah," I say. "I know where his house is. We could go now, if you like."

"Thank you," the man says. "You're being very kind."

"That's OK," Jamie says.

Anna says, "Where do you live?"

"Rome, at the moment."

"Oh. I don't know Rome very well. My family live in Vicenza."

"Yes," he says. "I've been there."

"Where were you born?"

"Naples."

"I've been there," Anna says seriously. "Is that where you grew up?"

"Yes." He shifts again a little, and I see his face twist for a moment as he moves.

"We'd better get going," Jamie says.

Anna doesn't seem to hear him. She says, "Did you live there a long time?"

For the first time, a shade of irritation crosses the hermit's face. "Yes," he says. "All the time I was growing up. Please, now—"

"Yeah," Jamie says. "Come *on*, Anna."

"Oh. Yeah," Anna says. To the hermit she adds, "We'll try not to be long, OK? You should get some sleep if you can. We'll be back soon."

"Thank you," the man says; it seems to me that his voice is fainter than before.

We go to the door. Sneaking a quick glance back, I can see that the hermit has closed his eyes again, just like Anna told him.

Outside, we stand in the searing afternoon sunlight and look at each other.

"This is really exciting," I say.

"You shouldn't have talked to him, though," Jamie says to Anna. "I mean, he could have been dangerous. He could have been anyone."

Anna doesn't say anything.

"He wasn't, though," I say. "He knows Signor Ferucci. I *told* you he was the hermit."

"Don't be silly," Jamie says. "He's too young."

"Well, maybe he's another hermit."

"No he's not. You heard what he said. He lives in Rome." He suddenly grins at me. "You and your hermits. Anna? Are you OK?"

She seems to be staring at nothing. After a long moment, she blinks and shakes her head slightly.

"Anna? What is it?"

"He said he grew up in Naples," she said.

"Yes," Jamie says slowly. "That's right."

There's another silence. The afternoon buzzes and hums around us. I can see Jamie is getting impatient; but he's also curious, wants to know what has made Anna go like this.

At last, she says, "He said he crashed his car."

"Yes."

"He said the road was near here. A farm road that comes down steep from the main road. That's right, isn't it?"

Jamie is nodding. "Yeah, that's what he said. Why?"

Anna doesn't answer him. "You reckon we could find that road?"

Jamie's impatience finally gets the better of him. "Anna, what is it? We've got to go and find Signor Ferucci. Come *on*."

She shakes her head again. "No. No, we have to go and see."

"See what?"

"Where the car is. If it's like he says."

"We can do that afterwards," Jamie says. "It'll be there for days, probably."

"No. We've got to go now," she says simply.

Jamie and I stare at her. Jamie's mouth is slightly open, as if he's searching for something to say that will shake this abrupt, unexplained stubbornness.

I say, "Why do you want to see his car?"

A strange look comes over Anna's face. She says, "I'm not sure." There's another impenetrable pause, and then she says, "I don't think he's telling the truth."

"About what?" Jamie says.

"I don't know."

"We have to get Signor Ferucci," I say, starting to feel nervous. The bushes near the side door of the chapel stir very slightly in a breath of air.

"No," Anna says. "We have to go and find his car. We'll do that first." She catches Jamie's eye, and grudgingly adds, "We can go and see Signor Ferucci then, OK?"

Jamie looks like he's struggling with something. Anna stares at him, her eyes dark. At last he shrugs, and the conflict in him eases.

"OK," he says. "But we've got to be quick. You just want to look, right?"

"I just want to look," Anna confirms, but I think that her voice sounds weirdly distant, as though she isn't really concentrating on the question.

"And then we'll go straight into town."

"Yeah. Of course."

"Right, then," Jamie says uncertainly. Anna is looking away from him, at the little door that leads into the cool darkness to where the hermit lies sleeping. For a long time it looks as if she's forgotten our whole conversation, and might be going to stand here until the sun goes down. I tug at the side of her T-shirt.

"Anna?"

She shivers. "Yeah. Let's go."

And we start up the valley together, heading into territory none of us have explored before, following the winding of the river and keeping our eyes open for a road cutting close by, down from the head of the valley.

*   *   *

Across the valley, back down towards where the wonderful blue of the Mediterranean comes up to fill the curve between the two shoulders of land, there is a white house on the hillside, behind a wall. Acres and acres of estate in there slide slowly into ruin, but the house itself always looks sharp and new. Sometimes there are cars on the wide driveway, and they are always shiny and clean, and not clogged with the red dust of the valley. The gates hardly ever open and when they do, the shiny cars hardly ever come down towards the sea: instead they drive off up the valley, going to places I can't imagine. Once in a while there is a tall man with a neatly trimmed beard in the town, but that is all; and that's only once in a while.

Unexplored territory. My mother says, "Thank God nothing like that ever happens here," and turns the volume on the radio down low when she sees me in the doorway.

If time had happened differently, we would have built a tree house, Jamie and I. Perhaps it would have had a rope to climb up, and perhaps it would have been high enough that we would be able to look down the valley and see all the way to the water. These things could have happened.

These things could have happened: a young couple could have gone to a jazz club one night, and they could have drunk beers and talked about an old friend of theirs, and they could have smiled at each other as they remembered. And they could have listened to the music, and let the memories that it brought wash over them, and hardly need to talk now because the music says so much, and they both know it so well. And then they could go out into the night, and fall into step, and have their arms around each other as they walk.

And then they turn a corner and the friend they've been talking about comes out of a bar there, and they are all surprised and amazed and delighted because they haven't seen each other in so long; and it's like, *Hey! What the hell are you doing here? Christ, it's good to see you. You know where we've just been? And we were talking—*

And the three of them have their arms round each other now, and behind them in the night the young people in the jazz club listen, and the musicians play, and the music keeps going until it's late, very late.

And the music doesn't stop—there's no end—and the three friends are talking and laughing and saying that they'll never lose touch like that again. And the night becomes morning and it's another day, and the musicians are tired and the friends are tired as the sun rises over the old city. No-one is dead, and no-one dies, and that is how it could have happened.

I cling to the photographs as if to a sea anchor in a storm, staring at them fiercely, trying to hold myself in the present by force of will. These paintings, at least, have nothing to do with the past.

Whatever it is that is missing here can't be understood with the images scattered round me on the floor. The exhibition will be linear, at eye level, a progression from past to present. I have worked my way round the living room, taping them to the walls: bisecting the room with an almost continuous line of images, broken only at that place where the wall dissolves into a swirl of brush marks and half-formed shapes. By chance it falls right in the centre of the sequence. It makes the whole thing seem in some way uneven, lopsided; but I have found I can't cover these new brush strokes, no matter how hard I try. Whenever I try to ignore them, they end up sucking me back in again. I know, suddenly, that I have to buy proper brushes; proper paints. I need to get colour into this scene: the leached, deadened colour of moonlight, with its heightened contrasts. I can't leave it the way it is.

I frown, shake my head and turn my attention from where substance is starting to emerge from confusion, to where the forms are already complete, finished.

Something is wrong here. I knew it in London, and it's the same now. I can't shake the feeling.

Faces stare out at me, fractured and distorted: a middle-aged woman writing by a window, her hand smoothing the pages of the book open in front of her. A man—a farmer, perhaps—crouched, holding a stone in his hand. It's not the faces. It's the eyes. The eyes look back at me from these paintings and there is something I am not understanding.

It takes us less than an hour to find the wreck.

The hermit's car is lodged at an angle in a patch of scrub, some way off a deserted farm track. It looks as though it has come off the road a little way back, and rolled to where it now is; the bushes behind it are torn and broken. It is a good eight feet below the level of the road surface; the earth has been eroded a small way so that a lip of concrete stands proud at the very edge of the road. Jamie, further along, finds a place where this lip has been scratched and broken away.

"It must have come off here," he shouts back to us.

Anna and I stand looking at the car. It is tipped over to one side, but not too much; the bushes seem to have cushioned it. The driver's side door is open. The near wing of the car is buckled and scratched, but even so, it isn't as wrecked as I have expected. Jamie returns and joins us.

"So he did crash," he says.

"Mm," Anna says. "Let's get closer."

We have almost missed seeing the car. From the road the bushes, and the drop and the way the land lies hide it quite effectively; it is only because we are looking that we spot it. Now, we scramble down the sharp incline, scraping up little avalanches of pebbles and dust, and work our way through the rocky debris in the bottom of the gully until we're round by the side of the car.

"It looks quite old," Jamie says. The car is grey—something else that has helped make it difficult to spot against the stone of the valley floor—and relatively small. Anna pushes her way through the bushes, ignoring the scratches she gets on her arms, until she can look inside.

"What do you see?" Jamie says, starting after her.

"There's all blood on the seat," she says. "Lots of it. And a kind of bandage. No, it's a hanky. It's got blood on it, too."

Jamie and I join her, and peer at the interior. "Yuk," I say.

"Yeah."

"That's why he's so ill," Anna says. "You're not supposed to lose a lot of blood. It makes you weak."

"I wonder where he cut himself," I say, looking. Anna goes still, and then turns sharply to me.

"What?"

I say, "I wonder where he cut himself. Cos he said he cut his leg in the crash."

"Yeah," Anna says. "That's right." Her voice is funny again, as if she's talking to herself. She stares around the inside of the car. "Jamie? Can you see anywhere?"

Jamie looks. "No. Maybe he cut it on the door, getting out."

"But the blood's all on the seat. It's not on the door."

I say, "This is like detective work."

"Forensic detective work," Jamie nods. "Like on TV."

Anna ignores us. "Where did he cut himself? He said he cut himself."

We all look into the car, puzzled.

"I thought it would be wrecked," I say. "All mangled."

Anna nods. "But it's not, is it? Not really. I mean, if it'd come off the big road, then it would've been. It would've been squashed up and probably on fire. But here it's like it just—came off the road and rolled down into the bushes here. It's not even run into anything, much. It's not a real crash, not really."

She sounds to me as if she's thinking aloud, as if she's searching for something that makes sense of it all. I say, "He said the world turned upside down."

Anna nods. "Yeah. I remember. And the windows aren't even broken."

Her frown deepens. Jamie looks around him, and shrugs.

"Well? What now?"

Anna starts to wade through the scrub to the front of the car. "I'm going to look in the other side," she says. Jamie and I watch her through the open door as she gets round to the passenger side. She tugs on the door there and it comes open a little way, and then snags on a bush. Anna gets her foot onto the bush and stamps it down until she can heave the door open properly. She leans into the car, glances at us, and grins.

"Be careful," Jamie says. "It's moving a bit."

He's right; the body of the car rocks soggily against the bushes that are under it as Anna supports herself on the doorsill.

"I want to look in here," she says, reaching for the glove compartment. She twists the catch and the compartment falls open. There's a pause.

"What is it?" I say.

"Nothing," she says, sounding disappointed. "Wait a minute." She heaves herself bodily into the car, and the whole vehicle lurches over as she does so.

"Careful!" Jamie shouts.

"I'm all right," Anna says crossly. "Shut up."

I can see her leaning over the seat back, checking the floor at the rear of the car.

"Anything?"

"No."

When she gets out, the car settles itself drunkenly. Jamie and I look at Anna through the two open doors.

"I thought there'd be something," she says vaguely.

Jamie looks uncomfortable. "We ought to go back," he says.

"Yeah. But I thought there'd be something," she says again.

"Like what?"

"I don't know."

Jamie glances at his feet. Then he looks up again, and says, "There's the boot. We could try that."

Anna blinks. "Oh—of course."

We fight our way through the tangled bushes to the back of the car. The rear wheels are off the ground. I duck down and look underneath; there is a biggish rock hidden under there, and I realize that it must be this which is taking the car's weight. The bushes are just supporting it at the sides, stopping it from tipping too far one way or the other.

Jamie runs his hands along the boot looking for the catch.

"I can't find it," he says.

"Maybe it's one of the ones that open from inside the car," Anna says. "We have one like that. Alex? Go and look."

"What for?"

She pushes past me. "Never mind. I'll do it."

I see her reach into the car once again, and after a moment or two, the lid of the boot jumps up.

"Got it!" Jamie calls.

We have to pull ourselves up a little to see inside, and the car tilts and rocks alarmingly. Anna says, "I see something. It's a case."

"Get it out," I say.

"We shouldn't," Jamie says, sounding worried. "It's stealing."

"Balls," Anna says through clenched teeth, her head in the boot and her feet dangling some inches off the ground. "I've got it."

She drags the case out and swings it down to the ground.

"It's heavy," she says.

"It's not a suitcase," Jamie says.

He's right. The case is black, and has two silver clasps. It's not very big; about half as large as one of the cases my parents have under the bed in their room. There is a handle. It reminds me at once of something, and in a second I have it.

"It's an instrument case," I say. "Like yours—only bigger."

Jamie looks at it, and then nods. "Yeah, you're right. It's the same kind of thing."

Anna is struggling with the clasps. "I can't get it open," she says. "You try."

Jamie kneels down. "Oh," he says. "It's locked."

"What kind of instrument do you think it is?" I say.

"I don't know. Maybe something like a trumpet or a trombone."

"It looks too big for a trumpet," I say.

"It's really heavy," Anna says again. The three of us look at each other.

"He must have the key," Jamie says. Anna is casting about her as if looking for something among the bushes.

"We can ask him," I say. "Maybe he'll play something for us when he's better."

Anna turns back to the case with a sharp, fist-sized rock in her hand. Before Jamie can stop her, she swings it down onto one of the clasps. There's a *clink* and a little puff of dust. The clasp buckles.

"Christ!" Jamie says. "What are you doing?"

"Anna, it's not ours," I say, suddenly nervous.

"Shut up." She hits it again and again. Jamie and I look on helplessly. Then the clasp springs apart, little pieces of it scattering in the sunlight.

"There," she says, and turns to the other one. *Clink. Clink.*

Jamie says, "Stop it, Anna."

"No."

"We'll get in trouble."

"Shut up."

The second clasp comes apart and Anna stops. She turns the case so it's resting properly on its side, and opens it up. We all crowd around it, and our shadows merge together as we lean in.

It takes me a moment to understand what is in the case. Jamie's breathing catches for a second, and I know he knows, too.

Anna says, "Fucking hell." There is awe in her voice, and excitement, and something else which I can't identify. She doesn't sound scared. She sounds—alive. "Fucking—hell," she says again, quietly, shaking her head slightly.

She glances at Jamie and me, and her eyes are bright and glittering and alive. To my amazement, a grin spreads over her face. "What should we do now?" she says.

9

*W*e have ice-cream and Cokes in a side-street *Gelatería*. There are little cast-iron tables set out in the street behind a ragged cordon of shrubs growing in old lead troughs. Anna gets ice-cream on her fingers and licks them. She looks almost guilty, and I laugh.

"It doesn't taste the same," she says.

"The same as what?"

"The same as it used to. At Toni's." She pauses, tries the ice-cream with a spoon this time. "No. It's better, I think, but it doesn't taste the same."

"Well, that's true. Does it bother you?"

"No. It's only ice-cream."

I watch her as she eats, and occasionally, to hide the fact that I'm watching, I take a spoonful of my own ice-cream and eat it. I hardly notice the taste and whether it has changed. I am too caught up with seeing her: the way she lifts the spoon, the way she pokes her teeth with her tongue when they get too cold, the way she focuses so entirely on this one simple thing. When the bowl is empty, she puts the spoon down and takes a sip of Coke, and notices me looking at her.

"What?"

"Nothing," I say.

"You were looking at me."

"So?"

"Well—stop it!"

"Shan't," I say. Her eyes glitter and she grins.

"You haven't finished your ice-cream."

"You can have some if you like," I say.

"OK." She steals spoonfuls, her eyes darting up every so often to see if she can catch me looking at her again. After a time, she says, "It's been a long time since I had ice-cream."

"I know. Me, too."

"I mean—ice-cream like this."

"I know."

"I don't know what I mean. I mean—it's been ages, and I—Christ. I don't know what I mean."

"I missed you," I say.

"Yeah? Really?" She glances across the street at some people walking by in the shadow of the building opposite.

"It's strange, isn't it? Sometimes it feels like no time's passed at all—like you just went away for the weekend or something, and now you're back. And other times, it's like it's been years."

"It *has* been years," she says.

"Yeah, I know it has."

She fiddles with her spoon. "Alex . . ."

I wait for her to go on, but she's silent. "What?" I say.

"It's just that—the way you talk? It makes it sound like we're just the same people as we were. Like everything's the same as it was."

"Oh," I say. "No, I didn't mean that. I mean—I know things aren't the same. But at least we're here, and we're the same."

"No." She shakes her head emphatically. "That's it. I'm *not* the same person. That was five years ago. I've changed a lot since then. Christ—it's not even five years, not really. When was the last time we really talked? Ten, twelve years ago? We were children then. I'm someone different now."

I'm not sure what to say; there is a kind of edge to her voice that surprises me, as if she's trying to tell me something and I'm not understanding. I say, "Everyone grows up, Anna. Me, too."

A quick grimace flickers across her face, as if I've said the wrong thing. Then she smiles slightly, and says, "Yeah. I suppose." She drinks the last of her Coke, and adds, "Look at us. Alex the famous artist. Who'd have thought *that*?"

I laugh a little. "Not famous yet."

"Yeah, but you will be," she says dismissively.

I am uncomfortable with this. I say, "What about you? What's it going to be? Politician? Political historian? Some kind of academic?" Even as I say it, I know it's impossible—not the Anna I know, anyway.

"Maybe."

"Haven't you decided yet?"

She glances across the street again; I turn instinctively to see what she's looking at, but there's no-one there. She says, "Oh, there's plenty of time to decide. The thesis is going to take another year at least."

"You'll have to tell me about it some time."

"Oh, sure. But it's pretty dry stuff."

"I'd listen."

"I know you would. Thanks."

"I'd be interested, too."

"Do you really think so?" she says.

"Why not?"

A slight smile twitches the corner of her mouth, and I can't tell whether she's teasing or not when she says, "Well, you seem so buried in the past. All this stuff you like has already happened, hasn't it? What I'm trying to deal with is what's happening *now*."

I finish my Coke. "Is that what you think? That I'm only interested in the past?"

She's quiet for a moment. "Sometimes."

I sit, looking at her, trying to work out whether she's teasing me or whether she means it. At last, when the silence is starting to be uncomfortable, I search for something to say, and it just comes out.

"Why didn't you come to his funeral?"

A flash of some emotion crosses her face, and is stifled. She looks away from me again, across the street; and when she turns back, her face is composed and serious. All the playfulness—the delight in the ice-cream, the shyness at being looked at—is gone, and she stares at me like an adult talking to a child.

"You know why. I couldn't. I wanted to, Alex, but I couldn't. I had—something else. I told you all this."

"It was important," I hear myself say. I can't understand why I'm saying these things.

"I know it was. Death is always important." She shakes her head, as if she's said something stupid. "I mean, I understand. I wish I could have been there. But there was just no way."

"What was it? Some family thing or something?"

"Yes," she says, shortly. Then, "Look, Alex. It wasn't as if I'd even seen him for two years. Just that time here, when you two were on that trip thing. And that was only a week." Her voice is meditative now, as if she's only half aware that she's talking to me. "I mean, sometimes you have to make decisions that aren't easy, you know? Sometimes it's difficult. But you have to decide because that's what life's all about, and some deaths are more important than others."

"What?"

She blinks, looks at me quizzically.

I say, "What does that mean? 'Some deaths are more important than others'?"

She shakes her head with a kind of weariness. "Nothing. Nothing. Just something going round in my head." She stands up. "Would you get the bill? I'm just going to—wash my face, something."

"Are you OK?" I say.

"Yeah. I'm fine." She hesitates, and then adds, "I know you don't understand why I wasn't there. I wish I could explain it better, so you'd get it. But you just have to believe me. It was important, and there wasn't any other way."

I nod. "I do believe you," I say. "I just wish it had been different."

"I know. But just leave it now, OK? It's in the past, so let it lie. Let's think about something else."

I nod again. "OK," I say. "OK."

Lena is in the kitchen when I arrive home. I am out of breath from the journey down the valley—I have run as much of the way as I am able. Jamie, running with me, controls his impatience when I get winded and have to slow down. I have been watching him, and have seen the nervousness in him. When we reach the place where the farm track joins the road to our houses, he pauses for a moment.

"How much money do you have?" he says.

"Not much." It's true; I've spent most of my pocket money on sweets.

"Well, get what you can. You remember the rest of the stuff?"

I nod; Anna's instructions are still very clear in my head.

"OK then. See you by your gate in five minutes."

"Right," I say, almost overwhelmed with the gravity of the tasks in front of us. Jamie sprints down to his driveway and vanishes inside, while I run more slowly down to my own house.

"You look tired," Lena says critically when I appear in the kitchen doorway. "Have you been playing?"

"Yes," I say. "Hide-and-seek. Don't tell anyone I'm here."

She smiles. "I won't."

"Where's Mummy?"

"She's having a rest. Don't disturb her, now."

"OK," I say, carefully keeping my voice neutral. My father is away in Salerno today, and with Mummy asleep, there will be no trouble getting to the bathroom unnoticed. "Bye," I say to Lena, and slip out of the kitchen and up the stairs.

In the bathroom there is a mirrored cabinet over the sink. There is another one like it in the bathroom just off my parents' bedroom, stuffed with packets and bottles and shaving stuff and soap. This one in the main bathroom has pills for headaches and plasters for cut knees. There is a cupboard under the sink here, too. One side of it has loo paper. The other side, which nobody ever opens much, has some old towels and linen, and a little first-aid kit with a red cross on a white square. Keeping my footsteps quiet on the creaky passage floor, I get to the bathroom. I remember carefully what Anna has told me. I lift out the pile of old linen and work my way through it until I find a pillowcase. I put the rest back, and then put the first-aid kit inside the pillowcase, which is like a little sack. I open up the mirrored cabinet and stare helplessly at the contents. There are lots of little pill bottles and plaster boxes and unidentifiable things in here. I take down aspirin, which I recognize—I can read the word easily—and several of the others at random. Hidden at the back is a roll of white gauze, like a bandage. I know we want something like that, so I take it, with a quick flush of pride at having come across something so useful. Anna will be pleased.

The stairs creak sometimes, but I know how to get around that: I make my way down laboriously, legs stretched apart, stepping only on the very sides of the stairs. I don't make a sound coming down, and I go out the front door, closing it silently behind me. Lena will think I'm hiding upstairs. I grin to myself at the cleverness of the deception, though even being clever for once doesn't completely subdue the sense of anxiety that has been building in me all the way down the valley. Some part of me keeps insisting that, no matter what Anna might say, we *are* just kids, and that the right thing to do would be to call the police.

When I meet Jamie, it is clear to me from his face that he's been thinking the same thing. He looks openly worried, standing by his front gate and glancing up the valley every so often, as if expecting something to happen all of a sudden. When he sees me he looks a little relieved, but only a little.

"Did you get anything?" he says.

"Yeah. Lots."

"OK. Here." He has a carrier bag behind his back, and from it he stuffs some more things into my pillowcase. The last of the items is a big, heavy book. "What about money?"

I shake my pockets empty. "That's all."

"I've got a bit more," he says. "I don't think it's going to be enough, though."

"It might be."

"I don't think so."

We look at each other uncertainly.

"Alex?"

"Yeah?"

"Do you think . . ."

"What?"

"Maybe we should tell someone?"

He's said it at last. With Anna there, neither of us have dared voice any doubts. But Anna isn't here any more; she's still up the valley, lugging the heavy case across to the chapel where the hermit—who isn't really a hermit, I know that now—is lying asleep, or unconscious. If Anna were here, maybe we'd be thinking differently; but she's not.

"I don't know," I say. "Maybe."

"I mean—it could be dangerous."

"Anna says he's hurt badly," I say. "More than he says he is."

"Even so."

"But what would happen if we *did* tell?"

"I don't know. They'd come and get him, I suppose."

"Oh." I think about that. "What about his grandmother?"

"I don't think he has a grandmother. I mean, I think that was a lie, don't you? Just like Anna said."

Anna. It keeps coming back to her: that she seems to understand things we don't.

"How do you think she knew?" I say.

"I don't know."

We glance around us, but the road is empty still.

Jamie says, "I wish I knew what to do."

"We should talk to Anna about it," I say, and the moment the words are out, we both know they're right.

"Yeah," Jamie says with relief. "Then we can decide together." He thinks a while longer, and then goes on, "I mean, nothing's going to happen right away. We can get the stuff like she said, and then go back to the chapel. Then we can all come back down together and tell someone. That's the right thing to do."

"I think he's hurt pretty bad," I say seriously. "I don't think he can walk."

"He walked to the chapel," Jamie says.

"Yeah . . . but maybe he's weaker now. Like Anna said, about losing blood and all that."

Jamie nods slowly. "I think you're right," he says. Then, "OK. You go up and find Anna. Tell her not to go in the chapel, OK? She shouldn't go near him. Wait for me outside, and we'll talk to her, and then we'll all come down together." He sounds pleased with the way he's planned things out. I feel some of the guilt and anxiousness fade inside me.

"OK," I say. "I'll see you up there, then."

"Bet I catch you halfway," he grins.

"Bet you don't."

"We'll see."

"All right." I think of something, then. "Jamie? You know when we were going to go, and then Anna said stop?"

"Yeah?"

I say, "The hermit said something."

"What?"

"I don't know. It didn't make sense. But then I thought maybe it was English. It kind of makes sense in English."

"What was it?"

" 'Name angel,' " I say.

Jamie frowns. "What does *that* mean?"

"I don't know."

"It still doesn't make any sense, then."

"But the words do, kind of."

"Maybe you heard it wrong. Maybe it was just—you know, sounds."

I nod, reluctantly. "Yeah. It might have been. But it sounded like 'name angel' to me."

"Well, what do you think it means?"

I shrug. "I don't know."

"Well, then." He grins. "I'll see you later, OK?"

"See you."

He waves, and starts to trot down the road into town, stuffing my money into his jeans pocket as he goes. I heft my sack of supplies on my back and start in the opposite direction, trying to run a little even though my legs are still wobbly from the journey down. Once Jamie is out of sight, though, I quickly slow down, and let myself settle into a steady walk instead. The pillowcase is heavier now that it has the big book in it, and it bumps steadily against my back as I go.

The afternoon sun is getting lower in the sky as I turn the corner into the farm track, and another pang of worry crosses my mind: we are going to be late home if we're not careful. I find myself half hoping that we are; if we're late, there might be a row, and then I might be forced to say where we've been and what we've done. But then I remember: we're going to tell everyone anyway. We're going to talk Anna out of keeping it all a secret.

It's strange, though, that even though Jamie and I have decided this, it still doesn't feel to me like it will actually happen. Something about Anna's determination—the fierce look in her eyes when she argues with us at the side of the road where the car is crashed—seems impossible to overcome. I wonder if Jamie and I can manage it.

When I reach the empty river, I manage to break into a gentle jog, and hold the pace for a while. Around me, the valley moves slowly past, and little puffs of dust are struck up by my feet and trail behind me as I go.

When I reach the chapel, Anna is nowhere to be seen. It crosses my mind briefly that she might not have arrived yet, but even I can see that she must have been able to make the journey to the chapel in the time it's taken Jamie and me to go all the way down the valley and back. Still, standing in the sunlight with the blank face of the dandelion clock staring impassively at me, I hesitate. If she's not out here, she must be inside; and I don't like the idea of going into the solemn coolness of the chapel without Jamie.

Tell her not to go in the chapel, Jamie has said. *She shouldn't go near him.* I scuff my feet through the pine needles and walk about a bit, swinging my pillowcase, feeling worried and confused.

"Alex!"

Anna's voice comes from somewhere, but I can't see her. I look round, turning this way and that.

"No. Up here."

I look up, and have to squint my eyes against the bright blue of the sky to see her: she has her head and shoulders sticking out of one of the apertures in the belltower, and is looking down at me.

"I saw you come up the valley," she says. "I was watching. I saw you a long way away. Did you get everything?"

"Some of it," I say, hefting the pillowcase to show her.

"OK. Bring it up here, then."

Going to the belltower means crossing the chapel floor, where the hermit must still be. I stare at my feet for a moment. The darkness of the chapel, and the bloodstained hermit—

"Come on," Anna calls down.

"You come down," I say, playing for time. I can almost hear her breathe out in exasperation.

"He's asleep. Stop fussing, Alex. Just go quietly."

I think it through, and realize that when the hermit wakes up again, he will be between us and the chapel door. We might end up trapped in the belltower, unable to get out. "No," I say, more firmly. "You come down."

"You're *such* a pain," she says. "All right. Wait there." Her silhouette disappears from view. I squint up at the tower for a while longer, but there is only the clockface there now. A long time passes, and I see a bird swoop across from one side of the valley, flutter for a second, and vanish into the same window Anna has been staring out of. There is a sudden twist of tension in my stomach as I realize that perhaps the hermit has already woken; that perhaps Anna has been caught. Tentatively, I creep to the corner of the chapel and look round it. The little side door is there, in the shade of the clump of bushes that partly obscures it. I watch, my throat dry, for what seems like an hour. Then Anna's slight figure eases out of the doorway, slowly pulls the door closed, and steps out into the sunlight.

"What did you get?" she says.

We sit ourselves on one of the piles of timber near the stone pines and I open the pillowcase to show her.

"Plasters. The first-aid box. Pills—I got some but I don't know what they all are. I found this," I say, holding up the roll of bandage.

"Good," she says, and I feel warm inside. I knew she'd be pleased.

"Jamie's found the book," I say. Anna lifts it out and studies the cover. "It's the encyclopedia," I add, pleased that I know the name.

"I wanted something on—you know. Medicine and that stuff."

"Oh, it'll have that," I say. Jamie has shown me how the encyclopedia works. I take it from Anna and look at the spine. "It goes from Fa to Gen," I say.

"What use is that?"

I think about it. "I don't know," I say. "But Jamie will." I know he's bound to have got this one for a reason.

"It's in English."

"It's Jamie's father's," I say.

"English is no good," she says crossly.

"We can tell you what it means."

She shrugs. "Yeah, I suppose." She drops the book back into the pillowcase and takes out the first-aid kit. The inside is stuffed with more plasters, two more rolls of gauze, and several little packets. Anna scrutinizes them closely.

"I don't know what these are," she says.

"Maybe the book will tell us."

"Maybe."

Something has been nagging at me while we've been talking. I say, "Where is it?"

She looks at me blankly. "What?"

"You know. The gun."

"Oh, that." She closes the first-aid box and puts it back. "It's in the tower, by the bell. I checked he was still asleep first, and then I took it up there. It's really heavy."

"Why'd you put it there?" I ask.

"Well—it's up all those stairs, isn't it? With his leg the way it is, he can't get up there. So it's safe."

"Oh. I suppose," I say, impressed despite myself by the way she seems to have thought it through.

Anna stands up and walks a little way out from where we've been sitting.

"We're going to have to be really careful," she says quietly. "We can't let anyone know we've come here."

I watch her, thinking to myself that I'll wait for Jamie before explaining to her that we have to tell someone—the police, our parents, someone. But looking at her back, the way her shoulders are so straight and her feet so firmly placed on the ground, she looks like nothing we say will ever make any difference. I swallow, and wonder how long Jamie will be.

The hermit is still lying against the end of the pew where we left him. The three of us lean cautiously in round the door, letting our eyes adjust to the gloom.

"He's sleeping," I say.

"He could still be dangerous," Jamie mutters. I can tell he's not wholly convinced by what Anna's told him; but as I have suspected, none of our arguments have had the slightest effect on her. For my part, I don't know what to think. I want to do the right thing, and Jamie says that not telling anyone could get us all into trouble—real trouble, not just trouble with our parents. Secretly I think he is right. But Anna is adamant that her plan is the only one which makes sense. When we press her for details and ask her why, though, she becomes first vague and then angry, shouting at us both and saying that we're being ridiculous. The hermit isn't dangerous, she keeps saying. After all, he's hurt;

there are three of us and only one of him; and we're the ones with the gun now.

"Besides," she says, looking rather distant, "perhaps he'll turn out to be nice."

Jamie looks disbelieving when she says this, but I wonder. The hermit, when he talked to us before, sounded very pleasant, even though I have to keep reminding myself how the story about his grandmother was probably all a lie.

Anna stares critically at the dimly lit figure. "We ought to talk to him," she says. "We'll have to wake him up." She starts inside the chapel, and reluctantly, Jamie and I follow.

When we get close, however, it becomes clear that the hermit is already awake. His eyes are half closed, but I can see the dim red and blue of the Madonna and Child reflected in them. Anna kneels down on the floor beside him, and his eyes move to follow her.

"We're back," she says softly. Jamie and I are standing, keeping a little way off. Anna glances back at us, and then goes on, "Sorry we were so long. We had to go all down the valley. Do you feel better after your sleep?"

The man blinks slowly. He seems to be digesting what Anna has said. Then he says, "Signor Ferucci—you've told him, yes?"

"No," Anna says. "We went to his house but he wasn't there. The housekeeper says he's gone away."

"For how long?"

"I don't know. Maybe he's on holiday."

The hermit doesn't look like he's at all pleased to hear this. He thinks for a while, and then says, "Did you tell anyone else?" His voice sounds a bit strange; weak, and slightly hoarse.

"No. You said not to," Anna says, sounding a little surprised. "We were very careful. Nobody knows we're here."

Jamie flinches very slightly when she says this, as though he's worried she's done something stupid. I can't work out what, though. Anna keeps her voice low and her eyes on the hermit.

"We saw your car," she says.

"What?" He sounds surprised, and a bit dazed.

"We went up the track a bit. We saw where it had come off the road. There was a lot of blood."

"Yeah," Jamie puts in, his voice tense. "You must have cut yourself pretty badly."

"I told you I did," the man says.

"How did it happen?" Anna asks.

"I can't remember, not properly. I think there was some metal torn on the door frame," the hermit says. His mind doesn't seem to be properly on the conversation, though. He has a faraway look on his face, as though his brain is occupied with different thoughts entirely. He says, "You're sure you couldn't find Signor Ferucci?"

"He's gone away," Anna says. "I don't know when he'll be back. We could ask his housekeeper next time we're in town."

"Yes," he says. A shadow of pain crosses his face and he draws his breath in sharply.

"You're not well," Anna says.

"I'm fine."

"You need a doctor."

The man closes his eyes briefly. "No. No doctors or hospitals. I told you."

"But supposing you don't get better? What if you get worse?"

There's a long pause, and I wonder if the hermit has gone to sleep again. But then his eyes open, and he looks at her. The look is close, appraising, as if he's searching for something in her face.

Anna meets his eyes evenly. She says, "We don't know when Signor Ferucci will be back. Your cut might get worse. In the—when we looked in the car, there was a lot of blood. That makes you weak, doesn't it?"

After a second, he nods.

Anna says, "You weren't telling the truth, were you?"

The man continues to stare right at her. "I don't know what you mean," he says.

"About it only being a small cut. It must be bad, to bleed that much."

His face remains neutral. "Oh," he says. "That. Well, perhaps. I didn't want to frighten you."

"I'm not frightened," Anna says.

"I can see that," he says. There's an odd quality to his voice, quite apart from the hoarseness which, I have decided, must come from the pain.

Jamie says, abruptly, "Are you a musician?"

The man blinks. "What?" he says.

Jamie says, "We found a case in your car. Like an instrument case. I play the clarinet," he adds, casually.

"You do, do you?" the man says. "What did you do with it?"

"With the case?"

"Yes."

"It was locked," Anna says. "We put it in a place in the rocks near the car. It's hidden, I mean. We thought maybe if we left it in the car someone might take it. Jamie said it looked like an instrument case. We thought it might be valuable."

The man considers this. His eyes continue to reflect the dull light of the window, and as I shift awkwardly from foot to foot, they seem to change colour: blue to gold to blue. Then he says, "That was a good idea. You've been very thoughtful." He turns his head a little and looks at Jamie. It feels like the first time he's taken his eyes off Anna since we came into the chapel. He says, "So you play the clarinet, yes? That's pretty impressive. Have you played for long?"

"Oh, three years, nearly," Jamie says. "What about you?"

"Yes. I'm a musician," he says. "I play—saxophone. Tenor. It's a big instrument. Heavy, too. You'll know that if you carried it any distance."

Jamie looks blank for a moment, and then nods quickly.

The man's eyes sweep round us. I watch them, fascinated by the changing colours, held by their sudden sharpness. He says, "Jamie. Anna. Alex. That's right, isn't it?"

"How do you know our names?" Jamie says, sounding panicky.

The man grunts a half-laugh. "You said them before, remember? You were talking to each other. And I asked Alex his," he adds, nodding at me. "So. Jamie, Anna and Alex. I want to thank you for helping me so much. But I think perhaps I may have to ask you to help me some more."

Anna nods. "We know," she says. She reaches to me and I hand her the pillowcase. She tips it up and the contents tumble out onto the floor. "This is all we could get straight away," she says. She spreads the empty pillowcase on the dusty floor and sorts through the items, putting them neatly into rows on the linen. "Jamie?"

Jamie opens the shopping bag he's brought. In it is bread and bottles of water, a big stick of salami sausage, some fruit and cotton wool.

Anna says, "We can get more. We didn't know quite what to get. This seemed like the best stuff to bring."

The hermit looks at the accumulation of provisions and medications wordlessly for a time. His brow is lined with an expression that is partly pain from his leg, but also something else which I can't properly identify; as if he's trying to solve a puzzle in his head, maybe. Then the look clears a little. He glances up at Jamie and me.

"Jamie and Alex," he says. "English names, yes?"

"Yes," Jamie says.

"Your Italian is very good," he says. "I wouldn't be able to tell if it weren't for the names." He takes a breath. "You're sure no-one saw you come here?"

"Yeah," Jamie says. "Nobody ever comes here any more."

"All the same," the man says. "Could you two go and check outside? Just have a look round the building—maybe have a look at the tracks and so on. Just to make sure."

"OK," I say. The idea of getting out of the murky chapel is appealing. I am beginning to think I am able to smell the metallic tang of the blood on the hermit's clothing.

Jamie, though, doesn't seem so eager to leave. "Anna?" he says. "You come, too."

"That's all right," the hermit says easily. "Anna can tell me all about these things you've brought me."

"Anna," Jamie says. There's a detectable urgency in his voice. "Come on."

Anna gets up and the three of us go over to the door. Once there, though, she stops, and drops her voice to a whisper.

"Just go and look round," she hisses. "It's OK. I'll be fine."

"We shouldn't leave each other alone with him," Jamie says, slightly desperately. "You don't know what might happen."

"Don't be silly. Just go and check like he says."

"There's nobody there," Jamie says. "You know that."

"For God's sake," she says, angrily. "Don't be so *wet*."

Jamie flushes at the insult, but he stays where he is. "It's not safe," he says.

"Yes it is." She softens her tone a bit. "Look. Only a couple of minutes, all right? What's the harm in that? Then you can come straight back."

"Why are you taking his side?" Jamie says. "We don't know anything about him."

Anna shrugs. "He won't do anything. We're looking after him. He needs us."

Some logic in this makes sense to Jamie. He hesitates still, but Anna takes his arm and gently pushes him out the side door. The light outside has changed; it's getting to be evening.

"We can't stay much longer anyway," she says. "Just have a look round and check. I'll tell him about the stuff we've got."

She shuts the door after us, and Jamie and I are left standing by the side of the building, looking at each other.

"Where should we look?" I say.

A kind of rebellious anger takes hold of Jamie. "I'm not leaving," he says, and he squats down in the dust where he is, putting his eye to the keyhole of the door.

I glance around nervously; all the talk of being followed and checking for people has made me uneasy. Jamie shifts slightly. I say, "Can you see anything?"

"Not much," he says. "I can see Anna and I can see his legs. She's kneeling beside him again."

"Can you hear anything?"

"No," he says.

"What's happening now?"

"She's just sitting there, I think," he says. "I can't really see much. Maybe they're talking."

"Nothing bad's happening?"

"No."

"Oh."

"Alex?"

"Yeah?"

"Do you think we're doing the right thing?"

"I don't know."

"Me neither."

"What's happening now?"

"Nothing."

I wait while Jamie continues his observation. After a minute or so has passed, he stands up. "We could go back in now," he says.

"We haven't checked."

"It doesn't matter," he says impatiently. "There's no-one. I don't know what Anna's up to."

"Is she up to something?" I ask.

"Well, I don't know. But she's acting really weird, don't you think?" I consider this. "Yeah," I say.

"Well then. I just wish I knew what she was doing."

"She always has good ideas, though," I say. "Like going to the car and stuff."

Jamie nods reluctantly. "Yeah, that's true. But why did she want to go there? It's like she knows stuff without—without having a way to know it." He wanders in little aimless circles for a while. "It's all really weird."

"Let's go back in," I say.

"OK." But he doesn't go back to the door. Instead, he stops walking and stares up the valley at the hills there. He says, "Where d'you think he came from?"

"I don't know. Somewhere over the hills, I suppose."

"Yeah. And why did he come here?"

"He knows Signor Ferucci," I say. Instinctively, my gaze darts down the valley to the distant white house on the hillside.

"Mm." Jamie is lost in thought. When, after a moment or two, he shows no sign of moving, I tug at his sleeve.

"We ought to go back in," I say.

"Yeah. OK."

We open the door quietly and slip inside the chapel again. Anna and the hermit both look up briefly. Anna is kneeling by the hermit's side, just like Jamie has described to me. I am reassured; the hermit hasn't hurt her or tried to hold her hostage or anything like that. In fact, it isn't at all clear to me what, if anything, they've been doing. Perhaps Anna has been showing him all the things we've brought, just like she said she would.

She comes over to us. "His leg's hurt pretty bad," she says.

"Thought so."

"We need to put a bandage on it, I think."

"It's getting late," Jamie says. "What about dinner?"

For once Anna doesn't tell him not to be silly, or to stop being so wet. She frowns. "Yeah. We mustn't let them worry. But I don't think it's a good idea to leave him alone."

"We can't stay here all night," Jamie says.

"Not all of us. But one of us could, if we were careful."

"How?"

She ignores the question. "And we need other stuff. I keep realizing. Lights of some sort. More water—we need to wash his leg, probably. Blankets and stuff. It must get really cold in here at night."

I think about that, and realize she's right. The thought sends a little shiver down me.

"That's a lot of stuff," Jamie says.

"We could do it. If we all work together."

She's looking straight at Jamie now, her brown eyes almost black in the dim light.

"Please, Jamie."

Jamie looks away, then looks back at her. Finally he nods. "Yeah, all right. What about dinner?"

"You'll have to cover for me. Is there a way to do that?"

Jamie thinks for a moment and then nods again. "Yeah. Yeah, we can do that. I think we can do the night thing too."

"Can you get back here after dinner?"

"Yeah."

"Then let's do that. I'll stay with him for the moment, and then you guys come back. We'll plan it all out properly then."

"Right," Jamie says. "You sure you'll be OK?"

"Yeah. You'd better get going. It's getting late."

Jamie and I take a final look around the darkening chapel—at the paler shape of the hermit's figure leant against the pew back in the shadows, at the huge daubs of colour cast by the stained-glass window, at the upstretched arm of the wood and plaster Christ over by the wall. Then we duck outside, and the remains of the afternoon's heat wash round us. We pull the door closed behind us, and I catch a quick glimpse of Anna standing there staring after us, hands by her sides, the smear of blood on her T-shirt just visible as the shadow from the moving door closes over her. Then we are completely outside, and there is no way of telling that there is anyone in the chapel at all. The afternoon is still and humming with insects, and our feet crunch drily on the grit and pine needles. Jamie looks at his watch.

"Is there time?" I say.

"Only just. We'd better run," he says.

"I've run everywhere today," I complain as we trot across the church-yard to the fence.

"Yeah."

"Jamie?"

"Mm?"

"Are we really going to stay here all night?"

"I'm not sure," he says. "Maybe. I think Anna wants to."

"It might be spooky," I say.

"Yeah, I know. Don't worry about it now, though."

In the dry riverbed, we lengthen our strides and I try to keep up with Jamie's pace.

"Jamie?"

"What?"

"He's going to be all right, isn't he? The hermit."

"I hope so," Jamie says.

"What if he dies?" I say.

"He won't."

"He might die," I say. "Maybe he'll get sick and die."

"That won't happen, Alex. Don't say things like that."

"It might, though."

"Shut up."

We run on in silence for a while.

"If he dies and we were supposed to look after him, are we mur-derers?"

"He's not going to die, Alex. Be quiet now. We've got to get home. We can talk about it after dinner, OK?"

"OK."

I am out of breath from the running already, but Jamie doesn't slow down like he sometimes does. I force my legs to work harder, to keep up; and to my surprise, they somehow manage it. We jog steadily down the river towards home.

"We've got blankets and sheets," Jamie says, laying them down. "And we filled these up with water. And we got candles because Alex says they never use them in his house unless there's a power cut. And my torch. And scissors this time, but we've got to take them back cos Lena uses her sewing box quite a lot and she'd know if they went missing. And biscuits and comics," he finishes, slightly embarrassed.

Anna doesn't seem to notice his embarrassment. "That's good," she says quietly. "What happened with dinner?"

"Oh, it was easy. We told my mum and dad we were going to Alex's, and we told Alex's mum and dad we were going to our house. Then we went round the back and hid."

"I got us food," I say.

"We did the same thing with tonight," Jamie goes on. "Told them all we were staying at the other house, you know? It's fine. Nobody minds."

Anna grins. "Excellent," she says. "We could do this a lot."

"I don't think so," Jamie says. "I mean, this once, yes, but if we do it more often, they're bound to realize. All they'd have to do is go round or something and we wouldn't be there."

"Oh. Shit. You're right."

"We'll have to think of something else."

"Yeah. We can do that later."

"How is he?"

A shadow of worry passes across Anna's face. "He's sleeping again," she says. "But he's got very hot. He's sweating."

"But it's cold," I say.

"I know. I think it's bad."

"What do we do now?" Jamie says.

"I think we need to bandage his leg properly. He was going to try to do it himself when you went, but then we didn't have scissors or anything and it hurts him a lot to move. His leg seems to have gone all stiff, so he can't move it so easily."

"Oh."

Anna says, "I suppose we'd better get started, then."

There is bright sunlight on the stairs. How can there be sunlight? The chapel is dark—

The front door stands wide and bright sunlight comes through and spills up the stairs. I straighten, and for a long moment I am not sure whether this is afternoon light or morning light. My head spins a little with standing, and there are tense muscles in my legs. I stretch, breathing in deeply. I feel I could drink this sunlight.

Tools are scattered on the floor. I must have been working hard. I have my sleeves rolled up; there is plaster and dust and flakes of old paint on my forearms. There is dust on the photographs that ring the walls, too. I stink of sweat; I need a shower.

I wonder what day today is.

Time seems to have been slipping by me again without touching me properly. Things are being done, it seems, but hardly with my knowledge. I must be doing them, because I can see the house changing in front of me: a cupboard door fixed here, a loose window-frame seated properly here, a missing tap and a cracked tile replaced here and here. The house changes around me and I seem to drift through the changes, doing them but at the same time only noticing them when they're done.

In the living room, the scene on the wall is taking form into itself, gathering substance and weight. I am almost frightened by how it is happening. Around it, framing it, are the perfectly ordered photographs whose order I know to be flawed. In London, they will be the same; but the eyes—the eyes tell me I have understood things wrongly. This is not how they should be.

I feel out of control, but there is nothing—nothing at all—I can do about it.

What day is it? It must be Monday. Or Tuesday; Tuesday at the latest.

I should call Max. I should go into town now.

The chapel keeps pulsing in and out of the corners of my perception, as if it is all about me, but hidden behind the merest fraction of a hair's breadth. I feel the house could turn in an instant to dust, and leave me stranded in the past, with no way of getting home.

I can feel my thoughts reeling and making no sense. I try to hold onto them, to pin them down and keep them from whirling like this, but it is too difficult. I can't move fast enough to catch them.

We should have told someone. It was Anna's fault, what we did; it was her idea.

No. It was all our faults. It was my fault too. I was there, and I could have done something, and I didn't. A sin of omission, then.

The paintings stare down at me from the walls, and I hardly recognize them any more.

I want to turn back the hands on the clock and change it all, make it different; three friends who build a tree house, and who meet up by chance in an old city and share a beer and laugh at old stories and old jokes. But it wasn't like that; and the clock has no hands, so I can't turn them back.

10

*J*amie lights candles and places them in a circle around where the hermit is lying. He has his torch, too, and sets it so that it shines straight onto the hermit's leg. The encyclopedia is on one of the pews, held open at the pages on first aid. It is a big section, all about what to do in emergencies, and there are diagrams, too: how to give the kiss of life to a drowned man. How to make a splint for a broken bone. How to make a sling.

Anna and I crouch at the hermit's side. He is awake again, though I can see that his face is glistening slightly in the candlelight. The shadows around his eyes look very deep now that there is no more light from the window to reflect in them.

He says, "You will have to bandage the leg. You understand this, yes?"

I nod. Anna says, "Yes."

"And clean it, too. That will help stop infection." Infection is something we're all worried about now; the hermit has explained to us that just stopping the bleeding may not be enough. The encyclopedia says that something called Sulfa will stop infection, but none of the bottles or packets we've brought has this word on them. There is a cream which Lena puts on my knees when I graze them, though, and we are going to use this instead.

"You'll have to cut the trouser leg, I'm afraid," the hermit says apologetically. "I don't think I can move the leg enough to get them off."

"That's OK," Anna says. "We've got scissors."

The hermit takes a breath, and for a moment his gaze drifts away from Anna and out into the darkness of the chapel. Then he blinks, and seems to see her again.

"Where was I?" he says.

"You said we had to cut the trousers away," Anna says. She glances at Jamie, who is looking worried.

"Yes. That's right. And then there's this." He moves his hand on his thigh and I see something I haven't noticed before. The dim lighting and the darkness of the blood staining the cloth have hidden it. The hermit has a belt wrapped around his leg, right up near the top.

"What's that for?" I say.

He moves his head to look at me. His movements are slightly uncertain, and sometimes his voice slurs a little, like some of the men in town when they've been drinking beer in the afternoon. He says, "This is to stop the blood. If you keep it tight, not so much can get into the leg. But you mustn't have it too tight, or not enough blood will come down and the leg will die." He tries a smile, but it looks sickly. "That wouldn't be good, would it?"

I shake my head. The idea of the leg dying while still attached to the hermit makes me feel very queasy.

"So, little Alex, you will have to hold on here." He shows me the end of the belt. "Just hold on, all right? Don't pull. But if suddenly there is a lot of blood—new blood—then pull it tight, you see? Try to stop it. And when it's stopped, let it go slowly until it's like it is now again. Do you understand?"

"Yes," I say, trying to keep my voice steady.

Anna says, "So we wash it, and then put the cream on, and then bandage it up?"

The hermit's gaze has drifted again. He looks at Anna, and it seems like it is a big effort to do so. "What?"

"We cut the trousers, then we wash it, and put on the cream, and bandage it up?"

"Yes. That's right."

"Where's the cut?" she says, peering at the dark fabric. "I can't see."

"Up here," the man says, pointing. He pauses for a second, and then takes a breath. "There will be another one, too. On the other side."

"What?" Anna says.

"At the back of the leg. Another—cut. But maybe worse than the one at the front. I think the one at the front will be—quite small."

Anna nods, though she looks puzzled.

"You will need to turn me, to get at the cut at the back," the hermit says. "That may be difficult. Do you understand?"

"Yes."

"And it may be that I lose consciousness. If that happens, don't worry. Just get the leg cleaned and bandaged. All right?"

"Yes," Anna says. "I understand."

"You're sure you remember everything?"

"Yes," Anna says.

"All right." He leans back, exhausted, and closes his eyes. Anna turns to me.

"Get hold of the belt, then," she says. I nod and take the end of the belt that the hermit has shown me firmly in both hands. I can see the buckle now, deep in a fold of cloth. It looks like it must be quite tight. I think of winding threads of cotton round my thumb, watching the tip turn pink and then darkly red. I understand what the hermit meant.

Steadily, Anna starts to cut up the trouser leg from the ankle. The scissors make a neat little sound as they bite through the cloth, and it reminds me of Lena on sunny afternoons, sewing in the kitchen. I am careful not to let myself slip away, though; Anna and the hermit need me to be right here, all the time, in case I have to pull on the belt. Jamie has come closer as well, holding the torch so Anna can see more clearly what she's doing.

"OK," she says. "Now we need to cut round."

Sometimes, when she is concentrating hard, the tip of her tongue pokes slightly out of the corner of her mouth. She cuts round the outside of the hermit's thigh, and then looks up at Jamie and me.

"We'll have to move him a little," she says. "I can't get the scissors underneath."

I have thought that the hermit has fallen asleep, but when Anna puts her hands under his knee and gently lifts it, he draws in a ragged, painful breath. His eyes stay closed, though.

"That's enough," she says after a moment. Her hands are small, and she's able to reach underneath now and continue cutting. She has to crouch down low against the floor to see properly. Then she changes hands with the scissors and finishes the job, cutting down the inside of the thigh. The cloth flaps away to either side and she pulls it clear. "Get the pillowcase," she says. Jamie passes it to her and she puts it on the floor under the leg.

We can see the leg properly now. It's covered in old blood, turned dark and almost black in places. Halfway up the thigh is a small, round hole, so small it looks like I wouldn't get my little finger in it. The place around it looks swollen and blotchy. There is fresh blood here, trickling down the side of the leg. I steady my grip on the belt.

"It's so small," Jamie says in wonder.

"Let's get it clean," Anna says.

We have the bottles of mineral water ready, and Anna takes pieces of the cotton wool we've bought and wets them. She works slowly and methodically, cleaning the blood from the skin, working gradually towards the wound itself. The way her hands are when she's working remind me a lot of Jamie; there is the same precision and competence there. Her movements are gentle but definite, with no hesitation or uncertainty. When she gets very close to the wound itself, the hermit grits his teeth and his breath comes more quickly. Anna glances up.

"Is it all right?" she says.

"Keep—going," the hermit says, forcing the words out. Anna nods to herself and bends back to the work.

Soon the whole of the top of the leg is clean, and we can all see the little round hole much more clearly. It's hardly bleeding at all now. I try to keep my tension on the belt as gentle as possible, reminding myself of the horrible possibility that I might kill the hermit's leg by pulling too hard, but my hands have cramped up into clenched fists, and it is difficult to control how hard they pull. I am shivering slightly, which is strange, because I don't feel cold.

"There," Anna says at last. She blinks, and stretches, and puts the cotton wool she's been using onto the little pile of blood-soaked rubbish that is growing beside her. "That's the top. We need to turn him now."

"Onto his front?" Jamie says.

"Just onto his side, I think," she says. We all wait a second for the hermit to confirm this, but he is silent, his breath shallow and quick.

"He looks really hot," Jamie says.

"I know. But we have to turn him now."

"OK."

It is difficult, turning the hermit. He is a fully grown man, and he weighs a lot more than any of us would have guessed. Jamie takes his shoulders and Anna takes his knee, and I try to hang onto the belt and push a little at his hip. Jamie counts softly to three, and we all heave. The hermit's body turns, and then he lets out a huge cry of pain. It startles us all so much that we jump back.

"Shit!" Anna gasps.

The hermit crashes back into place, his face white and sweating. I have lost my grip on the belt, and suddenly there is more blood on the leg—a lot more.

"Alex!" Anna snaps. I seize the end of the strap and pull on it hard, and keep pulling. The hermit is breathing very quickly now.

"Shit," Jamie says. "What do we do now?"

"We do it again," Anna says. She sounds furious, and I wonder if she'll tell me or Jamie off for letting go. But she doesn't. After a while I remember that she let go as well; perhaps she is angry at herself too. "Let me clean this first," she says, and she wipes away the fresh blood from the leg. Her hands and arms are streaked with blood. She throws the used cotton wool onto the pile and looks up at both of us.

"All right. Again. And don't stop this time, no matter what he does." She sounds fierce. Jamie and I nod instinctively.

"One. Two. Three. Now."

We turn the hermit onto his side. He doesn't shout this time. His head is still rested against the end of the pew.

Anna says, "Get the sheet for a pillow."

"What sheet?"

"The one I brought. It's over there." Jamie nods.

To make a theatre. Anna's note feels like it comes from years and years ago.

I keep holding onto the end of the belt while Anna starts cleaning the back of the leg. "I can't see," she complains after a while. "Can you get the torch round here?"

Jamie, who has done his best to prop the hermit more comfortably, comes round. He shines the torch where Anna is working.

"Christ," she says softly. "Can you see this?"

"Yuk," I say faintly. I look away. The candles dance and jump excitedly around us, their flames twitched by the moving air we are all stirring up as we move and breathe. I stare at them, watching the way they make shadows leap on the walls of the chapel.

The back of the hermit's leg is a mess. It is nothing like the neat hole, only as wide as a pencil, which is at the front. It looks like something has been torn out of him. There are flaps of flesh there. I stare at the candles and breathe in and out.

Anna is still swabbing old blood away. I can see her moving out of the corner of my eye. Jamie's hand is trembling on the torch—I can see the beam shaking—but Anna doesn't say anything. Every so often she turns to drop another used ball of cotton wool onto the pile.

It feels like a week passes before she says, "There. That's it, I think." She straightens for a moment, and then says, "How much water is there left?"

"Most of a bottle," Jamie says.

"Give it here."

She sloshes the bottle over the wound. The hermit doesn't make a sound; he is lying completely still. For a second I can't hear him breathing, and I panic—am about to shout out—but then I see his mouth move a little. Anna keeps sloshing water over the leg. I swallow, and take a quick look at what she's doing. The water runs out of the wound slightly pink. The floor around where she is kneeling is slick, shiny.

"OK," she says at last. She puts the bottle down and gets more cotton wool. "We have to dry it now." She pats carefully, working round the area like she did when she was cleaning it. She dabs the leg dry on both sides. When she's happy with it, Jamie hands her the tube of graze cream. She squeezes lots of it onto both sides of the leg, all around the wounds.

"Pass me the bandage stuff, then."

The hermit has explained to us how to make a bandage. Anna rinses her hands with the last of the water, and then tears open one of our packets of gauze.

"Jamie?"

Jamie holds the leg at the knee, keeping it up enough that Anna can wind the gauze round and round. The gauze quickly turns red where it touches the wounds. I strengthen my grip, but it makes no difference. Anna goes round and round until the first pack of gauze is all used up.

"How much cotton wool is there?"

"Some," Jamie says.

She opens the other pack of gauze. She makes thick pads of the remaining cotton wool and puts them over the two wounds, and she binds them in place with the rest of the gauze. By the time she's finished, the hermit's thigh is all wrapped up for about six inches, and there are two bulges, one front and one back, where the cotton pads are pressed into place.

"Get me some plasters. The big ones," she says.

Jamie cuts her off a strip of plaster from a thick roll of it that has come from his house. Anna uses it like sticky tape, to fix the loose end of the gauze in place. Then, blinking slightly, she sits back on her haunches.

"There," she says. "That's got it."

"Is it all done?" Jamie asks.

"I think so. How is he?"

Jamie is quiet for a moment. "I don't know. His breathing's funny. He feels hot still."

Anna stands up, her knees cracking. "Maybe he'll get better now it's bandaged," she says.

"Yeah."

"Can I let go now?" I say.

Anna looks at me as if noticing me for the first time in ages. She says, "Oh. Yes, I think so. Gently, though. Just a bit at a time."

I do so. My hands are numb where they've been gripping the leather.

Jamie says, "Should we turn him back the way he was?"

"I don't know. It might start him bleeding more."

"He doesn't look very comfortable like he is."

Anna thinks. Then she says, "You're right. Let's turn him back. It won't be so hard this way."

For the last time, we take hold of the hermit and roll him as gently as possible back. His face is ashen, and his mouth hangs open a little. I can hear him breathing again, though, which is a relief. Even though the breaths are fast and so light that they're hardly there, it means he's still alive.

"What do we do now?" Jamie says.

We all stare at the hermit, sleeping now in the middle of his ring of candles.

"I like this one," Mr. Dalton is saying. "The way the lights ring the figure like this. Interesting use of light on the face, too." He looks closer at the picture. "Kind of Christ-like, isn't he?" he says.

"I suppose," I say.

"Is that intentional?"

"Kind of."

"Well, I'll tell you what I first thought of when I saw it," he says. "You see how the edges of the lights take on a spikiness when you paint them with a cubist sensibility? Well, I saw this man, looking a bit like a kind of Renaissance Christ, ringed round with spikes, and I thought 'Crown of thorns.' Or is that pushing the symbolism too much?" He looks at me, smiling mischievously.

"I don't really know," I say. "It wasn't supposed to be a crown of thorns."

"Ah, well, that's the trouble with putting your stuff up on a wall," he says, standing back and surveying the collection of drawings and paintings. "Once you do that, you see, it stops being entirely your property. Oh, I know you painted them and all that, and they're yours for as long as you don't let anyone else see them. But the moment you go public, everyone has their own idea of what you meant and what the pictures mean, and everyone's filtering what they see through their own ideas and experiences. Who's to say you're right and they're wrong, eh?"

"Well—I did do them," I say.

"Sure. But you're giving them away when you let other people see them. You have to."

"I never thought of it like that," I say.

The Art department around us is dark, only this little gallery lit. The whole wall in front of us is my work, the papers and canvases spread out linearly, labelled neatly. Two other walls have other boys' work on them, but they are both sixth-formers, and I am just a fourth-former. This is my first proper display of work—almost an exhibition,

I tell myself—set up here in readiness for the school's annual open day. Tomorrow, there will be parents and old boys of the school, with their school ties and tweed jackets with leather patches at the elbows. I have seen this all happen before, last year, but this is the first time I have been properly—involved. People will be in this room tomorrow, with glasses of white wine supplied by the department, and canapés, nodding and talking and looking out for the work of boys they know—sons or nephews or grandsons. And my work is up here on the wall—a great spread of it.

The pictures are dark: night scenes, and scenes by candlelight, with heavy shadows and deep wells of darkness behind the figures that inhabit them. It is difficult to see who the figures are; often they are indistinct, lost in the shadows that flood in from the corners of the pictures. But sometimes you catch a clearer glimpse. Mr. Dalton turns to one where a girl's face is just visible, lit with strange, dull, bold colours: red and blue and gold.

After a moment, he says, "Well. It's late. Enough art for one day. Have we finished here?"

I look around. Everything is labelled, properly mounted, properly hung. "I think so," I say.

"We'd better lock up, then. Tomorrow's going to be a big day."

"I suppose."

It's late when I get back to the house. All around, people are tired but excited. I am not the only person preparing for tomorrow; there will be cricket matches, and displays of shooting and fencing and karate, and rowing and sculling on the river, and concerts by the School Orchestra and the Chamber Orchestra and the Jazz Band.

Jamie will be playing. Perhaps I'll see him, and be able to wish him luck; but probably I won't.

The valley below us is asleep; I can see moonlight on the water far down in the bay. It is very quiet in the belltower. Above us, in the rafters, there come the occasional soft sounds of the roosting birds there.

Jamie says, "What time is it?"

Anna looks at her watch. "Half-past one."

"I'm tired," I say.

Anna drags the case out from the wall and sits down on it. Jamie leans against one of the stone sills. He says, "What about tomorrow?"

"We'll do it in shifts. And we're going to need more stuff. The book says you have to change bandages, doesn't it?"

"Yeah."

"So we'll need bandage stuff. And more water, cos we've used it all up."

"I'm worried that he's so hot," Jamie says.

"Me too."

"Is there anything we can do about that?"

I say, "Lena puts a wet flannel on my head when I'm ill, sometimes."

"We could do that," Jamie says. Anna nods.

"Yeah. That's good. Maybe we can find other things, too." She thinks for a while longer. "We ought to get stuff to make him a bed. You know, blankets and so on. It's not good where he is at the moment."

"Yeah." Jamie turns and glances out the window, down the valley. "We need to have a system," he says quietly.

"What kind of system?" Anna says.

"I don't think we can stay here all the time," he says. I can tell from his voice that he's thinking aloud. "They'd notice. We'll have to be there in the morning, and at lunch, and at dinner and bedtime. Maybe we can pretend to be one place or the other sometimes, but it won't work every day."

"Mm," Anna says. "Yeah."

"So we'll have to have a system. If one of us is here, the other two can cover. Sometimes we can all come up—like in the afternoons. Nobody cares what we do then." His tone is more animated as he gets to grips with the problem. "The real thing is nights. We'll have to go to bed, and then get out later when they're asleep . . ."

For a moment I find myself caught up in the idea of adventure and midnight meetings, but then I remember that it will mean walking through the valley at night, and being alone in the chapel with the hermit. Suddenly I am scared by the idea.

"We should come together," I say. Anna shakes her head.

"No. It's too much work like that. It's better if it's one of us at a time."

Jamie says, "What if something goes wrong? Supposing we need help, and there's only one of us here?"

Anna frowns. "I don't know."

We both turn to Jamie. There is a long silence, and then he says, "There's a way. Here's how we'll do it."

Anna and I listen attentively while he explains the system to us. At the end he says, "What do you think?"

"We're not going to be getting much sleep," Anna says.

"No. But there isn't any other way, I don't think."

"Right," she says. "You've both got alarm clocks?"

"Yes," I say. Jamie nods.

"Then it should work."

"And we should synchronize our watches," Jamie says.

"What's that?" I say.

"Make sure they all have the same time."

We fiddle with our watches until they're all the same. Jamie hands Anna the torch. "Green for OK, red for danger," he says.

"I know."

"What about tonight?" I say. "Who stays tonight?"

"I'll stay," Anna says. "I don't feel tired yet."

"Are you sure?"

"Yeah. You two go home. I'll see you for breakfast."

"All right," Jamie says. Anna gets up and pushes the case back against the wall.

"You brought comics?" she says.

"Yeah."

"At least I'll have something to do."

We file across the organ-loft and down the stairs. The hermit hasn't moved. The candles in the part of the circle nearest the chapel door flutter in a draught; they've burnt lower than the others. Mentally I note that we'll have to be careful to conserve our candles.

Outside, the valley is dark. There is a sprinkling of lights down towards the bay, and the stars above are hard and bright, but the land itself, and the rising hills around us, are black. There is the soft crunch and light springiness of gravel and pine needles under our feet as we walk to the end of the chapel. Anna has the torch, but it is switched off. Everything is still; not even the bats that you see in the late evening are out now.

"What time should I start back?" Anna asks.

Jamie says, "Six o'clock to be sure."

"OK."

"And remember, every hour, OK? Start at—" He thinks for a second. "Start at four. We've got to get home."

"I will," Anna says.

We are at the end of the chapel, under the belltower. Above us, on the wall, is the dandelion clock, its shape only just visible. In daylight, it is dark against the whitewashed wall, but now everything has been leached of its contrast and identity. I catch glimpses of the clock out of the corner of my eye, but when I look straight at it, it somehow vanishes.

"You sure you'll be OK?" Jamie says, his voice low.

"Of course I will be," Anna says. I am expecting her to say, Don't be so silly, but to my surprise she says, "Thanks."

Jamie says, "We'd better go."

"Wait," Anna says.

"What?"

She steps a little closer to us. "We ought to swear," she says. "Promise not to tell."

"Of course," Jamie says.

"No. I mean—*really* promise. Not to tell anyone. Ever. No matter what."

Jamie says, slowly, "But supposing he gets worse, and we—"

"No," Anna says. "He's not going to get worse. He's going to get better. We have to swear."

"But Anna—he might—"

"*No,*" she says. She grabs Jamie's wrist, and he looks down in surprise at her hand there. I can see her fingers, tight, digging into him. "You have to promise."

"Why?" Jamie says. "You know we wouldn't tell."

"Because sometimes you have to promise," she says earnestly. "It's only us three that know. It has to stay like that. We have to keep the secret."

Jamie stares at her for a moment, and then tries to shrug her hand off. He can't. Anna holds onto him, her eyes bright and fierce again.

"Let go," Jamie says.

"You have to swear."

Jamie looks at me helplessly. I can tell that he doesn't know what to do. If it were another boy, I think to myself, Jamie might punch him—like that time in the playground when I was in Salerno. But Jamie doesn't hit girls. Besides, looking at Anna's face, it seems suddenly obvious to me that if he did, she would hit him back; and then where would we be?

Anna says, "You have to." Her voice is very quiet, but I think I can hear it tremble slightly.

I say, "I swear."

Jamie glances at me in surprise. Then he blinks, and looks back at Anna. After a long moment he says, "OK. I swear too."

"Swear never to tell anyone about the hermit, for as long as you live. Swear to keep it a secret. Only us, all right?"

"I swear," Jamie says.

I echo, "I swear."

Anna says, "I swear."

Silence steals over us. Anna seems to notice that she's holding Jamie's wrist still, and she lets it go suddenly. I can see the white marks of her fingers on his skin. Jamie makes a little movement as if he's going to rub the wrist, but then changes his mind, pretends to scratch his leg instead.

Anna says, "Well. OK, then."

"Yeah," Jamie says. "We'd better get going."

"See you tomorrow," Anna says.

"It's today," Jamie grins.

"Oh. Yeah, I suppose."

"Well. See you."

She nods, and taps the torch on her leg for a moment, and then she grins, too. "See you," she says, and turns and walks back round the corner of the chapel.

The department is crowded out with people. Upstairs, in the area where we usually work, there are displays of ceramics and print-making and sculpture. Downstairs there are drawings and paintings. And off in the little exhibition gallery are the three showcase walls, one of them mine.

I am dressed in the dark suit which is the proper thing to wear on days like this, though with the sunshine and all the people, the art building is baking in heat. I feel hot and uncomfortable, but also proud.

My name is on the wall—*Alex Carlisle*—on a separate piece of card. I want to drift casually past the people looking at my pictures and hear what they're saying, but I'm too nervous, too shy. I am terrified someone will recognize me and say something—anything. I am terrified they will be complimentary and tell me how good I am. I am terrified they will be critical. I end up skulking at a distance, stealing glances through the length of the gallery every so often.

A lot of people are looking at my stuff; more than are gathered in front of the other walls.

Mr. Dalton appears and hands me a glass of wine. "You're allowed one," he says. "And get something to eat while there's still anything left. The hordes are truly ravenous."

"I will," I say. "Thanks."

"You seem to have drawn quite a crowd in there," he says. "I'm going to go and eavesdrop. See you in a bit."

He walks casually away, stopping to chat to parents, laughing, smiling, pointing out work by boys they know. I fade further back into my corner of the room.

Suddenly I see Jamie among the people. He is walking quickly, head down, away from the display of my work. He heads out of the gallery area, and I see him near the foot of the stairs, looking around sharply. He looks almost angry; I wonder what has happened.

I hurry through the press of people into the lobby and see him by the door to the lavatories. He is scanning the crowd edgily. I make my way towards him, and at last he sees me. His expression is furious.

"What is it?" I say. "Is something wrong?"

"Not here," he says. He ducks quickly inside the door to the loos and, bemused, I follow him.

There are three cubicles and two hand basins. The cubicle doors are all open; there's no-one here.

"What is it?" I say again.

He is pacing back and forth, his movements incredibly tense, as if he might shatter. He pushes a hand through his hair. His eyes are darting around the room, unable to stay still on anything.

"Jamie," I say. I am casting about to try and imagine what might have done this to him—a fight of some sort? Getting into trouble? I have never seen him this angry.

I don't know what to do. I put my hand out to touch his arm, to try and calm him, and he slaps it away violently. I am completely unprepared. I stagger back. The wine glass I'm holding in my other hand jars against the wall and shatters. The hand with which I've reached out stings sharply with the force of the blow.

"Fucking hell, Alex," he says, not shouting, keeping his voice tightly under control, but still so angry. "What is that in there?"

I don't understand him. "What?" I say.

"That—that fucking wall of stuff," he says. He's pacing again now, back and forth, back and forth. "What's the matter with you—are you retarded or something?"

"I—"

"You *drew* all that?"

"I—yes—"

"And then you put it all up on a wall so everyone can see it?" He sounds incredulous. "What the fuck were you thinking?" He rubs both hands across his face.

"Jamie, I don't understand."

He stops walking and suddenly he is standing right in front of me. His fists are clenched. He says, "My parents are here today. Yours too, I imagine. They can go in there and they can see all that shit you've drawn. Christ, Alex, what's with you? You don't just break the promise, you paint the whole thing on big fucking canvases and stick it on a fucking wall so everyone can see it. I mean, why not put it *all* up there? Not just the hermit and Anna—you could have everything else as well. You could have little fucking stickers saying, This is a boy I knew called Jamie and when I was twelve we went to the beach and he—"

The door opens and a younger boy comes in. I know him, vaguely; he's often in the department but I don't speak to him much. He stops dead, staring at us. Jamie is frozen for a moment, and then a kind of forced, artificial casualness comes over him. He takes a step away from me.

The boy says, "Carlisle—you've cut your hand."

I look down and he's right. There is a thin, curved cut, like a crescent, on the side of my finger. On the floor little spatters of blood twist in the spilt wine and among the scattered shards of glass.

"It's OK," I say. "I broke a glass."

"Yeah," Jamie mutters. "We should—you should wash it. Here." He reaches into his pocket and takes out a clean handkerchief.

"Thanks," I say. I rinse the cut under the tap and dab it dry with paper from the dispenser. I wrap Jamie's hanky round it. I am aware all the time that the younger boy is staring at us both.

Jamie says, "There's glass on the floor. We'd better clear that up." He glances at the boy. "There are other loos upstairs. Use those, OK?"

"Should I get someone?" the boy says. He looks like he knows it's not just a broken glass.

"No," I say. "It's nothing. Go on."

He hesitates, then turns and leaves.

"Shit," Jamie says quietly. He lets out a breath—a long breath. The tension is gone out of him now. "How's your hand?"

"Can't feel it, really. I hadn't noticed I'd done it."

He walks to the line of cubicles and then back again, slowly. His head is down and he's looking at his feet while he walks. He says, "What were you thinking?"

I finger the hanky round my hand gently. I say, "No-one will know anything. They're just pictures. I bet if you didn't know, you wouldn't recognize a thing."

"I recognize me."

"Well—only because you know it's you. Nobody else has said anything."

"Really? You're sure?"

"Yeah. Besides, so what if they do? Everyone knows we were— we knew each other in Italy. They'll just think you're in a few of them because—well, because I remember you from there. That makes sense, doesn't it?"

Reluctantly, he nods. He's still not looking at me. "I suppose."

"I didn't break the promise, Jamie."

"But why did you do them at all? Why couldn't you just—let it all alone?"

I shake my head. "I don't know. It's not like that." I struggle to find the right words to explain it to him. "It's not like I *choose* to do this, you know. It's just—what I paint."

"Everyone else paints still lives and all that crap."

"Yeah. Me, too. But this is different—this is what it's *for.*"

"Can't you just—stop? Do something else?"

"I don't think so. And nobody's going to know anything, are they? Like I said—if you weren't there, how would you know?"

"What about your parents?"

I manage a smile. "Well, they weren't there either, were they?"

He looks up at last. "I suppose not." His eyes meet mine, and I see the last of the anger drain away. His expression softens, and a smile tugs faintly at the corners of his mouth as well. He says, "Well. So maybe it isn't as bad as all that."

"It's not. Really."

He sticks his hands in his pockets. "Sorry I was so wound up."

"It's OK."

"Is your hand really all right?"

I glance at it. "Yeah. Stings a bit now, but it's clean."

"Wine's probably a good disinfectant."

"Yeah," I say.

"Especially the cheap shit they lay on for stuff like this. Probably plenty of antifreeze and stuff to—you know, kill the microbes and stuff."

"Yeah," I say. He tries the smile for real now, and I feel myself grin a little back at him. Then it fades, and he's just looking at me. Outside, I can hear people talking, and footsteps on the staircase, and the clink of glasses and an occasional voice raised in comment or laughter.

"What are you—I mean, how long does this thing last?" he says.

"Until twelve. When are you on?"

"This afternoon. Orchestra at two, Jazz Band at four-thirty."

"Good luck," I say.

"Thanks."

"I'll come and listen."

"Don't. Well, not the orchestral thing, anyway. Maybe the jazz."

"Yeah."

He scuffs one toe on the floor for a while, and then says, "They're really good, you know."

"I know. I heard some of the rehearsals last week."

"No," he says impatiently. "Your pictures. They're really good. The ones of Anna."

"Oh," I say.

"And that one with the ring of candles. I—when I saw it—" He breaks off, looks at the door, takes a breath. "I mean, it was the weirdest thing. Because I—" He stops again.

"What?" I say.

He's not looking at me, and his voice is low, strange. "I don't know. It's weird, Alex. Since we came here, you know, it's like I've started to forget stuff."

In my head, a voice from long ago sounds again.

That's another thing about growing up. What to remember and what to forget.

I say, "Like what?"

"Like—I don't know. Like what he looked like, exactly. What his face was like. I remember some stuff so clearly, but then parts of it all get—blurry. Like they might not really have happened. Like maybe I dreamed them. And then when I came in here, it was like there was a whole wall of it—all the stuff that I was forgetting, all the stuff that had just—slipped out of my mind, you know? And suddenly there he is—his face—only you've done it in that way like it's all broken up into pieces, yeah?" He steals a quick glance at the broken wine glass on the floor. "Well, it was like seeing him again—but different. Almost more real than what I have in my head, cos I don't remember so clearly." He laughs, almost. "But then you *would* remember it all, wouldn't you?"

Slowly, I shake my head. "It's not like that," I say, and my voice sounds in my ears like his—hesitant and low and unsure, as if feeling its way in darkness towards something. "Not any more."

"What do you mean?"

"I can't do that any more. The thing I used to. It's gone."

His face changes, and I see a kind of regret, and sympathy, in his eyes. "When?"

"When I came here," I say. It's almost the truth, after all, and perhaps it's kinder.

"Really? All of it?"

"Not all of it. I can still—see things, you know. If I really try. But I can't—go into them."

"I'm sorry," he says; then, "You didn't tell me."

"No. I would have, but you—"

He nods, and suddenly he is looking sad, terribly sad. "Yeah," he says. "I know."

We stand there, staring at the floor and sometimes at each other. The sounds keep on outside, the bustle of people, until there is a hush in the background murmur of noise, and then a spatter of applause. Jamie looks up.

I say, "They're doing speeches now, I think."

"Right. Lots of that going on."

"They're pretty boring," I say.

"Do you want to hang around?"

"Not really."

"All right. Let's go."

I sweep the broken glass under the nearest hand basin with the side of my foot. Outside, the parents are gathered listening to Mr. Dalton talk about what has been happening in Art this term. Probably he will be going to say something about me, and normally I'd want to stay to hear what it is—even if I keep at the back. But it's not important any more. As we slip out the side door, Jamie turns and looks at me, and for a moment there is the shadow of a smile on his face—a smile like the ones I remember.

The late morning sunshine is warm. We go together towards the music schools, and we talk as we go.

My driveway is swathed in shadows when I wave Jamie goodbye. I can see my bedroom window, open six inches, from the side of the house, and it is not too difficult to climb up the trellis at the end of the patio and find my way along the kitchen roof until I'm under it. Fleeting images come to me of lying out here on the still warm tiles and watching the Perseids, some long time ago.

My bed is fresh and cool. I strip my clothes off and get in, remembering at the last minute that I will have to make the bed myself the next morning. Jamie and I have worked it all out walking home—for once, there has been no need to run. The deception has to be carried all the way through; it will be an early start for me, to be up before anyone else, to get dressed again, to make my bed and to get out of the house. And when my parents get up, they will find—as will Jamie's—that their son's room is empty, his bed unslept in. Which is how it should be, because he has spent the night at his friend's house, and will only be back later in the morning.

Where Jamie and I will be during this time we don't know yet. Perhaps watching the lizards blink their slow, early morning eyes behind the wall, or perhaps deep in the lemon grove waiting for Anna.

Carefully, I set the alarm clock. It is a quarter to three. I remember to check it against my watch, make sure that it shows the right time.

My eyes close and my head nestles against the pillow, the hard shape of the alarm clock hardly softened through the feathers. Still, I am so tired. There has been so much—the hermit, and the journeys up and down the valley. My legs feel like over-cooked spaghetti. And Anna and Jamie, and the case in the belltower . . .

It takes me a long while to realize what the sound is: a thick, throbbing, angry sound. I blink, and frown, and then I remember. Reaching under the pillow I quickly shut the alarm clock off. It is such an effort to sit up, not to sink back into the warmth and comfort of sleep; but I mustn't let them down. We have to look out for each other, Anna says. I think to myself, as I struggle out of bed, how I will feel when it is my turn; when I am the one with the torch, staring at my own watch in the candlelight of the chapel, with only the hermit and the sleeping pigeons for company.

I go to the window and look out up the valley. It is difficult to see exactly where the chapel is, so I just fix my eyes in the right direction and gaze vaguely.

Minutes pass, and my eyelids feel very heavy. I wonder if Anna has forgotten. Or maybe she has fallen asleep. If she's asleep, there's no point in my waiting; I can go back to bed.

But we have promised each other things, and so I have to wait.

At last—six minutes past the hour, by my watch—it comes. A green light, high up the valley, winks out three times. There is a pause, and then another three. It's the signal. All my tiredness is gone, and I am full of the excitement of being part of this. I run quickly to the door, and flick my light switch on and off three times. I can't see from my room, of course, but in his house Jamie must be doing the same thing. I go back to the window, and sure enough, Anna's response comes a second or two later: three more green winks.

It's green: she's safe. I smile to myself, and gradually my limbs start to get heavy again, and my eyes start to want to close. I fumble with the alarm clock, reset it for five o'clock. Jamie is right; we're none of us going to get much sleep. But we have to look out for each other, too. That's the most important thing.

I make myself comfortable, and close my eyes. If I listen carefully, I can even hear the ticking of the clock through the pillow.

*   *   *

It is evening. The day has gone, and I have not even known what day it has been.

I find I hardly care.

There is too much to be done; too much to put right again. The whole house is filled with things that need attention, things broken or missing or damaged in some way. There may never be time to make them all right again. And there is a boy standing naked on a rock in the moonlight, and that has to be—finished, too.

I have to work harder. It is not a matter of whether or not there is time; these things have to be done. Time may have to move aside to let them through. I have to rebuild—I have to rebuild. Things have been lost and broken. I have to make them new again.

11

I break the tab from a new phonecard and dial, waiting while the line clicks and hums gently and the connections are made through exchanges, over landlines, maybe even off satellites, all the way to London.

Halfway through the sixth ring, he picks up.

"Yes?"

"Max, it's me."

There is a long silence at the other end of the line. Then he says, "Tell me you're at Gatwick right now."

"I'm sorry, Max," I say. "It's been—"

"What's going on, Alex?" he says. His voice sounds strange; not only far away, but also muted, as if he's walled in behind glass or something.

"There's so much to do here."

"No there isn't. You went to put a house on the market. It doesn't take more than a day or two."

"Well," I say, "I know it's been a little longer than that, but there have been—"

"It's been nearly three weeks," he interrupts. It's an insane thing to say; we both know I can't have been here more than—well, not more than a week, maybe ten days? Three weeks is absurd. That would mean the exhibition—

"Max—what's the date?" I say.

"For God's sake, Alex!" he shouts. The line distorts and his voice crackles against my ear. It makes me shiver as if I've been stung. "You've got four days. *Four days.* Now get on a plane and get back here." There's a slight pause, as if he's taking a breath; then he says, "What do you mean, what's the date? Don't you know what *day* it is?"

"You don't understand," I say, lamely. "I have so much to do—"

"I have no time for this," he says abruptly. "This is your exhibition, Alex, not mine. It's your reputation on the line here. I have better things to do than sponsor your fucking mid-life crisis, OK? Get yourself together, for God's sake. You need to work out what your priorities are in all this. Chances like this don't come round twice, you know. This is it. If you fuck this up, it's thirty years wasted. You understand that? When you get into London, call me. Now get to a fucking airport."

There's a click and the line is dead. I stare numbly at the display, still holding the receiver, not able to move or even think much. My finger hovers to call him back, to try and explain all this to him—how important it is. But I know I won't be able to make him understand. I can picture him in his office, his head in his hands, furious, frustrated, wanting answers. Wanting some kind of understanding that I know I can't give him.

Has it really been three weeks?

I try to remember the days, one at a time, but I can't. They shift and come apart and before long they are other days; days when I was seven or thirteen or twenty-two. Not these days. I have hardly been living these days, so perhaps Max is right; perhaps they've slid past faster than I have thought.

I keep trying to count them, the phone humming by my cheek, but they elude me, slide away faster than I can get a grip on them.

I feel regret that I am letting people down. If it was just me, it wouldn't matter, wouldn't even cross my mind. But there are other people—Max, Julia Connell, the people running the gallery—everyone else. I should be there; I know I should. I should go back.

Carefully I replace the receiver, remove the card. Well. It hurts me to think about it. I feel responsible for them all.

I need food. I have a sense that I may not have been eating as regularly as I should. In the kitchen this morning I have found a half a loaf of bread and some cheese, nothing more. And the bread is very hard, hardly edible unless I dampen it with water. I must try to remember to eat properly, and now that I am in town I will buy food. But materials first; like Max has said, priorities have to be decided upon.

I need wood glue, and varnish, and masking tape, for all the things that have to be mended. And I need paint: deep blue and black for the waves, and dusty brown to temper the black bulk of the cliffs, and white and cream and blue again for the figure of the boy who is standing over the water, tensed, waiting to dive.

The sunlight is very warm. The spring is ripening, starting to turn over into summer.

I can't leave it like this. It has to be done right.

We have crossed through town, past Toni's and the empty school playground, and are on a little track leading up the far side of the valley. It twists and turns through the cypresses. It is early—only just gone nine—but for us it feels already like half the day has passed. We have been up since six, hiding, maintaining the deception of where we have spent the night. My bed is neatly made; I have struggled over it for some time. I creep out of the house in the twilight of dawn, when the valley is still in the shadow of its own hills, and wait for Jamie. The two of us read comics in the lemon grove until we see Anna coming down the road. She looks tired, but her pace is steady.

We leave it long enough to seem credible, and then announce our return in both households, Jamie's first, following immediately with the news that we are going to spend the day at the beach. We get money for lunch and ice-creams and are out before anyone can quiz us closely on what we have done since yesterday.

When I go to find my mother to ask her for lunch money, she is talking with my father. The radio is on, the news. My mother is saying, "Thank God nothing like that ever happens here." I wonder what she's talking about—something on the radio, presumably—and I hesitate in the doorway. From the little portable set comes the newsreader's voice:

". . . though his condition remains critical. Police will be seeking to interview him once doctors pronounce him stable enough to undergo questioning. Meanwhile, it was announced early this morning that police will be widening their search—"

My mother reaches for the radio and turns the volume down. "What is it, dear?" she says.

"Can I have some money for lunch? We're going to the beach."

"All right," she says, after a second. "Ask Lena for it, will you?"

"OK," I say. A question comes into my head. "Thank God nothing like what ever happens here?"

My mother smiles. "Don't worry. It's just something a long way away, that's all."

"Oh. All right."

"Run along now. Have you had breakfast?"

"Had it at Jamie's," I reply promptly, pleased with myself for keeping our story straight.

"All right."

I go to the kitchen to see Lena, and she reaches down into the big jar where she keeps loose change and household money. "There you go," she says. "Now remember to buy some proper food at lunchtime, yes? Not just ice-creams. And don't go swimming for at least two hours after lunch."

"OK," I say. "Why not?"

"You know why not. It's bad for you."

"Why?"

"I don't know. But it is. Now go on."

"Bye!" I call to her as I run out the kitchen door.

Now, as we trudge up the dusty path higher into the foothills of the valley's side, Jamie says, "How is he?"

Anna says, "He's sleeping. He slept all the time I was there, mostly. Sometimes he sort of moved a bit in his sleep, but not much."

"How's the bandage?"

"It's OK," Anna says. "But we'll have to change it today."

The encyclopedia is very clear on this point: bandages—which it calls "dressings"—have to be changed regularly.

"We don't have any more," Jamie says.

"We'll have to buy some."

"How much money do we have?"

I dig in my pockets for what Lena has given me. Anna and Jamie are searching, too. We hand it all to Jamie and he counts it.

"It's not much," he says, doubtfully. "Maybe enough. But not for lunch, too."

Anna looks from Jamie to me. "We can go without," she says.

Immediately she says it, I start to feel hungry, and it's only nine. I can tell from Jamie's face that he's thinking the same thing.

"He might die," Anna says.

Jamie shakes his head. "All right," he says. "All right."

"And we need cotton wool. And water."

Jamie looks up the track ahead of us. "Hey," he says, and his voice is suddenly hushed. "Look there."

We stop, breathing a little hard from the climb. The path curves off to the left, but up ahead through the trees and bushes there is a glimpse of white: a wall.

"Come on," Anna says. She leads the way off the path, scrambling up through the loose earth and scree of the slope, clinging to bits of bushes to give herself a hand up. Jamie and I follow. The wall is further away than it first looks, and when we reach it, we're tired out from the climb.

"It's tall," Jamie says breathlessly.

Anna looks back and forth along the length of the wall. "It goes on for ever," she says.

"Yeah."

"Why does he need a wall, anyway?"

"I don't know. Maybe when there were vines and stuff people used to steal them."

"Here," she says. "Give me a hand up."

"You can't go over," Jamie says, shocked.

"I'm not. I just want to see."

"Well, be careful. If anyone sees you we're in big trouble."

Jamie crouches down and makes a stirrup with his hands for Anna, and a moment later he's lifted her by one foot. I see her grip the top of the wall and crane her neck over, staring around her. I say, "What do you see?"

"It's all just land," she says. "But I can see the house, too. It's a long way away. There's a car out front, and—and it's a really big house. That's all."

Jamie lets her down. "What now?" he says.

Anna shrugs. "Nothing. I just wanted to see, that's all."

Jamie says, slowly, "Now that we're here—I mean, he's probably up there inside."

"He never comes out," I point out. "So he's bound to be inside. Well, he hardly ever comes out."

"Now that we're here," Jamie repeats, ignoring me, "why don't we go and—you know. Tell him. Like the hermit said."

He's been looking at the ground while saying this, but now he looks up at Anna questioningly. I look at her too.

"No," she says.

"But why *not?*" Jamie says, sounding slightly desperate. "What's wrong with telling someone?"

Anna's eyes have a far-off look in them, as though she's hardly here at all. She says, "We can't tell anyone. He's ours. We found him. He's all we've—I mean, we're all he's got."

"He asked for Signor Ferucci," Jamie says. "Why did we—why did you lie?"

"We weren't the ones that lied," Anna says. She's staring at Jamie now, and her eyes are clear of the distance I've seen in them before. She's staring at him, hard. "*He* lied to *us*. Remember? About the car crash and everything. And what we found. He's still lying, I think."

"How did you know he was lying?"

The farawayness comes back. "I don't know," Anna says. "I just thought he was."

"Even if he did lie," Jamie says, "shouldn't we tell someone now?"

"No." Anna's voice is calm. Jamie's voice has had a slight tremble at its edge that I know means he's upset or angry. Anna says, "It's too late now. We have to look after him. Besides, you swore."

Before I can stop myself, I say, "Yeah, Jamie. We did swear."

Jamie flashes a look at me that is surprised—hurt. Then he says, "I know that. But—what if—"

Anna's voice is soothing. "It's OK. It's all going to be all right. He needs us. That's all. That's all we need to think about, OK?"

Jamie looks at her, hard, and then shrugs reluctantly.

"Come on," she says. "We'd better be getting back."

As we file down the hillside, away from the house where Signor Ferucci may be lurking behind the dark windows and high walls, I keep glancing back; and after a time I notice Jamie doing the same thing. Only Anna keeps her eyes firmly on the path ahead, down into the basin of the town. I know what Jamie's afraid of, even though I can't put a name to it myself: a kind of huge, ill-defined awareness of things going beyond our control, and of us letting them slip by. Anna doesn't seem afraid, though. She seems excited: as though the things that are scaring Jamie and me are lighting her up from inside. I watch her, and I don't understand her.

We've sworn. We'll tell no-one. That's all there is to it.

Anna says, out of nowhere, "I wonder how the hermit knows this Ferucci man, anyway?"

"Everyone grows up, Anna. Me too."

Somewhere in the darkness is a voice. I know I am sleeping—I can feel the heaviness of sleep all around me, and this is a dream, not a falling back into the past. But the voice is a voice from the past even so. It comes out of the darkness from a great distance, from so far away that to start with I can't hear what it is saying, only the cadences of the words. The rhythms of the language are strange to me, unfamiliar, as if something has become jumbled across the distance between where the speaker is and where I am. It might be a dream-voice, speaking nonsense; but I know it isn't.

There is something strange. The sound of the voice is muffled, closed in, as if shut away tight inside something heavy and musty. But it shouldn't be like that. I should be able to hear a slight echo. The voice should be bouncing off stone and plaster, through empty volumes of air, to reach me.

Someone has shut it away in something and it is trying to get out—

With a struggle and a gasp I am awake.

For a strange, disconcerting moment I am not sure where I am—where this place is—and then I know. This is Florence, a hotel room. It is somewhere in the small hours of the morning.

I dream so rarely that the process of dreaming always surprises me. I remember people I have spoken to who dream every night, remembering all the stories and images that go through their heads. I have read that dreams are the mind's way of sifting what it has encountered, making sense of it all. If so, my mind must have a different way of ordering itself. But sometimes there are dreams, like this one; impressions of things. Faint images. Certainly what I remember of the dream has that sense of surreal dislocation that seems to be the nature of dreams.

But I know that the impression is wrong. There is nothing surreal or distorted about the voice in the dark. It really was like that. The words really were alien, making no sense to me, feeling ill-fitting and uncomfortable in my ears. And it really was dark, too.

I wonder for a moment why I should be dreaming about this, now; and then I know the answer. I look across to Anna's bed. She isn't there.

She is sitting by the window. She's taken the chair from the writing desk in the corner, and has pulled the shutter open a little. Her arms rest on the sill, but she's looking at me; she must have heard me wake. I prop myself up on one elbow.

"What're you doing?"

I see her smile in the faint glow of the street lamps. "Nothing. I woke up and couldn't get back to sleep, that's all. What about you?"

"Just a dream," I say.

"Yeah? You were thrashing about. Was it a nightmare?"

"No," I say. "I stopped having that ages ago. Just—kind of weird."

"Oh," she says, and I can hear that she's smiling. "*That* kind of dream."

"What?"

"You know. A sex dream. Was it like that?"

"No," I say. "Just an ordinary weird dream." I can feel myself blushing.

"You can tell me, you know. You won't shock me. Was it kinky?"

"Anna, it wasn't a wet dream, for God's sake."

"Are you sure? You were kind of breathing heavily for a while." She's still smiling; I can hear the mischief in her voice.

"It wasn't like that," I say.

"Boring."

I think of something to change the subject. "How long have you been there?"

"About twenty minutes." She's wearing a long T-shirt that comes down to her knees. Her arms and legs look fragile in the almost-dark. I look at my watch.

"It's twenty-past four," I say.

"So?"

"Well—so you woke up at four o'clock."

"And?"

I wait for her to make the same connection I have, and, eventually, she does.

"Don't be daft, Alex. I don't wake up on the hour, every hour, you know."

"You used to," I say.

"Yes," she says, and turns to look out the window. "But that was a long time ago."

"Still . . ."

"No, Alex. I just woke up, that's all."

I lie there watching her for a while, but she doesn't say any more. At last I say, "You can talk about it, you know. We don't have to go on pretending that nothing happened."

"Is that what you think we're doing?" she says. Her voice is detached, distant; I can't see her face properly any more. The edge of the shutter cuts across it.

"Well—sometimes I think that—"

She interrupts. "I told you. We were kids. That's what it was. People change. There isn't anything to talk about."

"Not even Jamie?" I say, but she doesn't reply.

I stay awake, watching her, for a while, but she doesn't turn and she seems to have forgotten about me. Eventually I put my head back on the pillow and close my eyes. The air coming in at the open window is cool at last, after the day. I can picture Anna at the window, can imagine the view she can see: the little square, the line of mopeds at one side, the plane trees at the other, the little church she pointed out to me on our first day here. I can imagine the low clouds over the city, catching the light from the street lamps, bathing everything in a dull orange glow. When the cloud is right, you feel you could just reach up and touch the sky. You know how it would feel, too; like cold velvet.

The thought puts into my mind a memory of another sky, which I really could reach up and touch. The sky Anna made.

I am almost asleep when something she has said before comes back to me. *Some deaths are more important than others.* What did she mean by that? But before I can work it out, the words are gone, lost in the memory of her voice and the soft touch of the darkness.

The valley swelters in the heat, and I wish to myself that the lies we told were true: that we were heading for the beach, to dive and splash and have swimming races, rather than for the chapel, to tend to the hermit. Everything about the hermit worries me or scares me now; his leg, which may be dying; the lies he has told us; the secret of the gun, hidden in its case in the belltower. All these things press in on my mind, and as we walk I stare down at my feet and imagine the trouble we might be in if anyone were to find out.

Jamie opens the chapel door, and I see his expression change to a kind of panic.

"Shit," he says, and runs inside.

"What is it?" I say, hurrying after him, but a moment later I can see for myself.

The hermit is not where we left him, against his pew. He is halfway across the floor to the chapel door, and he is face down; his arms are spread wide and his wounded leg has dragged a long smear of blood on the floor. He isn't moving.

"Is he dead?" I say.

Anna crouches at the hermit's side. "I can feel him breathing," she says. Her voice sounds thin and frightened—I've never heard it like this before. "We need to turn him over."

Jamie and Anna take the hermit's shoulders and I take hold of the leg that isn't wounded. We turn him over. The hermit doesn't make a sound; his face is flushed and sweating. His mouth is open slightly. The dust from the floor has made his clothes grey, and it strikes me unnervingly that he looks like a ghost. His head lolls loosely as we drag him back to his place.

"He's dying, isn't he?" I say. Jamie glances at me, and I am expecting him to tell me to shut up, but he doesn't. Anna is watching the hermit closely, staring into his face. His eyes are closed. His breathing is quick and shallow.

"The bandage is all dirty," Jamie says, pointing. He's right. Where before there was a neat, white dressing, there is now an untidy tangle of bloodied cotton and dirt from the floor. The hermit has dragged the bandage half off himself.

"What was he trying to do?" Anna says to herself. She's already set to work, getting water and fresh bandage out of the bag we've brought. I watch in silence as she strips off her T-shirt and puts it to one side.

"OK," she says. "We'll have to do it again. Jamie, come here and hold him. Alex—"

"I know. The belt," I say.

"Yeah."

We know what to do now, and we work more efficiently. Anna swabs the wounds clean and flushes away the stale discharge from them with water. I keep the tourniquet tight while she works. She wraps the new bandage steadily and carefully, packing it with cotton wool. I can see her ribs move as she breathes, pale in the chapel's strange, coloured light. There is blood on her arms and hands, and in one long streak across her belly, before she is finished. The hermit doesn't move at all. Jamie cuts strips from the sheet Anna was going to use as a curtain, and she finishes the dressing with those, fastening them securely in place with the sticking plaster from the roll. She brushes her hair back with her forearm, and I notice she is sweating.

"There."

We look at the hermit, and at each other. I slacken my hold on the belt.

"He must have been trying to get outside," Jamie says.

"Why would he do that?"

"I don't know."

Anna says, slowly, "Maybe he was—you know. When people are ill and they don't think straight."

"Maybe," Jamie says.

"Do you think he'll die?" I say.

Jamie says, "No, Alex." Anna is silent. After a moment, we both look at her.

"I don't know," she says at last. "Maybe."

"*Maybe?*" Jamie says. "You said he would be OK! What do you mean, 'maybe'?"

Anna looks at him steadily. "We've done everything we can," she says. "We shouldn't have left him alone, that's all. From now on, we never leave him alone, OK? Never. Not till he's well again."

"What do you mean, 'maybe'?" Jamie says again.

Anna is silent for a time. Then she says, "We'll just have to see."

"What happens if he dies?" Jamie demands. There is anger and panic in his voice. "What happens to us then?"

"I don't think he'll die," I say, trying to sound confident.

"Christ, Anna! What if he dies and we haven't told anyone?"

"Better for him if he dies than if we go and blab about it," she says.

"What does that mean?"

"You know."

"I don't know," Jamie says hotly. "What?"

"You know he doesn't want anyone to know about him. He trusts us."

"Yeah," Jamie says, with disgust. "He trusts us. What about us trusting him, then? You know what—what must have happened to him."

"Maybe it was a mistake."

"What about . . . ?" Jamie nods his head upwards towards the bell-tower.

Anna says, "Look, we're not going to tell anyone, OK? We've got to look after him."

"Why?"

She leans closer to Jamie; her expression is fierce. "Because there isn't anyone else. We've got to look after him as well as we can."

I am beginning to realize that I don't understand parts of the conversation. "What happened to him?" I say. "What was maybe a mistake?"

Jamie and Anna stare at me for a moment. "His leg," Anna says.

"Of course it was a mistake," I say. "He wouldn't have cut it on purpose."

She shakes her head. "He didn't cut it, Alex," she says. "It's not a cut, is it? You saw what it looked like." She turns back to Jamie. "We have to stick together," she says. "We have to. We can't get scared now."

"And if he dies?"

"We'll think about that when it comes," Anna says. She sounds calmer now, more in control. "Maybe it won't come, though. He looks strong, don't you think? Maybe he just needs to sleep for a while."

I am picturing the wounds in the hermit's leg. Anna is right; they don't look like cuts, not really. They look different—more like—

Abruptly I can see that what I have thought of as two wounds might actually be *one* wound; that instead of something cutting the hermit's leg on the front and at the back, something might actually have been forced right through it, making a neat, small hole at the front and—somehow—a larger, ragged one at the back. I blink. I start to see what Anna has meant.

She and Jamie are still talking, but the tone of their voices has quietened. I know Jamie's fears will go away eventually. I know also that there is no question now of us telling anyone. There never has been any question of it; it has been decided right from the start that we shall look after the hermit. Anna has decided it. Right from—when? I think and think, but I can't remember at what point the decision is made without slipping away, and Jamie has told me not to do that around Anna. I tell myself that I must ask him about this: about whether I should still be careful, or whether Anna is now enough of a friend for her to know about the going places in my head business as well.

Anna is saying, "We need to make him some kind of bed, too. It isn't right keeping him like this. We can do that and then move him onto it."

Jamie nods. I nod too, joining in the decision even though I know it makes no difference. I feel again like things are shifting reluctantly in my head; the same way I have felt around Jamie when things he has said have opened up corners of my understanding. I am beginning to understand the hermit. There is a mystery here, but it is one that is starting to reveal itself to me.

What's strange is that at the same time the hermit is becoming more understandable, it feels as though Anna is becoming less so. I steal a look at her as she is examining the hermit's face, and what I see in her eyes makes no sense to me. Jamie is right to want reasons and explanations for what we are doing, but he doesn't yet know—as I do—that he's not going to get them. It is a strange thought, but it comes to me with a great weight of certainty. Anna's reasons are hidden away somewhere deep inside her, and it may be that we'll never know what they are. I think for a moment, with a kind of satisfaction, of her naked body tiny against the dark bulk of the cliff, and know that she will never make sense to me.

I wake late, and my eyes feel sticky and still tired. For some reason it feels a lot as if I haven't slept at all, and I wonder briefly whether the patterns of my sleep have been disturbed some way. I remember waking in the night, and seeing Anna by the window; that, at least, suggests that my normally deep sleep has become erratic.

Anna is gone, her bed empty and the chair where she leaves her clothes bare. I get up, stretch, and see that there is a sheet of paper on the writing desk: a note.

Gone to the dandelion clock. Got an idea to make a theatre so I've taken a sheet. Come and meet me.

It doesn't say that, of course. For some reason, memories of the dandelion clock—of that time—keep intruding. I recall a vague impression of a voice in the darkness, but muffled somehow; part of the dream that woke me. I pick up Anna's note and skim through it.

Letting you sleep cos you look like you need it. I've gone to check out the times for this lecture thing; I'll see you for lunch—how about 2 o'clock by Santa Croce? Same place as yesterday. PS. Do you know you snore?

I smile to myself and put the sheet of paper back. It's only a little after nine; she must have made an early start. I find myself wondering if she ever went to bed at all, after I saw her. Perhaps she stayed the rest of the night looking out into the sleeping city. She looked like she had something on her mind, and I wonder, as I pull my clothes on, what it might have been.

The lecture is part of her excuse to be here: something political. She has told me about it on the bus, briefly; the details are complicated and she glosses them quickly. Some political theorist will be giving a series of talks, and one of them may be relevant to her thesis. It means she can take time off to make the trip and still claim it as research. It means we can be together for a while, which is all that matters.

Her suitcases are still in the corner of the room, slung in a pile. It is strange how Anna can sometimes be so neat—almost fastidious—and then sometimes be so casual. Jamie would have stacked the cases properly, I know.

There are little stickers on the bag she took with her on the plane: travel stickers with the names of places on them. Some are old, very worn and faded; others are newer, the colours bold. Kenya. London. Rome. Paris. Florence—quite an old one, that; perhaps from the last time she was here, with Jamie and me; perhaps even bought the morning before she stumbles across me sketching in the shadow of the Campanile. Bonn. Prague. Budapest. Bucharest. The cities form a strange, poetic map in my mind's eye as I fumble with socks and shoelaces. I feel I could reach out and trace Anna's past through them: the past we have shared in some way (Rome, Florence, London) and the past that has formed this other Anna, the Anna that I begin to feel I don't really know at all. The scuffed edges of the stickers could be a pattern, I feel; like a join-the-dots, where the picture that emerges once the connections have all been made is a picture of Anna, a key to understanding her. I sit on the end of her bed and stare at them, try to imagine where she has been, what she has done and seen, the people she has spoken to. All of these things must have helped shape her—or at least, shape the Anna I don't know.

It's then that it happens.

It is like an impact. The city lurches away from me, seems to shift, and then lurches back in place again; but it is wrong. It has changed somehow. Something is different.

I stare around me at the room, but nothing is altered in the slightest. Outside, the sounds of traffic and people are the same. Everything is normal, except that in my head I know that the city has—moved, changed, somehow. I can still feel my head reeling with the sense of sudden movement.

I sit for a long time, wondering what has just happened to me.

When I finally leave the room and go out into the city proper, I keep looking about me, as if to catch a clue out of the corner of my eye. There is nothing. The river is bright and there are crowds on the bridges as I pass by. Florence is just as it has always been.

I sometimes think I have never understood anything in my life—never really learnt anything—until it is too late, and the knowledge is useless to me. Things have passed by, and by the time I have worked them out, they are gone. There is a kind of torture in seeing the past so clearly, so close to me, and not being able to change it, to step in knowing what I know now and do the right thing. Of course Florence didn't move; but Florence *did* move, all the same. The dream was right, too; the hermit was gone, long gone, but there was a shadow of him in some dark, enclosed space. The hermit was still there, and there were things I knew were wrong, and *I should have known*. There's no dodging that; I should have known. But I was distracted—by her beauty, and by the way that the sunshine in the old city made it feel like nothing could ever be wrong again. It was that simple.

High up in the valley I can see the headlights of a vehicle trailing across the hills, but otherwise everything is still. There are the lights of the boats out in the bay, and the town itself glowing sleepily in its low cradle of land. It looks peaceful and safe, like my mother always thought it was.

12

*T*he bright morning sunlight catches the colours of the pictures, brings them alive. The living room is filled with images—a lifetime's worth. Moving among them, I am caught in a flow of paintings, and the more I feel them around me, the more I know they are wrong.

To begin with I think it is the arrangement. I try to group them on the walls in ways that will make more sense of them. The linear chronology of the gallery is all wrong: I'm convinced of that now. So I try other ways to hang them. I put them in clusters, clumped together by theme or colour or the predominant tone of the composition. Each time they are as wrong as they were before. There is something about the eyes of the figures, too: the eyes that look back at me from the subjects. It has always been people, for me, never objects or empty scenes: there are always people in the paintings. Studies sketched out in retirement homes and shopping arcades and offices and bus-stops all come together here. It is a sea of faces, and the more I look at them, the more there is something about the way their eyes look back at me that stirs unease—even panic—in me.

I am beginning to feel that I don't know these paintings—don't know these people. Wherever I look, I can feel it: these are not my pictures. I don't understand it. I can remember painting each one, can remember the thought processes and the physical application of media that have gone into their construction, the effort and struggle to get them right, the abandoned attempts that went before, the bundles of working sketches used to rough them out. They can't belong to anyone else; and yet still I keep feeling that they're not mine.

I tear them all down and lay them out again, and again. Each time the pattern alters, I think that this time they will reveal themselves to me—that they'll make sense and, with a deep breath of relief, I'll see that they *are* my own work, that I have done these things, that they haven't—escaped from me, somehow.

Each time, when they're back on the walls, it's the same. I can still see that they are the paintings I have made, over the years; but they are alien to me. It's as if I've been blind all along to what I've really been doing. Like the way the house is getting fixed around me while I am stumbling in memories, these pictures now look to me as though someone else has made them through me; as if thirty years of work has all been a sham.

In their centre, breaking the sequence, the plaster of the wall is covered with streaks and clots of paint, lines and blocks of dark, night-time colour, defining shapes. A rock. A boy, standing, about to dive.

Max's words echo faintly in my head. A mid-life crisis—is that all this really is?

I tear them down, put them back. And they're still not mine.

The signal is there: the quick green blinks of light. I go to the wall switch and click my room light in reply; and then, picking up my shoes and treading slowly and quietly, I make my way to the door and out into the corridor.

This will be my first night with the hermit. As I round the corner of the gate and start up the road towards the farm track, I can feel my stomach turning uneasily. All day, ever since we decided on the rota, I have been wondering if there is any way I can escape being with the hermit in the chapel at night. In the day, I tell myself, it wouldn't be so bad; but in the awful darkness anything might happen. The chapel alone would be bad enough; but the chapel with the hermit in it is worse.

The empty riverbed at night has a peculiar, alien feel to it. The moonlight and starlight have robbed the land of colour, and the dark green shrubs and pale brown grasses and red dust underfoot are all reduced to different shades of grey. The dust is eerily light, like sand. In one of Jamie's books on stars there are drawings of the surface of the moon: the flat expanses of dust rising to distant low mountain peaks. The dust could be moon dust; the little spurts and puffs of it that rise from underfoot drift lazily in the still night air, as if in low gravity.

With a start, I remember something: that the great dust-plains on the moon are called *seas*. The Sea of Tranquillity. The Sea of Serenity, The Seas of Nectar and Showers and Crises and Fertility. Jamie's charts have them all marked out, the old Latin names first and then the English ones underneath. The Ocean of Storms and the Bay of Rainbows and the great crater, Copernicus. The names are a litany, like a poem. Dry seas; and I am here, walking on a dry river.

It's weird. I feel myself tugged by the understanding of what it might feel like on the moon, and for one heady second, it is almost as if I might suddenly be tugged all the way there—that I might finally realize Jamie's ambition of transporting myself to wherever I want, just by thinking it.

Somewhere out in the valley, an owl calls, and the moment vanishes as silently as a bubble. My feet continue to kick up puffs of dust, but now they are just the normal dust of the valley, turned an unfamiliar shade by the faint light of the night sky. My body, which has for an instant felt light as a feather, is its usual weight again.

I walk quickly, but it is still nearly one when I first catch sight of the chapel ahead. The pale walls of the building are just visible between the dark shadows of the trees that cluster round it. I climb the riverbank, feel my way to the railings, and clamber over them. Up above me, I catch a glimpse of a green light flickering on and off; Jamie is making the one o'clock signal to Anna. There are the piles of masonry and wood, and the stone pines, and the end of the building. I round its corner under the ever constant gaze of the blank clockface, and go to the side door.

Inside, a single candle is burning at the back of the building. The hermit is out of sight; we have moved him, after replacing his ruined dressing, to the space under the little organ gantry, where the chapel feels more enclosed and homely. Anna has made him a bed there with the blankets we've taken; the jumble of old pews blocks off that corner of the building and makes it more secluded.

Jamie is sitting on the bottom step of the stairs that lead up to the balcony and the belltower. He must just have come down. The candle is on the end of one of the pews near him, and by its steady yellow light I can see he has been reading. He looks up as I approach, startled for a moment, then recognizing me with relief.

"You were quiet," he says.

"How is he?"

"He's sleeping still. That's all he seems to do, sleep."

"Maybe he needs it."

We make our way out softly into the night. Jamie gives me the torch so I can find my way around the chapel. It is set to white at the moment; when I make my signal, I will need to change it to green with the special ring in the handle. We stand under the wall of the chapel and scrape our feet in the dirt and talk about nothing. We have both been seized with a reluctance to let go. The loneliness and isolation of the chapel at night fill me with uncertainty and foreboding, and these feelings seem to have seeped into Jamie as well, so that he finds it difficult to leave me here alone. We check the torch over again.

"He just mostly sleeps. Sometimes he makes some noises, but not much."

"Yeah."

I play with the torch. Jamie stares round at the sleeping valley.

"I s'pose I should go."

"Mm."

"I'll watch for your signal," he says, a little uncomfortably.

"Yeah," I say. Then, finally finding the courage to give him permission, I add, "You'd better go." He nods, and smiles quickly. I watch from the doorway as he walks away down the length of the building, the night breezes stirring the bushes nearby.

As he reaches the corner, though, I call softly after him. "Jamie!"

He stops and turns. I run to catch him up. "What?" he says.

"When you're walking back," I say, "look at the dust in the river. It looks like moon dust."

His eyebrows go up, and he smiles, pleased. "OK."

"I noticed it on the way up."

"I will," he says.

We hesitate as if caught at the corner of the building, being pulled in different directions. At last I say again, "You should go."

"Yeah. All right. See you later, then."

I nod. Jamie walks quickly below the trees to the fence, turns, gives me a wave, and then is over the palings and into the long grass and scrub beyond. I see the bushes waver where he moves through them, and then he is out of sight down the curve of the riverbank. I wait a while longer, in case he comes back into view, but he doesn't; and after a minute or two more, I trudge slowly to the chapel door. Now that Jamie is gone I am entirely alone; well, except for the hermit, and that presence is little comfort.

I close the door on the night valley and on Jamie. I am in the chapel now, where the hermit is, and it will be four hours before I can signal to Anna that I am ready to leave. I stay at the altar end of the building, pretending to look at the niches that once held statues and at the boarded-over windows, while back by the steps the candle twinkles away and the hermit, hidden in the shadows, gets on with the business of living or dying.

"Did you find out about the lecture?" I say.

Anna nods, spooning up *ribollita* hungrily. "Mm. There's a whole series of them over the next ten days. I'll catch the one on Friday, I think."

"Who is he?"

"Just this guy. One of my tutors is really keen on his ideas. He's controversial, though; far-right stuff tarted up to sound good."

"Oh. Not your thing, then?"

She shrugs. "Well, you have to listen, don't you? Freedom of speech and all that."

"You don't *have* to listen," I say. "You could not go."

"Yeah, well, it could be useful to see what he has to say on some things—eugenics and genetic manipulation, mainly. It's all relevant." She laughs suddenly; she seems excitable, vibrant this morning. "Believe me, Alex, after a while *everything's* relevant. You can't see someone pissing in the street without thinking of a footnote."

I raise my eyebrows. "You must have weird footnotes."

"I do," she grins. "Here, try some of this. I love it."

"Bread soup?"

"It's fantastic. God, I'm hungry."

"You sound like you've had too much coffee," I say.

"Haven't touched a drop all morning. Sorry. Am I being hyper?"

"A little," I say. "It's OK, though. I like it."

She scrapes the bowl empty and pushes it to one side. "You said something last night. I asked if you'd had a nightmare, and you said no, it had stopped years ago, something like that."

"Oh," I say.

"So? What was it? I didn't know you used to have nightmares."

"Not nightmares," I say, vaguely. "Not really dreams. Just—a thought, I suppose."

"Just one thought?"

"Well—yes, I suppose so."

She's looking at me curiously. "Tell me."

I blink. "I don't have it any more."

"I know. You said. Tell me."

"Why?"

"I want to know. Go on."

I say, "Well. It's difficult to explain, really. I—I used to think sometimes that perhaps everything that was happening to me—my whole life—was just a memory. As if one moment I could be eleven, and playing in the sun, and the next I might—*wake up*, somehow, and find I was old and—and dying, and that the day when I was eleven was just a bright, clear memory. I used to be afraid it could happen at any moment, that everything could be snatched away." I look at her, to see what she's making of this. She looks horrified.

"Jesus. That's grim. Grim and weird. Why would you think that?"

Of course, she can't understand. I've never told her what I told Jamie—about how my mind used to work back then.

Jamie. I say, "At his—at the funeral, there was a part of the service. 'In the midst of life we are in death.' I remember thinking that it could have been meant for that eleven-year-old me. That was my fear, back then."

"You said it stopped?"

"Yeah. When—when I was twelve. It just—stopped happening." In the avalanche; swept away by the same roar of change that blocked up the door in my head. But I can't explain all that to her now. Maybe one day.

"Well," Anna says, uncertainly. "It's still the scariest thing I've heard in a long time."

"I know," I say. "That's how it felt to me, too."

"Tell you what," she says suddenly.

"What?"

"We should go out tonight. Somewhere loud and modern and shiny. Lots of chrome and music and lights. Lots of young people. Get you out of all this moping around in the past."

"Um—all right."

"Don't look like that. You'd like it. I saw this little place in the university quarter that looks perfect. You'd like it," she says again. "Really."

"What kind of little place?"

"It's a jazz club," she says. "They do all sorts of stuff. I can't remember what's on tonight. What do you say? Do you want to?"

I smile; it's impossible not to smile when she's like this. Her eyes are bright and alive and fixed on me, pretending to plead, knowing she's already got her way. "Sure. Why not?"

"*Ottimo.* Cool." She grins and pours herself more wine from the carafe. A slight chill has come over me, though; the way she's just spoken has sounded too much like—I can't be sure. Another time, maybe, or something someone else once said. I shake my head, and the feeling is gone.

"I hope they hurry up with the veal," she is saying. "I'm starving."

"Have some more bread," I say, and watch, amused, as she tears it apart and wolfs it down. I wonder what it is that's got her so worked up.

The place at the bottom of the stairs where Jamie has sat is comfortable enough, but I can't read. The hermit, though silent and motionless, fixes me to the spot as rigidly as if he were awake and staring right at me. I sit with the candle by me for what feels like an hour at least, and at the end of the time I casually check my watch to see if I'm right. But only a few minutes have gone by. I stare at the watch face, holding it closer to the flame to see it clearly, and the second-hand is still ticking round regularly; the watch hasn't stopped. But the minute-hand is hardly moving at all; no matter how closely I peer at it, its gradual, insectile creep doesn't alter. And it has to go all the way round the numbers before the first hour is up; and that is only the first hour of four. I know, deep in my stomach, that I am not going to be able to do this.

Then the hermit moves. His head turns, though his eyes are still shut, and one of his hands flutters for a moment, weakly, before dropping to the floor. His face, catching the light a little now, is shiny with sweat.

I am frozen to the spot: even my breath has stopped. But nothing more happens. The hermit stays as he is, head over to one side, sleeping again. Slowly, very slowly, I let myself relax.

Time passes.

I am on the road into town and it is noon when I see the snake. It is to one side of the road, not in the middle, and the wheel of a car has gone over it and mashed its body into the asphalt. It looks dead, but even dead snakes can be dangerous, I know.

I get a stick from beside the road and, crouching down, prod cautiously at the snake's head. The place where it has been flattened and split is further back, and there is a good foot or more where it looks undamaged. It is a big snake, dark in the sun, and it seems to be baked onto the surface of the road.

When my stick touches it, the snake moves. I give a twitch and almost drop the stick, but then I see that the snake can't harm me. The way it moves isn't like a snake any more: not oiled and fluid like a snake in the scrub grass, but just a slight contraction and pulling away. Its mouth comes open a small way and I think I see its teeth folding out, but then the mouth falls closed.

With a kind of horrified curiosity, I push the stick close to its head again. The snake's eyes, dusty with the dust from the road and unblinking—not a lizard's eyes, and I certainly can't stare for that long—see the stick and it makes again its spasming, sluggish movement. The mouth comes open and seems to fumble for the end of the stick, but I pull it away out of reach. I don't want the snake to get hold of my stick and pull it from me; and I don't want it to bite the stick, and for me to pull at it and for the snake to come away with the stick. The place where it has been burst open and welded by the heat of the sun and the asphalt into part of the road looks like it might tear away and leave me with a part of the snake—the living part, even if only sluggishly alive—suddenly free.

Once the stick is away from it, the snake stays still for a while. Then a strange little tremor kicks through the length of its body, once, twice; there is a tiny, flat sound as its head knocks against the road. I wait, my mouth open, for a long time. Then I push the stick in close again, but the snake doesn't move any more.

I get bolder, and push its head round a small way with the stick's end, and feel the slow heaviness of the snake's body transmit itself up the stick to my hand. But the snake doesn't move at all any more.

After a while, I stand up, looking down at the dead snake. I throw my stick far away into the bushes by the roadside; I don't know why, but it feels somehow like the stick might now be contaminated in some way, might be able to hurt me or infect me or something. I shiver, even though the sun is very hot, and rub my hands on the sides of my shorts.

I take a step or two back, and cross the road to the other side, and only then—at a good distance—pass by the snake. When I have gone some way, I turn and look back. It is still visible, a dark line on the reddish road, and the heat-haze trembling there makes its body seem to waver and float a little. But I know it is still dead. I hug my arms round my body and walk on into town.

There is the sound of a voice in the darkness, and I strain to catch the words—but they aren't real—

The hermit is talking. His voice is low and hoarse and the words make no sense to me; just sounds. His voice doesn't sound like it did when he was talking to us all, when he was properly awake; it sounds different, frightening. Instinctively I try to move away from him, but in getting to the next stair my foot slips and scrapes and makes a noise. The hermit is suddenly quiet, and I look up. The eyes are open in the glistening, flushed face, and staring about, looking for something.

It takes him a long time to see me, though I get the feeling that this is not because I'm hidden, but because his eyes are not working properly. Then he focuses, picking me out of the other shapes around him.

He starts to say something, and then stops; clears his throat; shifts slightly. He uses one hand to prop himself up against the folded blanket and pieces of timber that we have used to make him a crude pillow.

He says, "Alex?"

His voice is still low and different—rusty-sounding—but not the voice of a demon or a monster from a comic book. In Jamie's comics the monsters' words are sometimes written in a different way—dripping with slime, or shaky. In my head I imagine how they would sound, and Jamie and I try them out on each other. But the hermit's voice is not like that. It is the same voice: roughened and dry-sounding and weak, but the same. I find, to my surprise, that I am suddenly not afraid any more.

"Alex?" he says again. "Is that you?"

"Yes," I say, and I get down from the step and come out into the chapel towards him. "Are you OK? Are you better now?"

He doesn't seem to be listening properly. He says, "Water. Please."

"Oh," I say, understanding. The water bottle is where Jamie has shown me; I pick it up and go over to the hermit. It isn't as difficult getting close to him as I have thought it will be. "Here," I say.

I have to support the bottle as he drinks, because although he brings his hand up to it, he doesn't seem able to grip the plastic right. He takes a few swallows of the water and some of it spills down his face and onto his shirt. His eyes close briefly and I take the bottle away.

"That's good," he says.

"How's your leg?" I ask.

His face twists a little. "Hurts," he says briefly.

Tentatively, I touch my hand to his arm. "You're really hot," I say.

He nods slightly. "Yes. I know. I feel it." Speaking seems to exhaust him; he closes his eyes again for a long minute. When he opens them again, he says something I don't understand: the sounds are strange, unfamiliar, and though I struggle, I can't make sense of them.

"What?" I say.

He blinks, and his eyes pull round to me with difficulty. "What is this place?" he says.

"It's the chapel," I say. "You remember. You came here after you hurt your leg."

He frowns. His breath comes in short, tight gasps. He says, "You mustn't tell anyone."

"We won't," I say.

"You haven't told anyone, have you?"

"No. I promise. Anna said not to."

He nods at this, as if satisfied, and his eyes start to close. Then all at once they are wide open and he has gripped my wrist with his hand. His grip is fiercely strong, and I struggle and fall to one side, twisting my arm. He doesn't let go. "You haven't told anyone?" he says.

"No! Stop it—you're hurting."

Abruptly his grip slackens and I wrench my arm free, stumbling backwards against the big locked double-doors of the chapel. The sound of me slamming into them booms around the chapel and I lose my footing, falling to the floor. My wrist aches where he has held me.

I scramble to my feet and run wildly across the room, echoes of my footsteps clattering off the stone walls. Out in the main body of the building, I turn, waiting, but everything at the far end is silent. I wait a while longer, and then I creep back, watching all the time in case the hermit is only pretending, and actually hiding there ready to grab me again. But when he comes into view round the end of the pews, I can see that he has his eyes shut once more, and that his breathing has subsided into a faint murmur. The hand that held me is lying out to one side of his body, and he has slumped a little sideways against his makeshift pillow. I stand watching him for a long time, ready to bolt, but he doesn't move. My heart slows from its pounding in my chest.

In the end I sit down in my place on the stair, as before. The bottle of water has been kicked over in my struggle with the hermit, and I can see the trailing line of it from the bottle's mouth across the dusty floor to the doors, and out under them. If the hermit wakes and wants more water, there won't be any; but it is his own fault, not mine. We will have to bring some more later.

I sit, with the candle at my elbow and the comics in a low stack by my foot, watching the hermit, waiting for the hour to go by.

The night breezes sift gently through the open apertures of the bell-tower. I sight precisely down the valley with the torch. It's already switched to green; I have done this long since. I aim at Jamie's house, though it is difficult to make it out accurately in the darkness. The torch has a clever switch, which you push back and forth to turn it on and off but can also press in, to flash the torch; so it is this that I do.

One. Two. Three. I wait a second, and then repeat the signal. One. Two. Three.

It is two minutes past the hour when I see it: Jamie's room light blinks on and off three times in response. I grin to myself, knowing that he's seen me, that he's been there by his window watching for me. Happily, I put the torch down on the floor, and start to drag the case back to from where I took it.

As I am doing this, though, it starts to come to me that there is now another hour before I can contact Jamie; another hour to be spent in the chapel with the hermit. I slow in my dragging of the case until I have stopped completely, halfway across the raised wooden platform of the tower. I don't want to go back downstairs just yet.

Above me, the pigeons shuffle and warble quietly in their sleep. I sit myself down on the floor and stare at the case.

The clasps are scuffed and one of them is shattered from where Anna hit them with the rock, but the other, we have found, works just well enough to hold the case closed, though it is no longer locked properly. You can get it open very easily, by prying at it with a thumbnail. I reach out and stroke the surface of the case, which to me still looks like an instrument case, like Jamie's.

Almost without deciding to, with my brain still thinking vaguely about instrument cases and not wanting to go back downstairs, I fiddle the catch open and lift up the lid of the case.

The gun is inside, just as we left it. It is big—a rifle, not a handgun—but it is broken into several pieces. Just as when I first saw it, it takes me a moment to assemble the thing in my mind, to make a whole shape out of it, though the clues that it is a gun—the trigger and handle part, and the barrel part—are all there. It's just that they are spaced apart from each other in an unfamiliar way, dislocated. And there are some parts that I am hard put to find a name for, and whose purpose I can only guess at.

Each of the parts of the gun has its own home in the grey rubber foam that lines the case; the compartments have been cut away neatly and each piece fits snugly in its gap. I reach out, hesitate, and then touch the wood of the handle. It is cool and smooth, the surfaces sculpted and planed with extreme precision. I know, looking at it, that in some ways it is a very beautiful thing; a piece of craftsmanship like a carving or an antique or something.

Behind the handle and trigger part is a big, solid-looking block of curved and smoothed wood. The rifles I know best come from television, and the Saturday cowboy films that Jamie and I sometimes watch together. This wooden part is the part, then, that goes against your shoulder when you lift the rifle to shoot. But it looks much bigger, and more solid, than the ones on the TV, and the back part of it seems to have been carved or moulded to fit smoothly against the curve of a man's shoulder. There is a small panel here with writing on it. I run my fingers over it gently, and then bend close and click the green light of the torch onto it for a moment to read the words.

MAUSER-WERKE OBERNDORF GmbH.

It means nothing to me. There is a number underneath the words, too. I click the torch off and set it down beside me.

The moon is quite low in the sky, and there is enough light through the four windows of the tower for me to see the rest of the pieces in the case clearly enough. There is a longish wooden part with a stubby barrel protruding from its end. There is another, separate barrel, too, set above it in the case, and for a long time I can't understand how these two barrels work together. Then I see the clean glint of light on one end of the second barrel, and touching it can feel the screw-thread there. So— this second barrel screws into the first somehow, to make it longer.

The guns on TV always have a little metal triangle at the end of the barrel, which the cowboy lines up with his target when shooting. But this gun doesn't have anything like that; just a smooth bulge at the end of the metal tube, punched through with regular slots on all sides. Strange.

There are a couple of other things in the case. In one corner there are a series of six small troughs. Three of them are empty, but the other three contain what I quickly realize are bullets: slender cylinders of two different coloured metals, one gold, one greyish-silver. Each is as long as a cigarette. I wonder briefly where the three that went in the other troughs have gone. I think also of the gunfights on TV, and think it rather brave and perhaps foolish of the hermit to carry only six bullets. In all the fights I've seen, you need a lot more than that.

Right at the top of the case, near the hinge, is a thick cylinder as long as my forearm and flaring out slightly at each end. It is the only part of the gun I can't readily identify, now that I've worked out how the barrel goes. It is dark metal, with a dull finish. I sit looking at it for a long time before touching it; and then, with great care and trepidation, I put my fingers under it and ease it gently from its bed.

It is much heavier than I would have thought. The solidity of it surprises me, but also feels satisfying, pleasant in my hands. It is cool to the touch, like all the parts of the gun I've actually felt. I lift it out from the case. It doesn't look like any part of the gun that might go off suddenly; I have been very careful not to touch the trigger or the bullets. In fact, it hardly looks like part of a gun at all. It reminds me of something, though; and as I turn it in my hands and catch the gleam of light on curved glass at its end, I suddenly realize what it is. It is a telescope, like Jamie's, only smaller and much heavier.

I examine the little telescope until I am satisfied that this is all it is; and then a great thought comes to me. With the hermit's telescope, and Jamie's, perhaps we can actually see each other along the whole length of the valley: perhaps, rather than click lights on and off, we can point our telescopes at each other and wave and hold up messages written on paper and read them, even over that distance. Eager to see whether my telescope is good enough to reach down the valley—though it is heavy, it is also small, and might not be as powerful as Jamie's—I go over to the window.

I prop my elbows on the ledge and set the telescope to my eye.

What I see makes me start, and the device almost slips from my hands. I clutch it quickly, and set it down on the ledge rather too fast. It clinks against the stone, but nothing breaks.

The few dim, distant lights of the town have sprung close to me, sharp and crisp in the centre of the telescope's eye. For the second or so I've held it, my hands must have wavered because the view shudders and twitches and drifts this way and that; but it isn't this which has made my heart race all of a sudden. It is the one thing in the view which hasn't trembled or shaken at all, but remained starkly constant. Three neat black lines: one from each side, one from the bottom, all nearly meeting in the centre, their ends defining a tiny open space where the lines almost touch, but don't.

I have never seen this on TV or in the comics—not quite this—but I know at once what it is. The comics even give me the words: *telescopic sight*. It's subtly different from comics and the TV in the way that I know real life often is subtly different. Comics and TV show things more clearly, in brighter colours. In a comic this would have cross-hairs and circles and read-outs, not just three stark, mundane lines. It would look much more exciting, but, I now know, much less real. In reality you wouldn't want all those things getting in the way of what you're looking at.

Not looking at. Aiming at. That little gap is meant to be filled by—by something.

It is much better this way. I can see that.

There are only three bullets in the case, but there is room for six. What does that mean? Has the hermit killed three people?

Maybe the bullets are still in the gun. Maybe the hermit hasn't killed anyone.

I think of the bullets, of the shape of them. As long as a cigarette, but not very wide. Less wide than my little finger. I have never seen a bullet before. They are slender, pointed, purposeful.

If a bullet—a real bullet—went through you, what kind of hole would it make?

It feels like information stacked up in my head over the past few days is starting to fall, one piece against the next, starting a tumble of bits and pieces which, once they have all fallen and the crashing has stopped and the dust has settled again, now form a pattern I can see and understand.

I whisper to myself, experimentally, "The hermit shot someone." I glance across to the gun. The missing bullets; the telescopic sights; the gun hidden in the car. It sounds right, then.

I try another. "Someone shot the hermit. Maybe they shot him back." The hermit's leg hasn't been cut in the car crash. Anna is sure of that, and we have never found the sharp place where he might have cut it. And it doesn't look like a cut. It looks like something else. I've known that all along, but I've never known *what* else. Now I do. The hole a bullet would make.

And the blood in the car must have come from the hermit's leg while he was driving. Driving away from somewhere; away from where he shot someone and someone shot him.

I say, "A long way away. It's just something a long way away, that's all." And, a moment later, "Thank God nothing like that ever happens here."

Saying the words out loud is a good test. None of them sound wrong in my ears. I know I have understood it all at last. I start to wonder how much of this Jamie knows already, and Anna.

All these times when I think that I finally understand; and each time, the real understanding is still waiting, waiting to come to me too late.

The hermit says something I can't understand. *Mi ez? Hol vagyok? What is this place? Where am I?*

Lying in the darkness of the living room, the candles blown out and the faint rustlings of the garden bushes in the air the only sound, the same fear comes back to me: that even this, where I have at least the illusion of control and command of myself, might still be just a dream. I am waiting now to fall asleep, but any moment I may actually be waking up—and waking up to a time and a reality that, just for the moment, elude me. I might be dying; it might all be too late once again.

From the edges of the darkness I imagine I can hear another voice. The words, again, make no sense; are meaningless in my ears.

Tudni akarom. Könyörgök—mondj el mindent.

But then the incomprehension softens, blurs away, and I understand them.

I want to know. Tell me everything—please.

Strange words in a deserted chapel where the echoes come faintly from the stone. When I first hear them, they won't fit properly in my ears; but now they do. I know them too well now.

But the voice this time is not the hermit. It is Anna.

13

*J*amie and I have to get to know each other again. It is a slow process, because although it is really only two years, it is two years that have meant a lot to both of us. We have a lot of catching up to do, and we no longer have the endless, timeless mornings and afternoons of Altesa in which to do it. We have our lessons; Jamie has his music and I have my art. There are sports for Jamie, though fewer for me. It is difficult to talk in the house, where there are always other boys around; and because we are in different years, the easy conversations which can occur between boys of the same age are less easy for us.

In the end, it is the music and the art that come to our rescue, and give us the places we need.

The music schools are an old building, tall, buried away in trees at one side of the school grounds. Upstairs, there are practice rooms, the thick, heavy doors insulated against sound, with little rectangular windows set into them so you can check if the room is occupied without opening the door. All the doors leak just a little, though, and to go upstairs is to enter a strange corridor of sounds: scales going up and down, fragments of pieces repeated and repeated to the same point, where a finger mistimes or misplays and forces the player to try again, and the sounds of stringed instruments being tuned, and percussion sounds, and sometimes voices singing or occasionally laughing. It feels to me like a beehive of music, with all the cells buzzing with activity. There is a friendly feel to the building, too, and the boys I meet in the corridor are, like those in the Art department, quicker to smile or say something affable in passing. It is, I begin to realize, another haven in a school which sometimes threatens to overwhelm me.

The Art department is my own territory by now—somewhere I feel as completely at home as I ever can in England. I can go there whenever I want. So it is in the Art department in the evenings, or one of the practice rooms of the music schools in the afternoons, that Jamie and I are able to talk.

We have missed out on two years of each other's lives somehow. We don't talk of that last summer before Jamie went away; neither of us seems able to think very clearly about that. But the two years that follow it we are eager for, and as we tell the stories of them to each other, it feels more and more like we are not standing behind a canvas screen with paint-stained coffee mugs on the windowsill beside us, or sitting on piano stools while Jamie idly picks out notes on the keyboard, but instead cross-legged on the floor of a room somewhere a long way away, surrounded by sunlight and comics.

For me, of course, the great news is that I have at last discovered what it is that I can do; what my hobby is, as Jamie once put it. Jamie knows this already: even in the year here where we have not spoken to each other—the year that finishes with my first exhibition, and Jamie breaking a wine glass in his anger and yet somehow finding a way for us to talk again—there has been comment around the house of how well I'm doing in Art. There are the pictures on the walls of my room; and though, at the start, Jamie never comes in there, he hears about them when the boys of my year are talking between themselves. So he knows quite a lot about me, I realize, though obviously he knows more now that he has seen all that I've drawn and painted, and now that I've explained some of it to him—what I'm trying to do, and what other pictures have inspired me, and what scenes or people I've chosen to concentrate on.

At the same time that talk around the school has let Jamie in on what has been happening in my life, so I have been hearing about him. I have heard, straight off, Mr. Dalton say *Musician, isn't he?* when he sees Jamie's face in my picture; and from this I know that even people who are not musicians themselves know who Jamie is, and what he does. It doesn't surprise me. I can remember how good he used to be on his clarinet, and I assume that he's got better.

He has; but there's more than just the clarinet, though. One afternoon, he shows me: a saxophone, bright and heavy and cold in its case. He takes it out, fits the pieces together, softens the reed for a while in his mouth, and plays for me. The sound is so different to what I'm used to from the clarinet that it takes me a minute or two to realize what should have been obvious right from the start: that he's captivating. The sound swoops and murmurs, is sometimes husky, sometimes strident and wailing. I can't believe how he can be so good at this so fast. There's something else, too, which it takes me longer to figure out. While he was always good at the clarinet, I can now hear something in the music that was missing before. I decide it's passion, love. He loves this instrument in a way he never really loved the clarinet.

"You've only been playing a year?" I say, incredulous.

He nods. His face is lit up, grinning, alive with excitement. "I know. It's amazing. I mean—it's surprised me too. But this is it. This is what I'm good at."

"Do you practise a lot?"

Another nod, emphatic. "Sure. All the time. Well—two, three hours a day, most days. But it's not like practising, it's like—well, it's not work, you know?"

I think of losing myself in painting, and I nod. "Yeah. I know."

"I thought you would."

A thought strikes me, and I am puzzled. "How come I haven't heard you before? I mean, in the orchestra or something."

"They need me on clarinet in the orchestra," he says. "There's a guy in the sixth form who's OK on sax."

"What about the Jazz Band, then?"

A slight shadow crosses his face, as if he's not sure what to say. Then he shrugs, and the look lifts. "It's weird. I don't want to play it in a band or in the orchestra. My teacher wants me to enter this competition next term, but I don't want to do that either."

"Why not? You're good enough, I bet."

"I know. But—it feels like something I want to keep for me, not for the school. They can have the clarinet if they like."

I try to understand what he means, but it's difficult. "So who do you play to?"

"Nobody. You, if you like. Just to myself, really."

"Oh," I say.

"I love it," he says. He's looking out the window of the room, not at me, not at the sax which he's laid back into its case. "It's like I forget where I am and—and everything—when I'm playing."

"How do you find time for all that practise?"

"How do you find time for all that painting?" he says, looking back at me, with a grin.

"Yeah, OK."

"You know something?" he says.

"What?"

"I'm going to be good at this."

"You are already," I say.

"No. I mean *really* good. I'm going to make something of this."

I look at him, and at the certainty on his face. "I know," I say.

Later—much later—I realize that Jamie has said something which, if I examine it properly, surprises me. I know, after all, that I am an outsider in this place; I feel it deep in myself. It is only in the Art department and sometimes in the music schools that I feel I fit. Belonging is something I have to earn, by being good at drawing so that people will admire me; by bringing credit to the house in Art festivals and competitions the way some boys do on the sports pitches. But Jamie has never had to work to be accepted or liked, and it's the same here as it was back in Altesa when we were six or seven. Everyone knows him by name, and everyone likes him. The confidence that I see in him at first—the confidence that comes from having been at the place a year longer than I have—stays with him, until I just assume that it is the way he is. But when he looks out of the window at the trees there and says, *It's like I forget where I am and—and everything*, there is something hidden in his face and voice that I don't understand—hardly notice—at the time. It is to do with being an outsider.

The quickness with which Jamie seems to understand my own worries about fitting in is no surprise to me, because Jamie has always understood me better than anyone else. It never occurs to me until much later that his empathy might come from something more central than just having known me a long time; that he, too, might be feeling alone.

The bells of the town are distantly audible as I sit out on the verandah with my lunch. I have bought myself some proper food. The garden is warm; there is the smell of summer properly in the air now: of hot lavender and the resin from the big pines, and rock dust, and melting asphalt. I tear bread and salami and make a crude sandwich, and while I am watching the end of the garden, a stealthy movement catches my eye.

It is a grey cat, slender, moving between the bushes low down by the wall. The sun casts a thin sliver of shadow here, and the cat is keeping to it, head turning slightly from side to side. I remember it; it is the same cat I saw jump up onto and over the wall when I first saw the garden again. I wonder if it belongs to someone, or if it is wild.

I whistle gently between my teeth and the cat's head snaps round. It watches me warily for a long second, but doesn't run. I take a piece of the salami and throw it a little way out onto the grass—away from me, but not all the way down the lawn. The cat follows the movement, and I see its ears strain forward and its body tense as it stares at the scrap of meat. Then, always watching, it comes out of the shadow and across the grass, picking its way delicately, sometimes looking up at me to check what I'm doing. I sit still, and whistle occasionally, quietly, just to let it know I'm here.

It sniffs the piece of sausage discerningly, and then glances at me. The glance looks accusing, as if it doesn't approve of my taste in salami. But it eats it nonetheless, and I find myself smiling. I tear off another little piece, and throw that, this time slightly nearer. The cat stares at me with eyes whose pupils, in the bright sun, are hardly more than black lines in the green, and then it pads up and takes this second offering.

"Do you live round here, then?" I say quietly. The cat's ears twitch at the sound of my voice, and it seems to consider the question. "You look familiar," I tell it. Its tail waves slightly, and then it sits down on its haunches and begins to lick one paw clean.

I wonder if it is some distant descendant of the cat I saw playing in the grass, the day that Anna was under the lemon tree. There must be a whole tribe of wild or half-wild cats in the valley, living off scraps and what's left out in the dustbins, and lizards, and whatever else they can catch. But this one does, I tell myself, have something about the narrow shape of its head that I seem to remember.

A grasshopper whirs past the cat, and it stops its cleaning for a moment to watch; but the grasshopper doesn't interest it. It turns back to me, watching me steadily. I prepare to give it something else to eat.

It is nearly six o'clock in the morning when I finally crawl through my bedroom window and take off my clothes.

Anna arrives to relieve me at just before five. She brings a message from Jamie that he agrees about the lunar sand, and she's clearly nettled that he has refused to explain to her what this means. I give in and tell her, but she doesn't seem to get the same sense of satisfaction from the comparison that Jamie has. I tell myself it's probably because she doesn't read as much about the moon and space as Jamie does.

We check the hermit together, but he is asleep again. Anna looks at the bottle of water that's been knocked over, and then at me; I read the question in her face.

"I gave him some, and then he knocked the bottle over," I say.

"We'll have to get some more."

"Yeah. I'll tell Jamie."

She is looking at the hermit, concentrating, her eyes focused tightly on him. She looks like she is trying to make him well again by sheer force of will.

In my room, I turn the events of the night round and round in my head. Outside it is getting light now; I watch conscientiously until I just discern Anna's signal from the belltower, and then I get into bed. My eyes are already half-closed, which surprises me; I have thought, walking back, that I feel remarkably lively and awake. Now I find, all of a sudden, that I'm not. Instead, the cool pillow and comforting blankets drag me down into sleep. I am trying to decide what I think of the hermit, now that I have understood what the gun really means; but the thoughts are heavy and difficult to move about. It is too much effort.

Jamie and I arrive at the chapel at nine, having managed to obscure Anna's absence with a good deal of running between households and shouting and generally making enough noise and commotion for three. The scant two hours' sleep I've managed after getting back makes me a bit groggy to start with, but after breakfast and some of Lena's lemonade I start to feel brighter. Jamie, meanwhile, secures more water for the hermit, this time in a big, plastic bottle that used to hold Coke.

Anna is there to meet us.

"I've been thinking," she says. "About the car. Someone's going to see it sooner or later."

We are outside, in the shadow of the belltower. The hermit is sleeping, though Anna says he has been awake for at least some parts of the night. We are keeping away from him so our voices don't disturb him.

"There's nothing we can do about that," Jamie says.

"We can hide it," she says. "I told you I'd been thinking. It's in all those bushes, right?"

"Mm," Jamie says. I can see he's thinking now as well; and his thoughts race ahead to catch up with where Anna already is. "Yeah, we could use them. Branches and stuff."

"It's quite a stone-coloured car, anyway," Anna says, echoing something I've already thought. "If we cover it up a bit it won't show nearly as much."

"Yeah. OK. Who stays here?"

"It's your turn," she says. "Alex and I can do it."

"You sure?" Jamie doesn't look very certain.

I say, "Of course we can do it."

"Yeah," Anna says with a grin.

"Well, OK. But be back by twelve cos his bandage will need changing."

She nods. "Of course. See you then."

"Yeah." Jamie watches, rather disconsolately, as we run across the churchyard and start up the valley. I know how he feels; on a day like this, I'd rather be outside in the sun than inside with the hermit.

When we hit the roadway along which the hermit's car has crashed, Anna says, "Last night—"

"Yeah?"

"Was the hermit asleep all the time?" she says. "Or did he—you know—talk to you and stuff?"

"No," I say. "Well, a bit. He asked for water and he knocked the bottle over."

"Oh," she says. "Yeah, you said."

"And then he went back to sleep."

"So he's mostly been asleep?" She seems very focused on this point.

"Yeah," I say. "Why? Did he wake up when you were there?"

She is scanning the road ahead. There's no traffic, no pedestrians. Everything is quiet. She says, "Sometimes. He didn't seem very—you know. Like he wasn't sure where he was."

"I know," I say.

"But yeah, he woke up sometimes." She skips off to the other side of the road and picks up a long piece of stick, which she swishes through the air. She clearly finds the sound it makes satisfying. She comes back to my side with the stick still in her hand.

"What did he say to you?" I ask, wondering if the hermit has started making more sense after I have left him.

"Not much," she says vaguely. Then, "I wonder what actually happened?"

"When?"

"With the hermit. I mean, what the real story is."

I say, "I think he shot someone. Like an assassin, on a roof or something." This is how I picture it. "But then someone shot him back, and got him in the leg. That's where the bullet went through, that hole. And then he drove here, cos it happened somewhere else, somewhere—a long way away. And that's why there's blood in the car, from where he was driving." I think for a moment, and faint voices come and go in my head and the world blurs over briefly. "Oh, and I think he shot two people. One of them died. And the other one's"—I concentrate—"in intensive care, where his condition remains critical." I nod to myself, pleased at having caught these fragments; the voices have been very faint, heard only down the hall as I approach the door to the living room.

I have walked on a few paces before I realize Anna isn't with me. I stop and look round. She's standing in the road, staring at me, her mouth slightly open. She doesn't move.

I say, "What is it?"

She shuts her mouth, then opens it as if to say something, then shuts it again. At last she says, "How do you know all that?"

"I was thinking," I say. "I had a look at the hermit's gun. It's like an assassin's gun, isn't it? With telescopic sights and everything. And I heard something on the radio, too." I can't quite read her expression. "Don't you think that's what happened?"

After a moment, she nods. "Yeah. I think you might be right." She shakes her head as if a fly is bothering her, and then walks to catch me up. "Yeah. You know, I—" She pauses.

"What?"

"I didn't think you knew any of that."

"I was thinking last night," I say.

"Yeah."

"That is what you think, isn't it?"

"You say he shot two people?" she says.

"I think so. I mean, there were two people on the news. And there are only three bullets left. So perhaps he shot three people."

"What? Which three bullets?"

"In the case. There's room for six, but there's only three there."

"Oh," she says. "I didn't notice that."

"So I was thinking maybe he shot several people, but then one of them shot him back. And that's what happened to his leg." I glance at her to see if she agrees with this. "Do you think that's right?"

She says, "Yeah, Alex, OK. I think that's right." She thinks to herself for a second, and then adds, "You mustn't tell anyone any of this. You know that, don't you?"

She's speaking to me as if I were a little kid or something. I say, irritated, "Of course not. I know that."

"Well, it's just—" She shakes her head again. "How come you know all this stuff?" she says, not really asking the question, just saying it because it's bothering her.

"I told you, I was—"

"You were thinking. Yeah, I know." She sniffs. "You say there was something on the news?"

"I heard a bit of it. One man dead and another where his condition remains critical." I hesitate. "That's bad, isn't it?"

"Yeah."

"Does that mean he might die?"

"I don't know. Maybe."

"Perhaps the hermit's condition remains critical too," I say, secretly quite pleased with the heavy importance of the words.

Anna says, "So he drove all the way here." She looks at me again. "Where from? Did the radio say where it all happened?"

I concentrate.

"Alex?"

There's only the sound of voices—radio voices—this far back down the hall. I can't make out what they're saying until I get closer to the doorway.

"Alex? Are you OK?"

"Mm," I say. "No, I can't remember."

Anna is looking at me curiously. "What were you doing there?" she asks.

I say, "Just thinking. Trying to remember."

"Oh. Your eyes were funny."

"Jamie says I go dreamy sometimes," I say carefully.

"Yeah, I heard him say that. So. He came from somewhere else . . ."

"A long way away," I say. "All the way with a bullet in his leg."

"I don't think the bullet's *in* his leg any more," Anna says. "I think it went right through. That's what the hole at the back is."

"Oh," I say. "Of course." I knew this really.

Anna says, "I wonder why he came *here?*"

This is obvious, so I tell her. "To see Signor Ferucci," I say.

Anna stops dead a second time. "Yeah," she says. "Yeah, that's right. That's what he said. But he might have been lying . . ."

"I don't think so," I say. "He wanted us to go and get him, re-member?"

"That's right. He did." I can see she's thinking hard now. She says, "Then Signor Ferucci must know."

"About what?"

"About the hermit."

"Oh," I say. I wonder exactly what she means by this.

"Look," she says. "There it is."

We've been thinking so hard that I've forgotten that we're supposed to be looking for the hermit's car. Anna points off the road to where it's lodged, and again I'm struck by how easy it is to miss. We jump down into the rain gully and scramble down the incline, kicking up big swirls of dust.

"Right," Anna says, when we're at the bottom and surveying the car. "We'd better get started. Pull off branches and we'll put them over. We ought to cover the shiny things, like the lights and the radiator bit, first."

"OK," I say.

The bushes are tough and gnarled, and pulling a branch off one of them is a laborious task. You have to bend the wood back and forth over and over until its fibres part and tear. It takes time, but eventually Anna has got one free; and a few seconds later I manage my first as well.

"There!" she says, pleased.

We throw the branches onto the body of the wreck and bend back down to the bushes again.

"Ready?" she says.

"Yeah," I say.

"How are the sketches?"

"They're good." I take one last look at the drawings and then turn them face down on the bed. "A good day's work."

"Good for you. You deserve an evening out, then."

"If you say so."

The streets are starting to fill with the evening crowds, and there are entertainers and musicians on many of the corners as we cut up through the city towards the university quarter. There is cheaper accommodation here, like the rooms Jamie and I were staying in on the school trip where we met Anna, some seven years ago.

It's as if the thought passes straight to her. She says, "Remember before?"

"Yeah," I say. "I was just thinking about it, in fact."

"I enjoyed all that. It was good fun."

"You were impressive," I say. "It's a shame you haven't gone for a career where your acting skills could be put to better use."

"What acting skills?" she says.

"You know. Boyfriend and girlfriend and all that."

"Oh, right. Well, don't be so sure," she says. "There's a lot of use for acting in politics. And in academia, too."

"Yeah, well," I say, not sure if she's kidding or not, "not the kind of acting you managed that time."

She giggles. "I made a pretty good femme fatale, didn't I?"

"It wasn't fair. None of us could see properly through our hormones. Teenage boys are easy targets."

" 'None of us?' " she says. "You don't mean you were letching too?"

"Well—" I hesitate, not knowing quite what to say.

"Alex!" She sounds shocked, and it takes me a second to realize she's only feigning it. "I thought you were above that kind of thing. You're supposed to be my *friend*."

"I try," I say, uncomfortable.

"Besides, you're an artist. You're used to the female form." She grins. "I didn't shock you or anything did I?"

"Well—" I say, smiling, a little embarrassed. "What did you expect?"

She's quiet for a moment; then the grin catches the corner of her mouth again. "Well," she says. "Maybe it wasn't *all* acting."

"Why?"

She's quiet for longer this time. "I'm not sure," she says at last, and the kidding has gone from her voice now. She sounds thoughtful, introspective; it's unlike her. She says, "It's just—I think I'd got so used to you looking at me like a friend. You and Jamie. I think I wanted you to see me in a different way for once, that's all."

"Well, you certainly managed that," I say.

"You really were shocked, weren't you?" The amusement's back again now.

"Well—it was a surprise, I'll give you that much," I say, managing to keep a note of detachment in my voice. An idea comes to me. "But it wasn't like it was anything new."

"Oh, really? Were all your life-models seventeen, then?"

"That's not what I meant," I say. I have to watch the street ahead, not look at her, to keep from laughing and spoiling it. It isn't often that I'm one step ahead of Anna in anything. I go on, "What I meant was— well, you were only topless, after all. I've—um—seen more than that, in the past."

"I bet. Who? Tell me about it. Or do you just mean porno mags and stuff like that?"

"No," I say. "I mean you."

"What?" She is genuinely puzzled.

"I've seen you," I say. "Naked. As in, no clothes? You know?"

"When?" she says, slapping my arm. "Come on, tell all. Were you watching at my keyhole or something?"

"No," I say. "It was an accident."

"When?" she says, impatient.

"You were very pretty," I add, stalling, enjoying teasing her.

"Oh, balls, Alex. Come on. Tell me."

"All right," I say, giving in. "It was the first time you came to Altesa. I was eight, you were ten, I think. We went swimming and there was a place for diving from, on the cliff—remember?"

She nods. "Oh, that," she says, and there's a faint note of relief in her voice. "That doesn't count. What's there to see at that age? Besides, we kept our pants on."

"Not afterwards," I say.

"What?"

"You know. You went back. You said you'd dropped your watch, and then you went back and dived from the ledge higher up. We'd all agreed it was too high, but you did it anyway."

She's frowning a little. "Yeah? I don't remember."

"You did," I say. "And you took off all your clothes that time."

"Are you sure?" she says. "We were all doing it, I thought. Jumping off that little ridge place. Then we went back home."

"No," I say, starting to be puzzled. "You went back again. I remembered something and I followed you and then there you were, up on the cliff. I wanted to stop you, but I didn't know how."

"Oh," she says. "Well. I can't remember that."

I don't understand how she can not remember. I say, "There must have been a reason. I mean, you really wanted to do it. You waited till we'd gone along the cliff path a way and then you went back. You told me to go on. I mean, you didn't want me to see you or anything."

"It must've been a spur of the moment thing, then," she says. "I don't remember it. Sounds a bit stupid, really."

"I always wondered why you did it," I say. "I wanted to ask you. And now I finally can, you don't remember?"

"Don't get upset," she says. "It was probably just some kid thing. You know how kids are—they do weird things for no reason. Probably something like that."

I can hardly believe it is Anna saying this. "Don't you remember?" I say. "None of us were kids, and none of us were weird."

"Yes we were," she says. "We were all kids, and you were *really* weird sometimes. And if I did what you say, then so was I. So yes we were kids, and yes we were weird."

"No," I say. "It wasn't like that."

"You sure?"

"Yeah."

"Whatever. So," she says. "You were watching this, yeah? There's me with no clothes on, halfway up a cliff, about to do something really stupid and dangerous, and there's you watching me. What next?"

"Well, you dived," I say. "I thought you might never come up. And then you surfaced but you were screaming. And I thought maybe you were hurt, but then I realized you were shouting because you'd done it. Managed to do it. And then you came out and got dry in the sun."

"Cool," she says. "Did you get a good look?"

"Um . . . yes."

"Was I any good?"

I don't know what to say to that. "You were ten," I say. "What do you mean?"

"Well, you must have felt *something*. You know. Did it turn you on?"

She's grinning again. I say, "Well—kind of, I suppose. It didn't feel like that, though. I just thought you looked—nice."

"*Nice,*" she says, sounding disgusted. "God. How awful. *Nice.*"

"Well, that's what I thought."

"What about later?" she says. "In your room in the hostel. Did you think I was *nice* then?"

"I thought you were even nicer," I say.

Anna laughs aloud, and pushes me away from her. "You're useless," she says. "The things I do for you, and look what gratitude I get."

"Nobody asked you to do anything," I say.

"Oh, come on. You desperately needed the kudos. I bet you were the talk of the town when you got back to England."

"You could say that."

There must be something in my voice. She stops, turning to look at me. "What is it?"

I can feel the struggle to pretend it's nothing going on inside me. But perhaps it's something about the night, and the feel of the city around us, and how good she looks right now. I say, "Don't you get it?"

"Get what?"

"I always fancied you," I say. I feel like I could stammer into silence at any moment, so I plunge on anyway. "Right from back then when—when I saw you on the cliff. I didn't know it then, but I think it was—that. Seeing you then was—I don't know. It changed things in me." I can feel other memories scraping at my mind, and I force them away. "It was *important,* you know? And now I tell you, and you can't even remember it."

"Really?" she says. "You fancied me? Like—childhood sweethearts, that kind of thing?"

I shrug. I feel helpless. I know she's finding this funny—that she's laughing at me. It's no use. I say, "I loved you, I think."

"Oh, God, Alex," she says. "You are just *too* heavy, sometimes. You didn't, you know. I bet I was the only girl you really got to know, that's all. Is that true?"

"It wasn't like that."

"Balls. Of course it was."

I know I have to try, because I know this isn't going to happen again. I won't be able to say any of this a second time. I say, "What about—now? Don't you ever feel like—"

She breaks in. "Alex, you know something? You're sweet. I really like you. Back then, you were—you and Jamie were—pretty much my only friends, you know that? I liked you a *lot.* I still do. And I'm really pleased—and flattered—to have been your childhood sweetheart. I think it's sweet. If I'd had a sweetheart it probably would have been you. But that was when we were—what, ten? I'm a bit old for carving love hearts in tree trunks and buying each other sweets and all that."

I just stare at her. It's more painful than I've imagined, even though I've known it was coming.

She points across the street suddenly. "There it is. We need to cross here."

I see the doorway to the club as we dodge the traffic. It's a basement place, a neon sign with an arrow pointing down some steps. On the pavement is a sandwich-board with the names of bands on it. A young couple are just starting down the steps when we get close, the girl hanging on the boy's arm, laughing. Far away through the city I can hear a siren, and then a bell chiming. At the far end of the street, I catch a glimpse of someone—a young woman with reddish streaks in her hair—looking our way before she turns the corner.

We reach the pavement and Anna says, "What do you think?"

"It looks fine," I say. It does. It looks familiar, too, though I've never been here before. It's the shadows of other clubs at other times, that's all. Still, something is too familiar for comfort.

"Alex—don't look like that. I'm still your friend."

"Yeah," I say. "I know. Thanks."

"You OK?"

I shrug. "Yeah. Sure. Let's see what's playing."

We start down the steps, and as we go she puts her hand on my arm and gives it a squeeze, for all the world as though we're a couple like the one I've seen a second before. Then there is a black door, and through it noise and laughter and smoke and lights. We duck inside and look around us: the place is getting full. On stage, a couple of band members are checking their instruments, tuning up. The pain of what she's said—and what she's left unsaid—is muted now. I'm caught up with looking around me, at this place that I've never seen before but which is already familiar. It even smells the same. I know I should feel something—should have some reaction—and I wait for it to happen, to grip me suddenly and unexpectedly. I even try to imagine him here, grinning at me through the crowd, waiting for his turn to get up on the low stage and play. I should feel something.

I wait to feel, but nothing comes. It's as if there's nothing here that means anything to me. Still, while Anna pushes through to the bar and buys us drinks, I keep waiting.

14

*T*he walls are lined with pictures. Some of the prints are speckled with paint or bits of plaster, or scratched a little, or creased with handling. It doesn't matter. I can see through the snapshots to the originals—big squares and rectangles of canvas hundreds of miles away. Tomorrow—I think it is tomorrow; I'm fairly sure it is—the doors will open, and people will walk in and look at these pieces. They will see them in the wrong order, laid out from first to last. They'll think they're my work, too, and they're not. The whole exhibition is a huge fraud, a smoke-screen, and the reality of it is hidden somewhere behind the surfaces of these images, and perhaps in that single painting that is growing and spreading on the wall.

I feel like I'm right on the edge of working out what it is I've done. All I know right now is that these paintings aren't my own; that what I've thought I was painting, year by year, isn't what is actually on the canvas. I have painted something different to what I had thought. I have fooled myself—or been fooled—and none of my work is really what I had thought it to be. The eyes are wrong. They aren't the eyes of the people in the pictures at all. The eyes are all the same.

I take them down from the walls, and I put them back up, and change the configuration of them again. There is a puzzle here I can solve if I can fit its pieces together in the right order.

My exhibition opens tomorrow, and the paintings on its walls are not my paintings. They're not the paintings I thought they were, anyway.

Anna's finger traces the empty cavities in the lining of the case. "You're right," she says. "There's three missing."

Jamie says, "So maybe he shot three people."

"I thought maybe there might be one still in the gun," I say. We all stare at the pieces of the gun apprehensively.

Anna says, "We covered the car up. At least we don't have to worry about that."

"Can't you see it at all?" Jamie asks.

"Well, a bit. But not as much as before. I don't think anyone goes down that road anyway."

"Yeah."

"How's he been?" she adds.

Jamie glances at the floor as if looking through it, down to the sleeping hermit. "He's still really hot," he says. "I put a cloth on his forehead—a wet cloth, I mean. But it doesn't seem to do much good."

"It's been ages," Anna says. "He hasn't eaten anything, either."

"But you don't eat when you're feeling really ill. I don't, anyway."

"I suppose," she says. "But he's got to start getting better soon, don't you think?"

"Well—probably," Jamie says. He doesn't sound sure, though.

"He asked me for water," I remind them. "Maybe that shows he's feeling better." I try not to think about the way he grabbed me, and the strange look in his eyes, as if he wasn't quite seeing what was around him. Anna nods.

"Yeah, exactly." She gets up, looks out one of the windows for a moment and then turns back to us both. "We'd better go and check on him."

Outside, the sunshine is heating the valley floor and the lizards are warmed up and moving. There are plenty of lizards around the chapel, living in the tumbles of masonry and piles of timber. Jamie and I sit with our backs to the chapel wall, feet in the sun, bodies in the shade. Anna is inside, looking after the hermit for the moment. Blue bees drone purposefully past us, examining the walls briefly for likely looking holes to crawl into, and then zoom off.

"Jamie?"

"Yeah?"

"I like it when Anna's here."

"Mm."

"What if she has to go home before the hermit's better?"

He tenses beside me. "What?"

"What if the holidays finish and Anna has to go home, and the hermit's not better? How do we take care of him then?"

Jamie shakes his head. "There's weeks yet. He'll get better before that," he says.

"Are you sure?"

"Pretty sure. Don't worry about it, Alex."

"OK."

There's the crunch of footsteps on the grit and Anna rounds the end of the chapel. She has a peculiar expression on her face; half amused, half worried.

"What is it?" Jamie says.

"It's the hermit," she says. "He's awake again."

"Is he all right?"

"Well—kind of," she says. Her mouth twists slightly, accentuating the weird look on her face.

"What?" Jamie says, curious.

Anna rubs one foot in the dirt for a while. Then she says, "He needs to pee."

"What?" Jamie says again, though I'm sure he's heard perfectly well.

"He needs to pee," Anna says again, and then suddenly she is overcome with giggles. Her hand flies to her mouth and she tries to hold them in. "I didn't know what to do," she says, breathless. "You'll have to help him."

"Why us?" Jamie says, which I think is stupid of him.

"Cos you're boys. Anyway, it's all Alex's fault. If you hadn't given him the water, maybe he wouldn't need to." Another burst of giggles come over her until she has to stop, coughing, to get her breath back.

"I'm not helping him," Jamie says, sounding faintly horrified. "I mean—what do you mean, help him?"

"I don't know," Anna says. "Boys do it standing up, don't they? You'll have to help him stand." She looks at us, and our expressions start her laughing again. She manages to gasp, "Maybe you'll have to get his thing out for him." Jamie's expression of distaste deepens.

"He can't stand up," I say, pragmatically. "His leg's hurt."

At that, Anna gets herself under control. "Oh. Yeah," she says, and all at once the moment of childishness is gone from her. She tilts her head slightly on one side as she thinks. "Well," she says. "He could do it lying down, couldn't he? If we had—I don't know. A bucket or something."

"We don't have a bucket," Jamie says.

"I know. That's why I said *or something*. Something like a bucket."

"There's the bottle of water he knocked over," I say. Anna says, "Yeah, that might do it."

"Will it be big enough?" Jamie says.

"Depends how badly he needs to pee," Anna says, grinning. "How much water did you give him, Alex?"

"Not much, I think," I say.

"Well, then. Yeah, it'll be all right." She stares at us. "Well, go on, then."

Jamie and I look at each other. I say, "We'll need to get him on his side, probably." Jamie nods.

"So?"

"Well . . ." I say. "We need three of us for that."

There's a silence. Then Anna says, soberly, "OK. We'll all go."

"I'm not getting his thing out," Jamie says.

"I was just kidding. He can do that himself," Anna says.

"All right, then. All of us."

Anna nods; after a moment so do I.

In the chapel, it is as if the bright, buzzing morning doesn't exist. In the shadows at the end the hermit is awake, and coughing; we can hear him as we go down the length of the building. When we get there, Anna kneels down beside him.

"We're going to turn you on your side," she says. "It might hurt a bit. There's a bottle you can—there's a bottle you can use."

The hermit nods. There is a strange expression on his face, too, and it takes me a moment to recognize it. He is ashamed. I feel suddenly sorry for him.

"Don't worry," I say, without thinking.

Anna seems to have noticed it as well. "I shan't look," she says seriously.

The man looks round at the three of us, and then his expression changes: he laughs, just a little. "Thank you," he says. "You're right. It's no good my being shy. Well. Let's get it over with."

His voice sounds almost normal this morning; I compare it to the harsh growl that came from him in the night, and can hardly recognize them as the same thing. But his face is still glistening, and when we come to turn him, I can feel the heat coming off him as if from the oven in the kitchen. We take hold of his shoulders and arm, and Anna takes his wounded leg, and we turn him as carefully as we can onto his good side. His face tightens and contorts quickly, but he doesn't cry out. He steadies himself on one elbow, and with his free arm he fumbles at the zip on his trousers. Anna passes the bottle to Jamie, who takes it from her with some apprehension. I am holding the hermit's shoulders, keeping him steady.

Jamie holds the bottle for the hermit, simultaneously trying to keep it in place near the man's groin and appear as if he's looking somewhere else entirely. He looks very uncomfortable indeed, and, in my safe position behind the hermit's shoulders, I'm glad someone else is doing the difficult part. Anna is right, though, to everyone's relief; the hermit gets his zip undone and his thing out with no help. Jamie, resolutely ignoring everything around him, shifts the bottle closer until the man can get his thing to the neck of it. Then there's a pause, and finally the sound of the bottle filling surprisingly rapidly. The hermit must have needed to pee pretty badly after all, I realize.

I steal a glance at the hermit's thing while pretending, like Jamie, to be absorbed with the chapel doors. I tell myself that, since I'm behind the hermit's head, he can't see me and so I won't embarrass him. What I see is surprisingly large and strangely muscular-looking. It is nothing like my thing or Jamie's. I blink quickly and look away, fascinated now by the stone of the pillar against which we've made the hermit's pillow. At the opening of the hermit's trousers, there have been a few twists of dark hair showing in the candlelight.

When the hermit has finished, and zipped his trousers again, Anna takes the bottle from Jamie and sets it aside while we turn the hermit onto his back again. His face, flushed with the pain of the movement, nevertheless has an undertone of relief. His eyes are closed for a short time, but then he opens them. He's actually seeing us, this time, not looking through us as he's sometimes done.

He says, "Thank you. That feels a lot better. You can imagine, yes?"

Jamie laughs a little, politely. Anna nods.

"Are you feeling better?" I say.

"A little, I think," the hermit says. "But—the fever's still here. I can feel that."

"What should we do about it?" Anna says.

"I don't think there's much you can do," the hermit says. "We just— have to wait. It should pass." He gives a half-laugh, and the sound turns into a coughing which lasts a minute or more. At the end of it he lies back, exhausted.

"Here," Anna says. She's got the fresh water in the Coke bottle, and she holds it while the hermit drinks a little. When he's finished, he turns his head and closes his eyes.

"Like little angels," he says faintly, and I can hear that his voice has that strange quality which I've come to recognize. It means he's not really with us any more. "Angels in the chapel to bear me up." And then he says something else, but the words are wrong again.

The stored words come back to me now, and now I know them. *Angyalok repítenek a fellegekbe.* Angels carrying me into the sky.

"Come on," Anna says abruptly. "Let's let him be for a while." She picks up the bottle the hermit has filled and starts off down the chapel. Jamie and I straighten. The hermit mumbles something I don't quite catch.

"Come on," she calls again. I'm slightly surprised that she wants to leave so suddenly; I had thought we might take the time to change the hermit's dressing again. But we follow her out into the sunshine anyway.

Anna empties the bottle in the bushes, and darts back into the chapel to put it away. Then she joins us at the end of the building.

"We can keep that one for him to pee in," she says. "Just as long as we don't get them muddled up."

"Yuk, no," I say, pulling a face.

She glances at us. "It wasn't too bad, though, was it?"

Jamie shrugs reluctantly. "I s'pose not," he says.

The bees are still sweeping the area industriously. The little shadow here, under the clock tower, has narrowed a few inches while we've been inside; soon it will pass over into afternoon, and the dandelion clock, above us in the wall, will start to catch the sun. Anna and Jamie and I settle ourselves comfortably on the pine needles.

I say, "Did you see the hermit's thing?"

There's a pause. Jamie says, "Did you?"

"Mm," I say.

"Me too," he says.

"Did you?" I ask Anna.

"Well, yes."

Jamie glances at her. "You said you wouldn't look," he says, sounding slightly shocked.

"Well, it was difficult not to," she says, not meeting his eye.

I say, "Wasn't it really big?" I feel vaguely, secretly worried about this.

Anna says, "It wasn't so big."

"Oh. I thought it was," I say.

I look at Jamie for support in this. After a moment, he nods very slightly, and says, "Yeah, me too."

"Well, I didn't think it was all that big," she says, offhand.

"What would you know? You're a girl."

"That doesn't mean I haven't seen—things," she says.

I am astonished by this. Apart from my own and Jamie's, this is the first man's thing I have seen. That Anna's experience here should be greater than mine is something I haven't anticipated at all. Something like the same sequence of thoughts must be going through Jamie's head too, because he looks as taken aback as I feel. Anna stares at us both.

"What?" she says. "Haven't you seen—you know. Your dad's?"

"No," I say. My parents have their own bathroom. The thought of my father ever being naked, and ever having a thing like the hermit's, strikes me at once as being quite unbelievable. Again, I look at Jamie.

"Well, no," he says. "Maybe once or twice. But not—you know—not that."

"Oh," Anna says. She sounds as frankly surprised as we have been. "Well, I didn't think it was all that big."

"So you've seen your dad?" Jamie says.

"He's not my real dad."

"But you've seen it?"

"Mm."

"When?"

Anna shrugs. "In the bathroom."

"Oh."

"So the hermit's wasn't really very big?" I say, trying to sort all this out.

"I don't know," Anna says. "I didn't think so." She hesitates, then grins; a little flare of mischief is in her eye. She says, "At least it wasn't—you know."

"What?" Jamie says.

"*You* know. At least it wasn't—like that."

"Like what?"

Anna shakes her head, still grinning. "Don't be thick. You're boys, you should know this stuff. You know—how it goes."

Jamie and I look at each other. Neither of us knows what Anna's talking about.

"What do you mean?" Jamie says.

Anna leans slightly closer and drops her voice. "You know. When it goes hard."

Jamie's eyes go wide, and then he blushes deeply. "How do you know about that?" he says.

"I know lots of things," Anna says.

I think fast and realize that Anna is right—that sometimes it is hard; mainly at night. It's just one of the things it does sometimes, and which I've never bothered to think about until now.

"Why does it go hard, then?" I ask.

Jamie looks flustered, and drops his eyes, staring at the ground between his knees. He waits for Anna to say something, but she doesn't.

When I look at her, she's looking away, at the hills at the end of the valley.

At last Jamie says, "Well, why does it, then?"

Anna says, "It's for screwing."

"Oh, that," Jamie says hastily.

I say, "How do you know all this?"

"One of the girls at school told me," Anna says.

"Oh." I think for a moment. "Screwing's rude."

"Well, of course," Anna says, in a matter-of-fact way.

"We ought to change his dressing," Jamie says. I am surprised and a little disappointed; I want to hear more. But Anna stands up.

"Yeah," she says. "You're right."

She leads the way in out of the sun. As I walk behind her I realize I am surprised there is anything anyone knows more about than Jamie; with his books and comics, he is usually the one who tells me new and wonderful things. But in some things, it seems that Anna is ahead of us both.

We have a table in a corner of the club. Anna has fetched two beers in tall glasses, while around us the young people talk noisily. At the far end of the room, the musicians on stage have finished setting up; a couple of them are taking sips from plastic bottles of mineral water—or at least, something that looks like mineral water—and conversing quietly. Anna clinks her beer glass against mine.

"Cheers."

"Cheers," I say. "What made you pick this place, then?"

"I told you, it looked good. Oh, wait—they're starting."

The band have finished tuning and talking and, as I turn my head, launch neatly into an opening I recognize: it's *C Jam Blues*, a piece I've heard Jamie play many times. There's scattered applause from the crowd, and then the room quietens down slightly, paying due attention to the music.

"Is it all going to be trad stuff?" I ask. I find myself hoping it will be; Jamie was always keener on trad than contemporary.

Anna shrugs. "I don't know. We'll have to wait and see."

The band have made it through the theme the obligatory couple of times, and the improvisation starts with the saxophonist. I turn my chair a little so I have a clearer view of the musicians. Beside me, Anna is tapping time with one finger on the table.

I say, "They're not bad."

She looks at me out of the corner of her eye, and then says, "You miss him a lot, don't you?"

It takes me by surprise. I say, "Yes. You?"

"Of course," she says. "Of course."

"He would have liked this kind of thing. Well, he would have been up there."

"He was really into all that, wasn't he?"

I nod. "Yes."

She says, "I kind of wish I'd been around to see that."

"You would have been impressed," I say. "I was. He was—really good."

It feels strange, talking about Jamie like this: painful, but also as if something inside is being slowly, slowly eased. We have kept him out of our conversation all the time we've been together, but it's been difficult; the sense of him has always been there. At least now, in this dimly lit room, we have said something aloud.

Anna says, "Yeah. I thought he would be."

In the band, the flow of the improvisation shifts to the bass player, and the mood of the music alters to accommodate the change. As I listen, a glimmer of memory starts to trouble me. Something in the street outside the bar. After a second, I have it: the girl down the street, red streaks in her hair, glancing our way and then turning the corner. There has been something about her that has felt—familiar. I can't be sure what. She has been a little too far away for me to see her face clearly, but still, there is—something.

It's puzzling. I wonder where I might have seen her—in another street perhaps, on our way here, or some other night out in the piazzas. Whatever. It's just a coincidence, but—

I can't place her. There was a time when I could have just taken a moment or two to drift sideways out of the room, and catch wherever it was that I saw her first; but that was a long time ago now. In any case— I glance around—she's not in the bar. I'll probably never know for sure.

Anna turns to me and says, "What sort of thing did Jamie play, then?" She hesitates, and then says, "Alex? What is it?"

I shake my head. "Nothing. I just thought I saw someone, that's all."

"Yeah? Who?"

"Just—someone I'd seen before. But I don't know where. Probably on the street."

"Yeah, well."

"What sort of thing did Jamie play?" I repeat.

"Yeah. You could tell me about it."

"OK. If you like." I wonder where to start.

So stupid. So stupid not to see it right then, to put the pieces together. Afterwards—when things have passed—it looks so simple that I can't believe I didn't understand at the time; but that is how it has always been for me. Perhaps it is how it will always be, too; and perhaps, of course, there is actually no time left for it to continue being that way, and I will open my eyes in a moment to find that it is *all* "has," all past.

Something is wrong in the club, but with the music and the conversation we're having I tell myself that the unease comes from remembering Jamie, and bringing out into the open for the first time things which Anna and I have left silent until this point. But it's not that; not really that at all. On the street outside I have seen a girl I have seen before, but I sweep the thought aside without giving it time to work its way through my brain properly, trigger the right associations.

It's easily done. Anna's eyes are bright and wide in the low light, the pupils large and dark. She's smiling as she talks, and all I can see is her face, and all I can hear is the music and her voice drifting in and out of it. She's like a drug; I can't take my eyes off her and I can't get enough of her. We talk about Jamie, about his music, about the time in England; we laugh again at what happened here in Florence; we make up for a lot of lost time. Anna's face is alive and bright in the dim room, as if caught with afternoon light through coloured glass. When she lifts her beer, the glass casts amber across her mouth and the side of her jaw, gold, like the gold of a halo.

The band work through the familiar numbers, and gradually they drift into the background. I find I am used to their style now, can anticipate what they will do enough that they don't grab too much of my attention. The room seems to fade out slightly, to become just that tiny bit more distant, except for a pool of reality around the table where we're sitting. Anna is real; I am real. The young people moving through the bar are like tangible ghosts. She's beautiful. I watch her, and we talk, and I let myself ignore things I shouldn't.

Jamie stays with the hermit while Anna and I go into town. We need food—for us; the hermit doesn't seem able to eat yet—and water, and other supplies. We're down to the last of our hoarded pocket money, and none of us is sure how we'll buy things when it runs out.

Anna kicks her feet through the hot dust of the empty river and says, "I wish he'd get better."

"Are you worried?"

"No," she says quickly. "I just wish he'd get better, that's all."

Something she said before comes back to me. I say, "Why isn't he your real dad?"

"What?" Anna says; then she understands. "Oh. My parents are divorced."

I nod. One or two children at school have parents who are divorced, so the concept is vaguely familiar. "Why?" I say.

"I don't know." She kicks a stone along the dry riverbed, and runs after it, kicking it again. I hurry to catch up. She says, "Mummy says sometimes people fall in love and then fall out of love again later. She says it wasn't really anyone's fault."

"Do you think that?"

"No," she says. "I think it was his fault."

"Your dad?"

"No," she says, impatiently. "*Him.*" She pauses. "I call him dad, now," she adds, rather distantly. "But he's not really."

"Do you like him?"

"No. He doesn't like me."

"Is he nasty to you?"

She thinks about that, and for a moment her face alters as if she's preparing to tell me some great story of how cruel he is. But then she shrugs. "Not really. He just doesn't talk to me a lot. I think he's boring."

"What happened to your real dad, then?"

"He went away," she says. "He writes to me, though. He's gone back home."

"Where's that?"

"Hungary." She catches my blank look. "It's another country," she says. "It's where he used to live. We all used to live there once, and then we came here when I was very small. I don't really remember. Mummy says it was the best thing we ever did, but I don't really know."

"We used to live in England," I say.

"I know." We walk on in silence for a while, and then Anna says, "Do you like your parents?"

This is another question I've never considered. These past few weeks have thrown up a whole lot of questions like that. I say, "I suppose."

"Do you think Jamie likes his?"

"I think so," I say. Jamie and I never talk about our parents. It seems a strange thing to talk about; when we are together, there's so much else to do.

"I think parents are crap," she says. "I think we should go off and live together somewhere."

"Really? Where?"

"I don't know. In a house of our own somewhere."

"They don't give houses to kids," I say.

"Well, in a cave then. Or build a treehouse like Jamie said. Just the three of us. I don't see why we have to have parents."

"Who'd cook meals for us?" I say, a little worried by Anna's angry enthusiasm for the idea.

"We could cook. It's not difficult, is it?"

"And who'd give us pocket money to buy food with?" I say.

Anna says, "Oh, shut up, Alex."

"Why?" I say, hurt.

"I didn't *mean* it. Of course we can't go and live together. It was just an idea, that's all." She adds, "I was just playing a trick on you."

"It wasn't a funny trick," I say.

"Well, I thought it was."

We continue for a while without talking, Anna a little way ahead of me, kicking stones and sticks and whatever else she sees. I trail along behind her, wondering why she's suddenly so cross.

Then she starts to talk. She doesn't look round, and for a moment it looks as if she's talking to herself, though she knows of course that I'm there. She says, "Grown-ups always pretend like they're in charge of everything. We always have to do what they say, we can't do what we want. And they're always the strong ones, and we're not." She pauses. I can't see where she's going with this, so I keep quiet. She says, "But they're not really strong, are they? I mean, the hermit's a grown-up but he needs our help. We have to help him or he'll die. If we don't help him, he won't get well. He can't even pee unless we help him. We're kids and he's a grown-up but he'd have peed in his pants unless we helped him."

I don't like the way her voice has gone; it's thoughtful, but strangely cold, too. I say, "But he's hurt."

"I know," Anna says.

"Well, if you were hurt, you'd need people to help you, too."

"Mm," she says, but she doesn't sound to me as if what I've said makes much difference to her. After a while she says, "I mean, we've even got a gun."

"So?"

"So—so if anyone we don't like comes we can point the gun at them and they'd have to go away, or we'd shoot them."

I'm not sure what she means. After a second, it occurs to me that she may still be talking about the house where she and Jamie and I are going to live. I say, "But we don't know how to use the gun."

"We could work it out. I bet it isn't that hard. I bet I could do it, if I tried."

I'm even more worried to discover that I believe this. Somehow, having the gun—which before had been a reassuring thing—is now less reassuring. It's almost threatening. The way Anna is talking isn't the way she usually talks. It's like she's not the same Anna any more, as if something's changed in her.

She looks round, and her pace falters. "Hey," she says. "It's OK. I was just thinking." Then she stops. "Hey, Alex. Don't cry. It's all right— I was only kidding you. We won't really put the gun together."

"I'm not crying," I say, rubbing my face. "I got—I got dust in my eye."

"Oh. Let me see." She holds my chin and tilts my head back a little. "It's a bit red," she says critically. "Does it feel better now?"

"Mm," I say.

"OK." She looks at me, genuine concern in her face. "You sure?" she says.

"Yeah," I say. "Thanks."

She stares for a moment longer, and then leans in quickly and kisses the end of my nose. I blink, surprised and strangely pleased. "There," she says. Then, "Come on. We should keep going."

"Yeah," I say. "I'm hungry."

"I know. Me too. And I feel a bit weird. I think it's getting up every hour. We need more sleep than this, I think."

"Yeah," I say. "But we have to look out for each other."

She smiles. "That's right. That's what we have to do."

"So the one in the chapel isn't really alone," I say.

"Yeah. I know. Well, that's how we'll keep doing it for now, anyway."

"Good," I say.

It's late now, and the band—who are not the same band as were playing at the start of the evening—shift from the jauntier numbers to mellower, more atmospheric pieces. The mood alters subtly, and there are more people staring at the musicians now than before; the conversation has dropped away a little, and a kind of pleasant tiredness and slight melancholy has come over the bar. Anna pushes her beer an inch or so across the table with one finger, and gets up.

"Where are you going?" I say.

"Loo. Back in a bit." She takes her bag from the back of the chair and eases her way through the crowd towards the band. I watch her go, and can feel myself smiling, just from watching her.

One or two people are still coming in to join the crowd. No-one much seems to be leaving. The bar is packed close.

"And some plasters, please," Anna says, handing over the last of our money. We put the roll of bandage and the pack of plasters in the bag and leave casually, two children on an errand from their parents. Anna is good at looking relaxed and casual; better than I am. I think how clever she is to be able to fool people like this.

She pushes her way back through the crowd. "God. The whole place is heaving," she says. She looks a little breathless, her face slightly flushed. She glances at the table. "You got more beer?"

"I thought it might be a good idea," I say.

"Oh. Right." She slips into her chair and slings the bag on the floor. "So. Where were we?"

"Swimming races," I say with a grin.

"Yes. That's it."

"You used to swear terribly when you lost, too."

"Still do," she says. She takes a long drink of the beer and wipes her mouth.

"I used to think that was pretty cool."

"Really?" She seems pleased at this.

"Well, I used to think a lot of what you did was pretty cool."

"Cheers," she says. "I don't get called cool often enough."

"No? I bet you do really."

She shrugs. "I don't think the kind of people who do political theory think of each other as potentially cool," she says, smiling slightly.

"You said you'd tell me all about that some time," I say. "You know—the thesis and so on."

"Yeah, sure. Some time."

"How about now?"

She puts her drink down and hesitates for a second. Then she says, "You know, perhaps we ought to go."

"It's not so late," I say. "We could stay for a few more songs."

"Yeah, but—" She glances across the room at the band. "I don't like this stuff so much. It's a bit sad, don't you think?"

"A little," I say. "But they're playing really well. Compromise. Let's finish our drinks first."

She grins and grabs her glass and downs it. "There," she says. "Come on."

"What is it, Anna?" I say. She looks edgy, excited. Her eyes are gleaming.

"Nothing. I'm just bored."

"I've heard that somewhere before," I say, laughing. "You always—"

"Alex," she says, and something in the way she speaks stops me dead. She puts her elbows on the table and makes a little platform with her hands to rest her chin on.

"What?"

"I really think we ought to go."

I blink. "All right. Why?"

She takes a breath. "Look—what you were saying before—"

I interrupt her. "I'm sorry. I shouldn't have—"

"No," she says. "You were right."

I stare at her. No words come.

She says, "You were right. I think part of me's been—waiting, for it. All this time. I think that's why I—did what I did, when we were here last. It just took me until now to realize."

She leans across the table and kisses me on the mouth. It's only the second time she's ever done that. There is the barest touch of her tongue against my lips and then she breaks away, keeping close but not kissing me any more. Her eyes are dark now, this close. She says, "I think we should go and fuck now."

I can't think of a thing to say. I nod dumbly.

She reaches behind her and picks up her bag, all the while looking at me. When we push our chairs back and get up, another couple are quick to move in to take them.

"Here," the young man says. "You've left your beer."

"It's OK," I say. Anna is leading the way through to the exit, and her hand has found mine and is pulling me after her. The young man must see something in my face, because suddenly he grins broadly.

"OK," he calls after me.

I turn to follow Anna. The room seems hazy, the music and the people all out of focus. For a second, I think I catch a glimpse of the woman I've seen before, in among the press of people, but I can't be sure.

The air outside feels cold as water, and clean. I pull Anna against the side of a closed-up newspaper kiosk and kiss her again. Each touch of our mouths feels like a jolt of some kind of drug, as though we are feeding off each other. She has her hands round my shoulders; my hands are in her hair and then on her breasts.

"God, yes," she says.

I go to kiss her again, but she pulls away fractionally.

"What?"

"Let's get back to the hotel," she says; and then puts her chin on my shoulder quickly. I feel the heat of her breath against my ear as she whispers, "I want you inside me. Come on."

We stumble along the street, arms round each other. At the junction with the next road there is a taxi rank and we get into a cab, clutching each other as we tell the driver where to go, and giggling like children.

*   *   *

Her head strains back into the pillow and she gasps out a kind of stran-gled, inarticulate cry. I feel her body clench for a second, and then she shudders and her muscles relax. There is a long silence broken only by the gradually less laboured sounds of our breathing. I can feel my heart thudding almost painfully in me, but slowly that too starts to be less in-sistent. One of Anna's hands stirs on the pillow, and then with a slight, heavy clumsiness, reaches for my hair. She strokes my head very slowly.

Outside, car horns and the waspish sound of mopeds signal that the city is still there. The window stands wide, and I wonder briefly what people passing by have heard.

"Oh, God," Anna says. "God."

She stirs under me and I move off her. She sits up and swings her legs off the bed.

She says, "I wasn't expecting that. It isn't usually that good the first time."

The easy comparison with other times shocks me for a moment, and I feel a twinge of something—regret, perhaps. Of course there have been others. I try to ignore it.

She says, "Well? What do you think?"

"I don't think I can think any more," I say. "Think about what?"

She gets up and stands in front of me naked, hands by her sides, not posing, just standing there. She says, "This."

I haven't really had the chance to see her. The only light in the room has been from the streetlights outside. I've touched her—felt her skin and her hair—but I've only glimpsed her body. The curve of one shoul-der, her belly, her hands, her breasts. I look at her.

"Good," I say.

"So you think tits are an improvement?"

"Definitely. I always thought that, though."

"Good," she says. "Just checking."

She goes over to the window and looks out. I say, "Careful. Someone might see you."

"Yeah, I know," she says. She doesn't move, though; she stands there with the balance of weight on one foot and one hand on the edge of the wooden shutter. The light from the street casts a narrow line of colour down her side, showing the curve of one breast, one hip, and the under-side of her arm, orange against the shadow that is the rest of her. The windows are tall, the windowsills low down, at thigh height. She says, "Don't you like that, though? I do. Like maybe someone I'll never meet and never know can see all of me right now, all my body, just for a moment. And they'll never know who I am, either."

I laugh. "You haven't changed," I say.

She is quiet for a moment, and then she pulls the shutter across. The bars of shadow fold around her body. When she turns back towards me, I can't see her face properly any longer. She says, "I'm going to have a shower."

The sound of running water from the next room beats a faint rhythm through the wall. On the bed, I drift gently between dozing and wakefulness, my mind stirring itself every so often to wonder at Anna—the smell of her, how she feels against me, the urgency and eagerness of the way she moves, the sound of her breathing.

Once in a while, as I drift, other thoughts fade through the haze of images and tastes and sounds, but they have nothing of the drug-like wonder of these thoughts of Anna. I push them aside, and they go easily enough. Instead I wonder whether, when Anna comes back, we can perhaps make love a second time; and it is as I begin to think that we will that I fall finally asleep.

15

*S*unshine is breaking through a crack in the shutters when I wake. For a while I just lie in bed, drowsily remembering last night. Anna, when I turn to look, is still fast asleep, her outline under the sheet breathing slowly and deeply.

I get up and go to the window. It's earlier than I expect, and the little grocery at the corner of the square is still setting out its merchandise on the pavement. I look at Anna's face as she lies sleeping, and can't bring myself to wake her. I decide instead to find breakfast and bring it back, to surprise her with croissants and fruit juice and stuff in an hour or so. I get dressed as quietly as I can, and do my teeth and wash my face with the water running slowly into the basin, and close the door of our room carefully and silently behind me.

Spring has reached Florence fully, and the air is warm and clear. In the street I buy myself a plastic cup of coffee and sip it as I walk. For some reason I can't bring myself to sit down indoors and drink a proper cupful; I feel I need to keep moving. The slow beat of my footsteps on the pavements and cobbles is pleasant, and I am looking at the city as if I haven't seen it before: details keep catching my eye, and more than once I see something which I would like to return to, later, to sketch. Faintly I realize that it's the same city, and that it is I who have changed; but the sense is pervasive.

Perhaps this is what I was anticipating when the city seemed to move.

How did it happen? I keep thinking. There was a moment, out in the street, when I was sure it was impossible. She sounded like she had never even considered this. Then—in the club—the moment when she tells me she's always wanted it. It's amazing—unbelievable.

Something else. There's something I can say, now. I can say it in my head—even say it aloud. I love her. I've always loved her. I can admit it now, and it's OK, because I know at last that she loves me as well.

I won't let anything go wrong this time. It's a second chance: I have to get it right.

Anna often reads a paper in the morning, I've noticed; it's something that strikes me as odd, at first, a habit too serious and sedentary for my Anna. But when I think it through I realize she must need to keep in touch with world events, for her thesis and so on. A pleasant idea comes to me: I shall buy her a morning paper, and buy it from the one newspaper kiosk which now holds more significance for us than any other in Florence. It's an utterly foolish notion; the kiosk and the jazz bar are a good half an hour out of my way. But it's still early, and I feel like walking; and so I start to retrace our journey of the night before, heading up towards the university quarter.

As I go, thoughts of Anna drift in and out of my head. Still it seems incredible to me what has happened to us. Once or twice, it seems more like a dream than something real, as though I might go back to the hotel to find that Anna doesn't know what I'm talking about, that—worse— she might laugh at me.

Oh, she says, laughter in her voice. *That kind of dream. A sex dream. Was it like that?*

Then I smile to myself, because I know really that it *did* happen— that at last, it did happen.

I wonder what we will do now; how this will change things.

I wonder where we will be in five years' time; in ten. It feels like anything could happen now. I think back over the years when we've been apart, when we've—drifted, and realize that they're over now.

Whatever happens, we'll never let those kind of distances get between us again.

I suddenly regret having waited so long. Perhaps, if I'd said something before—

But at least everything's all right now.

I round the corner into the street where the club is, and I'm looking towards where the news kiosk is, so it takes me a moment to realize that something is going on. There is a fluttering line of tape across the road, green and white, further down beyond the kiosk; and some police cars lined up against the kerb. A handful of people are standing about, watching something. Curious, I quicken my pace, and the tune I've been whistling slips my mind.

At the kiosk I hand over money for the paper and nod down the street.

"What's going on down there?"

"Bomb," the man says. "They're still clearing up. No-one's allowed past the lines until they know what happened."

"A bomb?" I say. "Where?"

"A club," the man says. "In the basement there, so there's not a lot to see in the street."

"The jazz bar?" I say, feeling suddenly hollow.

"Yes. You know it? Blew the whole place apart. Everywhere's crawling with police." He shakes his head, warming to the story. "It happened last night. Everyone in the street heard it, they were all out here. There was a fire, too."

I can see a blackened smudge of soot across the buildings further down the street. I say, "Were—was anyone hurt?"

He nods. "Eight people killed, and a lot more injured."

"Christ," I say.

"You all right?" the man says; then, "Hey. You don't look well. What is it?"

"I was there last night," I say, the words sounding as if they're coming from a long way away. "I mean—I was in there. I went there."

"Hey, calm down," the man says. "You look sick. At least you weren't there when it happened." A shadow of worry crosses his face. "You had friends in there? You should talk to the police, they know the names, I think. Is that it? You had friends in there?"

"No," I say. "It's OK. It's nothing."

"Well, you still look sick."

"It's OK," I say. "I'm fine."

"If you were there last night, that was a close escape," the man says. "I think I'd look sick too."

"Yeah," I say, not really hearing. I grip the newspaper in fingers that feel numb, and start down the street towards the police cars and the tapes.

The steps leading down to the bar are black with smoke and slick with water. Standing by the tapes I can see across the cordoned-off area to a fire truck on the other side. There are policemen and firemen standing about in huddles. In the street, apart from the water from the hoses, there is little to see. There are some glittering fragments of glass, but nothing else. There are no ambulances, and I realize that they must have been and gone long before I arrived.

"Hey," I call to one of the cops. He turns and sees me, but goes back to talking to his companion. "Hey," I call again. "What happened?"

He finishes talking, and comes over. "Explosion," he says.

"The man back there said it was a bomb."

"It might have been gas," he says. "We'll know more later. You should move on now."

"Was anyone hurt?"

"Yes," he says shortly. "Eight people killed. Maybe more by now. Some of the ones they took off to hospital looked pretty bad."

"Why?" I say. I don't mean to say it; it's almost as if I'm thinking aloud.

"You think the people who do this kind of thing need reasons?" he says. Then he hesitates, as if hearing how the words have sounded. "Well," he says. "It could have been gas. You should move on now."

"Yes," I say. "Yes, of course."

My feet carry me slowly back down the street, but the rhythm of my footsteps seems sprained, disjointed, as if some mechanism has broken. I am still holding the newspaper. I think, *Thank God. Thank God it didn't all—end there.*

Into my head from nowhere comes a dark night, rain hammering down, and her hand slipping out of mine—Anna falling backwards away from me, swept suddenly into darkness. I can't let it happen again.

Suddenly I am desperate to get back to her, to make sure she's really safe, to hold her, to hear her voice. Everything seems fragile, as if it could crack. I need to touch her, to make sure she's still there.

The disturbed nights are starting to tell on us all. Jamie has dark patches under his eyes and I find it more and more difficult to get up for breakfast. But we have to get up, so as not to look suspicious; and we have to keep waking up on the hour, every hour, because none of us wants to be the one alone in the chapel, with no reassurance that friends are thinking of them at the other end of the valley. Still, when the alarm clock goes to start me on my shift, it is achingly hard to drag my legs out of the cosy comfort of my bed, and pull on my clothes over my pyjamas. I have stopped bothering about getting properly dressed; it's easier this way to get back into bed once it's over for the night.

It is Anna's shift at the moment. I trudge up the valley, my feet walking in a mass of footprints left over the many days we've all made this journey now. The dry dust of the riverbed is still smooth and un-broken in some places, towards the edge; but we've kicked and scuffed and trodden in it all down the middle, wearing a band of darker, less crystalline colour through the soft red. In the starlight, of course, it's just another shade of silver-grey. Jamie reads that the colours don't go at night; it's just that our eyes can't see them any more. He tells me about it one afternoon when we are in his bedroom and Anna is keeping watch in the chapel; one of the few moments of normality we manage to snatch in the middle of all the pretending and planning and running and keeping watch that have to be juggled for the hermit's safety. Nor-mally I am fascinated by anything Jamie tells me, but this time, I am just too tired. My concentration wanders and my mind drifts away from Jamie's voice and before I know it I am asleep. Jamie has to wake me up. He looks almost guilty about doing it, as though he knows how I feel and would perhaps secretly like to join me; but we've promised Anna that we'll go back and join her by the end of the afternoon. I realize with astonishment that I have slept two hours away.

It has got so that I know the route of the journey perfectly in my head. I recognize particular bushes, particular shapes in the dusty sand, particular trees against the silhouettes of the hills. I can keep a good track of where I am, how much further there is to go. I play little games in my head: when I reach the tree that looks like an old man, I am halfway there. Then it's half the remaining distance to the flat stone low in under the bank. Then it's about half what's left to the bush which has night flowers that smell dully sweet in the late evenings. Half again to a little scatter of bones, some animal killed by a fox, or perhaps drowned when there really was a river here. Then halfway again . . .

I reach the chapel. We have worn a little way through the weeds up to the fence. In all the time we have been coming to the chapel, I have never seen anyone else near it, so the fact that we're leaving signs of our coming and going doesn't really worry me. The air cools and smells a little bit tangy as I pass under the stone pines; and then, at the end of the chapel, right under the dandelion clock, I stop, because I can hear something strange.

Very faintly, there is the sound of singing: a clear, high voice weaving through a strange, rather mournful tune. It's so quiet that I shake my head to see if I'm imagining it; but it's still there a moment later. Very slowly, I walk forward, to see if I can hear better. By the big double-doors of the chapel I stop again, and turn my head this way and that to catch the sound. I stare around the empty churchyard for the owner of the voice, but the place is deserted.

Then it comes to me that the singing is coming from inside the chapel. I step in nearer the door, and sure enough, the faint sound becomes fractionally clearer. I frown as I realize that it must be Anna singing. I've never heard her sing before. Her voice is sure, and in the still night air it sounds haunting and beautiful. But what makes me frown is that, though I can hear her properly now, I can't understand what she's saying. The words of the song make no sense.

I've heard something like this before.

Slowly, like the way sunlight fades out of a room when a cloud goes over the sky, a kind of coldness comes over me. I have the sense that I am on the edge of something I don't properly understand, that there is something here I must remember but mustn't mention. It isn't frightening; it is just—something.

The voice moves through the music, up and down through the phrases, but the words—the words are like the sound of water through gravel. Anna's voice changes with them, and it is unfamiliar, Anna's voice but also not Anna's voice.

Something clicks together in my head, a connection: this is like the moment when I see her poised on the lip of rock high up in the shadow of the cliff. They're the same thing. I shouldn't have seen that, and I shouldn't have heard this. They aren't supposed to be for me.

I'm not sure what to do, so I wait by the doors. It hasn't occurred to me before that, when one is outside the chapel and down at this end, the hermit's bed is of course only a couple of yards away through the arch here. Because the doors won't open, and we always go to the far end of the chapel, we have almost forgotten how the inside corresponds to the outside.

I wonder suddenly if I can see inside.

People are supposed to look through keyholes, but most of the keyholes I have ever tried to look through have been blocked up with stuff, and no use at all. I kneel down, making sure to let my knees down gently into the pine needles, and lean forward. I don't touch the doors. In the wind, they move and creak a bit, and they would do that if I touched them, I'm sure.

Anna's voice comes cleanly through the keyhole, but I can't see anything much. There is a dim, uncertain glow, but the angle or something is wrong for me to see the hermit.

There are cracks in the door, though. I try them one at a time, putting my eye up close to each one. And I find one that works.

There is a candle burning. We are all being careful to obey Jamie's injunction about wasting candles, and we only ever have one alight at a time. Sometimes they blow out, if there is a sudden gust of wind under the door, but that doesn't happen very often and the torch is always nearby. Even so, it can be a breathless few seconds before the torch is on and you can see again.

The hermit looks as if he's asleep. Anna is sitting by his head, holding him. She has a torn piece of sheet dampened with water, and she's holding it to the hermit's forehead. Although the candlelight is flickery and I can't see the hermit all that well, his face looks beaded with sweat. Anna's head is bent down, looking at him, and again I think of the *pietà*, the body brought down and cradled in the woman's arms. And all the while, Anna's voice lifts very softly in music I don't know and words I can't understand.

She's singing so quietly that it is only because I have passed so close to the doors here that I have heard. I wonder to myself if I would ever have known, if I had been a few yards further away from the building; if I had gone down to the far door and opened it. The door there makes noise coming open; she would have heard me, and I am sure she would have stopped. So I would never have known—just as if I had gone on into town that afternoon without making the connection about Anna's watch, I should never have known about her dive from the cliff.

I suddenly wonder how many other things there are about Anna that I don't know because I haven't happened to be in the right place, unnoticed.

I swallow, and then get up from my crouch. I walk briskly round the end of the chapel and down the side, kicking my heels through the grit to make sound. When I reach the door, I fumble the catch, rattle it a little as I pull it open. The sound clatters and echoes in the air of the chapel. When I step inside, the only sound is the last fading hiss of echoes from my own entrance. There is nothing of any voice, or any music. As I walk down the length of the building, Anna stands up from where she's been sitting, and comes to meet me.

A kind of deep, incipient tiredness has taken the edge of excitement from these night-time meetings, and Anna and I spend little time in conversation before she leaves. Looking after the hermit is becoming a routine: a routine that leaves us only half awake for most of the day. Anna looks eager to get back to her bed.

Once I've seen her safely round the end of the chapel, I go past the hermit, whose face twitches slightly in his sleep, and up the little twisting staircase and along the organ balcony and up the wooden ladder to the bell platform, and watch Anna out of sight through one of the windows there. I can make out her small shape mainly by its pale shirt; her jeans are too dark to show up well against the weeds and bushes. She scrambles through the undergrowth down to the riverbed, and is gone.

I stand in the belltower and look out at the night for a long time, caught by the silence. The night seems to have wrapped itself around the tower, and everything is very still and very calm. The sea, far away down the valley, is dark, and I can't see the horizon.

I shake myself, and bend to the gun case. I fiddle the clasps open and lift the lid carefully on the smooth, organic shapes of the rifle. The six little sockets are there, three empty, three filled. With my fingertip I pry each of the remaining bullets free of its resting place, putting them with exaggerated caution to one side. I have no idea how easy it might be to set a bullet off; if maybe dropping them or jogging them harshly or even letting them clink against one another might be enough. But I have to do this.

When they're all out, I close up the gun case again and put it against the wall. The bullets I wrap up in my hanky and slip slowly and steadily into my trouser pocket. Then I take the torch, and make my way back down from the belltower, and into the chapel—where the hermit is asleep, but still moving occasionally in his sleep—and out into the night.

The night-time air is faintly redolent of the scent of the pines. I have a place in mind which I have found during the day, soon after deciding to do this. It is on the side of the chapel which we approach from the river, but where there is no door. Towards the altar end of the building, the bushes start up more and more thickly, and it is difficult to get round under the great boarded-up stained-glass window for all the thorns and foliage. In the thick of this tangle of undergrowth I have found a hiding place for the hermit's bullets: low down in the wall of the chapel is an iron grating which has come loose, and there is a space behind it. I have worked out that it must be to let air into the chapel somehow. Whatever its purpose, it is a good place, and after I've put the grating back in place and scuffed some dirt and pine needles up around it, you would never notice it. Certainly you would never guess there were three rifle bullets nestling together just behind it.

At last I feel satisfied, as if I can relax. Now no-one can put the gun together, and no-one can get shot.

I have to look after the hermit now. I get up, and look around me at the night-time valley, and think of the hermit's face twisting in the dancing candlelight, and wish I didn't have to go back in. But it's what has to be done.

The hermit is dreaming. His eyelids tremble and his head sometimes jerks, as if he's suddenly heard a sharp noise in the silence of the chapel. Once or twice, his right hand, which is lying out from his side on the boards of the chapel floor, clenches and drags a little against the wood.

I sit watching. I have the cloth in my hand, the torn piece of sheet which we keep cold with water and use to mop the hermit's face and neck. The little pocket of air here at the back of the chapel is, I believe, warmed by the hermit's fever, so that the occasional draughts which come in under the double-doors feel cold on my skin.

The hermit's eyes flicker open for a moment, and he looks around himself, uncomprehending. Then they fall closed, and he returns to his twitching, febrile sleep.

I pat the folded cloth gently across his face and neck, as Anna has shown me. I know from when we have changed the dressing that the hermit's leg is no longer bleeding, but if anything it looks worse than when it was; the holes are puckered up, but the skin around them is mottled and taut with swelling, and the bandages which we remove and bury under rocks by the river-bank are stained with discharge.

The hermit's eyes open again, but they are rolled up towards the chapel roof and he doesn't see me. His mouth opens and I strain to catch the words.

"*Vizet.*"

It is the fever; I can't understand him. But then his eyes dart towards the bottle by my side, and I understand. I lift it carefully to his mouth and he drinks until the water spills down his chin and onto his shirt front. I lift the bottle away. After a moment, the hermit says something else; but again, it makes no sense.

I shake my head to show him that I don't understand, but he hardly seems to see me. His eyes move uncertainly around the chapel and then fix on something, and widen. Instinctively I look as well, to see what the hermit has seen; but there is nothing there except the bare wall. Whatever the hermit is seeing, it is in his head.

He's speaking again.

I shiver slightly. The sound of the meaningless words rings through the chapel, and the echoes seem to filter through to the hermit, because his voice stops, and a look of fear crosses his face. He glances this way and that, as if afraid that someone or something will creep up on him if he doesn't keep alert.

"It's all right," I say. "You're safe. You're in the chapel. Remember?"

Slowly, very slowly, as if fighting against some invisible weight, the hermit turns his eyes towards me. His mouth opens and closes twice, but no sound comes out. Then he seems to see me, because he tries to lean forward; but he can't. He falls back against the pillow and gasps.

"*Istenem!*"

It must be a curse of some kind. "It's me," I say. "Alex. Do you remember?"

The hermit flinches briefly, and then his eyes seem to find me.

"*Árpád?*"

It sounds like it might be someone's name. I say, "No—Alex. You remember me. We're helping you." The hermit doesn't look like he understands, so I add, "You hurt your leg."

There are more meaningless words. I shrug helplessly.

"I don't understand," I say. "You need to talk properly."

The hermit's eyes wander away from me and his head drops back; his breath sounds thick and painful in his throat.

"*Vizet.*"

I know that one now: *water.* I hold the bottle for him to drink a second time. When he's done, I dampen the cloth again and press it to his forehead. His eyes close and his breathing slackens and he is asleep again.

I watch him as he sleeps. Shadows lick around his face as the candle flame stirs, but he seems to be resting more easily. I wonder what has been coming and going in the hermit's dreams, and what he has seen on the chapel wall.

We wait together for the night to pass.

In the third hour of my shift, the hermit opens his eyes again. He looks around him for a moment, and then he sees me. A faint attempt at a smile touches his mouth. He says, "Alex."

He knows who I am for the first time tonight. I say, quietly, "Hello. How are you?"

"Thirsty," he says. He's shivering slightly, as if he's cold; but I know from the sweat on his skin and the heat coming off him that he can't be.

I say, "Here," and I offer him the bottle. He tries to lift it himself, but I have to help him. He drinks, swallowing rapidly, and almost half what's left in the bottle disappears down his throat. At last he signals that he's had enough.

"That's good," he gasps when I take the bottle away.

"Are you feeling better?" I say, cautiously.

"I don't know. I'm tired." He seems to be thinking for a moment. "How long have I been here now?"

"Three days, I think," I say.

"God."

"Maybe you're getting better now."

He tries to smile again. "Maybe I am."

I pat the cloth on his head and he closes his eyes. His face looks much calmer than before. I say, "You should try to sleep. Anna says sleep's good for you."

"Ah," he says, with his eyes closed. "Well, if Anna says it, it must be true, no?"

I'm surprised at how well he seems to understand what I'm saying. He hasn't been like this for a long time. I say, "I suppose."

"Yes," the hermit says, and his voice is quieter, fading. "I'll sleep. I'll sleep, little Alex."

A moment later his breathing slows, and his head turns a little to one side, and he is asleep.

I watch him. His eyes aren't trembling and darting behind the closed lids, as they have been, and the small shivers I've seen a moment before seem to have ceased. His breathing is slow, and deep, and regular, in and out, in and out. I keep watching him, and his sleep seems to be sound and undisturbed. The dreams have finished, then.

I leave him to signal on the hour, and when I come down from the belltower he has turned slightly, and brought his hand up against his face, but he is still sleeping as deeply as before. His breathing sounds easy for the first time since I've known him: no longer gasping, or shallow, or strangely quick, or strained in his throat. It's peaceful breathing, like Jamie's breathing when he has fallen asleep in the shade of the garden after lunch. It doesn't sound like the hermit's sick any more.

I wait, and watch, to be certain that nothing bad suddenly happens, and the hour wears round.

Jamie says, "You're right. He's not as hot, either."

He takes his hand from the hermit's forehead and sits back on his haunches. I say, "He's been like that all the last hour. It was really strange. Like one moment he was all strange and talking—weirdly. And then he went quiet for a bit. And then he woke up, and wanted water, and he wasn't strange any more. And then he went to sleep, really heavily, like he is now."

"Maybe he is getting better, then," Jamie says.

Early sunlight is filtering through the stained-glass window, and the gloom in the chapel is lifted. We kneel around the hermit in a semicircle, watching him sleep. At last, Anna nods.

"Yeah. I think you're right. It's weird. When I left he was worse than ever, and now—well." She rubs one hand over her face and through her hair, which looks tousled, as though she may have dozed off against the chapel wall. Jamie doesn't look much better. I stifle a yawn, and find myself envying the hermit his deep, unbroken sleep.

We trail outside into the bright air. Jamie sits himself on a big piece of timber, like a railway sleeper, and Anna lies down in the sun beside him, resting her head against the wood by his knee. I walk slowly round them, setting my feet very carefully one in front of the other, as if I'm on a tightrope.

Jamie says, "What do we do now?"

"How do you mean?"

"If he gets better, I mean. What do we—do with him?"

Anna's eyes are closed. "We'll see. I don't know yet. But—something."

I say, rather dreamily, "Perhaps we can take him to the beach. To go swimming."

Jamie looks at me, and after a second he bursts out laughing. In the dust, I can hear Anna snort loudly and start to laugh as well.

"What?" I say. "What is it?"

"I think we should take him home for dinner," Jamie says. "Proper dinner. To meet—to meet our parents." He hiccups and laughs again. "Good one, Alex."

Reluctantly, I grin, too. Anna, her eyes still closed, says, "Yeah. We can introduce him to all our friends."

Jamie says, "Can you imagine my father? 'Pleased to meet you. What do you *do*, exactly?' "

It's a good imitation. Anna says, pitching her voice low and gruff like the hermit's, " 'I kill people.' "

" 'Oh jolly good,' " Jamie says. " 'Have some more—some more wine.' " He hiccups again, and puts his hand over his mouth, still laughing.

"Well, I don't know what else we're going to do with him," I say, a little put out that they find me funny. "He can't stay in the chapel for ever."

"Well, we'll think about that later," Anna says.

"Yeah," Jamie agrees. "Not now. Don't make me think now. My head's all tight, like it's full up."

"I'm so tired," Anna murmurs quietly. "I just want to curl up and sleep for ever."

"I know."

"We should check on him," she says, muzzily. "Every now and again someone go check on him."

"How often?" I say. "I can do it. I've got a watch."

I wait for her reply, but it doesn't come. Jamie and I look down at her. She is fast asleep.

"She shouldn't sleep in the sun," I say critically. "Lena says it's bad."

"Why?"

"I don't know. That's what Lena says."

"It's not so hot," Jamie says. "Let's leave her a while. We can wake her up when it gets warmer." He stands up, stretching. "I know how she feels," he says.

"Yeah. Me too."

"You want to go and look for lizards?"

"OK," I say. "If we can lie down."

"You're on."

We wander away from where Anna lies sleeping, wrapped in a haze of soft dust and the shrill background buzz of the cicadas.

When I wake up, the sun is high in the sky. Jamie is nowhere to be seen. Groggily, I get up from where I've been lying in the warm dust and rub my eyes before heading over to where Anna's lying.

As I get close to her, I notice a faint but unfamiliar sound. It takes me only a moment or two to work out what it is. A big grin breaks over my face. Then I hear footsteps, and Jamie is running towards me from the chapel.

"Ssh," I say. "Listen. She's snoring."

Jamie stops dead, his face blank; then he hears it, too, and grins with me. "Yeah," he says quietly. We listen to Anna snore for a few more moments, and then Jamie snaps his fingers as if suddenly remembering something. "He's awake," he says.

"Oh," I say. "We should wake her, then."

Jamie leans down and touches Anna's shoulder. When she doesn't move, he shakes her slightly. She snorts and looks up. "What?"

"He's awake," Jamie says.

She scrambles at once to her feet, shaking her head. "How long have I been there?" she says.

"A couple of hours," Jamie says. "Well, more like three, actually. It's OK. I kept checking on him."

"I fell asleep, too," I confess.

"Yeah. Alex was face-down in the pine needles ten minutes after we left you," Jamie says, grinning.

"How is he?" Anna says. I know she means the hermit, not me.

"Well, he's—I think he's better," Jamie says. "I mean, he still looks ill, but—well, come and see for yourself."

We hurry into the chapel, blinking away the hazy after-images that linger from the bright daylight outside; once we can see adequately in the half-light, we follow Jamie down the building to where the hermit is lying.

He looks at us all, and his eyes are clear, seeing what is really around him. For a moment, I see him as he is when we first find him; the face shifts and then shifts back again, and I realize that the hermit looks a lot thinner than he did. But at the same time, I can see that Jamie is right: he also looks far better than he did the night before. Anna kneels down by the hermit's torso and touches the back of her hand to his head, frowning.

"Well?" the hermit says. Anna is startled, a little, by the voice, and flinches for a second. Then she puts her hand back again, checking.

"You're back to normal," she says.

"Completely?" Jamie asks.

"Come here," Anna says. Jamie crouches beside her and she takes her hand from the hermit's head and touches it to Jamie's. "You try," she says.

Jamie touches the hermit, and then Anna. He nods. "Yeah, I can't tell the difference."

"Can I try?" I say, not wanting to be left out.

"OK."

I come in close and touch first the hermit, then Jamie, then Anna. I frown, as if considering my response carefully, and then nod. "Yeah. They're the same."

The hermit is looking at us, his expression rather mixed-up and strange. For a moment he looks like he might be trying not to laugh, but since there's nothing funny to laugh at, I can't think that this is really the case.

Anna says, "How do you feel?"

"Better," the man says. "And hungry."

"That must be good," Anna says, glancing at Jamie and me.

The hermit says, "I think it is. The fever's broken. How long—"

He's asked this before. "Four days, now," Anna says.

"Four days," the hermit repeats. He sounds dazed. "Four days."

"It's OK," Anna says softly. "You're safe here. We haven't told any-one, and no-one knows."

"That's good," the hermit says, after the briefest of pauses.

"If we got you some food," Anna says, "do you think you could eat it?"

The hermit nods. "Yes. Something simple, like bread. I shall have to be careful for a while."

"OK. We can get that now, if you like."

"I think—yes. That would be good."

"Then we can talk," Anna says.

The hermit nods. "Very well."

Anna says, "We hid your car."

The hermit's brow tightens. "How?"

"With branches," I say. "So you can't see it from the road."

The hermit looks as if he's trying to puzzle something out. "Why did you do that?" he says at last.

Anna says, "In case people came looking. Probably they won't, but we wanted to be sure."

The hermit looks at each of us in turn, searching our faces with his eyes. Finally he says, "Ah. Well. You've—you seem to have thought of everything."

"You're safe here," Anna says again. "All right. We'll go and get food and things, and then we'll change your bandage, OK? And then we'll talk."

It's the second time she's said it. I see the hermit staring at her, appraisingly; and I realize all at once that he's probably wondering, as I am, just what it is that Anna wants to talk about so much. But in the end the hermit just nods, and Anna nods back, and then she stands up.

"We'd better go and get food," she says. "How much money do we have?"

"We don't have any," Jamie says. "We'll have to get stuff from the pantry."

"It's OK," I add. "Lena won't mind. Well, not if it's only a little."

But the hermit has been listening, and now he says, "Wait. I have some money, if you need it."

He reaches inside his jacket and, after a second, fumbles out a wallet. From it he takes a slim bundle of notes. "Be careful," he says. "It would look strange if you showed all this money. Use the small bills only, and keep the rest hidden."

"Yes," Anna says, grasping immediately what he means. She takes the money and sorts out a couple of the smaller notes from it, then folds the rest and puts it in the back pocket of her jeans. "We'll be back soon," she tells the hermit.

"Yes," the hermit says. "I know you will."

There's something strange in his voice, something which sounds a bit like amusement and perhaps a bit like admiration; but it's difficult to judge, and besides, Anna is hurrying me out of the chapel now. We close the door on the hermit—who, I remind myself, is better now—and start walking in the hot midday sunshine. And as we walk I find myself wondering vaguely at the way Anna and the hermit look at each other; at the way they seem to be understanding what the other is thinking almost before the words are out. It's a strange thing; but with Anna, many things are strange things, so perhaps this is nothing new.

Anna's face goes white when I tell her. "Are you sure?" she says.

"Yes. Last night, apparently. Right after we were there."

"Shit," she says. She gets up, paces the room. She looks unsteady, shocked, confused—she looks scared.

I say, "Are you OK?"

"Well—I think probably. But I mean—shit." She pauses, runs a hand over her face and into her hair. "Was anyone hurt?"

"Yeah. They were saying eight people died, and lots more were— you know. It was practically a cellar, for God's sake. And you remember how packed it was."

"Eight?" she says, unbelieving. "Christ. That's—that's awful."

"Yeah."

She stops walking, just stands there in her too-big T-shirt, staring at the wall. She looks suddenly vulnerable. I get up, go to her, put my arms around her. She clutches onto me, gripping the back of my shirt with her fists. After a moment, I feel her body shudder against me, and I hear her sobbing hard into my shoulder.

It's shock, I know; but it's also the way I feel. I could have lost her. Another few minutes—God knows what the real timing of it all was, but it could have been just a few minutes—and she might have been gone for ever. Another drink—another song—anything. With a start, I see that if she hadn't realized at that moment how she really felt about me—or if she'd hesitated—we wouldn't have left in time.

But she's here, and alive. I still have her. I hold on tight, not wanting ever to let go again.

16

$\mathcal{S}$omewhere back in London, the gallery doors are open and people are walking in, buying the programmes that Julia Connell has designed, passing through the cool, still air of the rooms and looking at the paintings arrayed there. I suppose, since Julia never got her interview with the artist and her insights into the themes that run through the paintings, that she will have had to come up with something else to fill the pages. And somewhere there will be Max, furious, disbelieving, not knowing how something like this could have happened. I had thought, before, that I would wonder what they all think of the work; would want to know what passes across the faces of the people as they see each image. But instead I find that I don't much care. I am staring at the faces in the paintings, and at the scenes, and over and over again, no matter how much I feel I am becoming inured to it, I am hit by what I've realized: that these are paintings I did not know I had done.

From the beach, the water reflects the spur of rock from which Jamie and I dive, and all you can see on the surface of the water is the shape and colour of the rock; but when you break the surface, everything changes, and the whole of the seabed is laid out below you in that moment. It's something Jamie and I take for granted; just something that happens, along with the sudden breathless cool of the water along your body and the dull underwater rumbling of the splash of the dive.

Here, though, seeing through this surface all at once, I can't bring myself to take it for granted.

I have always had the dream that my whole life may be snatched clean away in one moment, but it has always been a literal vanishing: a waking to realize that things have actually passed. This loss, though, has crept up on me, sneaked past me year by year, my own doing. I haven't painted these pictures; they have been painted *through* me. All along I have been fooled.

I have scraped paint onto canvases, working hard, trying to get some measure of my conviction and vision of how the painting *should be* down there with the pigment, and every time, something else has happened. Every time, the picture has changed, eluded me, and whatever I have been trying to paint has turned inevitably to the same thing. There is not one where it hasn't happened, somehow, in some way. It's in the eyes. The faces are all different, but the eyes are always the same.

The boy is at the edge of the rock, and the whole length of the beach is dark.

It takes me a moment to realize why it is that the little rectangles of the photographs are blurring, their edges trembling and swimming as if seen just under the surface of a rock pool; and then I blink, and rub my eyes.

High over the valley, the sun continues its slow traverse of the sky, and the shadows of the verandah posts crawl barely noticeably across the boards.

"Are you still hungry?" Anna says. "Look, we got you some stuff. Bread and cheese and some patés and things."

She lays the foodstuffs out carefully on a smoothed-out plastic bag by the hermit's side. The man looks at them, and I see a flash of naked hunger cross his face. He nods. "Yes," he says. "Yes, that would be good."

"I'll make you a sandwich," Anna says. She has Jamie's pocket-knife, and she saws off pieces of bread and a slice of cheese and starts to put together food for the hermit. Her movements are casual and she sounds as if she's at ease, but there's a slight vibrancy to everything she does that gives her away. Jamie and I are waiting for her to begin. We've talked it all through, know what has to be said and done, but Anna has to start it all off. Finally, she does. She says, "Where did you say you'd come from?"

"Rome," the hermit says.

"What do you do there?"

"I work in banking, in the city," he says. He looks round at us. "Not very interesting, eh?"

I say, "Rome. That's a long way away, isn't it?"

"Yes," he says. "I suppose it is."

"A long way away," I repeat, looking at Jamie. I can see from his eyes that he understands what I mean.

"Here," Anna says, holding out a crude sandwich to the hermit. He accepts it gratefully, tearing hard at the bread with his teeth. We watch him for a minute or more as he devours the sandwich, and then takes a swig from the water bottle, and at last relaxes.

"That's good," he says.

"You shouldn't have too much at first," Anna says. "Just in case your tummy's not ready for it."

The hermit laughs. "It's certainly a relief to know I'm in such good hands," he says. "You like looking after other people, no?"

Anna looks frankly surprised. She says, "Not really."

The hermit shrugs. "Well, you're doing a good job with me, at least." I think back over the careful cleansing and dressing of the wound, which has taken the full forty minutes before Anna's question about Rome. The hermit's right: we are doing a good job.

Anna leans close to him and holds the cloth against his forehead again. She says, "You shouldn't worry. You're completely safe. No-one knows, and we won't tell anyone. We promise."

"If we'd wanted to tell anyone, we could have done," Jamie says.

"Exactly," Anna says. "That's it exactly. But we haven't, and we're not going to. Do you believe us?"

The hermit looks at her, examining her face. He says, "I suppose I do."

"You trust us, then."

The hermit gives a dry little laugh. "Do I have a choice?"

Anna takes the cloth away, wrings it out, wets it again with fresh water, and applies it again to the hermit's brow. She says, "We just want to—to know things. We want to know what happened, and—and everything. That's all, really."

"You want to know what happened?" the hermit says. "What do you mean?"

"No-one ever tells kids anything," Anna says, but she says it almost to herself. Then she shivers, and when she looks at the hermit she's focused exclusively on him once again. She says, "We want you to tell us about it. What happened and—why it happened, and—well. Everything. I mean, we know some of it already, cos we worked it out, but it can't be *everything*. Only you know that. And you could tell us." She searches the hermit's face for some sign of acquiescence. "We'd never let on to *anybody*. We promise. We swear."

The hermit just looks at her for a long time. Then he says, "Well. I'll try." He shifts position slightly. "You already know how it was night when I was driving. Well, it had been a long day for me, you know? So I was already tired when I started the trip, and I suppose I'd left it too late anyway. I kept nearly dozing off but I didn't want to stop, and I thought I'd be fine if I just kept my concentration. But I suppose it must have been harder than I'd thought—"

We are all staring at him in disbelief. Anna turns once to look at Jamie and me, and her expression is almost comical astonishment. The hermit is still talking when she interrupts him.

"No. What are you doing?"

The hermit breaks off, surprised, I suppose, by her tone of voice. He looks startled and wary.

Anna says, "You *told* us all that shit about your granny and falling asleep. Haven't you been listening? We *know* that's crap. We've known that all along. We want to know what *really* happened. We've trusted you, after all—we've looked after you and made you get better. We won't tell anyone, really. But we want to know all about it."

The hermit's eyes are very narrow now as he looks from one of us to the next. Anna and Jamie and I meet his gaze squarely, though when he looks straight at me I'm glad that the other two are there with me. If I was on my own, I admit, I might be scared by the way the hermit looks right now.

"I fell asleep and my car came off the road," the hermit says steadily.

"Now, I don't know what adventures you've imagined for me, but you have to remember that real life isn't a story, is it? It's usually more boring than that. And this is probably more boring than what you've invented. Now, I'm grateful to you for all you've done for me, but I can't be something I'm not for you, can I? And I'm not some character in a story you've made up. Excuse me, but that's how it is. I know it must have been—" He searches for the right word. "Exciting, I suppose, all this. But for me it's just a bad accident that I want to put behind me. It's not an adventure for me. All I want is to get better and go home. I *don't* want to be caught up in a game that you're playing, or anything like that. I'm sorry, but that's how it is. Do you understand?"

His voice is very stern. I want to drop my eyes from his, and suddenly I'm consumed by a terrible doubt: what if Anna is wrong—what if we're all wrong—and the hermit is just a man who works in the city, in an office in a bank? We might be in real trouble.

Then I remember the gun, and I know—with a kind of strange, upside-down relief—that we're not wrong, and that it is the hermit who is making things up, inventing the stories.

Anna takes a deep breath, and then lets it out. She looks at Jamie, and then at me, and then at the hermit. "I suppose you have to, don't you?" she says. "Just in case. But it's not like that. We really know."

The hermit shakes his head. "Whatever you think you know—" he begins, but Anna cuts him off a second time.

"You shot someone in Rome. Two people. One of them died and the other one didn't. And then someone shot you, in the leg. That's a bullet wound, not a cut. And the bullet didn't stay in you—it went all the way through."

I say, "Two holes instead of one."

"Yeah," Anna echoes. "Two instead of one."

Jamie says, "And you made a tourniquet with your belt and you drove here."

The hermit doesn't say anything. He's just staring at us.

"To see Signor Ferucci," I prompt, in case he needs to be reminded; but he's still silent.

Jamie says, "But the car went off the road and you didn't know what to do. You didn't really fall asleep. We think you—you know, passed out cos of all the blood you lost in the car."

I say, "Yeah. There was loads of it on the car seat. You were lucky. You might've died."

"And then you came here, and we found you." Anna shrugs. "We know all this stuff."

The hermit looks dazed.

Anna says, "And we got your gun, too. The rifle. It's safe."

"Telescopic sights," Jamie adds. "A sniper rifle."

"Yeah. So." There's a pause. Anna says, "All we want is to know what really happened." She sits back on her heels and looks at the hermit expectantly.

The man doesn't seem to know what to say. He looks from one to another of us, his mouth very slightly open. In the end he just says, "Can I have—some more water?"

Anna frowns slightly, as if she is wondering whether he's just playing for time again. But then she hands him the bottle. As he takes it from her, I notice that the water inside trembles; his hands are shaking.

When he's had enough, the hermit gives the bottle back, and wipes his mouth, and is still for a while. Then he says, quietly, "You haven't told anyone."

"No. No-one." We wait for what he'll say next. When the words come, though, they're unexpected.

"Why not?"

Anna blinks, surprised. Jamie and I steal a quick glance at each other; it is strange indeed that the hermit also wants to know what is, secretly, still puzzling us both.

Anna repeats, stupidly, "Why not?" She doesn't sound like she understands what he means.

"Yes. Why haven't you told someone? If you know all this?"

The hermit doesn't appear to be pretending any more.

"Because—" Anna says, and then stops. She considers for a moment, and then says, "Because we want to help you. You needed someone to help you. Without us, you would have died."

I remember what she said to me in the empty river, about adults sometimes being weak, and about how the hermit would have peed in his pants if we hadn't helped him.

The hermit is saying, "But still—why not tell someone? They wouldn't have killed me, after all. They would have taken me to hospital. And you wouldn't have had to do anything. You wouldn't have been—there wouldn't have been any danger to you."

"They would have locked you up, after," she says.

"Yes. But why should you worry about that?"

Anna frowns, as if she really hasn't thought about any of this. I can't tell whether she really hasn't, or whether she's still playing some kind of trick on the hermit. She says, stubbornly, "You needed us."

"Well," the hermit says, after a second. "That's true enough." He thinks for a while and then says, "You're not scared?"

"No."

"Why not?"

Anna shrugs. "Why should we be?"

"Well . . . you know about—what's happened. Doesn't that scare you? It would a lot of—a lot of people." I am pretty sure, in my mind, that the hermit has been about to say *a lot of kids*.

Anna says, "We've been careful. We hid the car, and our parents don't know. Nobody ever comes up here. So we should be safe."

The hermit is shaking his head impatiently. "That's not what I meant," he says. "Aren't you scared of *me*? Of what I've done?"

Anna looks completely blank for a split second. "Scared of *you*?" she echoes. Then, shaking her head, "No."

I say, "Well, a little bit. At first."

The hermit looks from Anna to me, and nods slowly. "So," he says. "Alex. You were scared a little, yes?"

He's waiting for me to answer. Hesitantly, I nod. He turns to Jamie. "And you? Jamie?"

Jamie looks reluctant to admit it, but in the end he says, "Well. I thought we shouldn't—you know. Get involved."

"I remember. You were very sensible." Jamie drops his gaze. The hermit says, "And perhaps a little afraid, too?"

"Well," Jamie says, uncomfortably.

"Indeed. But you?" He looks at Anna. "You weren't even a bit afraid?"

Anna looks right back at him and shakes her head.

I say, "You were. You were afraid he was going to die."

Anna says, "Oh, that. That's not the same thing."

I think it is, but the hermit is nodding slowly. He says, "That's right. That's not the same thing at all." The words come from him thoughtfully, as if his mind is on other things. For a long while he is silent, and we just sit waiting for him to decide what to say. Jamie shifts a little on the boards of the chapel, and I fiddle idly with one of my shoelaces, but Anna is motionless, watching only the hermit. Then at last the man says, "This is all rather unexpected. You have the gun, you say?"

"Yes," I say. "It's—"

"It's safe," Anna interrupts, darting an angry look at me.

"That's what I was going to say," I say, put out that she thinks I would have forgotten that the gun's whereabouts have to remain a secret.

"Ah," the hermit says. He thinks briefly. "The case was locked," he says.

"We broke it open," Anna says, quite calmly I think, given that we're all sure she shouldn't have.

I wait for the hermit to be cross with her, but all he says is, "Ah."

Anna settles herself more comfortably, crossing her legs. "We just want you to tell us what really happened," she says. "And why. All that. And we won't tell, and we'll look after you, and it'll be a secret always. Promise." She is staring at him fixedly, as if willing him to believe her. "Well? Will you?"

The hermit shakes his head. "I can't," he says. "This isn't the kind of thing for kids to hear."

I know the answer to that. I say, "That's OK. We're not kids."

The hermit turns to look at me, and in his troubled eyes I see that he's almost ready to believe me.

At the same time as I am getting to know Jamie again, a strange thing is happening: he is changing. It is as though the Jamie I am trying to get closer to is constantly moving away from me, shifting direction, so that it becomes hard to follow him, hard to keep up. At first I can't understand it at all; whenever I think I've finally got to know him, I glimpse something else which makes me doubt that I've got close to the whole story. Gradually, a picture starts to emerge from it all, and I realize that it is a picture that worries me—and almost scares me.

Jamie has always been the one who works well in school, and does well—effortlessly well—at sports, and I have always been the one who struggles along awkwardly in his wake. But now, it is as though something has swapped over between us. I am making a presentable effort in most of my subjects, and in Art, of course, everything is very fine. But Jamie seems to have lost interest in the things that used to fascinate him: the stars, his sense of wonder at the world, the endless, tireless questions that used to pour out of him. Instead, he seems to be turning more and more inward, spending more and more time alone. Not from me, exactly; I am always welcome—or at least always allowed near him. But from the rest of the house, he becomes slowly aloof. No-one else seems to notice it, much; but one day I realize that, while they still respect him and like him, I can't be sure that he likes or respects any of them. It's a disconcerting and upsetting realization, because some of these boys used to be Jamie's friends. As I watch, he slowly withdraws into himself, and into his music, until the Jamie that one sees from day to day around the school is more like a ghost-image of him than the real thing.

I start to notice, also, something I haven't seen in his face since— well, since many years before, when the hermit was in the chapel and the darkness each night was interlaced with flickering signals up and down the valley. There are dark smudges under his eyes, the kind that come from not enough sleep; and he seems dozy and unable to concentrate much in the mornings.

"What's going on?"

He looks at me, slight puzzlement vying with a kind of veiled guilt. "What do you mean?"

"You know," I say patiently.

He shrugs. It's a mild day in the spring term, and the grounds of the school are bright with new greenery as we walk between the house and the music schools. "Nothing," he says.

"Something's wrong," I say. "I can tell. I *know* you."

He lets a breath out in a sharp little exhalation, and then nods. "Yeah. I know. But it's not something wrong, it's—well, it's something right, I suppose."

"You look tired," I say.

"I haven't been getting much sleep recently."

"How come?"

He pauses. "I—there's something I'm doing."

"I guessed that. So are you going to tell me about it, or do I have to keep coming up with questions and try to piece it all together?"

Reluctantly, he smiles. "Sorry. I don't feel—safe, really, talking about it all."

"Not even with me?"

He hesitates, and then the smile widens fractionally. "Well, OK. Sorry. Sometimes I forget I can really talk to anyone."

I wait for him to go on. It worries me, the way he's so cautious. Jamie and I used to tell each other everything, and I have thought, recently, that we've started to do the same again.

He says, "I've been going out."

"Going out? Where?" There's nowhere to go out *to* around our school; just a quiet little village half a mile away.

"Well—" He thinks for a second, and then stops, turns to me. For the first time all week he looks really awake and animated: his eyes are bright suddenly, with excitement and the exhilaration of confiding in someone. He says, "I could show you. Tomorrow night, if you can make it."

"When?"

"Nine."

I blink, uncertainly. "*Nine?* When do we get back?"

"About half-one, two o'clock."

"That's impossible," I say. "Someone'll miss us. You should leave it later—like midnight."

"I can't," he says simply. "I have to be there by ten."

"By ten? How long does it take? Where are we going?"

"We have to take the train," he says. "Don't worry. It's safe. I'll make sure no-one'll miss you either."

"How can you do that?" I say, impressed and fascinated.

"It's not a problem," he says vaguely. "You just have to convince the monitor on duty that it's OK. I can do that."

"OK," I say, not quite believing him.

"So—nine o'clock? Just after roll-call. Wear something—I don't know, something casual."

"Sure." I look around us; there's no-one nearby. "Jamie, is this—is it safe? You're not going to get into any trouble?"

He shakes his head. "No. I'm being careful, promise. I'm keeping up the schoolwork—well, pretty much. It doesn't matter. I can afford to slip a bit. But this is important. I won't get caught, and neither will you."

"OK, then," I say, still not sure about anything.

"Don't worry so much," he says, cheerfully. "This is the best thing that's happened to me in ages. I'm not going to risk fucking it up. I'm really careful."

"So—what *is* it?" I say.

He grins. "You'll have to come along and find out," he says.

"Jamie—"

He shrugs. "Live a little," he says. "You don't *have* to come, if you don't want to."

I laugh as we start walking again. "Of course I want to," I say. Briefly, some more words scatter through my mind—*you know I'd do anything for you*—but I keep them inside. We both know they're true, so there's no need to say them aloud.

The ease with which Jamie slips out of the school grounds, down a lane behind one of the maintenance buildings, makes me realize that he has done this many times before—and again I'm struck by the things I've missed, by what I haven't known. He's wearing jeans and trainers and a shirt, open at the neck, and a dark jacket. He's also carrying the rugged and battered case that contains his sax, and at last I have a clue as to what we're doing.

The train station is relatively deserted, but we're careful here in case some returning master or senior boy should spot us. In case someone does, Jamie has a cover story all worked out; and it reminds me of our contingency plans many years before, the methodical way in which he outlines it to me as we walk. In this, at least, Jamie has lost none of his precision.

The train into London takes the best part of an hour, but once there, we don't have far to go. In the lights of the city, a change comes over Jamie that surprises—astonishes—me. Suddenly, the awkwardness and almost sullen withdrawal that have seemed to characterize him recently fall away, and he is confident, talkative, excited. His pace picks up as we walk, and he laughs and talks and is, for these minutes between the station and the club to which he has at last told me we're heading, the same enthusiastic, vibrant Jamie that I have known before. For some reason, although I am thrilled to see him like this, it strikes a sharp note of sadness in me; and I realize after a minute or two why. It is the first time he has seemed really alive in a long while, and I see, all of a sudden, that this is where he really belongs, and that something about life at school is stifling him. Not the same claustrophobia that comes over anyone in an institution like a boarding school, but something far more personal and far more penetrating. It is like watching loneliness evaporate when someone is suddenly surrounded by friends; except that here, it is the buildings and the streets and the lights and the smells that wash away Jamie's loneliness. And it hurts me to realize that he has been lonely even when I am there, and that only this—only what we are doing now, whatever that is—really quenches the thirst in him.

"We're here," he says. "Back door. You can come in this way too."

It's a matte-painted fire-door in the blank brick wall of a little side alley. Jamie punches the buzzer at the side, and some minutes pass before a man pushes the door open for us. He recognizes Jamie, grins at him, glances at me.

"He's a friend," Jamie says.

"Fair enough. Your set's on in twenty. You want a drink?"

"Just one," Jamie says. "Alex?"

"A—a Coke, I think," I say, not knowing whether or not to say a beer. The man just nods, though.

"Right you are. Rest of the crowd's out front, I think, except Paul."

"Thanks."

We have made our way down a narrow, black-painted corridor to a set of swing doors which lead through into an untidy room. The walls here are painted garishly in bright primaries, and the floor is littered with old polystyrene cups and cigarette ends. Instrument cases and larger flight cases and some amplifiers are stacked round the walls. Sitting on one of these is a young man, maybe in his early twenties, fitting a new string to an instrument I think at first is an electric guitar, but which after another look I realize is a bass. Being around Jamie has taught me the difference. The young man looks up.

"James," he says. "Good to see you. Who's your friend?"

"This is Alex," Jamie says. "Alex—Paul, our bassist."

"Hi," I say. *Our bassist* echoes in my mind.

"Hello. How long have we got now?"

"Sammy says twenty. I'm going to get this thing warmed up."

As he talks, Jamie sets the saxophone case on one of the big flight cases and, opening it, starts to slot the pieces of the sax together. He glances over at me.

"This is our dressing-room," he says, grinning. "Impressive ambience, no?"

"Are you two part of a band, then?" I say.

"Yeah, kind of. Actually, Paul's in another band. So are the others, mainly. We're all kind of moonlighting."

I must look blank, because Paul says, "You know—we all play other music as well. More commercial stuff, usually. But James and I were talking, and saying how cool it would be to do some of the old numbers sometimes, and I knew some other people, and it kind of went from there. We're just not giving up the day jobs, know what I mean?"

I nod, understanding, though a hundred tiny parts of the story feel out of place to me. Whatever Paul's idea of a day job is, Jamie's day job should be being at school. Except he's not Jamie here; he's *James*. It sounds older, more grown-up. Looking at Jamie, blowing warm air through the mouthpiece of the sax to get the reed supple, I suddenly see how much older he looks, too; his hands on the instrument are confident, and he looks both calm and tingling with tension. It's controlled excitement, of course. His hair has flopped over one eye as it sometimes does, and he looks—I struggle to find the right words, but I can't fit them round the thought. He looks like he *fits* here; he looks at ease and—and right.

The man they've called Sammy, who seems to own the club, comes back with a Coke in a plastic cup and a beer in a proper glass, and sets them by Jamie. "How's it going?" he says to Paul.

"Sorted. What's the crowd like?"

Sammy grins. "Pretty full. Should go down well. Save a few real slow ones for the end, OK?"

Paul nods, and Jamie turns, smiling, and says, "Sure. They'll leave weeping, I promise."

"Good. Take care now, you've got another ten or so. I've got to go out front for a while."

"Sure. See you."

I can't get over the feeling that Jamie looks taller, somehow; as if he's gained stature since passing through the stage door of this place. He has his jacket open, but he hasn't taken it off. I watch as he adjusts the sling of the sax round his neck, and hooks the instrument in place; then he glances at Paul, one eyebrow raised. "Time for a quickie?"

Paul laughs. "Yeah, all right. Key of D, twelve bar." He starts to pick out a progression of notes on the bass, and though the instrument isn't live—isn't amplified yet—the room is small enough and I'm close enough that they sound loud. After he's made it through the progression and started on it a second time, Jamie joins in, very softly. I know how loud the sax can be; but here Jamie holds almost all the sound in, keeps the notes very low, so that they thrum gently in the air. All the time, from further along the corridor, has come the sound of music from what must be the bar itself: up-tempo stuff, loud and involved and exciting, and the sound of people clapping and cheering. But these sounds are slowly pushed back out of the doorway of the room by the gentler beat and pace of the piece Jamie and Paul are constructing in front of me. I lean back against the wall and watch in silence as they work through the different variations, as Jamie coaxes spirals of sound from the instrument, as they play with off-beat rhythms and counterpoints for little heady fractions of time, and then catch the beat again perfectly before the piece can come apart. And in the end, they close it all down, bringing all the arcs of notes together to one last two-note chord that hangs for a moment, and is gone. I clap, and Jamie smiles.

"Brilliant," I say. "That was brilliant."

"Thanks," he says quietly.

"It wasn't bad, at that," Paul says. "We should work on it, maybe use it some time."

"The old ones are definitely the best," Jamie says. "Well, I guess we're on. Quick slash before the set. I'll see you out front. Paul—you'll show Alex where to go, yeah?"

"Sure," Paul says.

Jamie grins at me. "Wish us luck," he says.

"Good luck," I say.

"Right." He backs out the door, protecting the reed of the sax with one hand, and vanishes up the corridor.

Paul stands up and unslings his bass. "You two are friends?" he says.

"Yeah."

"He's good with that horn," he says. "Young, too. I wasn't that good at this thing when I was his age."

"He's always been good with stuff like that," I say, thinking of the clarinet.

"And you? Do you play?"

"No," I say. "No, I—I don't."

"Well, at least you don't have to stay sober, then," he says with a grin. "Come on. I'll show you a good place to sit if you want to see what's happening."

"Thanks."

As we go out into the narrow corridor, he says, "You and Jamie been friends long, then?"

"All our lives, really," I say.

"Oh!" he says, sounding surprised. "Oh, right."

And then we are through to the main body of the club, and the sound of the band who are finishing their set closes in around us. Paul points through the crowd to a place at the end of the bar, and I nod to show I've got it. He gives me a quick thumbs-up, and then moves back against the wall, keeping his bass carefully out of the way of the press of people. I ease my way through the crush, wondering how, if I've known Jamie all my life, I can still be finding out so much about him.

"You know you'll really be in deep shit if anyone finds out," I say.

"Yeah," Jamie says.

"You're not worried?"

He is staring out of the window of the train at the darkness, and the occasional freckles of light from the little towns and villages we're passing. I can see a dark reflection of his face in the window glass. He smiles slightly. "Not really. I mean, what's the worst they can do?"

"They could expel you," I say, bluntly.

He gives a small shrug. "Well," he says. "I suppose."

"You don't want that, do you?"

He closes his eyes. "It's not a question of what I *don't* want," he says. "It's about what I *do* want. I have to do this. This is—important—in a way that the rest of it—well, it just doesn't compare. They're not the same. This is—" I watch him struggle for words. "This is the real me," he says. "The rest of it they can keep."

This is the real me.

I say, "How long have you—I mean, how long have you been doing this?"

"A while," he says softly. "Regularly, now, for a couple of months. Before that, just once in a while."

"And they let you?" I ask, meaning the people in the club. "You're only sixteen."

"I look older, if I dress right. And besides, I'm good. And I don't ask to be paid much. Sammy knows he's onto a good thing."

I think about that; Jamie's right. He does look older, in the club; older and different. And he is good. The band have been impressive— some of the numbers have been compelling. The applause and shouts from the crowd in the club are obviously genuine.

Jamie slumps lower into his seat. "I'm knackered," he says. "It really takes it out of you. Normally I have to keep awake so I don't miss the stop."

"I can keep an eye out," I say.

"Thanks." He still has his eyes closed. One arm rests comfortably along the top of the sax case on the seat beside him. His hair has fallen loosely across his brow and left eye again, and the tiredness which I have noticed in his face at school, and which has disappeared for the short time we've been in London, is back again. It is as though there is something poisonous about school, that the further from it we go, the more alive Jamie looks. In my head, I compare this to the artificial posturing of other sixth-form boys; their self-conscious attitudes of anger and rebellion, their drug-culture posters and statement clothes. I think of Jamie's neat, ordered room, and Jamie's quietly spoken conservatism in most matters, and wonder what these other boys would think if they knew as much about him as I do. Straight after that thought, though, comes the recollection that I can't be sure, any longer, how well it is that I *do* know Jamie. James. Whoever he is.

"Just be careful," I say quietly, but it seems that he's already asleep; his head has nodded down and I can't see his eyes any longer for the swatch of hair that covers them. His arm is still on the sax case, as if he has it round the shoulder of a friend.

I whisper, "Be careful, OK?"

Outside, the stations pass by one by one, as the train slowly clatters its way back towards school.

*   *   *

Through the next day, the memory of the bombing haunts my thoughts; it is as if my mind can't help playing with the terrible possibilities contained in it. That Anna and I might be dead now. That somehow I might have survived and Anna die; or be horribly maimed, something awful. I can't leave it alone. The way that something this huge can crash into our lives at random shakes me. I begin to realize that I have always trusted that, if you look both ways crossing the road, and if you keep back from the edge of the platform on the underground, and do all the right things, nothing really bad can happen. But this has happened, and has happened so close to us that it has almost grazed us with its force. We could have been in there, I keep thinking. If we hadn't left when we did—if we'd waited longer, kissing at the news-stand, perhaps some fragment of masonry from the blast might have—it is all too horrible to contemplate, and yet I can't stop myself. It churns over and over in my head until I feel almost dizzy from the repetitions. There are only so many times you can feel sick with the awful realization of what has only just passed you by.

At last, my nerves seem to steady somewhat. Anna, throughout the morning, has been subdued, unusually quiet; and this is so unlike her that I know she is feeling some of the whirl of emotions that I am. It seems better not to talk to her about it—at least, not just yet. Perhaps both of us need to settle ourselves somewhat, get back to believing that the earth is solid under our feet.

Late in the morning, a face in the crowd catches my eye and I turn. My heart is suddenly hammering. I stare at the woman—picking through the items spread on the blanket of one of the street-traders. I've never seen her before. Her husband comes over a moment later, looks with her for a while, and then they go off together. She is older, now that I see her clearly, than I have thought she would be. She has a red silk scarf tied into her hair, and it is this, I know at once, that has made me turn.

There was a girl outside the bar with red streaks in her hair. That is what I have thought I've seen.

Why is that important?

And I remember the feeling I had before: that I have seen this woman somewhere. Suddenly, finding in my mind where that place might be feels very important. The same woman, twice; and then the bomb.

Where had I seen her before?

Even though I can't just let myself fall away into the past and catch the answer in the swirls of images there, I know for sure that I *have* seen her before. If I can think where, perhaps there will be something— important—in that.

The confusion in my head is worse than ever. I take a breath, hold it for a moment, try to calm myself. The chaos of thoughts and specu- lation gradually drains away. Nearby, Anna is wandering between the stalls of the street market we've found, looking at clothes—jackets. She's managing to keep at least the outward semblance of calm. I fix my eyes on her: she's still here. I'm still here. The things that could have happened, didn't; we're safe. I keep these thoughts in me until they force out the last remaining shreds of panic and chaos, and then I let the breath out, and walk through the stalls to catch up with her.

17

"So he was a bad man, the man you shot?"

Anna's voice sounds small but sure in the echoing stillness of the chapel. Crouched round the hermit, we all wait; but the hermit is quiet for a long time, and at last I can see he doesn't really know how to answer.

"He was, wasn't he?" Anna says. She's staring hard at the hermit.

"Yes," the hermit says. "He was a bad man."

"And the other man was trying to shoot you?"

"Yes."

"So *that* was self-defence, at least."

"I suppose."

"Well."

The other man is the one whose condition remains critical. He is the second man the hermit has shot; the first—the man who's dead—is shot on the steps of the building he's leaving. I can imagine the way he must look as the telescopic sights of the rifle line up on him, his head neatly framed by the three thin hair-lines. The second man is a bodyguard or a policeman; the hermit isn't sure which. He's shot in an alleyway behind the apartment building the hermit is leaving. It is his bullet which has passed through the hermit's leg.

We all sit looking at the hermit for a while. He seems to be lost in his own thoughts. Then he looks up, and asks casually, "Where did you put the gun, by the way?"

"In the—" I say, before Jamie jabs his elbow into my arm. "Ow," I say, sulkily.

"It's safe," Anna says. "Don't worry about it. We've taken care of everything."

The hermit shrugs. "All right," he says.

"Tell us again," Anna says. "Don't leave anything out. Tell us from when you knew you had to do it right through to getting away afterwards."

The hermit shakes his head. "I'm tired," he says. "I should rest."

"You're much better than yesterday," Anna says. "Start from when you first got to the apartment, then."

The hermit looks round at us, and his expression is resigned. "Very well," he says.

I settle myself more comfortably to listen to the story.

"Is she still in there?" Jamie says.

"Yeah."

"She doesn't get bored, does she?"

I think about that, and it does feel strange to me that Anna can feel bored in so many situations that Jamie or I would find fascinating; but in the dim shadow-world of the chapel, listening to the hermit's stories, she never is. She sits endlessly, making him tell her things over and over again, and picking at him for further details each time. After a long hour or two of this, Jamie and I have become restless, and on the pretext of needing to pee we have escaped the chapel. To find that there is still sunlight and a valley outside feels a disproportionate relief, after so long in the echoing stillness.

"She's really interested in it all."

"Yeah, but even the really dull stuff. It's weird."

I have to agree; but then, sometimes Anna *is* weird. I say, "We can stay out, if you like. She probably won't notice."

"Yeah. Let's."

We sit ourselves down in the dust by the side of the chapel and set up a little chunk of wood on one of the big blocks of stone there, which we can throw pebbles at. Jamie is always better at this than I am, but sometimes I get lucky and knock the target over. Jamie takes careful aim and flicks a pebble; it bounces close, but doesn't hit.

I say, "Do you think he's telling the truth now?"

"Yeah, I think. Don't you? I mean, all the stuff he's said so far makes sense, doesn't it?"

"I s'pose so."

"He was lucky to get away," Jamie says judiciously.

"Yeah." I chuck a stone at the wood, but miss by over a foot.

"Alex? You OK?"

"Mm," I say.

"What is it?"

Something is bothering me about the hermit's first story of the morning—his account of the shooting. "He said he shot the man on the steps and then he went down to the back of the building he was in," I say.

Jamie is looking at me with a kind of cautious interest. "Yeah, that's right," he says.

"And then there was the other man—"

"The bodyguard or policeman. Yeah. And he called out, and then shot the hermit, and the hermit shot him back."

"Mm," I say.

"Well? What?"

"I don't know," I say despondently, and throw another pebble. It gets closer. Jamie spins one after it and the wood block tumbles off its place.

"Got it!" he exclaims with some satisfaction. "I'll set it up again."

I watch him trot over to the big piece of masonry and put our little target back in its proper spot. As he comes back to where we're sitting, he glances in the direction of the river and the road beyond it.

"Strange that no-one ever comes here," he says. "Not even kids from school. You'd have thought they would."

"Maybe they're afraid," I say.

"Why?"

"Chapels and churches are spooky, sometimes. People get buried in them."

"Not *in* them," Jamie says. "Outside."

"Sometimes in them."

"Well, this one isn't very spooky."

"No." It's almost the truth; I've stopped being as apprehensive about the chapel now that the hermit seems to be recovering. It's just a dark building, after all. Part of me is very proud of being grown-up enough to feel this way. Jamie throws a stone, and it skitters off one side of the wood, knocking it round a little way.

"Nearly," he says.

I say, almost to myself, "He went down the stairs and out the back of the building. There was an alley. The man came down the alley and shot at the hermit, and the hermit shot him back."

Jamie stops throwing stones. "What is it?" he says, curiously. "Is there something wrong with that?"

I shake my head. "I don't know. I just—it's like it's stuck in my head."

"Mm," Jamie says, thoughtfully.

I have noticed that, ever since I told Jamie and Anna about the hermit shooting two people, and about what I'd worked out about the gun and from the radio, they've listened to me more closely. It's as if they're surprised that I can work these things out, though of course I know that it's just putting together things I've seen and heard, and not real thinking at all. Still, it's nice that they think I'm clever about this. It's difficult to say, though, whether this one thought running round and round my head is worth bothering about or not.

"Is it about the bullets?" Jamie prompts. "You know, the way there are three gone and three left?"

"The hermit said he only shot him once," I say. "I mean, he only shot each of them once. So that's two bullets, isn't it?"

"But maybe the other one is in the gun still."

"Yeah."

We sit, nonplussed, for a while. Then Jamie says, slowly, "Wait a minute." His eyes are fixed on his trainers for a long time; and then his head snaps up suddenly. "Alex—he can't have shot the second man the way he says. That's what it is. He can't have."

"Why not?"

"The gun—the gun's in the case. Don't you see?" Jamie says, excitedly.

"What?"

"He's at the window. He shoots the man on the steps. Then he packs the gun into its case, and he goes down into the street. So when the man shouts at him and then shoots him, the gun is *still* in the case. He wouldn't have had time to unpack it all and put it together."

"Oh. Yeah," I say, seeing what he's getting at at last. "So maybe he was lying. Maybe he didn't shoot him."

"Yes he did," Jamie says impatiently. "It was on the news, remember? You heard it."

"Oh, yeah."

"So he had the case with the gun in, and someone shot at him, and he turned round and shot them back, and they fell down. That's what he said." Jamie gets up and starts to pace nervously back and forth, something he often does when he's thinking. "But he couldn't have, because he would have had to stop and get the gun out and put it together again and all that. So what happened?"

I say, "He could have had another gun."

Jamie stops in his pacing, and stares at me. "Yeah," he whispers. "Yeah, he could have. Like—a small one, ready in case anyone . . ."

His voice tails off.

"What?" I say.

"If he's got another gun, where is it?" Jamie says quietly.

"Maybe in the car."

"We didn't see anything." He looks at his feet, and then up at me again. "Maybe he's still got it. Maybe it's in his pocket or something."

I'm worried; I don't know quite what all this means to us. I say, "What should we do?"

"I don't know," Jamie says. "We should tell Anna, though."

"She's in there with him," I say, realizing. My tone of voice must panic Jamie, because he tenses at once.

"Shit. Yeah. Come on."

We race across the churchyard, kicking up a trail of dust, and along the side of the chapel to the door there. Jamie tries to control how he opens the door but we still burst into the chapel in a clatter of footsteps. As the echoes die away, I'm aware that another sound has been suddenly cut off—a sound we've interrupted. The last traces of it fade with the echoes of our entrance: laughter. The hermit and Anna have been laughing.

Anna has jumped up. "What is it?" she demands, looking scared. "Is someone coming?"

"No," Jamie says. "No, it's—I mean, it's OK."

"You scared the shit out of me," she says. "What is it?"

Jamie and I stare down the length of the chapel at her. The hermit is unseen in his jury-rigged bed. Anna's face is white.

Jamie mumbles, "We were just—playing something. Sorry."

"Well, keep quiet, for God's sake," she says. "And keep out of sight, if you're playing outside."

"Yeah, we know," Jamie says. He and I shuffle our way back out of the chapel. Behind us, the sound of voices talking starts up again slowly.

"Why didn't you tell her?" I say.

He shakes his head. "I don't know. It's—it's weird. I couldn't. I think—well, I don't think she would have cared, do you?"

"Oh," I say. I think about telling Anna. "No."

"And I don't think he'd—*do* anything, do you? I mean, if he'd wanted to—to shoot anyone, or frighten anyone, he could have already, couldn't he?" Jamie walks on, head down, for a while. Then he says, "After all, we *are* helping him. He needs us. So probably he wouldn't want to scare us."

"Maybe he threw the other gun away," I say. "After he shot the man."

"Yeah, maybe," Jamie allows. "Maybe."

"They were laughing," I say.

"Yeah, I heard."

"What do you think they were laughing about?"

He kicks a stone edgily. "How should I know, Alex?"

"I can't think of anything very funny to be laughing about," I say. "I mean, about shooting people and all that."

"Maybe they weren't talking about all that any more."

"But that's what Anna wanted to talk about," I say. "She went on and on about it."

"Maybe they got bored with it. They could be talking about something else now."

"I s'pose," I say. I can't understand why Anna would rather be inside with the hermit than outside with us, and the lizards and cicadas and bush crickets. "I wish we could go swimming," I say, looking vaguely towards the dry river.

"Yeah. I know. Maybe we will later."

"It's always later since the hermit came," I say, rather petulantly; but Jamie doesn't have an answer for that.

In the afternoon, my friend the cat comes padding through the garden. There are still some scraps of food, and I fetch them, throw them to the grass. The cat inspects them delicately and then eats the ones that it seems to feel are the most promising. From the verandah, I watch its movements. I have brought the photographs out here with me into the sun, and I am surrounded by a mosaic of images. Almost the entire exhibition is arrayed here on the boards, the ochres and earth-colours glowing in the afternoon sunlight. For one sad, brief moment, I wish very much that Lena could be alive to see them all.

There was a time, a few hours past, when for some unknown reason I couldn't stop myself crying. It was something to do with the pictures, and the faces in them, and the memories that have begun floating like disturbed sediment through this old house. But for the life of me I can't remember now what started it. It seems a frail and strange thing, to be suddenly at the mercy of tears like that.

Now, the cat steps carefully and curiously up the steps of the verandah, and finally sits in a wide patch of sunshine and starts to clean its head and ears with one paw. It is good, I think to myself, to have a friend on an afternoon like this, when so much seems—uncertain, and unclear.

Inside the house, on the wall, the scene I am painting—the scene I can't help painting—is beginning to come together. You can see the water properly, now, even through the dark; and in the evenings by the tentative flickering of candlelight, the figure in the foreground—the boy in the foreground—the boy standing about to dive—seems to flicker and tremble as well. Things are changing. Old things that have been eroded by the years are coming back. Sometimes it's fresh plaster on a damaged wall, or new boards in the corner of a room. And sometimes it's a beach at night, with dark cliffs and a sea limned with moonlight. Things are being mended, made good again.

My eyes drift over the surface of the photographs as if they are a landscape: a series of terrains seen from high, high above. I feel at an impossible distance from them, as if I am in a tiny aeroplane, or perhaps a glider, silent in the currents and ribbons of air that flow over them. I want to set down, to land, to put my feet on these landscapes and walk through them, get to know them, but I can't set down and I can't land.

I am trapped in a gulf-stream like the pull of a tide, and my little aircraft and I are incapable of choosing our own course. The paintings are clear to me from where I am; I can see every detail in them. But I can't get close to them. The distance between them and me is impossible.

I can hear their voices, low but clear, through the door. It is nearly mid-night, and soon I will have to go inside and relieve Anna from her shift. She is insistent that we keep up our watch on the hermit, even though he seems so much better now; and again, when Jamie and I press her on this, she becomes first vague and then angry, saying that it's just what we have to *do*. Jamie mutters later that he doesn't understand anything about Anna. I think to myself of her voice, softly raised in song, and of the words I can't understand, and I agree with him; but I keep my thoughts, and what I've heard, to myself.

Outside the chapel, in the afternoon, Jamie and I at last tell Anna what we've worked out about the hermit's gun, and the second man he shot.

"It can't have been the rifle, you see," Jamie says. "Because it was all in pieces. So—"

"Oh. Yeah," Anna says. "I see." She's quiet for a moment, thinking, and then she shrugs. "Well, I suppose he must have another gun, then."

Jamie watches her for a while, waiting for her to say something else. When it becomes clear she isn't going to, he says, "Aren't you worried?"

"Why?"

"He's got a gun we don't know about. He might have it on him."

"It's OK," Anna says blithely. "He won't hurt us."

"How do you know?"

"I just do."

"How do you know for sure?"

"He won't, OK?" she says. "He's—he's not like that. We're helping him. He wouldn't hurt us."

Jamie doesn't look at all sure.

Anna says, "I'll take the first shift this evening, OK? Stop worrying. Everything's going to be fine."

Now, her voice comes quietly through the cracks in the wood. I can hear everything she says, and this time, I understand; she's speaking Italian.

"Can I see it?"

"Why?"

"Please. Just to look." I wonder what it is she wants to see.

"It's not a thing for a girl to see," the hermit says.

"Why not?"

"It just isn't."

"Don't you have women, then? In your—you know. In what you do."

The hermit is quiet for a time. Then he says, "Yes."

"Well, then. Show me. I won't touch it or anything."

There's a pause, and then I hear a kind of rustling as the hermit shifts position. "Here," he says. "Now are you satisfied?"

"It's small," she says.

"Yes."

"It's all smooth, too."

"It's designed that way. It was designed for the Soviet security forces, to be concealed in clothing. That's why it's small, and why the surfaces are rounded like this." There's a pause, and then he says something that I don't catch.

Anna says, "I know. But it's easier in Italian. I—I think I forgot a lot."

"How long has it been, now?"

"A long time."

"You should try to remember," the hermit says. "These things are important. They make us who we are. They shouldn't be forgotten."

"I know," Anna says. Then, "You should put it away now. Alex will be here soon."

"Ah."

I nod to myself, wondering what she'd think if she knew I could hear her talking like this. Probably, she'd be cross. I will be certain to keep a secret of what I've heard, even though I don't understand half of it.

When the time comes, I trudge round to the side door and do my trick of making a bit of noise as I open it.

"It's me," I call down the body of the building; and in a second, Anna's voice calls back.

"Hi, Alex."

She meets me halfway. "He's sleeping," she says. There's nothing in her tone to give away the lie, to suggest that only a minute before, she was deep in conversation with the hermit. "He's pretty tired. Does your watch have an alarm?"

"Yeah," I say.

"If you like, you can set it for the hours and sleep as well. Just wake up for the signals. OK?"

"All right," I say.

"Just keep near so if he wants anything you can get it for him. Well, I'm off."

"Bye," I say.

"See you tomorrow," she calls quietly from the door.

I shake my head, and we both say it together, grinning: "No, today." Then she's gone, and the door is quietly closed. I make my way down the length of the chapel to where the hermit is, and locate the torch on the bottom stair. We've all got used to moving about the chapel in the darkness; I never stumble into anything any more, even without the torch. There is one candle stub burning on the end of the pew, but the shadow it casts falls right across the hermit's chest and head, and it's impossible to see his face.

I wait a little while, watching to see if the hermit makes any movements or gives any indication that he's actually awake. But he's still, and after a time I begin to think he must have really fallen asleep, while Anna and I have been talking. It seems believable to me. He must be tired, after all.

I climb the stairs and cross the balcony and duck into the soft moonlight of the belltower. At the top of the wooden staircase I check my watch again, lean out the arch, sight the torch down the valley and key its switch three times. I have to wait a while, and send the signal twice more, before Jamie's bedroom lights wink back in reply; and I wonder whether he has found it hard to get out of bed. It's sometimes a terrible struggle not to ignore the alarm clock under your pillow and just drift off again.

Satisfied, I put the torch down. The night valley is silver-grey, and the distant sea is very dark. Somewhere along the path of the empty river Anna is making her way home, and I wonder what she's thinking of as she walks: whether she is reliving in her head the conversations she's had with the hermit over the four hours of her shift. I wonder, too, what they have been, what the two of them have talked about. For a moment or two I allow myself to drift, and I catch the sounds of Anna's voice, small but still audible through the heavy wood. They are musical, but strangely rough-edged, and it surprises me again to find that she is capable of making such strange, unfamiliar sounds come out of her mouth.

Downstairs, the hermit doesn't move. I watch the dark shape that is his face for a while, but it seems that, even if he was pretending before, he is properly asleep now. I can hear him breathing, and the breaths are steady and slow and even—nothing like the harsh, tearing breaths that sometimes came over him when he was in his fever.

"Are you awake?" I say softly. The hermit doesn't reply, and he doesn't move, and that's enough of an answer. I settle myself on the bottom stair, resting my back against the stone of the big pillar that forms the middle of the curving staircase. The candle flame twists for a moment as the air tugs at it, and then straightens.

I say, "I know you weren't really asleep before." There's no response; the hermit's breathing is low and regular. I say, "Anna lied. She said you were asleep all along. But I know you weren't."

I fiddle with my watch until its alarm is set for just before one. I decide I will sleep in the belltower with the pigeons; being asleep right next to the hermit disconcerts me somehow. I remember what Anna has said about being there if he wants anything, but a moment's thought convinces me that he can always call out and wake me if he wants anything that badly. I stand up, gripping the torch.

"Anna says you won't hurt us," I whisper.

The hermit doesn't reply. I shrug very slightly, to myself, and turn, and start up the stairs again.

Anna says you won't hurt us.

She was wrong. He did hurt us. Things happened; there were—consequences, repercussions. And we were hurt: all of us. I remember how scared I became, after a time, that the hermit, though gone, was still with us. I remember in Florence the moment of terrible realization when the pieces of the puzzle finally gathered themselves in a manner I could understand, could interpret. It was as if all the small fears that had soaked into me over the years were gushing out of me together—*the hermit's here! He's still here!*—in a torrent of almost inarticulate panic. *He's here!*

That was right, and wrong. The pieces were all there, but what I thought was comprehension was in fact something else entirely; a mistake I've carried for a long time. Perhaps because of the panic, I made of the fragments I'd gathered a whole, which was my own fear, not the truth.

When the past is softened by memory, some of the hurt that comes from mistakes and stupidity and misunderstanding is damped down. Time passes, and draws you further and further from the things you did wrong; and perhaps you learn, and don't make the same mistakes again. But now it seems that I can't hide behind that softening. The past is right here. I walk through it every day. The house is more and more mended, and I am more and more—damaged. It is as though I have to feed parts of myself into the mortar and plaster, to get this place right again. I wonder, if I ever finish the house, whether I'll be left with a life that makes any sense at all.

Anna says you won't hurt us.

Maybe she believed it was true. But we were hurt, all of us; Anna, too. And I should have known, and I should have done more.

18

"*That's* stupid, though," Anna says. "You shouldn't do it like that."

I have a comic open on my knees. In the frame Anna's pointing to, a man is holding a pistol to another man's head. The man with the gun is saying, *Drop it!*—and the other man is letting a knife fall to the floor. It's early morning. The hermit has had something to eat—bread, again, but also some of Lena's cold chicken pie, flavoured with saffron and little shreds of fiery chilli, which Jamie and I like very much. He seems hungry, and we're having trouble smuggling food for him.

"Why not?" I say.

"It's stupid to put a gun right up against someone," Anna says. "If you've got a gun, you can shoot someone right across the other side of the room. Or further away, even, if you're a good shot. And they can't do anything to you, cos if they move or try to run or anything, you can shoot them. But if you stick it up really close like that, this guy's only got to pull the gun a little way away and you can't shoot him any more."

"But that's how they always do it on TV."

"Then they're always wrong on TV."

"It would be difficult, though," I say. "Look—he's behind him, and he's got his arm here."

"So? It's still better my way." She pauses, as if trying to remember something. "A gun's advantage is its range," she says carefully. "If you give up your range, you're giving up your advantage, and you might as well use a knife or something. Knives are quieter."

"How come you know all about this?" I say, though I find that I have a pretty good idea.

Anna just shrugs. "It's obvious, actually," she says.

I flip the comic closed. "You're talking to him," I say, accusingly.

"So? So are you and Jamie."

"No . . . I mean, about—stuff."

"Well?"

"Well you shouldn't."

Anna opens her mouth to say something, and then seems to think better of it. "I don't talk to him much," she says, scraping one finger in the dirt. "Just sometimes. It's—interesting."

"We should be careful," I say.

"Did you hide the bullets?" she says, out of the blue.

"What?"

"They're not in the case any more. Did you take them?"

I hesitate, not knowing what to say. "Why were you looking in the case?" I say.

"Well, why were *you*? You did take them, didn't you? Jamie wouldn't. I know he wouldn't." She stares at me, closely. Then she sits up, her back straight against the big piece of wood by which we're sitting. She says, "It's OK. I'm not cross."

"I was—playing," I say, vaguely.

"You shouldn't play with bullets, Alex. They're dangerous."

"Neither should you."

"I wasn't going to play with them."

"Well what were you going to do with them, then?"

She glances away. "I was just going to—look at them."

"I lost them," I say, decisively. "I dropped them by accident and I couldn't find them again."

She looks at me again, hard. At last she says, slowly, "OK, then. Well, if you find them, you put them back, OK?"

"If I find them."

"Yeah."

We sit for a while in the morning sunlight. Anna scratches her ankles. Jamie, who has had the early shift, is asleep in the shadow of the chapel wall, curled up with his head on his arms.

I say, "Anna?"

"Mm?"

"This isn't fun any more."

"What isn't?"

"The hermit."

She looks at me, a strange expression on her face, as if I've said something ridiculous.

I say, "We're all just tired all the time. And all we do is come up here and look after the hermit. We never do anything else."

"This isn't a *game*, Alex," she says. "It's not supposed to be *fun*."

"So why are we doing it?" I say.

"Because we have to."

"I want to go swimming," I say. "Like we used to. It's much better."

"Well, we can't. We have to watch the hermit."

"That's what you always say."

"Well, we do." She gets up, sticks her hands in her pockets. "Just try to understand, OK?"

"He's better now," I say stubbornly. "We could leave him for a while. Just for the afternoon, maybe. We could go to the beach." I pick up a fir cone and throw it at Jamie's sleeping figure; it bounces past his arm and his head jerks up, startled. I say, "Jamie!"

"What? I was—I was asleep. What is it?"

"I want to go to the beach," I say.

Jamie sits up, running one hand through his hair. He's slept on a fold of it, and it's sticking up at the side. "When?"

Anna says, "We have to stay and look after the hermit. I told him but he won't listen."

Jamie rubs his face and comes across to us. "Yeah, well," he says, rather uncertainly.

"What?" Anna says. "You know we can't leave the hermit, Jamie. You *know* we can't."

"I suppose," he says. "Alex? She's right. We ought to stay."

I kick the ground. "I'm *bored* with the hermit," I say. "There's nothing to do. We just look after him. It's no fun."

"I told you. It's not a game," Anna says.

"It's OK for *you*. You enjoy doing it all. But I think it's boring."

She looks for a moment as if she's going to argue back about this, but then she closes her mouth and looks thoughtful. She glances at Jamie and then says, "Well—I s'pose that's true. Are you really bored, Alex?"

"Yes," I say.

"Well . . ." She still looks like she's thinking. "We don't all have to be here, I guess. You two go. I'll be all right."

"Really?" I say. "Thanks, Anna."

"It's OK."

Jamie looks at her uncertainly. "Are you sure you'll be OK on your own?"

It's a silly question. I answer for her. "Of course she will. She *likes* being with the hermit. Come on."

The little cove that is our favourite place is empty. Although the day is bright and sunny, it's still quite early in the morning and there is only a scattering of people on Altesa's sandy beach. It's rare anyway for anyone else to make the trek along the cliff path and down through the scree to the rocky place there. Jamie and I trot down the uneven route to the beach with the confidence that comes of having retraced the same steps time and again—down from the top of the cliff, round the bulge of land where once I gripped the rock tight to try and stop Anna from falling, and down onto the tumble of loose rock and pebbles that is the beach. We pause for a moment here, to get our breath back and to survey the area: the sea swells and breaks lethargically against the promontory, and there is almost no breeze. The beach itself is sheltered, enclosed by the cliffs and shielded by the spur of the promontory, and although there is a strip of dark shadow running all along the base of the tall cliff—the diving cliff—the rest of the beach is catching the morning sun, and the rocks and dried seaweed are hot to the touch.

"Want to swim?" Jamie says.

"Yeah," I say. "Underwater."

"You're on."

I am hot and dusty from the long walk down the valley and the hike over the cliffs, and the thought of plunging into the cool water by the promontory is almost too enticing to bear. We hurriedly struggle out of our clothes and, being careful where we put our feet on the sharp-edged rock of the spur, we tiptoe out to where the water is good and deep.

"On three!" Jamie says. "One, two—"

We jump and hit the water at the same time: Jamie in a smooth dive, me holding my nose and going in feet first. The water boils and seethes with bubbles for a long moment, and then begins to clear and settle again. Every part of me is suddenly deliciously cool, and all the hot sweaty dust is gone in the blink of an eye.

As usual, I feel myself break the surface before I've got complete control of what I'm doing; but it's only for a moment. I take a breath, and angle myself the proper way, and kick down hard; and I'm under-water.

I can't find Jamie for a moment, and then I see him a little way off. He has swum right down to the bottom, and has his hand on one of the rocks there, holding himself down. With his other hand he gently moves some of the rocks on the seabed, looking for anemones and sea-urchins. Sea-urchins are nasty if you step on them; the spines break off under the skin and go bad. But if you curl your whole hand around them you can pick them up easily. Placed on a flat rock—or even on the palm of your hand—they will start to walk along on their spines, moving all the individual spikes in a complicated, laborious effort. We find dead ones as well, where the spines have fallen away; and the husks that are left are blue and pink, and divided peculiarly, like flowers, into fives.

We've found spider crabs down here, too, and brought them to the beach to watch them wave their delicate claws; and once, a small, black lobster, in a cleft in the rock. On the side of the spur itself there are starfish and limpets and more anemones and mussels and all kinds of seaweeds. Close in, you have to be careful, because the swell of the waves is sometimes stronger than you expect, and can slap you hard against the rock before you can put out your arms or legs to brace your-self. There are fishes, too; little silver ones that dart back and forth in shoals that turn as if all the fish are moved by the same remote control; and larger ones sometimes, as long as your hand, in smaller groups. Jamie says the bigger fish are further out, and don't come in so close to the shore.

In the water, Jamie's hair floats round his head like dark seaweed, and his body—which looks very pale against the dark green-grey rocks of the sea floor—is mottled with the ribbons of light which break through the surface waves above us. He turns his head as I kick nearer to him, and a thin stream of bubbles breaks from his mouth. Sometimes, when you're starting to feel that you need to take a breath, it's easier to let out some of what you have. When he sees me, he grins, and with his free hand gives me the thumbs-up. On the rock below him, I can see he's found one of the big starfish that we sometimes get in the cove: knobbly and sandy-coloured, with tinges of blue on its bumps. I nod enthusiastically and concentrate as hard as I can on thinking words at Jamie.

Good one!

Sometimes Jamie and I try this—try thinking ideas or words at each other. Sometimes it works, sometimes it doesn't. Our thoughts so often seem to be in tune that it's hard to tell whether our successes are genuine or not, but we still try. Sometimes we lie with our heads touching, to see if that makes it any better. Sometimes it does, sometimes it doesn't; it's hard to say.

Jamie lets go of the rock and kicks up to the surface for another breath, and I go with him. Our heads break the surface at the same time.

"Did you see?"

"Yeah!" I gasp. "That's a good one!"

"It's a big one. Maybe we'll find more."

"OK," I say, breathing in and out fast. The longer you do this, the longer you can stay down. "On three!" I say, when my lungs feel hot with it. "One, two—"

We jackknife and kick our way down again, fighting through the heaviness of the water to the bottom. The starfish is where we left it. If you find the right handholds, you can grab rocks and things on the seabed and use them to pull your way around, keeping close to all the creatures that inhabit the rocks and sandy patches without having to keep kicking with your legs. As we progress, looking for more starfish, I am struck by how strange we look, almost as if we are walking on our hands: Jamie's arms are stretched out to the seabed, his hands holding and turning and examining, but his legs and feet trail away upwards towards the light. I wonder briefly how we must look to the fish, and whether they are amused by us, or just curious. A stream of the little silvery ones winds round Jamie and then turns, flashing for one quick second with sunlight, and zips off out of sight. If they are amused, they have gone away to laugh about us in private.

Later, tired and breathless and dizzy from being under the water for so long, we sit on the hot rocks of the beach together, little pools of water running off us and turning the stone black and slick for a time before the sun dries it up again. Jamie makes a little pillow out of his clothes and rests his head on it.

I say, "I wonder what Anna's doing."

Jamie grunts. He has his eyes closed.

I say, "Don't you think sometimes Anna's—a bit weird?"

Jamie doesn't open his eyes. He says, "Well, a bit."

"Why didn't she want to come to the beach?"

"She likes looking after the hermit, I guess."

"I wonder why," I say.

"I don't know, Alex. She just does."

"Well, I think it's weird."

"Mm."

Jamie sounds sleepy, and I remember that I woke him up to come here. "Are you still tired?"

"Yeah, a bit. Sometimes I'm just sitting or something and I think I could fall asleep right there, just sitting up but asleep, you know?"

"Yeah." I think about it. "Do you think Anna gets tired?"

"She must do."

"She doesn't show it very much, though."

"Maybe she's been sleeping while she's with the hermit."

I think of what I've heard, and know that she isn't; that they spend all the time when she's there talking together. It is, I realize, probably what they're doing now. I wonder whether to tell Jamie about it, but for some reason it doesn't feel right to do that. I look at him. He has one arm back behind his head, helping to cushion it against the rock, and the other by his side. There are a few beads of water still on his skin, but he's drying off quickly in the sun. His hair is still plastered across his head, though.

I say, "Do you think—"

"What?"

"Well," I say vaguely. It has been troubling me, in an odd kind of way, for a while now. "When we're older, will we—I mean, will our things look like the hermit's?"

Jamie opens his eyes; he looks surprised. He glances down at himself and then across at me, and gives a kind of half shrug. "I s'pose so," he says.

"Oh."

"Cos they change when you're older. You get hair and all that."

"Mm," I say.

"Some of the older boys at school say they already have," he says.

"Do you think they have?"

"I don't know. Perhaps. Maybe they're just saying it, though."

"I wonder what that's like."

"Mm."

Jamie has closed his eyes again.

I say, "You mustn't go to sleep in the sun."

"I'm not going to sleep."

"Lena says it's bad for you."

"I know. She always says that."

"I'm hungry," I say.

"Yeah. Me, too. We'll go and get a sandwich in a little while."

"OK."

The beads of water on Jamie dwindle in the sun, and leave tiny, pale ghosts of salt behind them. I sit up and scan the sea for fishing boats; sometimes they cross the horizon between the far cliffs and the end of the spur. Today, though, the stretch of sea is empty. Jamie stirs, and stretches.

"God, I *am* falling asleep."

"I told you."

He sits up and yawns. "OK. We'll go now, if you want."

"Let's get some Cokes."

"If we can afford it," he says doubtfully. Money is a problem. We have the roll of notes the hermit gave us; but the small ones have been used up on supplies, and we are too scared of looking suspicious to use the big denominations that are left over. There is the pocket money that we get, but this week's amount is all gone; and we are left with only the change that Lena gives us for sandwiches and ice-creams. Of this, some has to be set aside for emergencies. Anna is very stern on this point.

"Well, let's try anyway."

We pull our clothes on slowly and lazily, feeling the ache of the swimming in our arms and legs. When at last we are ready, Jamie leads the way back up the beach to the cliff path.

"What shall we do this afternoon?" I say.

"Don't know. We'll think about it on the way."

With the sun overhead, and the last of the seawater evaporating and making our hair crisp and tangled with salt, it is hard to believe that there is somewhere a hermit in a dark chapel, and a gun in a case, and three shiny bullets hidden behind a grating at the foot of a wall. It could all be a dream, I tell myself: a strange and unfathomable dream. I try to pretend, while walking, that it really is a dream, and that we're going to meet Anna outside Toni's for ice-cream. It makes me a little sad, deep inside, when I realize that I would far rather that this made-up reality were the truth.

Now that I know where Jamie goes at night, he suddenly makes more sense to me. For weeks after he takes me to London, I keep seeing the city streets we walked along in my head, and keep seeing also how different Jamie looks here. It's as though the Jamie I see every day in school is an imitation, good enough to fool everyone else, but not quite enough for me. The Jamie I have seen backstage at the club, and playing the saxophone in front of the crowd of people there, is unfamiliar—but at the same time, he is also the Jamie I know. This is a new way to look at him, but underneath it, he has the same sense of adventure and discovery and searching for something that have been there all his life. Although he has clearly changed, at least I now understand what that change is; and it's in keeping with who I know him to be. Strangely, it satisfies me. There have been times when the peculiar distance that has come between us has seemed to have altered him, made him harder for me to understand; and now I understand him again.

So now we share the secret. It reminds me of the other things we keep between us; and it must remind Jamie too, because in some way it affects what we talk about. Our conversations drift around the subject of the hermit, and the past. I'm not entirely sure that I understand

everything about Jamie yet, but I'm ready to give him time—to wait—
to see what he chooses to tell me.

But as the term wears on, and the spring weather gets clearer and
warmer, more changes come over Jamie. His grades in academic subjects, which have been slipping steadily, now slump dramatically. He
shrugs it off to me, saying that he can catch up on the work whenever
he likes; that the night-time excursions are only once a week or so. He's
hard to argue with because I know he's right, that he could catch up if
he wanted; but whenever he has a free afternoon, or any scrap of spare
time that he could use for studying, he is always either in the music
schools or else catching up on sleep, or off on his own somewhere. It
isn't long before I am sure that he simply doesn't care enough to make a
fuss about his grades. It worries me a lot.

"They're really bad," I say, looking over his half-termly report card.
"You're failing these three. You've got exams next term, you know."

"Yeah." He is staring out the window of his room, tapping one finger impatiently on the sill. "It's not important, Alex."

"Well, it will be if you don't get any passes and they kick you out.
What'll your parents say when they see this?"

He shrugs. "I don't know. I mean it, I really don't. Maybe they'll think
I had an off day."

"You've had an off year," I say.

"Mm," he says, noncommittally. Then, out of the blue, he adds,
"Strange, isn't it. Calling it a dandelion clock. I mean, why a clock?"

I stare at him. "You know," I say. "You blow it to find out the time."

"Yeah. Still, why not—a dandelion wand? Hit it on something and
make a wish."

"I s'pose," I say.

"I just think it's strange."

"You sound like you did back then," I say. "Why are the rocks like
sandwiches? Why don't snakes blink? Why? Why?"

He's grinning. "Yeah," he says. "I remember that. Those were good
times."

"Yeah."

He's quiet for a moment, and then the smile goes out of him. "Sometimes I think leaving Italy was a really bad mistake. That I shouldn't
have come here at all."

"How come?" I say.

"I don't know. Things were—better, there."

"Well, sometimes," I say.

"All the time. Anyway." He swings his legs back and forth, kicking the wall under the window. "Too late now. At least I've found this one thing."

He means the music. I say, "Yeah, that's good."

"It's better than good." He manages a smile. "Sometimes it feels like it's all I've got."

"You've got other things."

"Like what?"

"Well—friends."

Jamie laughs, but the sound isn't a happy one. "Really? I don't know *anyone* here."

"Everybody likes you," I protest, shocked.

"I know. Everyone likes me and nobody knows me. They don't get to know you here; have you noticed that? They don't really—get to know you. There isn't anyone here who's a proper friend, who I can really talk to. That's why I need to—get out, sometimes, get to London. At least some of the people there—Paul, you met him—at least they actually— *talk* about stuff. Not just this being-nice bullshit."

I am surprised by the vehemence in his voice. I say, "What about— I mean, don't you—"

A flash of realization crosses his face. "Shit, Alex, I didn't mean *you*," he says. "You know I—you know I can talk to you." He shakes his head. "I didn't mean that. I meant everyone else."

"Yeah, I know," I say.

"I mean, we talk about everything, don't we?"

"Sure," I say. Inside, some small voice echoes *everything*?—but doubt-fully, as if waiting to be convinced.

Jamie says, "Only sometimes it feels like—you know, it's just us, and all around us everything's—blank, somehow. I feel that here all the time."

"But not when you're in London?"

"No. Not then."

I don't know what to say for a long time. In the end, I say, "You should still try to work a bit, you know."

"I guess."

I say, brightly, "I mean, think how it would be for me if they kicked you out. Then *I* wouldn't have anyone to talk to."

He grins weakly. "Yeah. I suppose so."

"So you'll try?"

"I'll do some," he agrees. "But not if it—interferes."

"Of course not," I agree with mock solemnity. "Our art before all else."

The grin widens. "Fuck off."

"Yeah, and you."

I go to the door, and he follows me, puts his hand out to stop me opening it. "Alex?"

"Yeah?"

"You were—it was kind of you, talking—" He stops, shakes his head. "I mean, thanks."

"For what?"

"For looking out for me."

"It's OK. You look out for me, too."

"Well someone has to."

"Oh, cheers."

He hesitates, and I think he is about to say something else; and then he just shrugs slightly. His hand, as he takes it away from the door, touches the side of my face for a moment before it drops to his side. He says, "And thanks for coming and watching me play."

"You were really good," I say. "Really cool."

"Yeah?"

"Absolutely. *Ottimo.*"

"Yeah," he says, very quietly, as though he's known it secretly all along.

"See you later," I say.

"Sure. Bye, Alex."

Outside, in the corridor, I pass little clumps and groups of boys—running, walking, chatting in their studies. I watch the faces as I walk past. A couple of people look up and nod at me or say *Hi, Alex.* Outside, there are boys on the sports pitches: football still, but there will be early cricket after the half-term, if the weather is right for it. And as I walk, and the sea of faces parts to let me through and closes again behind me,

I see that Jamie is right: it is only us two. None of the rest of the people here are real in any way. Even Anna, far away in a different country, is more real to me now than any of these faces. It's just the two of us—the three of us—like it always has been.

Gradually, the hermit's leg gets better. Each day we change the dressings, and each day Anna checks the two wounds; they have formed tight, yellowish-brown scabs now, and we keep the bandages looser to let the air in. The hermit is still weak, but is eating steadily, and is stronger. He is able to manage going to the loo on his own; and when I talk to him, on some of the evening shifts when I am alone but he is still awake, his voice is firm and controlled. He sounds like a man who is getting back some strength, and part of me doesn't know quite what to feel about this.

The hermit talks to me sometimes: about my life, and the valley, and what I like. It's not the way he talks to Anna, but it's friendly. I ask Jamie if the hermit talks to him about these things, and he says no. I am not sure whether Jamie knows what's happening between the hermit and Anna; he doesn't mention it, and I don't like to say anything. But when I go to start my shifts, I have got into the habit of setting off early; and through the chapel doors there are always two voices, low and serious sometimes, and laughing at other times, before I go inside and the hermit pretends to be asleep.

Knowing something like this about Anna feels unsafe—there's that same sense of almost electrical danger that I felt when I saw her on the cliff—but I can't stop myself doing it. Even though often the words make no sense to me, I feel like I want to hear them.

Anna looks after the hermit more and more, letting Jamie and me run off into the scrub of the abandoned fields up here at the top of the valley, or take whole afternoons to go to the beach. Even so, there are still the night shifts to be managed, and Anna still insists that we keep the schedule up. When I ask her how long we'll have to do this, she just says, *As long as it takes.*

We're all tired. We sleep against walls and with our heads pillowed on our arms, at nine in the morning or two in the afternoon, whenever we can. Only the sun and fresh air manage to mask the blotches of darkness under our eyes. Anna's skin stays fair, though, from being in the dim hollow of the chapel so much of the time, but no-one seems to notice that Jamie and I are tanning and she is not. To start with, she looks as tired as we do; but then, gradually, she seems to absorb the tiredness, draw it inside her and somehow force it down. She starts to look better, more alive. I wish I could do the same.

In the night-time, the signals flicker up and down the valley, keeping us all comforted in the knowledge that we are safe and that we aren't alone. Every hour, on the hour, we are all thinking of each other—even if that thinking is done through a haze of tiredness, the signals noted through eyes still only half-open. At least we're there. I think to myself, when it is my turn in the belltower with the torch, that it is a bit like reaching out and feeling Anna's and Jamie's fingertips brush against mine for a moment—just a whisper of contact, but reassuring even so. In the drifting air of the belltower, with the dandelion clock outside reading no hour at all and only the pigeons for company, that can feel like a lot.

The summer is starting to draw towards its end, and there are some days when the sky is hazy in the early morning, and some days when the haze doesn't burn away by midday. Once we see thunderclouds far away on the skyline out to sea; but they must pass us by, because we never see anything more of them. Still, the heat now sometimes has a sweltering humidity to it, making T-shirts stick to you even when they've been clean on that morning and you've only been outside an hour. The weather seems to know it's going to break eventually, and is gathering itself for it.

The chapel stays cool and constant. In the patchy, deep-coloured half-light that spills in through the stained-glass window, the hermit lies in his bed on the dusty floor, and heals.

19

*T*he school year comes to an end, and another one begins, and Jamie continues his night-time escapes to London. Some part of what I say to him about schoolwork must make sense to him, though, because when his exam grades come through, they're not as bad as I have feared: they are mediocre, it's true, and everyone knows he should have done better, but they're enough to keep us together.

Even though my father's job has brought my parents back to England as well, now, I see little of Jamie in this summer. His parents are moving house again, and rather than stay with them through the haul of removals and packing and unpacking, he spends the time in London. He tells them—and I tell them, too, when they ask me—that he's staying with a school friend, someone in his year, whose family have a flat there. I know the truth: that he's sharing a bedsit with Paul, and playing the clubs almost every night. When I do get the chance to go and see him, it's always like visiting another world—a world that surrounds Jamie and makes sense of him in some way, so that he seems at ease and properly alive. It is a world in which I feel curiously detached; not unwelcome, but as if I am a child in the company of adults. It is only when the autumn closes in, and school begins again, that he sinks back into a kind of frustrated lethargy.

Sometimes I go to find him and he's not there. I get to know the signs; a kind of tension builds in him during the day, and in the late evening when everyone else is sleepy and ready for bed, Jamie is faking his sleepiness. An hour or two later and he will be gone. Most of the time he's back before three, creeping into the house by secret ways and going silently to bed. Sometimes, though, it's later—four or five o'clock. I know, because sometimes I lie awake and wait to hear his door, further down the corridor, open in the darkness of the sleeping house. Now that I am sixteen, I have once again caught Jamie up, if only in the sense that our rooms are on the same floor.

After that first time, when he lets me come with him, he doesn't invite me along on these excursions. He says that he's afraid of getting me into trouble if he's caught, and I believe that this is true—or mainly true. It's OK to go and watch him in the summer, he allows, and in other school holidays; he'll tell me when and where. But I know also that he doesn't tell me everything; that sometimes when he goes to London the saxophone stays in its case in his room. It's more than just playing the clubs, then; but I can't be certain what more.

I worry all the time about what will happen if they catch him, if he's found out. When I try to tell him this, though, he just laughs about it, as though it wouldn't matter at all.

"Have you heard about this?" I ask him one evening.

"What is it?"

"They're doing a combined arts trip to Florence. Applications next week."

"Oh," he says. "You going?"

"Yeah. It would be cool, don't you think?"

"I suppose. Lots of sketching and so on, then?"

"And other stuff," I say. "I thought—well, do you want to come?"

For a moment he looks genuinely perplexed. "Why?"

"You know—just to get out of here for a while. It's a whole week next term."

Jamie looks dubious. "Would they let me? I'm not an artist."

"You're a musician. Look here."

I have copied down the dates and events, and the phone numbers of all the concert halls and churches where they're to happen. It has taken me most of the afternoon, and a huge amount of change, to find it all out.

"What's this stuff?"

"Concerts and musical evenings and things like that. All in the week of the trip. There's bound to be more, but this is all I could find that've been planned out this far in advance. If you take this to the director of studies, he's bound to let you go. I mean, combined arts means music as well as painting and literature and that shit, doesn't it?"

A slow grin is spreading over Jamie's face. "You really think they'd go for it?" he says.

"Why not? You're an artist. You want to go. You've done all this preparatory work, and you're really, really enthusiastic about it. You *are* really, really, enthusiastic, aren't you?"

"*Really* really," Jamie confirms.

"Well then."

"If the applications are next week, how come you know all about it?"

"I have friends in high places," I say.

"Dalton?"

"Yeah."

"Thought so." He takes the piece of paper from me and stares at it. At last he says, "Yeah. That would be cool." There's a distant, slightly dreamy quality to his voice, as if he's already there in his head.

I say, "You sure?"

"Of course. Hey, Alex," he says, as I open the door to go.

"Yeah?"

"What do you call a clock without hands?"

"A dandelion clock, of course," I say, and for some reason that neither of us properly understands, we burst into uncontrolled laughter. In the corridor, a boy in Jamie's year passing by shakes his head in exaggerated disbelief. When I've got my breath back, I say, "It's still a crap joke, Jamie."

"All the best ones are," he grins. Then, after a moment, "This is a good idea, Alex."

"I'm full of them."

He just grins, one eyebrow raised, doesn't answer. I close the door, smiling to myself; I haven't been sure that Jamie will want this, but I have wanted it very much. It feels to me like it could be good for him. I have been haunted by what he said a long time before, that leaving Italy was a mistake. I want to see him back there, even for a short time. Now that he's agreed to it, there's only one more thing I have to do. As I walk back down the corridor to my room, I find myself whistling.

I'm still whistling softly as I smooth the sheet of writing paper and write out the school address at the top. Then I stop for a minute, staring at the blank part of the paper, wondering exactly how to say it. It's been a while since I last wrote; it's become harder to endure the silent waiting for replies that don't come. But this one will be different: I'm sure of that.

I tap the pen briefly on the desk and then write,

Dear Anna

"You've been nervous all day," she says, mopping up the coffee I've spilt with her napkin. "What's up with you?"

"It's nothing."

"Well, you shouldn't be drinking espresso if you're already this jumpy." She hesitates, then looks at me more closely. "Seriously, Alex. What is it? Is it still the—you know, the explosion thing?"

"It wasn't just an explosion thing," I say. "It was a *bomb*. People were killed."

"Yeah," she says quietly. "I know. But not us; we're OK. And it's been two days. Why are you still thinking about it?"

It's instinctive to glance round, though the moment I've done it I feel foolish. The café table is on a busy little street corner, and anyone lingering near us in the bustle would be painfully obvious. Still, I do it; and then I turn back to her. I say, "Don't you ever wonder about him?"

"Who?" she says blankly.

"Him. The hermit."

A flash of something—surprise?—crosses her face. She says, "That was ages ago, Alex. What's that to do with anything?"

I say, "I know it was ages ago. But sometimes, when you forget things, they—" I can't work out what to say to make sense of it. I stumble on anyway. "We were warned, weren't we? Not to forget. That was the thing. But you sound like it's all—buried, all gone away."

"It's in the past," she says. "That's the same thing."

"Not always, it isn't."

She looks at me with amusement. "So what's all this about?" she says.

"I saw someone, at the bar. The night we were there, you know?"

"Right. So did I. Lots of people."

"Not inside. Outside, on the street. It was someone I'd seen before."

"Yeah? Where?"

"I can't remember," I say.

"Did you know him?"

"It wasn't a him, it was a her. A woman. I'd seen her somewhere before, and then she was there that night at the bar."

"Are you sure?" Anna says; she sounds doubtful.

"Yes. Really sure. I just—can't remember where it was I saw her first."

"Oh." She's quiet for a moment. "And?"

I can tell I'm not making this sound right to her. She thinks I'm being paranoid. I say, "Listen. You remember when—you remember the hermit."

Her mouth twists in impatience. "Yeah, Alex. What's that got to do with anything?"

I plough on anyway. "You remember you and he—talked about stuff?"

"We all did."

"No. You talked to him more. Jamie and I got bored, but you never did. You used to talk to him lots more than we did."

She shrugs. "I really don't remember. It was a long time ago."

"He must have told you things. Don't you remember any of what you talked about?"

"Not really," she says. She thinks for a moment, and then adds, "Well, there was some stuff about—you know, what he'd done. But I think that was pretty much it. I was always like that as a kid, wanting to know all about things. It wasn't just the hermit, it was everything, I think."

I think of the Anna I remember from those years—the Anna constantly craving more of everything, more sensation, more experience, always fighting away boredom, always taking the risks Jamie and I wouldn't dare—and what she says now makes no sense to me. It was Jamie who wanted to know all about things, not Anna; Anna was the one who *did* things, not the one who read about them or talked about them.

"What is it?" she says. "You looked strange there, for a bit."

"I was just—remembering," I say. "You didn't seem like that to me."

"Well, we were just kids," she says again. "Things always look different, I guess. Are you going to drink that or not? I'll have it if you don't want it."

I say, "You don't think he could have said something to you that was—I don't know. Important, somehow. Like—something you shouldn't have heard?"

"Why?" she says, sipping at the remains of my coffee and wiping her mouth with the back of her hand.

"Because—maybe if he said something, and you heard it, and then *later* he realized that he'd said it, then he'd—"

She's starting to giggle. "Just get it out, Alex," she says.

"Maybe they're trying to kill you," I say. The moment the words are out, I know how wrong they are; they sound ridiculous, melodramatic, insane, in the bright morning air. Anna throws her head back and laughs delightedly.

"Oh, Alex! That's good. Is *that* what's been bothering you?"

The laughter feels like acid to me; and a memory stirs somewhere, uneasily.

I say, hopelessly, "I mean it. What if the—if that bomb had been meant to kill you? Or both of us? I mean—we're the only people who—who *know*. About him, I mean. We know his face."

She's still laughing. "Oh, Alex," she says again. "God. I mean—are you serious? Like the hermit's stalking us?" She snorts laughter again, and I wait, flushed and ashamed, until she stops. She drinks the last of the coffee and sets the cup down.

I say, "Well, I just thought—"

She interrupts. "Look," she says. "It's just a coincidence, OK? If the hermit had meant us any harm, he could have done it years ago. He didn't, though. He's out of our lives and we're out of his. Why on earth should he come back now? It's just all been a—horrible coincidence, that's all. There's no hermit any more. Maybe he's dead now, or in prison."

"I don't think so," I say dully. "There's never been anything in the papers."

"You mean you read the papers—*watching?*" She sounds amazed, and perhaps appalled as well.

"Sometimes."

"Christ," she says. She shakes her head, and we're quiet for a minute or more. Then she says, very steadily, "Alex, it's really simple. We were kids and we helped someone. He's gone now, and he's not going to come back and—I don't know, blow us up or something. It just doesn't work like that."

"How do you know?"

"I know," she says firmly. She is talking to me as if I am seven again. She says, "It's all in the past, and the past is gone. What we've got now is the present. That's all that counts."

Very reluctantly, I let myself nod. "OK," I say.

"Right. It's a beautiful day, you're in a beautiful city with lots of shit to sketch and draw and all that, and you stand a very good chance this afternoon of screwing your childhood sweetheart—again. So stop all this—panic. It was just something that happened, but we weren't there. It happened to other people, not us. It was nothing to do with us. Things like that happen all the time, everywhere; it's just that this one brushed by close to us. But it *brushed by.* Nothing more than that. OK?"

"OK," I say. She's smiling at me, gently.

"I was scared, too," she says. "When you told me, I mean. But it's gone now. We only have a couple of days left here, and we ought to make the most of them. It's just us, Alex; there's no-one lurking in the shadows, waiting to get us. It's just us. OK?"

I think of the woman I am sure I have seen before, but even so, I say it. "OK."

"And that's all. Come on, I'll pay up. Let's go and find something to do."

She is getting up, taking her bag from the back of the chair, starting towards the counter inside. I can't stop myself: the words rise up unbidden. I call after her, "Name angel."

She stops dead, turns back to me; her face is white as paper, as if it is the voice of a ghost that's called out to her.

She leans on the low wall that runs along beside the river, folding her arms around her as if she's cold, though the air is warm. I rest my elbows on the stone as well. She's not looking at me, but staring out over the water to the buildings running along the waterfront opposite, many of them cantelevered out and supported on wooden beams or stone arches.

At last she says, "Where did you learn Hungarian?"

"Your father was Hungarian, wasn't he?"

She nods. "Yeah. But that was—ages ago."

"Have you ever seen him again?"

Another nod. "A few times. He's got another family now. He used to come and see me sometimes, but my mother didn't like it. I write to him. I mean, I used to. Sometimes."

"Is that why you wanted us to help him?"

I mean the hermit, of course; and for once she doesn't ask me who I'm talking about. "Maybe," she says.

"Because he was Hungarian, too?"

"Maybe." She's quiet for a time. Then she says, "How did you know that?"

"I didn't," I say. "It was a guess."

"But you learnt the language?"

I shake my head. "No. I just remember what he said. I'd like to learn it, though; one day. Perhaps you could teach me."

She looks confused; dazed, almost. "What do you mean, 'What he said'?"

"The first time we saw him. We were going to go and get some-one—an adult, an ambulance, something like that. We'd got to the door of the chapel and he said something. It didn't make any sense at the time—well, not to me. But it did to you. That was the start of it all. You were—you were like us, up to then. You were going to go and tell some-one, find an adult, call an ambulance, all that. And then he said it, and you—you changed." I pause, take a breath. "You wouldn't let us leave him, remember? You wouldn't let Jamie and me leave. And later, when he told us to go and get Signor Ferucci—you wouldn't do that either. All because of that thing he said." I stop, and look at her for a while. "What does it mean?"

She is silent, and I wonder if she's trying to develop a lie; but then she just says, "It means, 'Don't go.' *Ne menj el.*"

Name angel.

"Yeah," I say. "That's what I thought." I shake my head. "And that was enough to—to make you do everything else? Just knowing he and you were born in the same country? That was all?"

"You remember the strangest things," she says, not answering. "Christ. When you said it, I thought—I mean, it sounded like him. You *sounded* like him." She sounds as though she can't quite believe this.

I say, "I just said what he said." I know what she means, though; in saying the words, I have imitated the one time I've heard them aloud. It's not the hermit's voice that has come out when I've spoken, but something in it must be close enough to wake that memory in her. She still looks pale, even in the warmth of the sunlight here.

She says, "God."

I say, "Do you see what I mean now? About him being a danger to us?"

She shakes her head slowly. "No, Alex. It doesn't change it at all. If anything, it's why I know you're wrong."

I stare at her, waiting for her to explain what she means.

She says, "You were right about one thing. I did talk to him. I talked to him a lot."

"Ah," I say.

"But that's why I'm sure, Alex. Maybe if I hadn't talked to him I'd be as—scared as you. But I got to know him. He wasn't just the hermit, for me. He was—someone I knew. Like a friend."

There is a catch in her voice as she says the last few words, and at once, I understand what it is she's held back. I say, incredulously, "You know his name, don't you?"

She shakes her head quickly, and then swallows, and nods. "Just his first name. Don't look like that. It's quite a common name, back home. It doesn't—identify him, or anything like that."

I can't believe this. I say, "He told you his *name*?"

"Why not? We told him ours. We trusted him, and he trusted us."

"You make it sound so simple," I say. "Anna, he was someone who killed people for a living."

"Not for a living," she says, and there's a spark of anger in her voice that surprises me. "He wasn't like that."

"I can't believe you'd trust someone like that."

"You trust me, don't you?" she says. Her eyes are flashing with some hard, unflinching emotion that I can't properly read; mainly anger, but—something else.

I say, "Of course. But that's—"

"Why? Why do you trust me? I keep telling you you hardly know me. We haven't spoken properly for—what? Six years or something. How can you trust this person?"

"That's just stupid," I say. I can hear anger in my voice—and in hers, too. I say, "You're talking about totally different things. You're my *friend,* someone I know. He was a terrorist, for God's sake. They're cowards, Anna—they kill children with bombs and run away. Like at the club. We could have died because of one of them, and we wouldn't even have known what they looked like. So no, I don't understand how you can trust someone like that, and I don't understand how you can say he was your friend the way—the way I am."

Her face is white. "You don't understand anything," she says.

"What don't I understand?"

"Have you studied any of this, Alex? Do you know anything—one single thing—about how terrorism works?"

"You don't need to study it to know this kind of thing, Anna. It's obvious."

"No," she says. "It's not."

I can't understand why she's so angry. I say, "Look—let's go and get a drink or something."

"I don't think so." She takes a breath, lets it out. "Alex—I could do with some time to myself, OK?"

"Hey," I say. "I'm sorry. I just—"

"It's OK," she breaks in. "I just need a walk. Why don't you go and sketch stuff for a while? I'll just—you know. Have a wander round. I'll see you later."

I'm starting to realize that I've upset her somehow, though I still can't see how or why. I say, "I'm really sorry. I just don't understand."

"No," she says. "I know. It doesn't matter."

"I'll see you later?"

"Sure." She smiles, a small, uneven smile. "Don't worry."

I watch her as she weaves her way through the people, head down, in the direction of the Palazzo Vecchio. All I can think is, *Christ, Alex—how did you screw things up like that? What did you do wrong?*

But I can't work it out. And I can't see how she can think that the hermit was ever her friend. It makes no sense to me.

I'd like to learn it, though; one day. Perhaps you could teach me.

It's just a moment of language, then, that links Anna and the hermit: a momentary realization of a connection. It's so slight. Then, from that first tiny contact, there come conversations, and gradually laughter, and quiet songs with unfamiliar words in the night. Hiding a gun, and a car. Keeping watch. Not telling, never telling. All from three small words.

But it's years before I do learn the language; painfully slowly, over a long time. It doesn't come easily, but I do it anyway, though I'm never really sure why; there's no reason to learn it any more. It's just one of those things: a relic. I do it anyway.

As the heat of the summer starts to be charged with humidity, and we see storm clouds more often far out at sea, we have to spend less time with the hermit. It becomes more and more difficult to absent ourselves from home so constantly, and although we keep up the rota of night-shifts in the chapel, during the day we are sometimes forced to abandon the hermit for hours at a time. None of us is too worried about doing this, though; while the hermit is still unable to move any distance un-aided, his wound seems to be healing well, and he's able to feed and look after himself much better than before.

One afternoon, when we are talking together in the sun outside the chapel, Anna says, "What day is it?"

"Tuesday, I think," Jamie says.

"What date, I mean."

He looks at his watch. "The twenty-third."

Anna nods. "I'm going to be eleven tomorrow," she says.

"Really?" Jamie is surprised, and I am too; Anna hasn't said anything until now. "It's your birthday tomorrow?"

"Yeah."

"You should have said. We should have a party."

She shrugs, looking a bit uncomfortable. "It's OK," she says.

I say, "Why didn't you say anything?"

"I forgot."

"How can you forget your birthday?" I say, strangely impressed. I think of the weeks of planning that always go into my birthday; to forget that it's coming at all seems very strange.

Anna says, "We—don't do much about birthdays. At home, I mean."

"Well, we do," Jamie says decisively. "We should have a party. We'll have to plan it quickly, if there's only a day to go."

"Yeah," I say, seriously. "It's important."

Anna's uncertain look lingers for a moment, but then it's replaced by a kind of embarrassed excitement. She says, "Really? There isn't time."

"Yes there is," Jamie says. "We'll have to go and tell Lena."

"She does the best birthday cake in the valley," I explain, when Anna looks at me questioningly.

"And then we'll have to think about presents," Jamie says.

"You'll have to have a birthday dinner," I say. "You know. Tomorrow evening."

"Yeah?"

"Yeah, of course."

Jamie is thinking, and we wait for him to come up with a plan. At last he nods to himself, and says, "OK, this is what we should do. Anna, you and me'll go and see Lena and tell her. You can ask for the kinds of food you really like, too. And we should tell my parents, too."

"Don't they know already?" I say.

"Well, they haven't said anything, have they? Did *you* tell them?" he asks Anna.

"No. I told you, I forgot."

"Well, then, they won't know." Jamie is grinning with excitement. "This'll be fun."

"Yeah," I say, nodding agreement.

"Alex, you stay with the hermit. Then once we've sorted everything with Lena, Anna can come back and take over and you and me'll go shopping and get all the stuff. OK?"

"OK," I say. I'm a bit sad that I won't be there for the serious business of planning the meal, but I know Lena will tell me all about it later. Besides, it's Anna's birthday, and it is right that she should tell Lena what she wants herself.

"Right," Jamie says. "We'll be back by five, probably. Or Anna will. I might stay down there and wait for you."

"No problem," Anna says.

"Get sweets," I call after them as they run off towards the fence. "For after."

"OK," Jamie calls back over his shoulder.

I am left alone, shaking my head in wonder that something so important as a birthday could have been forgotten—could, in fact, have nearly slipped by us without any of us noticing. It's not a good thought.

Somewhere far off there is a faint, rumbling echo; thunder in the hills inland. I glance up, but the sky, though hazy, is free of clouds. In this weather, though, you can smell the resin from the pine-trees more sharply, for some reason, and I know that it means that the bright, clear part of the summer is now behind us. It always comes as a surprise; and I quickly push from my mind the thought that school is not far away now.

Feeling slightly melancholy, I trudge inside the chapel to check on the hermit.

He's lying as usual on his bed. When I get closer to him, I can see that he's got his wounded leg bent a little at the knee, as if he's trying to see whether it will move properly.

I say, "What're you doing?"

He looks up. "Hello, Alex," he says. He is always polite with us, and calls us by our names. I quite like it.

"Doesn't that hurt?" I say.

"Yes; it does, rather. But I want—" He gives a little gasp as he bends the knee further, and then he eases the leg down on the boards again, gently. "I want to see if it still works," he says, smiling a little.

"Does it?"

"It seems to. I shan't be walking on it for a while, but it's definitely getting better. You did a good job with the bandages and cleaning it."

"Oh. Good," I say, not sure how to reply to this. "It was Anna, really."

"I know." The hermit shifts himself until he's sitting up more. "Where are she and Jamie, then?"

"They've gone off to plan," I say, pleased to have someone to confide the whole story to. The hermit will do until I can talk to Lena.

"Really? What are they planning, then?" he says. He sounds amused and interested.

I say, "It's Anna's birthday tomorrow. We're going to have a party."

"Yes? How old is she?"

"Eleven. She's going to be eleven, I mean. She's ten now."

"Ah. Exciting, no? Have you bought her a present?"

"No," I say. It's something that's already bothering me. "She only told us today. She'd forgotten."

"Forgotten a birthday?" The hermit raises one eyebrow in disbelief. "That's quite something to forget."

"That's what I said," I say, pleased that someone else agrees with me. "I'd never forget *my* birthday. Or Jamie's," I add, after a second.

"No, I should think not," the hermit says seriously. "But perhaps she's had other things on her mind."

"Well, I s'pose."

"So what will you do?"

"About what?"

"About the present. You'll have to get her something," the hermit says.

I sit down on the floor beside him with a sigh. He's right, but we've used up all our money—and all his—buying provisions and medical supplies. "I know," I say. "But I can't afford anything."

"We shall have to think about that, then," he says. "Perhaps you can make her something instead."

"Yeah," I say, rather more hopefully. "I could, I suppose. But what?"

"That's the difficult thing," the hermit agrees. "We should think about that. It ought to be something that is special—that will remind her of you." He looks at me for a moment. "You like Anna, don't you?"

"Mm," I say. "Yes."

"So. Something to remind her of you. If I were you, do you know what I'd do?"

"What?" I say, entranced.

"I'd go to somewhere that you go together—that you both know—and I'd look around. I wouldn't go looking for one thing in particular; I'd just wait until the right thing caught my eye. It could be anything: you never know what you'll find when you're looking. But the right thing will be there, if your eyes are open. Do you know a place like that?"

"Yeah," I say. "Thanks."

"Don't mention it," he says. "It's the least I can do, after all you're doing for me."

"Well," I say, rather uncertainly.

The hermit doesn't seem to notice. "And you'll give her a party, of course?" he says.

"Yes. Tomorrow evening."

"Yes? That will be fun."

"Yeah," I say. "It's going to be great."

The hermit laughs at that, and nods. I am pleased that he cares about Anna so much that he's happy that she's having a party; and I'm pleased that he's given me a way to find her a present. For the first time, I start to think that perhaps I could get to like the hermit, the way that Anna seems to.

The skies are grey and overcast on Anna's birthday—the first dark skies for well over a month. The party will be in the evening, so I have time to find Anna a present.

"I'm going to the beach," I tell Jamie first thing.

He looks at the sky and looks at me in disbelief. "It looks like rain," he says. "Besides, there's too much to do."

"No, I really am," I say. Anna's in the kitchen with Lena, so I can talk openly. I say, keeping my voice low, "I've got an idea for a present for her and I need to find something on the beach."

"Yeah?" Jamie says, intrigued. "What?"

"I don't know yet."

"Then how do you know what to look for?"

"The right thing will be there, if my eyes are open," I say. Jamie laughs hysterically at this, though I can't see anything funny in it. Anna comes out of the kitchen.

"What's up with you two?"

"Nothing," I say quickly.

"Alex is mad," Jamie says, very seriously.

"Shut up," I say.

Anna comes close to us. "Someone ought to check on the—dandelion clock," she says.

Jamie has had the last shift. "Everything was OK when I came back," he says.

"Yeah. But still."

Jamie nods. "OK. I can run up there before lunch. Is Lena keeping you here?"

Anna rolls her eyes expressively. "She says I have to be involved in all the cooking. She says it's traditional. Is it?"

"Yes," I say.

"Yes," Jamie agrees.

"Oh."

"It'll be OK," Jamie says. "I'll go and check on—you know—and Alex can keep you company."

"Not for a while," I remind him. "I'm going—I've got somewhere I need to go."

"Very mysterious," Anna says, grinning. "OK. I'll see you later, then."

"Yeah," I say. Jamie nods.

"I have to cut shapes out of pastry now," Anna says. She makes it sound like she's going to have to eat beetles or something.

Jamie heads up the valley and I head down. I turn every so often in the road to watch his progress, until he fades from view among the undergrowth of the abandoned fields. I quicken my pace slightly: the sooner I can get to the little cove, the sooner I can find something for Anna.

The beaches are deserted, even the bigger, sandy one in the centre of Altesa's bay. A steady breeze is coming in off the sea, and although the air is still warm, the breeze, and the occluded sky, make everything look as though it should be cold. I find it rather disconcerting as I make my way along the cliff path and down onto the pebbles of the cove.

I try to do exactly what the hermit has said, and I wander up and down the beach vaguely, keeping my eyes wide and waiting for something to spring out of the background and grab my attention. There are pieces of driftwood washed up on the high-tide line, but none of them is very pretty or interesting. Sometimes you can find driftwood with twists that look like something—a face, maybe, or a hand—but not today. There is dry seaweed, but no matter how hard I use my imagination, I can't imagine how seaweed could ever be a birthday present you'd be pleased to get. There are a few shells, too, though not many, but I know that while shells might be fine for one of the girls at school, they'd be wrong for Anna.

In the distance comes the sound of thunder again, and despite myself I shiver; the rains are clearly coming. The whole beach suddenly seems very dark, as though it's dusk all at once. I imagine how nasty it will be to be outside when it starts to pour, and remember also that Jamie has said we shouldn't go along the high cliff path in thunderstorms because of the lightning. The cove, which is usually such a friendly place, feels threatening and hostile, and I don't like it.

It's right down by the water's edge that I see it, about a yard out under the waves. It's difficult to see clearly because the surface of the water is getting quite choppy, even here behind the rock spur. Still, what I can see is enough to convince me to pull off my shoes and socks, and roll up my trousers, and wade out until I can reach down through the water and pick it out from among its fellows. Out of the water, but still glistening with the sea, it's perfect: small and pale, the colour of moonlight. But the best part is at the top, and it's this which has given me the idea for Anna's present.

The money Lena has given me is in my pocket, and now it seems that I might have a use for it after all. A piece of string would do, of course; but for it to be a proper present, I know that I should really find something better—something more special. I know what I need, and it's something I'll need to buy and not find on the beach.

I make it to the shops and out onto the road at the edge of town before the rain starts. Then fat, heavy, warm drops start to pound the countryside. By the time I'm home, my shoes and trousers are stained russet from the dust-mud on the road, and I'm soaked through. The trees in the garden are hissing and dripping with rain, and all the smells of the lavender and rosemary are gusting out in great pungent waves. Further up the valley, where Jamie must be, the water is drifting in sheets through the air. I wonder what it must sound like, on the roof of the chapel; and I think of Jamie in there with the hermit, listening to the rain, and am glad I'm home with Lena and Anna. I hide my present in my room, under the bed, and join them in the kitchen to make food for the party, and to wait for Jamie to come back.

Jamie is sitting with his back to a tree trunk, watching the distant figures of cricketers on one of the pitches. I dump my sketch pad and books down on the grass beside him, and he looks up, startled.

"I've got it," I say. "We don't call it a clock because we tell the time by it. We tell the time by it because we call it a clock. Do you see?"

Jamie blinks. "What?"

"What you said—about it being weird calling it a clock. I couldn't stop thinking about it. So I went and looked it up."

A flicker of interest shows in his face. "Yeah? What did it say?"

"The Oxford English just says it's a name for a dandelion seedhead, and that kids play at telling the time by it."

"I knew that."

"I know. But it still didn't say *why*. But then I thought, it's French, isn't it? Norman French, from when we were invaded. Dandelion. *Dents de lion*, lion's teeth. From the way the leaves look—all jagged."

Jamie's nodding. "Yeah."

"So I thought, if the plant's French, perhaps the clock part comes from French, too."

"What's French for 'clock,' then?"

"No," I say. "That's the wrong way round. It wouldn't have *meant* clock, back then. It would have been a French word that *sounded* like clock, so when the English heard it, they thought that's what the Normans were saying."

Jamie's nodding, understanding at once. "Yeah. Of course."

"I thought *cloche* to start with, so I looked that up."

"Means 'bell,' " Jamie says.

"Yeah, that's what I found. But why would they call it a bell? It doesn't look like a bell."

"Maybe one of those round bells on a jester's cap or something."

"Yeah, but not much, does it? Look. Think of a dandelion clock. What does it *really* look like? Imagine it. If you had to use a word for it, what would it be?"

I can see Jamie's mind is working at it now. He's silent for a long time, and then at last he says, "It's kind of like a moon, maybe. A white sphere. But it looks soft. And the light comes through it—silvery. Like a bubble underwater, maybe."

" 'Like a bubble underwater,' " I echo.

"What?"

I can hardly stop myself grinning. "There's another word. It is pretty rare now, but I bet a thousand years ago it was really common. *Cloque*. And get this—it comes from the same root as *cloche*. They were the same once."

Jamie's staring at me. "What does it mean?"

"Mostly? 'Blister,' " I say, grinning. "But in one little region, they still remember another meaning, one that everyone else has forgotten. So there *cloque* also means 'bubble.' "

Jamie's face breaks into the look of triumph that I know comes when he has the answer to something. "Or bubble," he says softly. "Yeah. That's it. Are you sure?"

"No. It's all guesswork."

"The Oxford doesn't say anything more?"

"No."

"That's like the biggest dictionary ever."

"I know. I could be wrong. But I think we tell the time by it cos it's called a clock, not the other way round. And I think it's called a clock because—"

"Because it looks like a bubble," he finishes. "Yeah. Yeah, that's got to be it." He looks up at me, and grins. "Cool," he says. "Fields of bubbles. Good one, Alex."

The party is enormous fun. We eat Anna's birthday dinner in Jamie's house, and Mr. and Mrs. Anderson have decorated the room, just as it should be. There is a cake, hastily assembled by Lena and with eleven candles in a circle, and there are games afterwards. We can't play in the garden, because it's still raining; but otherwise everything is perfect.

I've taken my special present with me, still wrapped in its bag. When the games are finished my parents arrive, and the adults all go off into the sitting room to talk and have G-and-Ts and finish the Asti Spumante, of which we've been allowed little glasses because this is a celebration, and at last we're left alone. Jamie gives Anna a book he's bought, and I give her my necklace.

"It's from the beach," I say, feeling suddenly and inexplicably shy. "I found it."

"It's beautiful," she says, turning it over in her hands. "How did you make it into a necklace?"

"The man in the shop did it," I say. "I bought the chain." The chain is thin, and silver-coloured, and looks good with the colour of the stone.

"It's beautiful," she says again.

"Yeah," Jamie says. He sounds impressed. "It's a great idea. You were lucky to find one like that. They're usually bigger."

"Yeah," I say, pleased that he understands; but then, Jamie always understands.

Anna opens the clasp and puts it round her neck. It takes her a moment to fiddle it closed again. "I haven't had a necklace before," she says. "There." She raises her head and straightens the pebble. "How's it look?"

"Nice," Jamie says.

"Yeah," I say.

"It feels—weird," she says, and then adds hastily, "Nice, I mean. I'm just not used to it, that's all."

"Look in the mirror," Jamie suggests. Anna goes across the room and looks at herself carefully.

"Yeah," she says. "Yeah, I like it."

I realize I'm smiling widely, and hastily try to look more nonchalant. Anna likes it. It's difficult not to grin.

Later, upstairs, Anna and Jamie sit on the edge of the bath while I brush my teeth.

"What about—you know?" Jamie says.

I say, with my mouth full of toothpaste, "We could leave it."

"No," Anna says, as I've expected she will. "We should go. We needed to take more water in any case. Jamie?"

"Yeah," Jamie says reluctantly. "There's not much left."

"It's my turn," she says. "I don't mind."

Jamie glances at me, and then says, "No. I'll go."

"You're not on till four," she protests.

"It's your birthday," he says. "You should get a proper night's sleep. I'll go. I'll do the whole lot, if you want." He grins, tiredly. "The way I feel right now, it won't make much difference anyway."

Anna hesitates, and I know she's thinking of what it would be like to sleep all night in a bed, without having to get up every hour, and without having to trek all the way up the valley at some point. She says, "Are you sure?"

"Yeah," Jamie says. "Birthday present."

"OK." She's quiet a moment, and then she giggles. "God, yes. OK. You're right. I can hardly keep my eyes open."

"I'll go at twelve," Jamie says. "They'll be in bed by then. I'll take him some water."

"You could take him some Asti," I say. Anna and Jamie grin.

"Yeah. And a piece of cake," Anna says. She rubs her face with one hand. "It's been a great birthday. Thanks."

"It's OK."

She gets up. "I'm going to bed," she says. "Bed. To sleep for ages and ages and ages."

We grin, rather enviously.

"I might get up tomorrow," she adds, from the door. "Or I might not. I just—can't—tell."

"Night," Jamie says.

"Night," I say.

"See you tomorrow," Anna says. "Thanks again."

We hear her door close down the hall, and look at each other. "You're mad," I say. "Are you really going to do the whole night?"

"I can sleep in the belltower," Jamie says. "It's not so bad." He yawns. "Let's get a couple of hours, anyway."

"Yeah," I say.

I'm only half awake when he leaves. "Alarm clock's here," he says. "It's just midnight. Remember to watch for me at one."

"Mm," I say. "I will."

"It's still raining," he says.

"Wear your coat."

"I am. See you tomorrow."

"T'day," I mumble into my pillow. I don't hear the door close, but he must leave. Darkness swells round me and swallows me whole.

I'm bleary when I put my eye to the telescope to check on Jamie's signal; bleary and only murkily awake. Then suddenly my stomach gives a weird lurch, and the sleepiness is gone as if drenched away in cold water. I'm fully awake, and my heart's pounding. I run to the light switch, and my fingers judder off it before I calm myself enough to do it properly.

I toggle the switch briefly six times; not the acknowledgement I usually send, but the "send again" response that we're supposed to use to confirm an unusual or misread signal. Then I hurry back to the telescope.

It's the same.

I make the acknowledgement signal—three pulses—and then scramble to find my clothes on the floor. As I creep down the hall to Anna's room, my heart's still pounding: I can feel it, louder than my breathing.

I shake Anna's shoulder.

"Wha'?" she mumbles. "Go away."

"Wake up."

"Piss off, Alex. I want to sleep."

"Anna, wake up," I say, shaking her more desperately. Finally her eyes come open.

"What is it?" She sounds thoroughly irritated. "Read a book if you're bored. I don't want to play anything." Then she must see my face clearly, because her tone changes completely. "Alex? What's wrong?"

"The signal's red," I say.

Without the stars or the moon, and with the haze of falling rain thick in front of us, the night is horribly dark. We blunder along the farm track, only just able to discern the edges of the road.

"There it is," I say.

"Where?"

"There."

We cross the bridge and scramble down the sharp bank more by touch than anything. Anna is first down; I hear a splash, and her voice, high with shock, shouts "Shit!"

"What is it?" I say, but I'm slithering down the muddy bank too, and a second later I'm beside her and the question's answered for me. "Ow!"

The empty river isn't empty any longer. Fast-running water, sharply cold, is halfway to my knees. I can just make it out, swirling and eddying and sweeping past under the bridge. We're both speechless for a moment.

"We can go along the bank," I say.

"How?" Anna demands. "It's all bushes. We can't see a thing. It'd take us all night."

"The roads, then," I say, a little desperately.

"We don't know the way. We'd be lost." She lets out an explosive breath. "*Shit!* Why didn't we ever think of this?"

I don't have an answer, so I keep quiet. The cold is starting to seep up my legs.

"Come on," she says, and I hear more than see her splashing out into the middle of the river.

"We can't go up this," I say.

"We've got to. It's all right. It's not deep, and the bottom's not too muddy."

"I'm cold," I say miserably.

"Me, too. If we walk fast it'll help keep us warm. Give me your hand."

I splash after her and put my hand in hers. She grips it tightly.

"There. We won't let go, OK? It won't be so bad. Come on. We can tell stories and sing songs and stuff like that."

It feels like some of her determination is flowing through her fingers into me. I say, "OK, then."

"Yeah! Alex is *on the team*!" she shouts, which makes me grin. Then, "Right. Let's go."

We splash erratically up the river. The water is quick-moving and the surface of it is all hissing with the rain that's coming down, so the river, when we can see it, looks like it's boiling. It doesn't feel that way, though. It feels colder and colder with every step, and although Anna's right—I'm quickly out of breath and I can feel sweat on my forehead—my feet and legs are still chilled.

"Don't kick through it," she says after a time. "Lift your feet out and then put them down. It's easier."

I try, and she's right, though the peculiar, high-stepping gait feels uncomfortable and awkward. Thunder grumbles in the hills, and a couple of times there is lightning far off, which clicks a momentary brilliance on the valley; but mostly there is just the steady, unending sound of the rain, never varying, never slackening. It sounds as though it might just keep raining for ever.

"What songs do you know? We'll sing a song."

Sometimes I feel stuff in the water snag round my legs, and I have to shake it off to free them; there must be weeds and plants and things. Once, a piece of wood or something heavy cracks me hard across the shins, and I cry out.

"You OK?"

"Something hit me."

"Try to keep going. Let's have another song, all right?"

We sing, trying to be cheerful, but our voices sound thin and too high against the heavy wash of the rain, as though all the strength has been stolen from them. Anna tells me stories, and I try to think of jokes that Jamie and I have swapped in the past. Sometimes we laugh, but the sound is breathless and stilted, punctuated by the sloshing of our wading steps.

"It's getting deeper," I say.

"No it's not. It's your imagination."

"No, it is. It's deeper than before. It's up to my knees."

She's silent for a minute; then, "Yeah. Mine too. It's filling up."

"What'll we do?" I say, and real panic grips me.

"It's OK," she says. "It's only going up slowly. We'll be all right. Look, if it gets too high, we can get out and try to go along the bank like you said, OK?"

"OK."

"Don't worry," she says. "Don't worry. It's going to be all right. Don't worry." The words are hypnotic, like a chant. We thresh through the water, hanging onto each other's hands so hard it hurts.

"Anna? I'm scared."

"No you're not. It's not so far to go now."

"How do you know?"

"I saw something back there," she says, lying. "A tree. We're really close now."

"Are you sure?" I say. I know it's a lie but I want to hear her say it all the same.

"Yeah, I'm really sure. Not far now. Just keep going."

"Anna—"

"Yeah?"

"We're not going to drown, are we?"

She laughs, and it sounds shrill and forced, like it might shatter in the air. "It's only up to our knees, Alex! Don't be silly. It's just a little river."

"I'm tired."

"I know. Keep going. It's not far now."

"It's not?"

"No. Promise. I saw a bush back there. We're really close now."

"Jamie will be surprised to see us like this," I say. "All wet."

"Yeah. He'll probably laugh his head off."

"Anna?"

"Yeah?"

"It's above my knees now."

"No it's not. It's just slopping up when you walk, that's all."

"Is it?"

"Yeah. You can't really tell cos you can't see properly."

"Oh," I say. "Right."

"This is going to be really funny when we're all dry and warm," she says.

"Yeah!" I say. "Yeah, it is."

"Not far to go now."

"Yeah," I say. "I saw a tree back there, I think. I think I did."

"Me too. We must be pretty close now."

The rain hammers down on the swelling river, and we plough on through it. No matter how high I lift my feet, they're never out of the water now; and our progress is laborious and exhausting. Every step is an effort. We haven't much breath to sing or tell stories, and for half an hour or more all that passes between us is the occasional reassurance that we're getting close, that the water's not rising any more, that we're going to be warm and dry soon.

"I think—we're there," Anna gasps.

"Me too," I say dully. "I saw—"

"No, Alex," she says. "Really. Look—over there. Is that it?"

I peer through the gloom. There's a pale shadow just visible through the rain. "I think—yeah," I say. "Yeah, I think so."

"Thank God," she says. "Where's the place through to the fence?"

We fight our way in to the bank and along it. "Here!" I say. "It's here."

The bank is slick and muddy. I slip back the first time I try to climb out, but then I get a handhold on the thick stem of a bush and pull myself free. Looking back, I can see the water swirling thickly around Anna. She scrambles for the bank, and I stretch out my hand to her. She grabs it and has hauled herself part-way out when something gives way. There's a slithering sound, and her hand is wrenched from mine. She doesn't even have time to cry out. A splash, and she's lost in the dark water.

"Anna!" I shout, but there's nothing: only the sound of the rain hissing into the river, and the slop of water against the mud of the bank. She's gone.

I panic. I cast about in the little area of bank on which I'm standing, trying to get a clear view of the river. "Anna!"

There's a voice; or at least, I *think* there's a voice. I hear something. The wash of water sounds fills my head. Somewhere away in the darkness is a heavy splash; part of the bank falling in, perhaps. I think of where the river goes: all the way down through the valley, through the town in its concrete conduit, and out into the harbour, into the distant blackness of the sea. "Anna!"

"Alex!"

It's her. I can't see her, but I can hear her voice. I get down as close to the water as I dare, clinging to the bush I've found. "Where are you?" I shout.

For a long time there's no response. Then I see something: a slight, dark figure battling against the coursing weight of the water. A tree branch sweeps by me, and I see it flash past her and then disappear into the night. She makes her way closer in to the bank, where the water is slacker. I can hear her gasping for breath as she gets near, and I stretch my hand out towards her.

"I'm here," I say. I feel her hand—terribly cold—close over mine, and for what feels like ages she just grips it, so hard it hurts through the numbness of my fingers, just holding me. I squeeze her hand back. At last, she manages to pull herself out of the water and up onto the mud with me, and she sits down suddenly and heavily, with a thump. Her breath is still ragged, and she's drenched, her hair plastered down over her head. She's shivering and I can feel her body shuddering through her anorak. She looks up at me, and on her face there is an expression I don't recognize. It's halfway between fear and—I can't tell.

Suddenly she turns to one side and spits. "Shit. I've got—" She pauses, spits again. "Yuk. I've got the whole river in my mouth."

"Did you go under?"

"Yeah." She spits again, and wipes her mouth on the back of her hand. "Shit, I'm cold."

The shivering is worse. I say, "We'd better get inside. Maybe there's—"

"Yeah. Let's get inside. Come on." She drags herself to her feet, still gripping my hand. She glances down, and seems to notice for the first time that she's still holding onto me. Abruptly, as if she's suddenly embarrassed, she lets go. She leads the way up the bank, but I notice that her steps are uneven and look weak. We struggle through the undergrowth until we crash into the fence.

"Ow," she says.

"You OK?"

"Yeah. I banged my arm." Her words are indistinct; her teeth are chattering.

My legs are numb and feel wobbly. It's more difficult climbing the fence than I would have thought possible; on the other side, I almost collapse. Anna is bent double, holding her knees, panting.

"God," she says.

I struggle to my feet and she straightens up.

"Nearly there," she says, and this time it's a joke, and I manage a breathless laugh.

"Yeah. I saw a chapel back there."

"Yeah. Too right."

"This had better be important," she says. "If he's just—forgotten his comics or something, I'll—"

"Me too."

We round the end of the chapel and come up on the side door. It's open. Anna's first inside, and I follow.

Jamie has lit several of the supply of candles, and they cast a warm light on the pale inside of the chapel. I think briefly to myself that he's been wasteful to light so many; we're supposed to be saving them. I stop beside Anna. Jamie comes up the chapel towards us; he has the torch in his hand. He is staring at us, and for the first time I am able to look down at myself and see what he's seeing: I'm soaked to the waist, my clothes all slathered with mud and bits of grass from the river-bank, and pine needles. Anna is even worse. Water is coming in a steady stream from the hem of her anorak, and all down one side she's covered in ochre slime from the riverbed. Jamie's mouth is open, and I can tell he's shocked at how we look. Glancing at him, I see that only his shoes and the ankles of his trousers are wet; the river must have been only filling a little when he made his way up. For an insane second, it's all wildly funny to me, and I want to burst out laughing.

Anna says, sharply, "What's wrong?"

The urge to laugh dies in me. Even though she's drenched and shivering, Anna is still in control. "Is he OK?" I echo.

Jamie shakes his head. He closes his mouth, and swallows, and then says, "He's gone."

"What?" Anna says. She sounds like she hasn't heard him properly. Maybe she's shivering too much.

"He's gone," Jamie says again. "When I got here, he wasn't there. And he's taken the gun."

Anna and I stare at him stupidly. "But he can't walk," I say.

Jamie shrugs helplessly.

"Gone?" Anna says. "How?"

"I don't know. He just is."

The candles flicker and jump in the air coming in through the open door. Jamie and Anna and I stand there, not speaking, not knowing what to say or do. The hermit's gone, I think to myself; the hermit's gone. I'm so tired that the words don't feel like they've really got a meaning; they're just words, going round my head. Anna, beside me, is hugging her arms around herself, trying to keep warm. River water is in a pool on the chapel floor around our feet. The hermit's gone. It doesn't mean anything.

20

*W*e sit on the bare boards of the chapel, shivering. I can feel my teeth rattling together in my head, and Anna, when I look her way, is still shaking visibly. When she speaks, her voice trembles with cold.

"How did he know where the gun was?"

"I don't know," Jamie says.

"And how could he walk?"

I say, "He was bending his leg yesterday. But he said it would be a long time before he could walk on it."

"He lied to us," Anna says, incredulously.

Jamie says, "He must have got all the way up into the belltower."

"How did he know it was there?" Anna says again. Then, "Shit, I'm cold."

"Me, too."

Jamie says, "What happened to you?"

"The river's filled up," I say simply. "We had to wade through it. Anna fell in." Anna and I glance at each other, and a silence absorbs this understatement.

"It was only like a stream when I came," Jamie says.

"Yeah, well, it's full now."

"God."

I say, "Why did you signal us? You could have come back and told us he was gone. Then we wouldn't—" I gesture vaguely at our sopping clothes. A flash of guilt crosses Jamie's face.

"Well, I thought maybe—maybe he'd just gone a little way, and we could—you know, look for him. Together. But I looked from the bell-tower and there wasn't anything I could see. And—" He hesitates. "I wasn't sure I should walk back—you know. On my own."

I start to understand. In the dark, with the hermit maybe somewhere near, and the gun gone—

"But he's really gone?" I say.

"Yeah," Jamie says, sounding grateful for the things I haven't asked. "If he could get up to the tower and get the gun, he's probably miles away by now."

We sit in silence for a minute. Jamie is starting to look worried.

"You're going to catch cold if you sit here like this," he says.

"I know," Anna says. "What else are we supposed to do, though?"

Jamie says, "You should get warm. We need a fire or something."

"Can't have a fire in here," Anna says, her words muffled as she cups her hands round her mouth. "It'd burn. The floor's wood."

"Not at the end," Jamie says.

He's right. At the altar end of the chapel there is a step up, and then the floor is marble right to the wall under the stained-glass window. Suddenly the thought of a warm fire is right in the front of everyone's mind.

"There's bits of wood in the blue sacks over there," Jamie says. "In with the bricks and stuff."

"Yeah," Anna says decisively. "Come on. Before we freeze to death."

We get the fire going with candlewax and shreds of bandage, and soon it's spluttering away happily. The wood is old and tinder-dry, and most of it is in the form of slats which we can break easily across a knee. Jamie tends the fire and gets the hermit's blankets, and Anna and I take off our soaked clothes and wrap up in the blankets instead. Jamie hunts through the jumble of old pews and finds a kind of carved bench which, with a lot of effort, he is able to extricate and drag down to the fireside.

He hangs our trousers and pyjamas and Anna's top and anorak on it to dry.

"How're we going to get home?" I say. "The river's full now, and we don't know any other way."

"We can try the roads, once it's daylight," Jamie says. "Maybe we'll be able to find our way down."

"When's it light?"

"Maybe five o'clock. I can't remember. I think it's usually light when I'm coming back."

"Only if we're late they'll know we were gone. There's no-one to cover for us."

"I know," he says.

Anna says, half to herself, "I can't believe he lied to us." And then, "How did he know where the gun was? We said it was in the valley, behind a rock. How did he *know*?"

"Maybe he knew a lot of things," Jamie says.

Some time in the middle of the night, the rain starts to ease, and the thunder dies away over the hills inland. I stir uncomfortably; the floor is hard and difficult to lie on. Jamie is dozing against the end of the bench he's brought, and Anna is curled up beside me, fast asleep, her blanket wrapped tightly round her. She's sucking her thumb; I've never seen her do this before, and for some reason it makes me smile. The fire is dying down to a heap of red embers, and sleepily I take another couple of pieces of wood from the pile Jamie's made and push them in. There is a little rush of gold sparks that swirl in the air and are gone in an instant, and then the flames catch and the slats start to crackle. The fire has been a good idea. I feel warm and almost cosy, despite the unyielding surface of the marble.

Jamie stirs slightly, and makes a little sound; then he's still. I rest my head back on my arms and stare into the fire.

Dawn comes pale and washed-out over the hills at the head of the valley. Gradually, the chapel lightens almost imperceptibly, until the forms and shapes of its walls and pillars and organ-loft are all discernible. The fire looks dead, but when Jamie stirs it up, there are some hot parts in the middle. He feeds it sticks and pieces of bandage and more wood until it's blazing merrily, and then reaches across to wake Anna.

"What time is it?" she says.

"Half-four. The rain's stopped."

"Good." She sits up and stretches, and looks about her.

Jamie says, "How do you feel? Are you OK?"

"Yeah. I think."

"Alex?"

"Mm. I think so."

"They're not really dry," he says, pointing at our clothes. "What do you think?"

"I think we should go," Anna says. "We won't get home in time otherwise, and then they'll want to know where we've been."

"Yeah," Jamie says. "That's what I think, too."

"I don't want to wear wet trousers," I say.

"I know," Anna says. "Neither do I. And my top's wet too, remember? But we'll be home soon and we can get dry ones."

"Mm. OK."

"Right. Let's get dressed, then."

We make our way back by the roads. It's not too difficult to find a way through the farm tracks to the main road into town; then it's just a question of trudging steadily down it. To begin with we're all nervous, on the lookout for cars coming or going. We will have to jump down into the ditch if any do. But there are none; everything is still asleep in the grey dawn light. We soon lose our vigilance and concentrate on the simple process of walking.

My shoes squeak with every step; they're still sodden, and though when I put them on they're warmly damp from the heat of the fire, they become cold and clammy almost the moment we're out the chapel door. By the time we're on the road, my feet are starting to feel sore and aching at the sides and heels.

On the downturn where the road straightens, something catches my eye. It's just for a second, when the bushes at the side of the road thin out for a couple of paces and the far side of the valley opens up through them. Far across, on the low swell of land down towards the harbour and the sea, Signor Ferucci's house—normally so dark and silent and closed up—is all ablaze with light. The bushes close and for a long while I am left wondering if I've invented this; dreamed it. Perhaps I've fallen asleep on my feet for a moment. But then, a moment later, I see it again: low in the foothills there, all its windows are lit and alive. Below, the town is still sleeping; but above it, lodged in darkness, there is light where there never has been before, as if something huge and important is happening there.

I glance at Jamie and Anna, but they're looking at their feet, or at the road ahead, and they've seen nothing. I'm about to point and tell them, but then a strange feeling comes over me. It's as if I suddenly *know* something, though I'm not sure what. There is something happening in Signor Ferucci's house, and the hermit is gone; between these two facts there is some kind of territory to which I can't quite get access. But it's enough. I look down at my own feet, and I don't point or say anything. I don't know why I keep quiet like this, staring at the muddy asphalt. It just feels like it might be easier this way.

All along the valley, winding down to our row of houses, I find myself haunted by the dense little cluster of lights, and what may or may not be hidden behind them.

We get home some time before six, and the valley is starting to be properly light. There are still thick clouds all across the sky, but they are at least pale clouds, not the dark thundery ones of yesterday's storm. The gardens of our houses are still dripping, and there are puddles in the driveways.

We slip quietly into Jamie's house, and creep up the stairs, feet at the sides like always. For once, I'm less worried about the creaking of the stair boards than I am about the squeaking of my shoes; but Jamie and Anna say it's hardly noticeable.

We say good night to Anna on the landing. She looks haggard and exhausted and somehow much younger than she normally does; and I think of seeing her in the night sucking her thumb. It's something I haven't done for maybe three years. Her hair is a tangled, straggly mess from the rain and the river, and then from drying out by the fire, and her cheeks look white and hollow. The black smudges I've seen below Jamie's eyes and mine are under hers now as well.

"*Buonanotte,*" she says.

"*Notte,*" I murmur.

Jamie closes the door to his room and we get undressed. I'm fumbling with the alarm clock, setting it for an hour's time, when I remember we don't have to do that any more. The hermit's gone; there won't be any more signals down the valley. My pyjama bottoms are still clammy.

I hang them on the back of a chair and get into bed, drawing the covers round me and pressing my face deep into the comforting softness of the pillow.

From his bed, I hear Jamie say softly, "Night, Alex."

"Night," I say.

No-one comes to wake us. When we finally do get downstairs, it's nearly lunchtime. I notice the knowing glances between the adults, and realize that they think we've been up all night reading comics or telling ghost stories or playing games. The thought is almost enough to make me laugh aloud, and I can see from Jamie's face that he's thinking the same thing.

I have to wear a pair of Jamie's trousers; mine are still wet—I start to think they will never dry—and besides, they're covered with mud. All Anna's clothes are the same, but she has more in her suitcase. We put the dirty clothes in a plastic bag and take them to my house, where I know we stand less chance of being disturbed. In the upstairs bathroom, we half-fill the bath with water and stir the clothes round until the water's gone mud-coloured; then we let it out and start again. Eventually the water comes clean. We hang everything to dry on the towel-rail. Lena may see it, but I feel so tired and dazed that I hardly care. In fact, as lunch approaches, I feel less and less well; and at last I get so dizzy and weak that I have to sit down.

Lena puts me to bed. I have a temperature of thirty-nine, she says, but she thinks it's just a summer chill of some kind. She brings me lots to drink and says that she'll call the doctor in the afternoon if I don't feel better.

"It must be something that's going round," she says, as she tucks me in. "Mrs. Anderson was saying that Anna's not feeling so well either."

Something in Lena's voice tells me that she either knows, or suspects, more than she is saying; that she doesn't really believe it's just a summer chill. But she doesn't say anything more. Later, when I get up to go to the loo, I see that the clothes are gone from the towel-rail. Later still, waking from a fitful sleep full of half-remembered terrors, I find my trousers and pyjamas dry, and folded, and on the chair by my window.

That night I dream I'm fighting my way through an endless torrent of water. Anna is calling out to me through the darkness: *Get to the bank, Alex! This way!* But when I turn to look, I can't find her; and the banks of the river get wider and wider apart, so that no matter how hard I try I can't reach them. At last, the water floods over my head and cuts off my breath; and I wake with a start, smothering a sharp cry of fear.

Jamie and I sit next to one another on the train from the airport, and as the Italian landscape rolls past us, I can see him staring at it with a kind of amazement, as if he hasn't believed it possible we'll get this far.

There are nineteen of us on the trip, and two teachers. The other boys are mainly lower-sixth pupils, like Jamie, but there are a few from my year as well. The bulk of the group are artists, but there are some literature specialists also. Jamie is the only musician; as I've predicted, the director of studies finds it hard to argue with the itinerary we have produced for him.

"All the colours are different," he says, marvelling. "From England, I mean."

"Yeah," I say. I find it strange, a little, how struck he is by the countryside outside the window, as if he's forgotten how it looks. For me, with my paintings of Altesa, Italy has never been all that far away; but looking at him now, I can see that for Jamie the past four years have become a huge distance.

"Back again," he says quietly, almost as if he knows what I'm thinking.

"What time's your lecture thing, then?"

"After lunch. I've got some errands to run, though; I ought to give my tutor a call and stuff like that. How would it be if we meet up this evening?"

"Sure," I say.

"You won't be lonely?" she says, teasing.

"I'll manage."

"What're you going to do?" she says. She's dressed less casually today, more in the stylish manner that's actually more common among young Italians. I watch as she checks herself in the mirror.

"Sketching. In fact, it's quite good to have a day without any distractions. I was planning to do loads more than I have. I need to catch up."

" 'Distractions'?" she says, making a face. "Is that what I am?"

"Yeah," I say. "Too much so."

She finishes with make-up and stuff and turns round. "There. What do you think?"

"Nice."

"You have to dress the part for these things," she says vaguely. "Well—I've got to go. Sure you'll be OK?"

"Sure you don't want me to come with you?"

She shakes her head. "You'd be bored. No, get some proper artist stuff done and we can get pissed later, OK?"

"Sounds like fun," I say.

"See you around six, then?"

"Sure thing. Bye, now."

She winks at me quickly, and is gone.

Slowly, I start to gather the things I'll need for the day, putting them together in the bag I keep for what Anna's called "artist stuff." It's a fine day; the sky's clear and deeply coloured, and there will be plenty to see and draw in and around the street markets. I flick briefly through my sketches of people looking at statues. For a second, the aftertaste comes to me of the strange dislocation I felt looking at the stickers on Anna's travel bag, as if the city had somehow—shifted. But then it's gone, and I find I am whistling to myself as I pack the last items up.

She's taken the bag with the stickers, I notice, but she's left something, too: tucked down between two of the suitcases that are still there is a sheaf of paper. Curious, I go over, pull it free. *Of course*, I think, when I can see it properly, *the thesis*. It's a good two inches thick, clamped together down its spine with a metal binder.

Still with that vague curiosity in me, I take it over to the desk and open it. I want to see some of what she's written, to get an idea of what it is that's occupying her life these days. On the first page there is a little fragment of text, like a quotation; alone on the page.

In csak fegyver vagyok.

I frown, and leaf through the rest of the manuscript, the pages turning slowly in front of me. Page after page is the same, the words unfamiliar. Hungarian, of course; but it surprises me all the same. She is studying in Rome; wouldn't they want her thesis in Italian?

There's something else, too. Her name, on the first page, is spelt differently: *Ana*. It looks as unfamiliar as the words inside. Strange.

Perhaps she means to translate it when she's finished.

I flick through the pages again, and then put the sheaf back where I found it. I'm not sure whether she'd want me looking through it without her permission.

I find myself whistling again as I finish my preparations and leave: nothing can shake the kind of gentle elation that's in me today. From nowhere, a phrase pops into my mind: something I remember from way back when I was a child. *The hermit's gone.* Well, I tell myself as I lock the door after me, even if I was never sure that was true before, at least I am now.

It's in the shadow of the Campanile that I hear her.

"Alex! Hey, Alex!"

It's our first morning in Florence, and Mr. Dalton has sent us off from our little hotel in groups to do studies of buildings. I am with three other boys, sketching the side of the cathedral; the arc of the side of the Duomo itself is just visible from where we're sitting, sharp against the sky. All four of us look up at the sound of my name. Anna is standing out in the sun, grinning like mad, waving. I drop my pad and sketching pen and run over to her.

"Hey, you made it!" I say.

"Yeah. I went to your hotel and they said you'd all gone out. I left a message. Lucky finding you, yeah?"

"Yeah," I say.

"Where's Jamie?"

"I don't know," I say honestly. "He's supposed to be at some musical thing, but—he might not be."

"Oh," she says, one eyebrow raised. "Sounds ominous."

"It is, a bit," I say. "I think—well, I can tell you later, if you like."

"Yeah." She stares at me for a moment, and then grabs me and hugs me. "Alex! It's good to see you."

"You too," I say.

"You're taller."

"You too."

"Your voice is all deep."

"You too," I say, grinning.

"Oh, funny today, are we?" She steps back from me, still smiling, and we just look at each other for a second. Then one of the boys I've been sketching with comes over.

"Hey," he says. "Do you know her, then?"

Anna and I glance at one another, and burst out laughing. "Yes," I manage after a while. "Sort of." Then something strikes me. Anna and I have been talking in Italian, as always, but Tim's question has been in English. I look at her, puzzled. "How did you—"

"I'm learning English," she says, still in Italian. "I know quite a lot now, but it's easier to understand than to speak."

"Cool," I say, impressed. "Go on, give it a go."

"No," she says. "If they know I understand, they'll all try and chat me up. I can do without that, I think."

"Oh, modest today, are we?" I say, though I know she's right.

Tim says, "Aren't you going to introduce us, Alex?"

Anna's eyes meet mine for a moment, and it's all we can do not to burst out laughing again. Then I say—switching back to English: "This is Anna. Anna—Tim, Eddie and Jonas."

Anna says, smiling politely, "They all look like wankers. Are they your friends?"

"What's she say?" Eddie asks.

"She says she's pleased to meet you."

"Yeah? Cool. How do you know her?"

Anna says, "Hey—tell them I'm your girlfriend."

"Don't be silly," I say.

"No, go on."

Tim says, "Yeah, come on, Alex. How do you know her?"

"She's just a friend of mine. Stop letching."

"I *knew* you'd never get a girlfriend like that, Carlisle. Tell her I think she's cute."

"Oh, for God's sake," I say. Anna takes me discreetly by the hand.

"Come on," she says. "Let's go somewhere else."

"Yeah," I say. To the watching boys I say, "If Dalton comes by, can you tell him I've met a friend and I'll be back for lunch? He won't mind. I've done most of a sketch anyway."

"We'll come," Jonas says eagerly.

"Fuck off."

They retire to where we've been sitting, grinning among themselves. As Anna and I walk away, I hear Eddie call after me—"Let her go free, Carlisle! You wouldn't know what to do with a girl like that anyway!" There's some poorly stifled laughter. I grin at Anna apologetically.

She says, "You know, I *knew* your friends would be like this. I just knew it. I thought, it'll be nice to see Alex, but of course all his friends will be adolescent males. I nearly didn't come."

"Oh, cheers."

"You shouldn't have told them. It would have been much more fun if we'd pretended to be boyfriend and girlfriend. You could have pissed them all off enormously."

"Yeah, well," I say. For some reason I find myself feeling very self-conscious, especially when Anna talks like this about us being boyfriend and girlfriend. I wish she wouldn't. I've been thinking about seeing her for weeks, ever since I get her letter saying that she might be able to make it; but somehow I've never quite realized how much she will have grown up. Although I laugh with her at how transparently attracted to her my friends have been, I am nervously aware that I am, as well. It's not something I can control. She's a very beautiful young woman, and she has some kind of confidence that I'm horribly aware I don't possess—feel like I never will possess, no matter how much older I get. Even more than before, when I was twelve, I feel that she has left me behind somehow—that the two years that separate us have stretched and become the whole difference between a child and an adult.

If any of this is occurring to Anna as well, she doesn't show it. "Let's get ice-cream," she says.

"What, ice-cream and Cokes?" I say.

"Of course. Is there an ice-cream place near here?"

"Florence," I say, with the assurance of one who's been in the city a full eighteen hours, "is full of ice-cream. We're bound to find some somewhere."

"This is so cool," she says. "I've been really excited."

"Yeah?"

"Yeah. What about you?"

"Yeah, me, too," I say.

"I wish we knew where Jamie was," she says, after a moment.

"He'll turn up," I say.

She glances at me. "Is everything all right with you two?" she says.

"Yeah, of course. What do you mean?"

"I don't know," she says, sounding thoughtful. "It's just—in your letter, you sounded a bit—and now—I just wondered . . ." Her voice tails off, and she shrugs. "Well, if you're OK," she says.

"Yeah," I say, not sure what she's meant. "We're fine."

"She's really fit," Eddie is saying approvingly. "Italian, though. Doesn't speak English."

I smile to myself and say nothing, knowing he's wrong on both counts. Over lunch, Anna is the subject of conversation at our table, Eddie and the others filling in some of the boys who weren't there and haven't seen her.

"How fit?" someone asks.

"Really good," Eddie says. "Wasn't she, Tim?"

"Mm," says Tim through a mouthful of pasta. "Definitely."

"How'd you know her, Alex? From when you used to live here?"

"Hey," someone else says. "Is she the same girl that you used to draw? You had those pictures, remember?"

"Oh—yeah," Jonas says. "I remember those. You had drawings of her on your wall when you were in the third form. Is she?"

I say, "Yeah."

"Christ," he says. "She looks really different now."

I shrug. I'm embarrassed by all the attention and stir Anna has created; and at the same time, part of me is strangely envious of these other boys, the way they can talk about her and think about her. I can't do that. She's my friend, not just some girl I've seen in the street and fancied. Everyone at the table is jealous of me, for knowing her, for being able to talk to her, to *be* with her, and all the time I'm feeling—left out. It's stupid, but it's there all the same.

Jamie's late. When I see him come in, I ease my way out from where I'm sitting and go across to meet him.

"Hey," he says.

"Hey. Where have you been?"

"Around," he says vaguely. "You know."

"Want to hear something cool?" I say, unable to keep myself from grinning.

He looks at me curiously. "What?"

I glance around the restaurant. A couple of the other boys are watching us, "Outside," I say. Jamie raises one eyebrow, but follows me out into the street.

"What is it?"

"Guess who's here?"

He looks blank. "What?"

"Guess who's *here*. Guess who I met by the Duomo today."

An expression of mild irritation crosses his face. "I don't know, Alex. Santa Claus?"

I have to tell him. I can't keep it inside any longer. "Anna," I say, watching to see how he'll react.

At first he just looks disbelieving; then he peers more closely at me, and his face alters. "What, really?" he says.

"Yeah."

"Anna's here?"

"Yeah."

He looks almost comically shocked. "You're—I mean, how come? What's she doing here?"

"She's told her tutors she's doing some research. Political history or something. She's here for the week, too."

"Christ," Jamie says faintly. There is something in his face I can't quite read properly. He says, "She's here right now?"

"Well, not *right* now. But she's going to meet us this evening."

"Christ," he says again. And, "Anna. Shit. I mean, what kind of coincidence is—" He stops, and again looks closely at me.

"What?" I say.

"You told her?" he says.

"Well, I mentioned it," I say. I'm surprised at how he's behaving. I have played through in my mind what it will be like when he finds out: confusion at first, then surprise, then delight. The three of us are together again. Instead of this, though, he looks almost suspicious, as if I've played a trick on him.

"What? You wrote to her?"

"Yeah," I say, some more of my excitement draining out of me at the tone of his voice. I say, "What is it? Aren't you pleased?"

He hesitates then, and frowns slightly, and then rubs the hair back from his forehead. He looks at me, and blinks, and smiles slightly for the first time. Just a small smile. He says, "Yeah. Yeah, of course I am. Jamie and Alex and Anna." There's another pause, and his smile widens, becomes more the way I know it. "Yeah. Cool."

"Good," I say, relieved. "You looked a bit—well, a bit weird then."

"It's been a long day," he says. "I just wasn't—expecting anything. Anything like that, anyway."

"She'll be back at seven. What should we do, do you think?"

A slightly crazy look has come over Jamie's face. "We should go out," he says. "Hit the town. Get partied up."

"Can you afford it?" I say. Neither of us has much money.

Jamie just pats his pocket, and I hear the faint sound of coins there. "Don't worry. The cash flow situation has eased."

"Shit! What have you been doing?"

He grins, and the faint look of madness is gone. "That saxophone's already paid for itself twice over," he says. "Just give me a subway and some old favourites."

"What, you've spent the whole afternoon busking?"

He nods.

I shake my head. "You're insane," I say. "Pray nobody catches you."

"They won't," he says lightly. "They never have."

"You can't be lucky for ever," I say.

"Oh, shut up, Alex. You make your own luck. Come on, I'm hungry." He stops, though, just in the doorway of the restaurant. "Anna, yeah? Now that's weird."

"Not weird," I say. "Cool. It'll be just like old times."

"Yeah," he says. "I suppose."

Later, when the plates are being cleared away, I try to catch his eye across the room; but he's not looking my way. Around me, the conversation finally drifts away from Anna, as Eddie and one of his friends discuss how cheap the wine is in Italy, and how easy it is to buy. I let my mind drift, and the words just wash around me.

I am in bed with my temperature for two days; so is Anna. The doctor comes and says I'll live, but when he's gone, I can sense the suspicion from downstairs. The doctor has asked difficult questions. Have I been out in the cold? Sleeping with the window open in the storm? Walking around at night? I mumble and shake my head and deny everything, but I can see in their faces that they don't quite believe me.

I have blisters on the sides of my feet, and on my heels, from where my wet socks have rubbed. It's a small miracle that nobody notices this, and that I don't have to think of yet more excuses and explanations.

The two days feel like a week. It occurs to me also that Anna will be going away again soon, and this seems a miserable way to spend what little time we have left together.

At last, though, we're better. Lena tells us not to go so far out into the valley, and to be back for lunch each day; no more money for sandwiches. She says we're still recovering and we need to take things easy for a while. For the first time ever, Anna's natural energy and verve seem to waver, and she just nods; she still looks terribly tired, as though two days and nights in bed have done her no good at all. But then, I remind myself, neither have they me; I feel just as weak as I did when we staggered up Jamie's drive with the remains of the thunderstorm dripping from the trees around us.

We sit behind the wall at the bottom of the garden, and look at the side of the valley. The sun's out today, which makes everything look more cheerful, but there's no doubt that the proper part of the summer is gone. Every so often a cloud draws across and the rocks go dull around us, before brightening again a minute later, and there's a thin, but steady, breeze coming in from the sea. Jamie idly flicks stones at a tin can some yards away; I watch him. Anna has her eyes closed, leaning back against the bricks of the wall.

"Do you think he took the car?" she says.

"Maybe."

Jamie throws a stone and misses. "I'm glad he's gone," he says, with a sudden and surprising vehemence.

"Why?" I say.

"I don't know. I just am." He throws another stone, and the can jumps sideways with a *clonk*.

"I wonder where he is now," Anna says, half to herself.

"Could be anywhere," Jamie says. I think, instinctively, of what I've seen; of Signor Ferucci's house all bright with lights, as if it's filled with bustle and activity. But I still don't say anything. Even if it was the hermit there, he won't be there any more. He wouldn't have been there two hours after I saw it; I'm sure of that. And now it's been three days.

"I wonder if . . ." Anna stops.

"What?"

"Nothing."

A voice calls, "Jamie! Anna!"

"It's my mum," Jamie says, sounding surprised. We brush the rock dust and dirt from our jeans and trot round the end of the wall to the front of Jamie's house.

His mother is in the hallway. "Here," she says. She sounds both amused and slightly intrigued, as if she can't quite work something out. "This came. It's for you, Anna." She holds it out: a postcard.

Anna takes it and turns it over, and her face goes pale.

"What does it say?" Jamie says; his voice is shaky. Anna just holds the card out to him. I peer over Jamie's shoulder.

For Anna on her eleventh birthday. There's nothing else.

"Who's it from?" Jamie's mother says. "The postmark's Salerno, see?"

"Oh," Anna says. "Yeah. That would be—I have a cousin who lives there, I think. That would be—yeah, that would be her."

"She's a little late," Mrs. Anderson says with a smile. "But it's a nice thought." She goes back into the sitting room, leaving us alone.

"Yeah," Anna says. Jamie turns the postcard over. On the other side is a picture of a figure silhouetted under a tree at sunset; it's one of those rather slushy pictures you see a lot at news-stands. What we're all looking at, though, is the line of print along the bottom of the picture. Sometimes they say things like *You're cute* or *My friend* or something like that. Jamie's finger traces the words.

Thinking of you.

"Yeah," he whispers. "I bet."

Anna's hands, when she takes the card back from Jamie, seem to be shivering slightly.

"What does it mean?" I say. "It's him, isn't it?"

"Not here," Anna says shortly; and she leads the way back outside behind the wall. There, in the sunshine, we pass the card from one to another, reading and rereading it.

"Why?" Jamie says at last.

"I don't know. I think—" She hesitates.

"What?"

She rubs her thumb gently and slowly across the words the hermit has written, but the ink doesn't smudge. She says, "It's like he's gone, but—"

"I don't like it," Jamie says. "It scares me."

"No," Anna says. "No. It's not like that. It's not a—you know, it's not to scare us. It's just—a reminder. You understand?" She looks round at Jamie and me.

"Yeah," I say. "I understand." Jamie doesn't say anything.

It's a low, overcast sky that has settled on the valley when the time comes for Anna to go. It's been a strange week, since the hermit's disappearance; all of us feel it. Even after we're fully better from the summer chill, our games don't feel the same. We don't know what to do with ourselves any more. For moments, sometimes, we're able to lose ourselves in some fantasy and everything is the way it always was; but then something breaks the mood, and we remember that things are different now. I remember also what Anna said long before—that none of us is a kid, and none of us is weird. At the time, that made me feel very grown-up and important. Now, though, I find myself wishing sometimes that we could go back, and be kids again. I don't know what we are any more. I remember looking for lizards with Jamie, and swimming in the cove, and comics and theatres and all of that, and it seems like someone else's life.

The bus comes for Anna just before lunchtime. Early that morning, we set off up the valley for what will be the last time for ages. It's Anna's idea. She wants to see the chapel before she leaves, she says, and Jamie and I can't refuse her. The bed of the empty river is muddy and sludgy still, but at least the water is gone again. Lena was right; it only fills up sometimes. Debris has been swept down the watercourse from the hills, and the familiar little piles of branches and pieces of detritus along the way are all gone. It's just another thing that has changed.

At the chapel, the stone pines hardly cast shadows in the dull light. Anna walks slowly round the building, staring at it; staring at the bell-tower and the walls and the eaves high up where the roof starts. She goes inside for a time. Jamie and I stand at the door and watch her. The ashes of our fire are still on the marble at the altar end, but apart from that, the chapel is much the same as when we found it.

Outside, we stand under the dandelion clock. Anna looks despondent, as if she doesn't know what to do now she's actually here. On the journey up the valley she's walked purposefully, as if she has a goal in mind; now, she seems almost unsure of why she's come all this way.

"Will you come again?" I say.

She smiles a little at that. "Yeah. Can I? Next year?"

"Of course," Jamie says.

"I'd like that," she says. "I really—I mean, I've—"

"That would be great," I say.

She looks around. "I really like this place," she says. I know she means all of Altesa, not just the chapel. "It's—I don't know."

Jamie looks at his watch. "We'll have to go soon," he says. "Or you'll miss your bus."

"I don't mind," she says. "They can go without me."

"What'll you do?" Jamie says, smiling, going along with her.

"I'll—I'll live here, of course. I want to be a hermit—only I'll be a *real* hermit this time. I'll live in the chapel, and I'll cook on a fire there at the altar end. And I'll pull down some of those boards over the windows so the light comes in and it's bright and all colours." Her eyes are bright, dancing with ideas. "I'll make a bed with straw from the fields and I'll sit up in the belltower and watch everything that goes on in the valley. All the people coming and going—and all the boats out in the harbour—and cars on the roads—and the houses at night, with the lights on. And I'll sing to myself to keep cheerful."

"Won't you be lonely?" I say.

"No. I'll draw people on the walls to keep myself company. And you and Jamie can come and visit."

"We can bring you sweets," I say.

"Yeah. And sometimes people from the town will come to ask the hermit's advice on something."

"And what'll you do with the rest of your time?" Jamie says. "You'd have a lot of time."

"You can play," I say.

Anna shakes her head. "No. I'd write a book."

"A book?" Jamie sounds intrigued. "About what?"

"About being a hermit, of course," Anna says, with a brilliant, mischievous grin. "So everyone would know how to do it. And perhaps one day everyone in the valley would decide to be hermits too, and they'd all have chapels and caves in the hills, and there'd be no-one left in the town at all. And all through the valley there'd be hermits, singing and watching and drawing and looking at each other from their belltowers."

We all stand silent, picturing Anna's valley of hermits. Then she digs in the pocket of her jeans and brings out the postcard.

"We have to promise," she says. "You both have to."

"Promise what?" Jamie says.

She puts the postcard down on a piece of stone among the pine needles, and takes out a box of matches. We watch as she lights one, and sets it to the corner of the postcard, and waits until it has burnt away to ash on the flat surface of the stone. When the last bright crescent of red spark has wandered across the charcoal and died, she kicks the ash to dust with one trainer, stamping it into the ground.

"You have to promise never to tell," she says. "Not to say anything to anyone, ever. If we keep our promise, he'll keep his."

"What's his promise?" Jamie says.

"It doesn't matter," she says, shaking her head impatiently. "Come on. We don't have a lot of time. You have to promise never to say anything, ever." She looks at me, and her eyes are frowning and hard and very serious.

I say, "I promise."

"Say, 'I swear by the dandelion clock.' "

I glance up instinctively at the blank face staring down at us, at the twelve hours ranged around it, but with no time passing through them, like sand frozen solid in an hourglass. The air under the stone pines here is suddenly chilly. I say, "I swear by the dandelion clock I'll never tell."

"Jamie?"

Jamie twists one foot in the pine needles, not meeting her eye.

"You have to," she says. "You have to swear. Please."

He looks up, at last, and says, "All right."

"Say it properly."

"I swear by the dandelion clock I won't tell."

Anna smiles at him quickly. Then she says, "I swear by the dandelion clock I will never tell."

We're quiet for a moment. It feels like something very important, what we've just done, but I'm not sure why. I was never going to tell anyone in any case.

Jamie says, "We ought to go."

"Yeah. I know." She's not looking at us; she's looking at the chapel, and then beyond it to the trees and the hills. She says, "You guys go on. I'll catch you up."

"You're sure?" Jamie says.

"Yeah. Really."

"All right."

He and I climb the fence and cut down through the vegetation to the river. I look back at one point. Anna is still standing there, staring away into the distance.

"Do you think she'll come?" I say, as our feet slap through the mud.

"Yeah."

"She's not going to really do it, then?"

"Do what?"

"Become a hermit, like she said."

Jamie laughs. "No. That was just a story."

"It didn't sound like a story."

"She's not going to become a hermit, Alex."

He's right. It's only a couple of minutes before we hear Anna splashing and slapping down the river behind us. We turn to watch her, but as she gets close she doesn't slow. She tears past us, grinning like mad, spattering red mud as she goes.

"Race you!" she shouts over her shoulder.

"Shit!" Jamie says, a lopsided grin on his face too. Then he shouts, "Come on, Alex! After her! She must not escape!"

We sprint after Anna, slithering and sliding in the inches-deep sediment. By the time we get halfway home, we're all out of breath and have to stop, gasping and snorting with laughter. Anna and Jamie are covered with mud—little dots and splashes of it are all over them. I realize after a moment that they're all over me, too. We look like we've caught some awful mud disease, and broken out in a rash.

"Look—look at you," Anna manages, hugging her sides.

"Shit," Jamie says. "What're—what're we going to say? They'll be furious."

"Doesn't—doesn't matter," Anna says, still grinning. "Screw them. What're they going to do? I'll—I'll say it was my fault."

"No," Jamie says. "No. They might not let you come again if you get in real trouble. We'll say it was my fault. Alex and I started it, teasing you. OK?"

She thinks for a moment, and then says, soberly, "Yeah, you're right. OK." She bends down and scoops up a handful of sludge from beside her foot.

"What're you doing?" Jamie says.

"Well, if it's going to be your fault, we might as well enjoy ourselves," she says. She prances a couple of yards away and hurls the mud straight at Jamie, and it bursts across his T-shirt with a wonderful slopping sound.

"Shit!" Jamie shouts. "What the hell are you—wait—"

Anna's got another mud-ball. I find giggles welling up in me, and in a second I've snatched a handful myself and hurled it wildly at Anna.

"C'mon, Jamie!" I shriek.

He only hesitates a fraction of a second. Then, with a whoop, he ducks out of the way of a handful Anna has thrown, and scoops up one of his own. "You're going to *die*!" he shouts.

Anna is laughing so hard she can hardly speak.

"You—you should know better—than to tease girls!" she shouts. "Ow—balls!"

"Get her, Alex!"

"No, Alex—get *him*! Be on my side!"

I can't stop laughing. We pelt each other with mud all the way down the valley. It's in our hair and mouths and ears by the time, tired and weak from running and laughing, we reach the track that leads to the road. When we get to the driveway of Jamie's house, we look at each other again, and more giggles overwhelm us.

"We can't let them see us like this," Anna says at last. "I mean—"

"I know," Jamie grins tiredly. "Don't worry. I'll get the hose."

We wave and wave until the bus is out of sight; long after we must have become invisible to Anna from her seat in the back. Still, neither of us wants to be the first one to stop.

I can hear thunder grumbling somewhere up the coast. It's going to be another storm. The summer is dying, and school is just round the corner.

We're in trouble because of the soaked clothing and the huge pool of river mud which, no matter how much we try to hose it away, now stains Jamie's back lawn. But it doesn't matter. Neither Jamie nor I would have done it differently.

The hermit is gone. There's nothing left of him now except a promise; no postcard, no gun, nothing in the chapel. Well, I remind myself, not quite nothing. But the three bullets are my secret, not anyone else's; and for all I care they can stay in their hiding place until they rust away to nothing. I don't want them back, and I don't need a promise to know that I'll never talk of them to anyone.

Anna will be back next year. It seems like an impossible time to endure, but I know it will pass, somehow. She'll be back next year. Meanwhile, there are still comics and stars and stories and all the things that we had before; perhaps they'll still make sense to us even after everything that's happened. And one day, summer will creep up on us, and it'll be time for birthdays and holidays and swimming at the beach, and Anna will come back.

21

"*I* always imagine you in your big English school with all the old buildings, and classrooms with panels on the walls and stuff," Anna is saying. "And now you tell me it's not like that?"

"Well—not all of it," Jamie says. "Some of it's quite modern."

"No, I don't want to hear." She takes another drink and shakes her head. It's amazing how easily we've all fallen together again, back into the old way of conversation and companionship. Except for the wine glasses between us on the table, and the changes of phrasing, and the city around us, it could all be six years ago. And the way Anna looks now, I add mentally. I glance at her: she's still speaking.

"I like my version better. All of you in rows, and a teacher with a cane at the front."

"Christ," I say. "Can you imagine Dalton with a cane?"

"Is he the guy in charge? I've seen him," she says.

"When?"

"Sometimes he comes and looks at your drawings and tells you stuff about them," she says. "Don't look like that, Alex. I wasn't spying on you. I was just in a café and some of your lot were drawing in the square there."

"Some of our lot," Jamie says, slightly morosely. "God. As if there *is* any 'our lot.' "

"What's up with you?" Anna says.

"Sorry. Nothing. I'm just—nothing."

She shrugs. "Well, I've seen him. I've probably seen everyone in your group now."

"How can you tell?"

"You go around in little groups. There are little groups of sketching boys all over the city. You keep bumping into them. And they look English."

"What's English look like, then?" I say.

"Sort of—different. You don't dress the same way. It's not a bad thing," she adds. "I quite like it. You'd think you'd all look the same, going to an old school and all that. But in fact, when you see you lot next to Italians, it's them that look all the same. Like they've got more of a uniform than you have."

Jamie's nodding. "Blue denim," he says. "They're all wearing blue denim this year. Trousers or jacket or shirt or something."

"Exactly," Anna says. "That's what I mean. Whereas you lot wear—different things."

"Just naturally free thinkers," I say.

"Maybe." She grins. "What's it like, being in a school with no girls?"

"Weird," I say. Jamie nods.

"Yeah," he says. "It's wrong, I think. I think they should all go mixed."

"Will they?"

"Doubt it."

"Half your lot look like they've never seen a girl before," she says.

"You shouldn't stir them up so much," Jamie says. "You do it on purpose. And don't call them 'our lot,' OK?"

"All right. And I don't stir them up. Well, not much. It would have been more fun if Alex had played along."

"What's this?" Jamie says.

I say, "Oh, nothing."

"I told Alex to say I was his girlfriend—just for fun, you know? But he went and ruined it all. It would have been cool. Never mind."

Jamie says, "I'm pissed, I think."

"Are you? Yeah, you probably are."

"What time is it?"

"Late. We should be going."

"Balls," Anna says. "Stay for another."

I shake my head. "No, we really should. We have to be back by eleven."

"Back by eleven," Jamie says. "What lives we lead."

Anna says, "Well, I'm staying."

"Really, Anna. We can't."

"Fine by me." She glances around the bar. "Plenty of men here who'd buy a nice girl a drink."

Jamie says, getting up, "Yeah, sure. But you'd have to supply a nice girl first."

She grins. "*Vaffanculo*, loser."

"Night to you too."

"See you tomorrow," I say, wishing she hadn't said that thing about letting someone else buy her a drink. I don't know if she means it, probably not. Probably it's a joke—a kind of tease. But I don't know for sure. At the door, we turn and wave, and she raises her glass in a kind of mock salute; and then we're out into the cool night air.

There are still plenty of people in the streets; once, we even glimpse three of the boys from Jamie's year down a side-street. They seem to be heading back also, and are passing a straw-wrapped Chianti bottle between them. Jamie sees them, and grins at me.

"The English abroad," he says.

"You're the one that's pissed," I say.

"A bit. Not badly."

"Fair enough," I say. "God, Anna drinks a lot, doesn't she?"

Jamie considers this, and then nods. "Yeah. And she looks sober at the end of it, too."

"I mean, she drank more than you did."

"I know." He's quiet for a while, and the street opens out into a little piazza before he speaks again. "You want to stop for a bit?"

"We're going to be late."

"Not for long. Come on, just for a bit."

"Why?"

"I just want a rest, OK?"

I look at him, curious. I know Jamie, and I know he's not really very drunk. "OK," I say.

There's a fountain at one end of the little square, water splashing down into a wide, shallow pool; and to one side of it there is a building with an impressive, pillared façade and a long tier of stone steps reaching down to the square itself. We sit on the fourth step, facing the water, and I wait for Jamie to speak. It's a long wait; he just sits in silence for several minutes, staring at the fountain. In the distance, I can hear laughter and the sound of voices in the streets, but this place is all but deserted.

At last he says, "I wish I hadn't come."

"What? Here? Why not?"

He takes a breath, and lets it out in a kind of quiet sigh. "I don't know. It feels like a mistake, that's all. It just—reminds me of stuff."

"What stuff?"

"I've done everything wrong," he says. "All of it. I shouldn't have gone away in the first place."

"That wasn't your fault," I say. "Your parents moved, remember? You had to."

"Yeah." He's quiet again. Then he says, "What about you? Why on earth did you go to England?"

I blink. "To be with you, of course."

"What?"

"Well—you know that, don't you? That's why I made my parents put me in for the school and everything. You remember."

"I remember all that," he says slowly. "But I thought—I thought maybe you'd changed your mind, but it was too late and they wouldn't let you."

"Why would I do that?" I say.

He just stares at me. At last he says, "You still wanted to, then?"

"Of course I did." I try to smile. "You were my best friend, stupid. Of course I did."

"Oh." He's quiet again for a long time. I see that he's shivering slightly, though I don't find the air so very cold. At last he says, "I feel like everything's—everything's going wrong. Like I haven't found a place to *be*. Sometimes all I can think is that ever since that summer—I mean, if we hadn't left Italy, everything would be OK still."

"And it's really not?"

"No."

I cast about for something to say. "What about London? You look—you look like that's somewhere you feel at home. I mean, the band you're in—that's good, isn't it?"

The ghost of a smile appears briefly on his face. "That's the only thing I've got," he says. "I think I live for that. Everything else feels hollow."

"And you've made new friends there," I say, carefully. "Paul, I mean. He's—he's good news, isn't he?"

Jamie looks up at me; his hair is hanging over his eyes the way it does, but I can see them all the same. "He's OK," he says.

"What, just OK? I thought—well, this summer and everything—"

Another smile that's gone almost as fast as it appears. "We—get on well, if that's what you mean. He's nice. He's very kind, and there's the music, too. But I think I care about the music more."

"Oh."

"I hadn't—I didn't know you knew. About Paul, I mean."

"Well—kind of. I kind of guessed."

"Oh. Right."

I want to say something more. "I like him," I say. "I thought he was nice."

Jamie doesn't reply. For a while I think he's just gone into another one of his long silences, and I wait for him to decide what to say next; but when I look at him, his face is turned away, and the slight trembling in his shoulders has become more like a shudder.

"Jamie?"

I realize, shocked, that he's crying.

"Hey," I say. "It's OK. Don't be—it's all right." I put my arm round his shoulder and pull him towards me, and hold him while he sobs. I don't know what it is that's started it. I think of how he keeps talking about wishing he'd never left Italy. Perhaps it's just the shock of being back here again. I hold him as if trying to squeeze the sobbing back inside, but it breaks out of him anyway, on and on. "It's OK," I keep saying. "Don't worry. Don't be sad. It's all OK." But he has his head buried in the crook of his arm, and I can't even be sure that he hears me.

Finally it seems to go out of him. His breath hitches a little, but the shuddering stops and he's quiet for a while. Then he sniffs and digs around in his pocket for a hanky. He's still trying to keep his face turned away from me, but I can see the smears on his cheeks and his eyes are still bright with tears in the glow of the streetlights. He blows his nose, and sighs, and rubs one hand over his face until it's patchily dry again.

"Sorry."

I shake my head. "It's OK."

He looks at his watch. "We're late," he says, sounding tired. "We'd better get back."

"Jamie—"

"No," he says. "Please. I'm all right. It was just—I'm just pissed or something."

"You're not pissed."

"I'm just tired, then. I'll be OK tomorrow." He looks at me properly for the first time since the crying started. "Really. I'll be fine."

"You're sure?"

He gives my arm a squeeze. "Yeah. Come on. They'll be sending out search parties before long."

We stand up. Jamie goes across to the fountain and dips his hands in the water; I see him splash it on his face. He straightens up, his back to me, staring at the water falling into the pool for a long while. Then he turns, and gives me a kind of half-grin which looks, strangely, very brave. We don't say anything more on the way back to the hotel.

Anna looks at me steadily. "So—what was he crying about, then?"

"I don't know."

I've told her everything about last night. I need her to help me make sense of it. After a while, she says, "I don't think he's OK, Alex."

"No. Me neither."

"You've met this guy—Paul?"

"Yeah."

"What's he like?"

"He's nice. I liked him, anyway. He was kind of cool."

"What about Jamie? How's he feel?"

"I don't know. He said he cared more about the music."

"Oh."

"I just wish he'd talk more. I know there's stuff he's not telling me. Sometimes I think he's—trying to protect me, somehow. As if knowing him better would be—bad for me. But I *want* to. You know what I mean?"

She nods. "I think so."

"I just wish he'd talk to me more."

"Maybe he will. Maybe he just needs time. It must all be pretty weird for him, don't you think?"

"Yeah."

"So maybe he'll talk to you when he's ready. You're his friend, Alex. He's not going to abandon you, you know."

I smile. "Thanks."

"Now, what was the other thing?"

I have to think for a second to remember. "Oh, that. Someone saw us, when we were—talking, you know. So now everyone's saying how we had our hands all over each other, that kind of thing."

Anna's face twists with distaste. "Wankers," she says. "What's Jamie say?"

"Nothing. I'm not sure he knows, actually. He's—he's kind of distant right now. I don't think he's taking much in. You know what I mean?"

She nods. "Yeah. So you're getting all the flak?"

"It's not so much."

"I bet."

"Well—I mean I can handle it. I just don't know what to say."

"What, haven't any of your lot put their arm round a friend?" Anna says.

"They're not my lot," I say.

"Whatever. You should have listened to me, you know. If we'd pretended like I said, none of this would have happened, would it?"

Her voice is joking, but I can't tell whether she means it or not. I shrug.

"Look, Alex, forget it. It'll be over in a week. They'll get bored."

"Maybe," I say. "But this kind of thing—I mean, how am I supposed to go around with Jamie if everyone thinks we're—you know—" I stumble awkwardly.

"What, lovers?"

"Christ, Anna."

"Well, that's what you meant, isn't it?"

"Mm."

"This is really a problem for you, isn't it?" she says.

"I—yeah."

"Well," she says. "Don't worry. We'll think of something."

The scenes fade through one another: static, but with the sense that there is potential movement packed into them, just below the surface, if only you could reach it. Here is Anna at the airport, at a distance, not yet seeing me. Her bags and suitcases are clustered around her. Here is when we meet—when I'm hugging her, and I can't see anything much but the arrivals and departures boards on the wall behind her. Pisa is a small airport, and the trains are right outside; I'm picking up her cases now, starting to head for the exit, when she stops me.

The cases are on the floor again, grouped around me: hers and mine. Anna is heading away from me towards the door to the loos, her shoulder bag with its stickers slung across her back. I stand and wait by a pillar, guarding the luggage, daydreaming about where we'll go and what we'll see; the conversations we'll have. My gaze, unfocused, rests on the wall to one side of the door to the lavatories.

There is something here; I'm sure of it. I just can't see it.

And then I do.

It's only a glimpse. I have my eyes fixed on the wall, so it's by chance that I see her as she comes out of the same door through which Anna has gone in, only a minute before. In the corner of my eye she's still clear enough: a young woman with red streaks in her hair. The same I've seen later on the street outside the club, at a distance, watching us. Following us.

I feel a surge of panic, and the image on the paper threatens to shred and tear. I fight the emotions down because I have to know this, have to see it properly. I can tell now that it's much, much more important than I've realized.

Then Anna is coming out of the loos, seeing me, smiling, walking briskly towards me. She looks happy, excited.

I try to put the pieces together. A woman I've never seen before brushes through my field of vision in an airport. Perhaps she's just come into the country. Anna and I have just come into the country too. Nothing so far; there are plenty of people at airports, and they've all come from somewhere, or are about to go. But then there is a jazz bar where Anna and I are sitting and drinking and talking. Outside, on the street, I have caught a glimpse of a woman: the same woman that has been in the airport with us. There's just enough time to spark the hazy blur of a recollection before she's gone; but for that second or so, I have been convinced that she is watching us.

Anna and I are intending to stay longer in the bar. I even buy more beer. But by chance we leave: and shortly after that, the room is swept by the blast of an explosion.

Set out like this—I can almost see the links on the paper in front of me—it becomes horribly clear to me that Anna has been wrong. The hermit isn't gone. The unsettling dreams I've had, hearing his voice, have been trying to tell me something, and I haven't been listening properly. For some reason, despite lying dormant these past sixteen years, what happened in the chapel in our childhood has come back. Someone is trying to hurt us.

Thinking of you.

The words come into my head unbidden.

It's not a—you know. It's not to scare us. It's just a reminder.

I can feel my heart thudding in me, and my breath is quick and sharp. I want to run after Anna, find her, warn her; except there's still something else here, something I haven't understood yet. The luggage: the bags. There has been something there all along, and I realize that now. But this—glimpsing the woman—isn't the same thing. She's another part of it, maybe; but it was Anna's luggage that was the first thing to needle at me. If I could understand that, perhaps other things would become clearer too.

Trying to breathe evenly and calmly, I bend my head back over the blank sheet of paper, and let my eyes focus just below its placid surface.

It's lunchtime on our last day, and the other boys are all in the restaurant across the street where Mr. Dalton has arranged cheap meals for us. Anna is sitting on the edge of my bed. We don't have much longer; I'm trying to say something, something that's always somehow been left unsaid since I've first known her. Always mundanities get in the way. I've told myself that this week in Florence I will say it—I'll get it out, finally—but now it's almost time to leave, and still it hasn't happened. I don't know why not. Every time, it seems to slide by me.

I say, "Do you remember—"

"What?"

"Once, you said something about how good it would be if we all shared a house together. We were going to get some place and just live there for ever. You remember that?"

She laughs, sounding delighted, and shakes her head. "No. Did I say that?"

"Yeah," I grin.

"God. I must've been off my head. Can you imagine? I mean, what on earth would *that* be like?" She shakes her head again, still laughing. I watch her, and it's like something is draining out of me as I do so. "God," she says again. "You remember the strangest things. Where'd you dig that one up from?"

"It was a long time ago," I say. "Ages."

"It must've been. Sometimes I think I was just the weirdest kid ever."

I try to laugh and go along with it. "Yeah, sometimes. You were going to be a hermit, too, at one point."

"I was?"

"Yeah. You were going to live alone and write a book."

"Well," she says, her eyes twinkling, "who knows? That's pretty much what university's going to be all about. Well, essays, treatises, not a book. Maybe I was right."

"I don't think so," I say. Then, "Anna?"

"Yeah?"

"Do you have a boyfriend?"

"What, like a steady guy? No."

"Oh."

"Too much hassle," she says. "No, Alex, steer clear of all that, trust me. Maybe when I'm older. Someone rich and very, very old."

I manage a weak grin. From down the hall comes the sound of a door slamming, and voices.

"Is that them?" Anna says.

"Sounds like it."

"Right," she says, jumping up off the bed and running to the door. "I'll see you before the plane, OK? By the Duomo, like before. Tell Jamie."

"I will," I say. "Hey—what are you doing?"

"Disinformation," she says.

She's pulled her arms in through the sleeves of her T-shirt, and I watch in astonishment as, reaching behind her back, she unhooks something; a second later, she's tugging her bra out the bottom of the shirt. "There," she says, throwing it on my bed. "Trophy."

The voices are closer down the hall now, and she grins at me quickly. "See you later," she whispers, and then to my amazement she hoists the T-shirt up to her shoulders. I have a moment's glimpse of small, pale breasts before she has the door to the room open and is out in the hall. She's shrugging the T-shirt back down as she goes, but anyone in the corridor outside must have seen much what I have. Anna's still looking back into the room, though, and I see her wink as she says—not quietly—"God, I needed that. Thanks, Alex."

The door's closed behind her before I realize she's spoken in English, not Italian. I stare after her—my eyes tracking across the plaster of the wall opposite as I imagine her progress down the passage outside. The voices out there have gone silent. Finally there's the slam of the main door closing, and then an excited, incredulous buzz from outside.

I sit back against the headboard of my bed and shake my head, hardly able to believe how she can do things like this—how she can shock me and surprise me and upset me and *affect* me so much, even after so many years. It seems to get worse each time I see her.

The door bursts open and Eddie and Jonas and several others are there, mouths open in disbelief. Across the end of the bed is Anna's bra.

"Black," Eddie says. "I *knew* she'd wear black. Jesus Christ, Alex, you fucking *bastard*. You didn't, did you?"

"I didn't do anything," I say, truthfully.

"Oh, bollocks. Dalton's still downstairs. Go on, tell us."

"Nothing happened," I say. "That's the truth." I snatch up the bra and stuff it deep in my suitcase. "Nothing. OK?"

Eddie lets out a kind of low moan of despair. "Oh, you *bastard*," he says. "You awful, awful bastard. How could you?"

He goes over to his bed and flops down on it. When he looks up at me again, he's grinning.

"Bastard," he says. "Good for you."

It's difficult to concentrate properly, now that I know I've seen her in both places. I have a couple of false starts before I can get back to the last thing I saw: that glimpse of her walking away through the airport. For a few frustrating minutes I get almost random things coming up on the paper—scenes from my childhood, moments from the past week, stuff like that. It's because of the sense of panic and confusion that's still inside, no matter how much I try to press it down.

Finally, the airport is back in front of me. Children running beside parents; people going past in both directions. The woman with the red streaks in her hair is gone, out of my field of vision, only to return days later on a night street near a bar. And now the door to the loos swings open, and Anna's coming out. The part of me that's detached—an observer—realizes with a lurch that they must have passed each other with only minutes to spare. If we had been a fraction earlier reaching that point, they would have seen each other.

But apart from that, everything's the same. Anna's got her bag over her shoulder. I pick up my holdall and her suitcases and she grins at me—a quick, excited grin that I take to mean she's also eager for us to be on our way. Here, and we're outside in the sunshine, piling our luggage on the platform as the train draws into sight.

My fingers, gripping the sketch pad, suddenly tighten; the fingertips are white with pressure. And my body goes cold, just like that—despite the mild, sunny day, and the sunlight just starting to come in from the window to the street. Now I can see it: everything. I was right; it *was* the bag.

The bag is different. It's the same make, the same kind of bag; there are the same stickers of cities and place-names and countries on it. It looks the same—almost.

The pattern of the stickers is wrong. It's not the same pattern that was on the bag to begin with, when Anna came through the arrivals gate and flung her arms around me. I must have glimpsed the bag twenty or a hundred times, one way and another, between the arrivals gate and the moment she goes out of sight through the loo door. The brightly coloured stickers draw the eye, and besides, I have found it almost impossible to take my eyes off her. It's as though, if I stop looking at her, she might suddenly vanish again: I have to try to keep her locked down with my eyes. And through that brief minute or so, between first seeing her and her saying she needs to stop for a pee, the shoulder bag has seeped inevitably into my visual memory, along with her clothes and the shape of her face and the way she's cut her hair.

It's not the same bag.

The stickers are worn and while some are bright, some are faded and uneven round the edges; just the same as Anna's. You couldn't pull them off and reposition them without tearing them. They're the same as Anna's, but this isn't Anna's bag. The pattern—the join-the-dots of the stickers—is different.

Christ, I think suddenly. *The city did move. All the cities moved.*

Something's wrong—terribly wrong—and at last I can see what it is.

The only thought going through my head is that Anna is in danger. The hermit hasn't gone, not really; Jamie was right. We were never safe, and now, it's catching us up. Whoever this woman is—the woman with the red streaks in her hair—she's done something to Anna's bag. No, not *done* something to it, just switched it—changed it for another one, almost alike but not quite. And Anna hasn't noticed. And that means—

"Christ," I whisper; and the pad, which has bent and warped along its edges where I've held it too tightly, drops to the floor as I get up. My legs feel numb, wobbly; but I get them under some kind of control.

On the writing-desk is a flier for the lecture. It has the address on the front. I could still be in time. I say it to myself over and over: *You could still be in time.*

Jamie would have made it twice as fast as I can; but once I'm out in the street, legs pounding on the pavement, there's no time to think of that any more. I just have to run, and hope, and keep the refrain going: *There's still time. You just have to warn her. Still time.*

I tell myself I believe it, as my sides ache and my lungs and throat burn with gasping in the air. *Jamie would have been twice as fast,* the thought comes again; but there's only me now. Me and Anna and, somewhere on the periphery of what we can see and understand, the hermit.

22

*I*t takes me a while to come fully to myself; but when I do, it is to find things nearly finished. The floor is strewn with tools and brushes, and debris, but the house itself—well; the walls are painted, the wood-work and plaster mended; everything is back the way it was. The whole house, as I walk through it, has migrated into its own past, become again what it ought to be; what it was.

There are little dabs and spatters of paint on the photographs that ring the living room and tie them, like a cord, to the picture that has grown and grown and is now also nearly finished in the centre of the wall. There are thumbprints in paint where the photographs have been taken down and the walls behind them painted, and then later put back again. I know still that the order is not right, that I am missing some way of articulating them with their position; but it's becoming harder to think clearly about that. There's so much else—in different places and times—that's pulling at me, that needs to be attended to first.

It is so nearly done. Everything except one last detail—the part I have saved for last. I have what I need: a tin of paint, blue, so dark it is almost black; a smaller tin of metallic silver. Two brushes: one larger, one small. A pencil for marking in the positions. I won't need a chart this time, like we needed before; I know that when I start, it will all come back to me perfectly.

I don't know what day it is, but it's a fine, clear morning as I start up the stairs with these materials, to put the last touch to the finished house.

After that summer with the hermit, other summers come and go. Each time the coach stirs its great dust-trail down from the hills, and then rumbles out of the square leaving her standing behind, it is the signal that the holiday has started in earnest: Anna is here, and now things can properly begin.

I am eight when I first know Anna, in the summer of the hermit and the chapel and the gun in its case and the hidden cache of rifle shells; I am eight and she is ten. As the years pass and our ages change, the thing that is always constant is the way we understand each other: the way we can pick up conversations where they left off ten months before; the way the same old jokes make us laugh; the way we tease each other in the same ways and about the same things. Jamie still beats Anna when they run races—nearly all the time, at least. And Anna is still as full of that mysterious aliveness that has captured me from the start, though turning it now in one direction and now in another. The start of a summer is a magical time. It is as though, for the greater part of the year, I am only two-thirds a whole person, but that with the arrival of the holidays and Anna, I become complete, fully alive, fully me.

In all that stays the same, though, there are changes: slow ones at first, but then starting to become noticeable. They don't feel like much to start with, it's true. But gradually—very gradually—I can feel them, and see them. Places where we used to play don't hold the same interest for us any more, and we find new things to do. Some of our games are dropped, new ones invented to take their place. Small things, to start with. And at the time it's that we just got bored of doing things that way; it's never that it's Anna who's bored, and Jamie and I who are shifting with her, even though that's the way it will seem to me one day.

And so summers pass, and years pass in the shadow of those brighter, more real, summer days. I get taller, but so do Jamie and Anna, and so I don't really notice that any of us are any different. But sometimes small places where I used to hide are too small now, and things which once seemed very big now look to me to be more normal. All the time, though, it's happening seamlessly, as though it's not me that's changing, but the rest of the world: I am held solid while things flow and meld and alter around me. That's the way it feels—if it feels any way at all.

But then things really do start to change, in a way I can't ignore. It's as if a series of tremors shudder through the calm of the valley, making the earth tumble from the hill terraces and the lemon trees shiver and rattle their dusty leaves, even though there's no wind. In one brief summer, all the change that has been building up around me unnoticed is let loose, unleashed in a brief series of convulsions that leave me gasping, my whole world suddenly different.

They start when I am eleven, when Jamie tells me about the school his parents want him to go to. A school in England. A school which will keep him away for all the term-times, and leave him free only in the holidays. A school that will pull the two of us apart, in those times of the year when Jamie is all I have. And there is talk, too, of the Anderson family moving to England: of Mr. and Mrs. Anderson selling their house at the end of the little row of four, and buying a new one there. It's to do with work, Jamie says bitterly. Slowly it is borne in on me that this will actually happen; that it's not just a story. Jamie will be the first to go—to get him settled there, Mr. Anderson tells my parents—and then they will follow. The thought of Jamie leaving the valley is impossible to examine. Distantly, I remember when he arrived: seeing him standing, staring at the hills on the horizon. I have never considered that he might go as suddenly or as easily. But it's going to happen; it's going to happen.

This, then, is the change that first shakes my sense of my world, and it comes in an autumn when I am eleven. But hardly have I had time to allow it into my head—to make space for it in there—than there are others. That year turns slowly on its axis, and the summer comes when I turn twelve. Already it is a summer whose heat and freedom are tainted. At its end, Jamie will be leaving Altesa, and I shan't see him again until Christmas. It will be like that from now on, I know. Trying not to think of this, I hug to myself the knowledge that Anna will be here soon. At least, I tell myself, we will always have the summers; that no matter how much distance comes between us the rest of the year, summer will always see us back here in Altesa, doing the same things, telling the same stories, telling the same jokes.

Even while I'm telling myself this, I think there is already some tiny, hidden part of me that knows this summer will be the last that we all share.

Anna says, "Are you looking forward to it?"

"I don't know." Jamie thinks for a moment. "I suppose—no, not really."

"Why not tell your parents?"

"I did. It doesn't make any difference. They're going to move there anyway, and I've got to go to school somewhere."

"That's crappy," she says.

"Yeah. It is."

The cove is baking in the sun. Anna has a pair of little sunglasses which she's pushed up on her head; secretly, I think they're very smart. She's thirteen now. Each year that passes is like a snap-shot of elapsed time: when she steps off the coach, she's always a little different from how I remember her. This time, though, the differences are enough that I have to look twice to make sure she's actually the girl we've come to meet. She's grown her hair long over the time since we've last seen her, and she's far taller than she was, too: taller even than Jamie, which shocks us both. At the beach, the changes in her are more obvious still. It's been several years since we last swam in only our pants; for some reason, Anna becomes suddenly self-conscious about underwear, and starts to insist that we wear proper swimming costumes. For the past couple of years she's had a mid-blue all-in-one swimsuit. Jamie and I can still swim in our underwear if we've forgotten to bring trunks, but if Anna forgets, she just sits out on the beach and watches us splash about, grinning at us when we wave.

This year, though, when she pulls off her T-shirt on the pebbles, she's wearing a proper bikini—a top part and a bottom part, cheerful red with white straps on the shoulders. My first thought is how grownup she looks, with her bikini and her sunglasses; my second—which comes as a kind of shock—is that she's sexy. For one thing, unlike the chest part of her old blue swimsuit, the top half of her red and white bikini cups small but distinct breasts.

"What are you staring at?" she says.

"You've—got a new swimsuit," I say quickly.

"Yeah. Do you like it?"

"Yeah. You look—really grown-up."

"Yeah? I think so, too. Jamie?"

"Mm?"

"What do you think?"

"It's nice," he says. "Bet it doesn't make you go faster than the old one, though."

Anna grins. "Is that a challenge?"

"Why? Think you might stand a chance this time?"

" '*This* time?' What does that mean? I beat you *all* the time."

"Yeah, right. Let's see you try. Alex? Umpire?"

"Um—in a minute." I still have my trousers on and I'm fumbling with my shoes. Anna and Jamie are already halfway along the spur.

"Alex! Come on! What's keeping you?"

"All right," I say. I fiddle with my trousers and pretend to have trouble getting them undone. The truth is that something has happened for which I'm utterly unprepared: for some reason, seeing Anna in her new bikini has made me wonder for a second what it would be like to touch her—to put my hand on one of her breasts, instead of just glancing at it. The thought's really only in my head for a moment before she asks me what I'm looking at, and quick shame and embarrassment drive it away; but now there is something else, something even more embarrassing. It's suddenly become very important that I keep my trousers on for a while longer. The material of my swimming trunks is quite stretchy, and if I take them off now, I'm sure Anna and Jamie will notice.

"Alex! Come *on*!"

"My zip's stuck," I say. "I can watch from here."

"Oh, all right," Jamie says. "Say one two three go."

"Ready?" I call. Their heads bob in unison, which makes me smile. "One, two, three—go!"

They both break the water at the same time, and I watch them all the way to the rocks which are always our target. It's neck and neck right up to the end, and I can't be sure at all which of them—if either—slaps their hand on the rock first.

I can see them treading water there, looking back at me expectantly. Anna calls, "Well? Who was it?"

I think for a moment of saying that it's a tie; and then I shout, "Anna—just by a bit, though." Jamie wins all the time anyway.

"Yes!" Anna's shouting. "She beats him again! *Another* world title to this incredibly talented newcomer!" Jamie, I can just see, is shaking his head, and I can imagine his rueful grin.

Now, lying on the pebbles and waiting to get dry—I have managed to join them in the water eventually—I say, "It's going to be strange, though."

"Yeah," Jamie says. "I know."

Anna says, "But you'll come back, won't you?"

"Yeah," Jamie says. "Of course. It's just that—well, it's such a long way away."

"It won't be the same without you here," I say, able at last to give voice in the mildest way to some of what I'm feeling.

"No. I know."

"Who's going to look at the stars with me?"

Jamie says, suddenly, "I'll leave my telescope. You can use it when I'm not here."

"No," I say, at once. "You need it more than I do. I mean—thanks. But you should take it with you."

"And I'll write to you," he says. "Lots. Every day, maybe."

"Yeah. And I'll write back and tell you everything that's happening here. That's a good idea."

Anna says, "I don't want to talk about this. It's sad."

"Yeah," Jamie says.

"We could go into town," she adds. "You know—get Cokes or something."

"Why not? That would be OK."

"And then maybe walk down to the harbour," she says. "We don't go down there very often. We could see what it's like."

"OK," I say.

Anna sits up and pulls her T-shirt towards her. "Hey, Alex," she says. "I've got something here—hang on a minute." She's digging in the pockets of her jeans now. "It's here somewhere," she says. "Yeah. Don't look."

I close my eyes, and hear Jamie say, "Oh, yeah, I remember that."

"You can open your eyes now," she says. When I look, she's got the necklace on that I made her years ago, for the first birthday party she had with us. The stone that's the colour of moonlight is just lighter than her skin, and the silver chain twinkles in the sun. As the summer goes on, and she tans, I know the contrast between stone and skin will get stronger.

"Hey," I say. "Yeah. You've still got it."

"Of course," she says, seriously. "I keep it for special occasions, though. It's too nice to wear all the time. It's my best piece of jewellery. I don't have much," she adds.

Jamie gets up and stretches. "Cokes at Toni's," he says. "Yeah, that sounds good."

"Just like old times," Anna says, but somehow her voice sounds kind of sad.

It's almost like old times, kind of like old times. Sometimes it's so close you can hardly tell the difference. Those are the times I like best—the times when the things that have changed fade into the background, and we're just Anna and Jamie and Alex, together.

It's Anna who says it. Jamie's having a bath—under protest, but Mrs. Anderson says he's got half the dust of the valley in his hair and clothes from the day's play—and we're sitting in his room waiting for him. I've got a comic open and Anna's sitting by the window, staring up the valley. Although we never go there now, I've noticed that she still likes to look up at the chapel, as if maybe she's expecting to see some signal from its belltower—some clue that the hermit's back, waiting for us there.

"You could go too," she says.

"What?"

I look up, the images and captions of the story fluttering away from me like gaudy butterflies.

"To school," she says, a little impatiently. "If you're going to miss him so much, you could ask to go too. Your parents might say yes."

I stare at her. It's such a simple idea, but for some reason—perhaps because the whole idea of England seems half like a fantasy to me—it's never crossed my mind. I say, "I'm not old enough."

"No, I know. Not this year. But next year you would be. Then you could be with Jamie and come back here for the summer."

I keep staring at her as the notion filters through my mind. She's right; if I were in England with Jamie, we'd be together through term-times as well. And England with Jamie would be better than Altesa without him, even though I'm sure England itself will be a colder and greyer place, with more heavy green curtains all the way down to the floor.

"Alex?"

"Yeah," I say, slowly. "Maybe."

"You can ask Jamie when he's out of the bath."

"No," I say, suddenly deciding something. "Don't say anything."

"Why not?"

"Cos my parents might not let me. Wait, and I'll ask them, and then we can tell Jamie."

She nods. "OK. That sounds like a good plan."

A grin breaks over my face. "Thanks, Anna," I say.

"No problem," she says, smiling back. With the window open behind her, and the valley stretching out to the skyline, I think she looks very beautiful.

When I go to buy sweets, Anna shakes her head. "I don't like those ones any more," she says.

"But they're your favourite."

"No. They're too sickly. Get me fruit-flavoured ones."

I say, "You really don't want the red ones?"

"No. They're really *too* sweet, don't you think?"

"Yeah," I say. "Yeah, I think so too."

The afternoon when we go to the harbour end of town is calm and still, and the heat hangs in the air all through the valley. Jamie and I just have shorts and trainers on; Anna has shorts too, but also a shirt that she's tied up so it shows her tummy. Again, I think how adult she looks like this.

At the far end of the bay, just past the main part of the harbour, there is a fish market and some big shed-like buildings where the fishermen keep things. We walk along the sea wall at the back of the harbour, looking at the boats moored there, hardly moving on the smooth water. Sometimes there is just the tapping of a rope against a mast in the quiet air.

Jamie says, "There's where the river ends."

We look, and nod. We've seen this before, but it's still weird to look at the rectangular concrete channel that comes through from the town and know that, if you were to jump down into it and walk all day, it would take you right to the top of the valley.

Anna says, "You guys want a drink? There's a bar."

"OK," Jamie says.

"Yeah," I say.

The bar is a little place, set back from the waterfront. There are plastic tables outside with colourful parasols sticking up on poles through their centres. Inside, the bar looks dark and cool and vaguely nautical, as though it must be crowded with old sailors and fishing-boat men in the evenings. Now, though, at half-past three, it's quiet. There's only one person—an old man who I'm sure is a sailor—sitting under one of the parasols and sipping a small glass of beer.

Jamie and I sit ourselves where we can see the boats. Anna finds change in her pocket, and Jamie and I hand over what we've got also.

"Get me a big Coke," I say.

"Hey," Anna says, suddenly. I know from her tone of voice that she's had an idea. Instead of going to get the drinks, she sits down, leaning closer to us. Jamie and I lean in too, instinctively.

"What?" Jamie says.

"Have you ever had beer?"

Jamie blinks. "No. Have you?"

"I've had wine lots of times," she says casually. "But not beer. You want to try some?"

"Um . . . all right," Jamie says. "Bet you won't like it, though."

"Bet I will."

"You won't. Girls don't drink beer."

"Well, I will."

"Get me a big beer, then," I say. I'm thirsty, and although the idea of drinking beer doesn't strike me as all that appealing—my father sometimes drinks beer, and I think the glasses smell rather nasty afterwards—I'm determined to be as casual as Anna is about the whole thing.

"All right," she says. "You sure?"

"Yeah," I say.

"Yeah," Jamie says after a moment. Anna gives us a conspiratorial grin and gets up, heading for the bar.

When she's inside, I say to Jamie, "Do you think she'll like it?"

"No," Jamie says. "Of course not. She's too young."

"She doesn't look as young as she did," I say.

"No. I know. But still," he says, reasonably.

"Might we get in trouble if anyone sees?" I say.

"Well," Jamie says uncertainly.

A shadow falls across the table and we both look up. There's a man standing there, watching us and smiling slightly. It takes me a moment to recognize the regular, handsome features, but when I do I glance instinctively at Jamie. I can see from the look on his face that he's made the connection, too.

"Hello," Signor Ferucci says. The sun is behind him and I have to squint to see him clearly.

I say, "Hello." Beside me, Jamie mumbles something inaudible.

Without being asked, Signor Ferucci pulls a chair out and sits down. There is still a faint smile on his face. I can see him much better now: the neat beard, trimmed short and starting to grey; the lean lines of his cheekbones and jaw. He looks ageless: a young man's vitality in an old man's face. His eyes are pale—almost grey—but when they catch the light they look both kind and terribly hard. There are little creases at their corners that might have come from laughter, but Signor Ferucci's face doesn't look as if it laughs a lot. I can imagine the ghost of a smile there widening, perhaps, but not actual laughter. I find I can't easily pull my gaze away from him.

"Has it been a good summer?" Signor Ferucci asks. He sounds interested, more than just polite. His voice is mild and good-natured.

Jamie says nothing, so I say, "Mm—yes."

"That's good. What have you been doing?"

I try to look to Jamie for some kind of support. I'm not used to talking to strange adults, and Signor Ferucci is more than just a stranger—he's a stranger about whom we've told stories, about whom we've theorized and conjectured a hundred times. He might be a vampire or a zombie, I remember rather crazily; he's certainly a recluse. He hardly ever comes out from his white house on the hillside, from behind his tall white wall over which we've peered many times now. And yet here he is, sitting in the sunshine with Jamie and me, and talking to us as if it's the most natural thing in all the world.

I say, "Mm . . . playing."

"Yes? Where? At the beach, maybe?"

"Sometimes," I say, rather guardedly.

"You mustn't go swimming too soon after your meals," he says, sounding like Lena.

"I know," I say.

"And what of your friend?" Signor Ferucci says. "Your cousin. Anna. How's she? I would have thought the three of you would be together on an afternoon like this. Everyone in the town says that you're never apart." He chuckles quietly at this. I wonder how Signor Ferucci manages to know what the town gossips about, since he's hardly ever in it. I could almost believe he has a telescope like Jamie's trained on the town square; except that wouldn't let him hear what people were saying. He adds, "How old would she be, now?"

"Thirteen," I say.

"She's growing up fast," Signor Ferucci says. "It doesn't seem so long ago that she was just ten, does it?"

I'm surprised. This is something I've found myself thinking more and more of late; I'm unprepared to hear Signor Ferucci put it into words for me. I say, "Mm."

"And you, too," he says, turning to Jamie. "You're off to school soon, if what I hear is right."

Jamie twitches in his seat when the man's eyes turn to him, as if I've pinched him. He says, but only just audibly, "Yes."

"That's going to be quite an adventure," Signor Ferucci says seriously. "A new school—new friends—lots of chances to do new things. And a different country, as well. You're a lucky young man," he adds. "It's not many people who have the opportunity to see so much of the world at your age."

"I s'pose," Jamie says. His voice isn't as tentative as before, and I can see that he's becoming reassured by the way the conversation is going. It's just the same kind of conversation we might end up having with any adult; except, I remind myself, that Signor Ferucci seems to know a lot about what's going on in our lives.

"England will seem very different to sleepy little Altesa, I expect. I should think it will be quite exciting, once you're there. Are you looking forward to it all?"

"Kind of," Jamie says.

Signor Ferucci nods, and in his eyes there is understanding and intelligent compassion. "But not entirely, perhaps? Well. That's in the way of things. When you move on, you have to leave things behind sometimes. Places, people." He shrugs. "That's part of living, part of growing up. In a while, you may find you don't miss Altesa as much. You'll have new places to call your own, and new friends, like I said."

I glance swiftly at Jamie. I don't like how this sounds: it's too close to some of the fears I keep hidden inside me.

Jamie says, more boldly, "I'll still come back, though."

"Yes?" Signor Ferucci seems pleased. "That's good. You'll be able to see Alex, then?"

Again, I'm surprised at how easily he seems to know what's in my mind. I say, "Yeah."

"That's another thing about growing up," Signor Ferucci says thoughtfully, as if it's just occurred to him. "Deciding what to leave behind and what to take with you. What to remember and what to forget."

Jamie shifts a little uncomfortably in his seat, and I think he's about to say something when he's stopped by a clink of glass on glass and Anna says, "I got them. This is yours, Alex, and this—"

Her voice stops dead as she reaches the table, and I know she's finally noticed the figure there.

"Ah," Signor Ferucci says, sounding surprised and pleased. "Anna. I didn't know you were here as well. I thought maybe the boys had abandoned you for the afternoon. I should have known better. Here, you can sit down, you know." He glances at the drinks she's brought. "Beer, is it? I'd join you, but there are a lot of things I have to do today, and I don't suppose there's time to sit and drink the afternoon away, pleasant though it may be."

Anna sits slowly, her eyes fixed on him. Something of the strangeness of the situation is starting to get through to me more strongly now. The three of us sit, waiting for what Signor Ferucci will say next.

For a while he just looks out at the harbour and the little fishing boats there. Then he turns back to us. He's looking at Jamie again.

"School," he says, as though he's just remembered something. "That's what we were talking about. Going away to school. Yes." He rubs his thumbs together, and seems to be thinking about something; his brow furrows for a moment.

Anna says, abruptly, "What are you doing here? You never come down here."

I'm appalled by her rudeness. This is the first time she's ever spoken to this man, and she sounds both fierce and angry, as if he's done something wrong.

Signor Ferucci's eyebrows lift momentarily, but he doesn't get cross. He says, still in his mild voice, "I didn't realize there was anything wrong with coming down to town once in a while. Actually, I'm probably here more than you imagine, you know. I just don't go to the same places you do. I don't have time to go bathing, I'm afraid, and I don't think I've visited a rock pool in fifty years. Perhaps that's my bad luck. As for what I'm doing here—well, given the number of times you've visited my house over the past few years, I thought it about time I repaid the courtesy." Anna's mouth has opened slightly at this, and Signor Ferucci smiles a little. "You should have rung the bell at the gate," he says. "There's not so much to see by just looking over the wall. The estate's been too badly neglected, I'm afraid; but the house itself has some good points. I have a small collection of sculpture of which I'm rather proud, and there's an old-fashioned walled garden at the back that's still kept up. You would have been welcome, you know."

We sit in silence, staring at him. Even Anna's boldness seems to have deserted her.

At last, Jamie says, "How do you—I mean—" His voice tails off, but Signor Ferucci seems to know exactly what he was trying to say.

"I like to keep in touch," he says, nodding to himself. "I imagine people must think that because I keep myself out of the way a good deal, I don't know what's going on around me. Well, perhaps that's true for a lot of things. But in certain things, I do take an interest."

"Like what?" Jamie says, and his voice has faded away almost to a whisper. Anna, I notice, is just staring at Signor Ferucci, waiting to see what he'll say next.

"Like you, for instance." Signor Ferucci smiles more broadly as he says this, and I notice that the corners of his eyes do wrinkle up a little. I still can't imagine him laughing aloud, though. "It's not every day that someone takes as big a step as you're about to. I wanted to wish you luck, for one thing."

"Oh," Jamie says blankly. Then, "Thanks."

"And I'm pleased that you're going to keep in touch. Like I said, it's important to decide what you want to remember, and what you want to forget. England is going to feel like it's a long way from Italy, after a time; and perhaps all of this—" He sweeps his hand around to take in the town, the harbour, the hills. "All of this will seem very long ago. Do you understand what I'm saying?"

Anna says, "Nobody's going to forget anything." Her voice is cold as stone.

"No. I didn't think so. That's best, I think." There's a pause, as if Signor Ferucci is trying to think of the right words to say something. "Sometimes," he says eventually, "we do things that—later—might feel different to us than they did at the time. That's because we change, as we get older. Our ideas, our minds, our perceptions—they alter. But what's been done is what's been done, and *that* doesn't change. So—" He looks at us, and gradually his smile widens again. "I don't need to say this, do I?"

"Nobody's going to forget," Anna says again.

"No. All right." He takes a breath, and then shakes his head, smiling to himself. "Well. Do you know, the older I get the more I realize something: and that's that no matter how old you are, you're not too old to learn something new. And I think today has been a day of learning for me." He stands up. "I must be going. You don't want your beer to get warm, do you? Have a good time in England, Jamie. I meant to congratulate you on your exam results, by the way—especially the music. Perhaps there's a career there one day, eh? To think that once upon a time we'd all have sworn it was to be astronomy. That's something that's changed, without a doubt. Alex. It was good to see you again. Remember me to your parents, and Lena. And Anna—" He pauses, looking at her. "Well. Perhaps we'll meet again some day. I really should have invited you up to the house before this, but the summers always seem to go by so quickly, and by the time I think about it, you're gone again. Still. You can drop by any time. You'll always know where to find me."

"I suppose you'll always know where to find us, too," Anna says quietly.

"Anna," he says, curiously gently. "I try to keep in touch with friends. That's all. There's nothing to worry about—nothing to be afraid of."

"I'm not afraid."

"No. I know." He looks out to the sea for a second. "I must be on my way. Enjoy your beer, Alex."

We watch him as he walks down to the harbour wall, stares out at the boats for a while, and then continues on towards the south side of the valley. I look at Jamie; his face is ashen, even though the heat is back in the afternoon again.

Jamie says, "He knows everything about us."

"Yeah," Anna says. "But you heard him—it's OK. There's nothing to be—"

"It's *not* OK!" Jamie shouts, loud enough that the old man at the table across from us looks up, frowning. "It's not fucking OK!"

"Quiet," Anna says, looking round. "Keep it down."

I say, "What did he mean?"

Anna says, "He just meant we shouldn't forget. That's all. And we won't." She looks hard at Jamie. "We won't, will we?"

Jamie says nothing. He's looking at the sea wall, where Signor Ferucci stood for a moment before he passed out of sight.

"Jamie," Anna says, quietly. "Jamie, it's OK. Really. He was just— reminding us."

"Warning us, you mean," Jamie says.

"No. Just reminding us."

"Well I wish he hadn't," Jamie says. "I don't want to be reminded. I didn't *need* to be reminded."

"No," she says, soothingly. "I know you didn't. But I know you better than he does, don't I?"

Grudgingly, Jamie nods.

I have understood what the conversation has all been about. I say, "Why did he leave it until now? Why didn't he say something before?"

Jamie says, "Because I'm going away. Where he can't—keep an eye on me. That's why." He slips back into a morose silence.

"Well," Anna says. She's quiet for a while, and then she says, "Do you like beer, then?"

We all pick up our glasses and sip at the beer. It's gone a little warm in the sun, and it's bitter and metallic to taste.

"No," Jamie says. "Not really."

"Me neither," I say. I try some more. "It's nasty, don't you think?"

"Oh, I don't know," she says. "It's not so bad."

Jamie lets out a low breath and his shoulders, which I now realize have been tensed up, slump a little. "Oh, screw it," he says. "I'm not having this ruin my summer. Screw it. Let's go and fish for crabs or something."

"Let's finish our beer first," Anna says.

We're lying out on the gentle slope of the roof outside my bedroom window one night, watching the patterns of the stars. Anna and I always listen while Jamie tells us their names, and points them out; some of the names have stories that go with them, and Jamie tells these, too.

"You know," I say, "I always dream of sleeping out here. Just looking up and falling to sleep with the stars looking back down at me."

"Shooting star," Anna says.

"I see it."

Jamie says, "Yeah. But you'd get cold."

"I know."

"It would be good, though."

"When you're grown up, you could have a bedroom with a glass ceiling," he says after a moment.

"What, like a greenhouse?"

"Yeah."

"That would be weird."

Anna says, smiling, "Yeah. It'd be hot. You'd boil in the day."

"I s'pose," I say.

She's quiet for a minute. When I look at her, she's got a slight frown of concentration on her face.

"Shooting star," Jamie says.

"Yeah."

Anna says, "There's something we *could* do, though."

"What?" Jamie says.

"We could try tomorrow. We'd need a bit of money."

"I've got some left over from my birthday," I say. "Why? What is it?"

"Not now," she says. "I'll tell you tomorrow. I need to think about it."

Jamie raises his eyebrows at me, and I grin back.

Jamie brings his star charts while Anna and I clear all the stuff out of my room and into Lena's room at the back of the house. It takes us three goes to get the bed through the door, but Anna's stronger than I'd imagine, and we manage it in the end.

"There," she says, when the room's clear. "Now the newspaper."

We spread the newspaper all over the bare floor, which looks very strange now that everything's gone. Anna brings in a stool from the kitchen, and sets out the pencils she's brought on the windowsill. My mother's agreement to Anna's plan has been won only after many assurances that no harm will come to the carpet, or any of the furniture. In fact, when we leave her, she seems to be starting to like the idea; I've wondered if she will. It's good luck that my father's away today, since I am pretty sure that he wouldn't approve.

Jamie comes back with the star maps and we spread them out on the floor and kneel over them, planning, working things out. While Anna and Jamie start to pencil in the positions of the constellations, I lie on my back on the softly rustling newspaper, guiding them, letting my mind's eye fill in the gaps from the star chart I now have in my head.

By the end of the morning the whole ceiling is covered with a dense rash of pencil marks. Anna and Jamie, who've spent more time tilting their heads back to see than I have, rub their necks a lot when we finish. I've been lying on the floor so my neck's OK, though I do find that when we leave the room the haze of pencil dots floats down the corridor in front of me for a while. Anna says, "It's nearly done. We just need to finish off the bit by the window, and we can start with the paint."

After lunch—during which Lena quizzes us about what's going on upstairs, and we resolutely stick to telling her to wait until it's finished, that it's a surprise—Jamie is dispatched into town with my birthday money and instructions on what to buy. Anna and I set to work completing the design. We know now where the remaining stars should lie, so I hold the chart for her while she works.

"It's going to be good, don't you think?" she says.

"Yeah," I say. "It's going to be great."

She's quiet for a time, and I can tell something's bothering her.

"What is it?"

"Do you think he was right?" she says.

"Who?"

"Signor Ferucci. When he said that Jamie would—would forget stuff. When he went away."

"No," I say. "Of course not. I mean—what stuff?"

Anna's eyes are fixed on the ceiling while she draws the dots in. "Well—stuff about Altesa," she says. "Stuff about us."

"Jamie wouldn't forget anything like that," I say. A thought strikes me. "You go away," I say. "And you don't forget things."

"Yeah—I know. But this is . . ." Her voice trails away.

"What?"

"It's different, don't you think? They're going to live there. It's like . . ."

I wait for her to go on. She takes a breath, and the arm holding the pencil drops to her side, though she's still looking upwards.

"It's like everything's changing. I just think—nothing's going to be the same any more. What's going to happen next summer?"

I blink. "We'll—we'll all come back here, I guess. Jamie'll come back."

"His parents might be moving then. He might not be able to."

"Of course he will," I say. "He can stay with me. So can you. Nothing's going to change."

I can see her bite her lip. "I think things have already changed," she says.

I want to tell her she's wrong, but I know she isn't. It's in the air, like the smell of hot resin from the stone pines. Even painting the ceiling of my room like this is part of it. I look up at the star patterns, and somewhere deep inside me I already know what they really are: something to remember Jamie and Anna by, when they're not there any more. A keepsake. I want to say that we'll always be the same, and everything's going to go on next year like always, but I know—some part of me knows. Things *are* different now. When I look up at Anna, reaching above her to draw in the positions on the white plaster, the shape of her body under her T-shirt and jeans, and what it does to me inside, is only part of what's different. The rest of it I can't even begin to understand.

I say, "Yeah."

"Hey. Don't be sad."

"I'm not."

She gets down from the stool and looks at me, concerned. "I didn't mean to upset you."

"I'm OK. I just—I miss him already. And you."

"Hey. But we'll do something, you'll see. We'll get together somehow."

I smile bravely. "Yeah. Of course."

"Maybe you'll get to go to school there, too."

"Yeah."

"That would be good, wouldn't it?"

I think of it: how it would make me closer to Jamie; and how it might make me further away from Anna. Italy—Altesa—the valley—this is our place, where we're supposed to be. We're supposed to drink Cokes at Toni's, and dive from the spur at the cove, and watch the water in the lion's-mouth fountain, and remember other things: a clock with no hands, and an empty chapel, and a big old white house on a hillside looking over everything from behind its high walls. I try to imagine the three of us some other place—England, maybe; anywhere—and I can't do it. This is where we're supposed to be. Going with Jamie is the only thing I can think to do, but in some awful way it feels like it will tear us apart just the same.

She seems to understand instinctively what I'm feeling. She says, "I'll be OK. Don't worry about me. I'm used to looking after myself."

"But I—" My mouth falters, and I don't know what to say. Something like, *I'll miss you.* Or maybe something else. In the end, all I can manage is, "I won't forget anything. Jamie won't either, but I won't. Not anything. I promise." Suddenly, I want to pour out everything: how she's locked in my head for ever—grinning at a joke, hair plastered back with seawater, tightening a bandage in the murky dimness of the chapel, shrieking as Jamie hurls mud at her, climbing trees in the lemon grove, peering over the high white wall of Signor Ferucci's estate—everything from the moment I first see her, sitting under a tree watching a kitten in the dry grass, through to the way she bites her lower lip slightly as she lines in the positions of the stars on my ceiling. She's there for ever, and all I have to do is let my eyes and mind drift, and I can see her again. All at once, I don't know why I haven't explained all this to her before. I should have. It was Jamie's idea not to, but I think now he was wrong; that Anna needs to know, too. And I have half opened my mouth to say it—to tell her everything—to try to put into words the feelings I've always had about her, and which although they're changing now are still the same, really—when the door opens and Jamie comes in.

"You got it?" Anna says.

"Yeah. It's all here." He lifts the paper bag he's got under one arm.

"Great," she says. "We can get started right away, if you like. Alex?"

"Yeah," I say, numbly. "Yeah. Let's do it."

We start at the door and work our way towards the window, taking it in turns to stand on the stool. If you load the brush only a little, the paint doesn't drip or spatter too badly; we learn quickly what's the right amount to use. Gradually, a wave of darkness spreads across the room: blue so dark it is almost black, and which looks deep as the sky. We work steadily and carefully, leaving little areas of white unpainted where the stars will be. The ceiling slants down from the door to the window, and to begin with, only Anna can reach it properly; but then Jamie can take over halfway, and by the time we're three-quarters done, I can take my place on the stool. It makes my arms ache, all this reaching up, but when you sit back down on the floor and see how it's starting to look, it's worth it.

When the blue's done, we sit and wait for it to dry, reading comics and talking and laughing. The whole room has the heady and exciting smell of fresh paint, even with the window wide open. Then, at last, it's time to start on the silver: the smaller pot that Jamie's bought, which we shake up vigorously before beginning. We have a special small brush for this, too.

The small stars are just a dot of paint, but the large ones we make bigger. Slowly, a scattered pattern of silver starts to take shape over the spread of the ceiling, replacing the plain white with glittering constellations. Anna's hands move smoothly and confidently, the paintbrush eight inches above her nose as she gets closer to the window. Then it's Jamie's turn, and mine. We're sure to keep our stars the right sizes for their different magnitudes, and when there's any doubt, Jamie checks the chart to make certain.

And then it's finished. We lie on the paint-spattered newspaper, our hands behind our heads, staring at what we've done. It looks like the top of the room has been lifted off and the universe left clear. The silver paint winks and shines and glimmers in the blue-black, and although

I have been reaching up to paint it myself just a few minutes before, the ceiling now looks terribly far away, as though you could never touch it no matter how high you stretched.

Anna says, "Hey. Not bad."

"It's perfect," I say. "It's amazing."

"Yeah," Jamie says. "It's pretty good." He sounds impressed. I stare around my personal sky, and am amazed at what has been done with only paint and brushes and an afternoon. It hardly seems possible.

"I wonder how it'll look at night."

"You know what?" Anna says. "You need to keep a candle burning so that they twinkle. Like real stars. Just one candle should do it."

"Yeah," I say, imagining how that would look. "Yeah, that would be good."

"I'd like to see that," Jamie says.

"We should," Anna says. "We can sleep over tonight, can't we, Alex?"

"Sure," I say. "Of course you can."

"Then we'll try it together," she says.

We lie on the floor of my room. The newspaper's cleared away and my bed's back, and my books and small amount of clutter. We don't see any of that, though. The room is dark: it's one in the morning. The rest of the valley is asleep, but in some strange way this time—this middle-of-the-night time—is almost more ours than the bright afternoons at the beach or the mornings down in the town. We've made it ours. We've covered the valley from one end to the other in these early morning hours, and seen its hills and fields by moonlight and starlight. None of us is scared of the night any more.

Like Anna has said, a single candle flickers and trembles in the slight breeze from the open window. Above us, the ceiling of stars catches its light in its silver paint, glittering and shimmering; and the blue soaks the rest away into itself. By candlelight, the blue is deeper and further away than ever.

"Hey," Anna says, pointing. "Shooting star." And for a moment, I believe her.

"Have you asked your parents, then?" she says.

"Not yet," I say. "But I will."

"Yeah."

Jamie's in town on an errand, and Anna and I are in the lemon grove. The lemons are fat and ripe in the trees, and Anna reaches up and picks one down, scratching the skin of it with her thumbnail and holding it out for me to sniff.

"Nice," I say.

"Hot lemons," Anna says, smelling it herself. The lemons get warmed up in the sun and it seems to waken the smell of them somehow. She bounces it in her hand. "Like a scent grenade," she says, with a grin, and hurls the lemon off into the undergrowth. "Blam! There it goes."

I laugh at the image.

She says, "If you go to England—"

"Yeah?" I say.

"Oh, nothing." She kicks her feet through the dust as she walks.

"Anna?"

"Yeah?"

"If I go to England, I'll write to you. Lots. OK?"

She smiles. "Yeah, OK."

"Thanks for my ceiling," I say. "I really—I mean, it's good. Really good. I—I really like it."

She stops walking and turns to look at me. I stop, too. "You really like it?" she says.

"Yeah. It's the best ceiling I've ever had."

She throws her head back and laughs at that, while I stand there watching her, pleased at having made her laugh. It's her last day, and she's been quiet and a little withdrawn all morning.

"You know something?" she says.

"What?"

"You're quite cute sometimes."

I don't know what to say to this. I can tell I'm blushing. I can't decide whether being cute is good or bad.

Anna says, "Here." She puts one hand to my face, and leans in, and kisses me quickly on the mouth. It's only a moment: I feel her lips touch mine, and then an instant of pressure, and a kind of tingle as they pull away again. I feel my mouth come open in surprise. Suddenly, my whole body feels lighter, as if it might float.

Anna bites her lip for a moment, still looking at me. Then she grins.

"What?" she says. "Didn't you like it?"

"No!—I mean, yes. Yes," I say, flustered.

"Hey, you're blushing."

"So are you."

"I'm not."

She isn't. I say, "What was that for?"

"Wasn't for anything. I just felt like it." She pulls another lemon from a branch above us. "Doesn't mean we're engaged or anything."

"Oh. Well," I say.

"Maybe Jamie's back now," she says.

"Maybe."

"We could go and look."

"Yeah," I say. "Let's." But I don't move. There's always the chance that she'll do it again. If she does, I think my feet might actually lift off the ground. It's weird. It's not the kiss itself, it's what it does to you inside. I wait to see what will happen.

Anna trots past me. "Well, come on, then," she calls over her shoulder.

It takes me a moment to get my co-ordination together enough to run after her.

Jamie sets the suitcases down on the pavement at the side of the square and looks at his watch. "Not long," he says.

"No."

"You've got a book to read?"

"Yeah. I've got two."

"That's good."

We lapse into an uncertain and awkward silence. Every so often I think I can hear the rumble of the bus, but minutes pass and it doesn't come.

Anna says, "When's school start?"

"In a week."

"When do you fly out, then?"

"Six days. You have to be there early, to settle in."

"You taking your telescope?"

"I don't know. Maybe."

"Maybe it'll be nice. It might be nice. You never know."

"Yeah, that's true."

It won't be nice. We all know that.

"Alex'll be in the top class now," Jamie says. "You get to do some stuff you don't get in the other classes."

"Oh. Yeah."

I hear something, and strain my ears to catch it; it might be the bus, or it might just be a car in one of the other streets. Or it might be nothing at all.

I say, "You'll come and see us next year, though?"

Anna opens her mouth to reply, and then shuts it again. Her lip trembles for a moment, and I realize—shocked—that she's trying not to cry. I've never seen Anna cry before. It's peculiarly distressing: I cry sometimes, and sometimes Jamie does, but Anna's older and stronger than us, and things don't hurt or upset her the same way. She's never scared of the things I'm scared of.

"Hey," I say.

There's a squeal of brakes, and the bus turns the corner into the square.

"It's here," Jamie says, unnecessarily. He picks up Anna's suitcases as the bus grinds to a stop beside us.

"Are you OK?" I say. Anna nods, and rubs her face quickly, and sniffs.

Jamie hands the cases to the driver, who stows them in the big baggage hold. Then it's time for Anna to go.

She grabs Jamie and hugs him, and I hear her murmur something that I don't quite catch. Then she grabs and hugs me, too, and says, "Bye, Alex. Be careful, OK?"

"You, too," I say. "I—Anna, I—" But whatever it is, I can't make it work out right. Instead I hear myself say, "Don't get sick on the bus."

"I won't."

Then she's climbing the steps, and we see her thread her way down the central aisle to her seat at the back. And we watch as the bus pulls away, turning round across the square and then climbing back past us. I can see Anna in the window, and as the bus comes by on its way out of the square again she lifts a hand and waves, and Jamie and I wave back. I'm sure I can see tears on her face, and I can't understand why she is suddenly so sad. We'll see each other again. It's not as if this is the last time we'll be together.

The bus is gone now, and Jamie and I start slowly back along the road to home. Anna's gone, too; it's just the two of us left. And in a week—in six days—Jamie will go, and I'll be alone. And as we walk, I start to realize what it is that's made Anna cry; until I can feel hot tears pricking at the corners of my eyes, too, and have to blink them away in the haze of dust left by the passage of the bus over the hot asphalt of the road.

23

"*D*o you know where he is?"

I shake my head.

"Do you know when he left?"

"No, sir."

"But you've known this has been going on?"

I don't know what to say to that. I stare at the carpet between my feet. It's some time in the middle of the night, and I'm standing in slippers and pyjamas and dressing-gown in my housemaster's study. I've known all along that something like this would happen eventually; it had felt inevitable from the start, right from when Jamie first took me into his confidence. It's six months since we came back from Florence, and, if anything, seeing Italy again seems to have spurred Jamie to even more flagrant night-time absences. It has to be noticed in the end—it's just a matter of time. This time, it seems, his luck has run out.

"How long has this been going on?"

I shrug helplessly. Since the first thudding knock on my bedroom door, I've known what it would all come down to: being asked to betray Jamie. But there's nothing to betray: there's nothing I can tell them they don't know already. Jamie's gone. He'll be back, I expect, some time. There's nothing more I can say or do. I don't know, in all honesty, where he is, though I could of course guess at a few places. But I won't say them. I stick to the absolute truth, which is that I don't know when he left, where he's gone, how long he'll be away—anything. It's all I can do, shivering slightly.

Dr. Cooper rubs a hand wearily across his eyes. I can guess he's more worried than I am, because he doesn't know that Jamie is capable of looking after himself. I have no worries. With a sudden spark of insight, I realize that he's afraid, too; afraid of what this means for Jamie, for him, for the house and the school. It's too bad, I think to myself. His fears don't mean anything much to me.

"Alex," he says, trying to keep his voice conversational yet serious. "We know he's done this before. He's your friend. It's very important that we find where he is, and get him back. This is a matter of the greatest seriousness. You do understand that, don't you?"

I nod. "Yes, sir."

"You must tell me right now if you have *any* idea where he might be."

I say, "I think he goes to London." They can search London all they like.

"Why? To do what?"

"I don't know." It might be any one of a number of things.

"Alex—answer this truthfully, now. Do you think Jamie's taking drugs?"

It's so incongruous I actually laugh aloud. Dr. Cooper's face flushes, and hastily I try to compose myself, get control again.

"No, sir. I don't think he'd do that."

"How can you be sure?"

I can feel giggles welling up inside me, and I have to force them down. "It's not really his style, sir."

"Not—his—style," Dr. Cooper says slowly, meditatively, as if the words are in a language foreign to him. Then, "I hope you're right."

I glance at the clock on the wall. It's twenty-past three. I wonder how long all this will last.

"Alex?"

"What is it?"

"Jamie's back." The monitor sees my questioning glance, and shakes his head. "I don't know. I think it's pretty bad. He missed all Saturday school. I mean, there's no way he wasn't going to get caught. Fucking stupid."

It's Sunday morning. Jamie has been gone since some time Friday night. During the past thirty-six hours, the whole school has come to know of what's happened: it's the only subject of conversation wherever you go. I've heard that he's skipped school to go to a disco; that he's had a nervous breakdown and gone home; that he's run off with a girl from the nearby town. This last one makes me smile for a moment before I remember how bad it's all going to be for Jamie. Not just pretty bad, like the monitor says; very bad.

"Oh," I say.

"Cooper's seeing him now. They were shouting down there when I went by." He sounds impressed; people don't usually shout at Dr. Cooper. "Christ. Some weekend, yeah?"

"I suppose," I say. I don't want to talk about it—gossip about it. I want to know what's happened to Jamie, if he's all right. But there will be more phone calls to his parents, and to the headmaster, and more rows and shouting in the study downstairs before any real information will leak its way to me. I lie back on my bed and close my eyes, and wait.

In the end, it's not information that makes its way to me in my room: it's Jamie.

"Hi," he says.

I sit up. "Shit, what're you doing here? Have they let you off?"

"Hey," he says. "Hang on. No, it's not like that." He comes in, closes the door behind him. He's wearing the jacket and jeans I've seen him wear to play the clubs, and his hair looks tousled, as though he might have slept on the train. He paces up and down the room.

"I'm supposed to be in custody," he says after a moment, with a grin. "Cooper's in seeing the head at the moment, and I'm supposed to wait in his study like a good little boy while they decide what to do with me."

"You shouldn't be here," I say, caught between wanting him to stay and being afraid for him if he does.

"Oh, it won't make any difference."

"It won't?"

"No. I'll be out of here by Monday, I guarantee it. After what I said to Cooper, I'd be surprised if they keep me overnight."

"What—what did you say?"

His grin broadens. "He wanted to know where I'd been. What I'd been doing. He went on and on about it."

"Yeah," I say. "He thought you were doing drugs."

Jamie laughs. "Really? Cool."

"So what'd you tell him?"

"I said I'd spent the weekend in London. He said he knew that, and he wanted to know who I was with and where I'd gone and what I'd done." He sits down on the end of the bed, still smiling. "God, it was funny. I said OK, I was with my boyfriend, and where we'd gone and what we'd done were our business, not his. You should have seen his face."

"I don't s'pose he was expecting that."

"No," Jamie says. "You could be right there."

"Were you? With Paul, I mean."

"Yeah. But not in the way I made it sound. There was a festival on, and we played some sets through Friday night and Saturday. That was all. Besides—Paul and me—well. It's a bit much to call him a boyfriend. I think he knows that too."

"Is he OK with it?"

"Think so."

"So what happens now?"

"Once they work out where I am, they'll send me home, I guess."

"What'll your parents say?"

"I don't know. I don't know if I mind all that much. I've got some money saved; I can get work easily enough. There's a lot of people on the circuit know me now. I'm actually pretty OK."

"Good," I say.

"You know what I'm thinking?"

"What?"

"I want to get enough together to go back to Italy. I could do it, I think. Work London until I've made a stake, and then get back there. Try playing in Rome for a while. There's bound to be stuff. I think that's what I'll do."

"Sounds good to me," I say.

"And I was thinking something else," he says.

"Yeah?"

"Once I'm out there, we could—I mean, you and me, we could maybe go back to Altesa one summer. You know, just—get together and do all the old things together."

"What, like read comics?"

He nods. "Definitely. Get some Judge Dredds and Silver Surfers and just chill out. Make lemonade."

I grin, nodding with him. "Yeah. And spy on Lucia."

"You reckon she's still there?"

"Bound to be. Witches never die."

Jamie snorts with laughter. "Yeah. And watch the stars, and have Cokes at Toni's. All that shit."

"I'd like that," I say.

"Really?"

"Yeah, really. It would be cool. I—I miss all that, sometimes."

"Me too," he says.

We're quiet for a moment. Then I say, "Maybe we can actually build that tree house we were always talking about."

"Definitely. Has to be done."

"And I'll referee your races."

He looks blank for a moment, like he doesn't understand what I've just said; and then a weird expression comes over his face. I'm puzzled. He looks like he's suddenly sad.

"What?" I say.

"Nothing," he says; then takes a breath, and lets it out slowly. "Nothing. Hey. How is Anna, anyway?"

"She's OK," I say. "She's looking for university places now."

"Yeah?" he goes quiet again. Then he says, "You write to her a lot, don't you?"

"Sure," I say.

"Does she write back much?"

I shrug. "Sometimes. I don't think she has a lot of time."

"No. Of course not."

"But she does sometimes. Postcards, sometimes."

Jamie says, "What actually happened, in Florence? There were loads of rumours going round."

It's the first time he's mentioned it. I laugh, a little awkwardly. "Oh, that. It was nothing. She was just kidding around."

"Oh, right."

"You know—pretending we were—you know, boyfriend and girlfriend and all that. She really fooled the other guys. You should have seen the looks I got, afterwards."

"I bet. Alex the great lover."

"Yeah, exactly."

"It's just, I thought you looked kind of weird afterwards. Like you were sad about something."

I blink, surprised. "No. Like what? It was really funny. She's always like that—you know, joking and that."

Jamie says, "Alex, I've known you since you were six, for God's sake."

I say, "Well—yeah."

"You fancy her, don't you?"

I don't know what to say. To anyone else, yes; but to Jamie, I'm lost. In the end, I manage, "I—I don't know. I suppose so."

"You suppose so. Jesus. It's worse than that, isn't it? You *love* her." There's a kind of pain on his face, as though he can see inside me, know what's really there. "That's it, isn't it?"

"I—I don't know."

"How long?"

"I—well, kind of—kind of right from the start."

He's nodding, slowly. "Yeah. Yeah."

"But it didn't feel like that to begin with—I mean, you know how it was. We were just friends—and just kids. And then it got so I just—kind of knew."

"All that stuff in Florence—pretending to be your girlfriend and everything. She doesn't know?"

I swallow. My throat feels tight and my hands are cold. "It's not— I mean, she doesn't seem to think about me like that. She doesn't really—"

"Yeah," he says. "She made a joke out of it, didn't she? Jesus, Alex." He's quiet for a moment. Then he says, "I'm sorry. I really am."

I don't know what to say.

"Why don't you tell her?"

"I don't think I can. It's been too long. In Florence, I just—I just looked at her, but I couldn't make any words come out."

"Yeah. I know."

"It's horrible."

"Don't be sad." He reaches out and squeezes my hand briefly. "Maybe one day it'll work out, yeah?"

"Maybe," I say. "Yeah, maybe."

He's quiet again for a long time. Somewhere in the distance there's a bell ringing; it must be time for lunch or something. I hardly notice it. Jamie says, meditatively, "Right from the start."

"I think so."

"What, when you first saw her?"

I think. I can feel my brows draw together. "No," I say. "Not right then, I guess. That first time she was just—a girl, you know? Someone I didn't know."

"And then you got to know her?"

I'm still thinking back. It's not easy. "No. Not like that. There was a moment. There was this thing that happened, and afterwards, it was like I'd got her in my head and I couldn't get her out again. Just this one thing. Other stuff happened afterwards, but it all felt like it was part of—part of the same thing."

"What was the thing that happened?" he says, surprisingly gently, as if he's coaxing it out of me.

I say, "You remember when we first went swimming? The three of us, I mean. There was a ledge in the cliff we used to dive from."

Jamie nods. "Yeah, I remember."

"And there was another one, higher up. Right up in the cliff face."

"Yeah," he says.

"I never told you before. It was when you'd run on. You went to get Cokes or something."

"Go on," he says quietly.

When I've finished, Jamie leans back against the wall. "So that's when you knew?" he says.

"I know it doesn't make sense. But yeah—that was when."

"It was a dangerous thing to do."

"I know," I say. "Everything Anna did was dangerous; did you ever think of that?"

He considers this for a moment. "Yes," he says. "Yes, I know what you mean. I used to think that, too."

"It was like there was some part of her that wanted to be—I don't know. On the edge of a drop that might be too big. All the time. Even in Florence, she was playing around with stuff like that. I mean, how many girls do you know who'd do something like she did, just for a laugh?"

"Not many," he agrees.

"It's something in her," I say.

"And that's what—that's what makes her special?"

It's a nice way to put it. "Yeah," I say. "I suppose so."

He thinks for a while. "And it doesn't scare you?"

"No. Why should it?"

"I don't know. I think it would scare me," he says.

"You're not like her, though," I say, and something I can't quite catch flickers in Jamie's face. "I mean—you're not really scared of her, are you?"

"I don't know. I don't know if I even know her, any more. It's been a long time."

"Well, we're going to change that," I say, trying to lift the air of strange sadness that seems to have come over Jamie.

"How?"

"You remember—your idea. The three of us back in Altesa, just like old times."

"Oh," he says. "That. Yeah."

"You always have good ideas," I say.

"One of us has to," he says, but the old rejoinder just sounds tired and out of place.

"I'm going to go," he says.

"You don't have to go yet," I say, dismayed. "They'll be looking for you for hours."

"Yeah. But they might find me before that. I kind of want it all to be over with anyway. And I want to—I want to say goodbye, without being—you know, dragged off."

"Oh," I say.

He gets up and goes over to the window, staring out at the school grounds. "I'm not going to miss this place at all," he says quietly.

"I know."

"I wonder what we'd have thought—you know—back then. If someone had said things would turn out like this."

"Laughed at them, probably."

"Yeah. Probably."

I say, "Jamie—"

"What?"

"Are you sure you're going to be OK?"

He gives me one of his lopsided half-smiles. "Of course I am."

"You really mean it about going back to Italy?"

"Yeah. I really do. I'm going to do it, Alex."

"Good," I say.

"And if you ever want to come and visit—you and Anna, I mean—you know. Just give me a call."

I say, "You keep leaving me, you know. And I keep following you around and then you do it again." I'm trying to make him laugh, and I get a slight grin out of him.

"Is that what's happening?" he says. "I s'pose it looks that way. Look, Alex; I'm going to go. I hate all this shit—goodbyes and so on. So I'd better go."

I stand up too. "OK," I say.

"Keep at it," he says. "Keep on with your painting and stuff. You're going to be good, some day."

"Fuck 'some day,' " I say. "I'm good now. And you know it."

He laughs a little at that. "Yeah, I know."

"You're good too. Don't forget your sax."

"No."

We stand, awkward, not knowing what else to say. Then Jamie turns and goes over to the door.

"Bye, Alex."

"Wait," I say.

He looks at me.

"I need to tell you something," I say.

"You don't. You don't need to tell me anything."

"That summer," I say, rather desperately. "On the beach."

"Alex—don't," he says, but I can't stop.

"I lied," I say. "I lied to myself. I told myself I didn't understand."

"Alex—"

"But I did. I did understand."

"You don't mean that."

"Yes I do. I understood because—because I felt the same thing." I can feel my eyes pricking with tears, and my heart's hammering; but I have to say this. Jamie is my best friend in the world. I say, "I felt the same thing, but—but she—I don't know, Jamie, I don't know—"

"Hey." His voice is soft, and he steps close and puts his hand to my arm, and it hesitates there a moment, and then he brings it up and touches the side of my face. "Hey. Don't. You don't have to say anything. I don't want to hear it."

"Jamie—" I say. I want to tell him something to make everything feel better, but I don't know what. I see him smile, and shake his head.

"It's all right," he says. "I'm all right. Don't do this."

We stand there frozen for an age of time; and then his hand drops to his side, and he turns back to the door.

"You should—you should say something. To Anna, I mean. You should tell her what you really feel."

I stare at him for a long time. He stands framed in the doorway, his hair tousled and dusty and his clothes rumpled from having worn them through the weekend. His hands are the hands of a musician: slender and precise and strong. His face, half hidden by the shadow where his hair falls across his brow and eye, is these things too: and full of sadness and beauty. I want very badly to run to him and hug him and not let him walk out of here and be gone, but my feet are fixed on the floor and I can only look at him. He is the best friend I have in the world.

I say, "Bye, Jamie."

He smiles, one last quick smile, and opens the door, and goes out without looking back. The door closes after him, and after a time I hear the door at the end of the corridor swing shut; and he's gone. I stand motionless for what feels like hours and hours, watching the grain of the wood in the door where, before, his face was; and then I slowly make my legs work again, and go to the desk under the window, and sit down, and look out across the playing fields and trees of the school grounds.

I say, "Everything Anna did was dangerous; did you think of that?"

And Jamie says, "Yes."

He says, "I think it would scare me."

But for me, trust is an easy thing. It is understanding—always understanding—that comes hard, and too late. We should have talked more, Jamie and I, and we should have told each other so many things that we hadn't had time to say. But before I know it, a year has passed, and Jamie is dead; and all I have left are a few letters and postcards and the memory of how he looks as he smiles and turns and leaves. It's not enough. Even now, thirty years later, it's not enough.

My arms ache from reaching above me, but the pattern on the ceiling is starting to emerge, the way it ought to be: another join-the-dots.

I can feel the scar in my shoulder burning softly from the exertion. For a second I hesitate, and put my finger to the place; I can just feel the slight, dimpled depression through the cotton of the shirt. Another dot to be joined into the pattern of stars and snap-shots and fragments of the past.

My feet pound down on the city pavements, and my breath comes in short, hot gasps. Where there are loose crowds I push my way through, not stopping to apologize, just shoving the inert bodies out of my way. I know they are staring at me, but it doesn't matter. Nothing matters but getting to Anna before they hurt her. For once, I tell myself, I've understood things in time to do something about them.

My legs ache with the pace, but I know I have to keep going. Jamie would keep going. Jamie could have run there in no time. I have to do the same, because I don't know what might happen if I can't. I don't dare think what might happen.

Anna is the only thing left for me. I won't let them hurt her—not now.

The buildings of Florence hurtle by me in a mass of jumbled, blurred shapes. At the edges of my vision, a kind of haze starts to creep in, crowding the periphery of what I can see. I'm suddenly afraid I'm going to pass out, here in the street. I'd be taken to hospital, maybe, miles from here. I force myself to slow, to let air get into my lungs properly; and gradually the haze clears.

All the cities moved, I think, the thought feeling as uneven and shaky as my body. *All the cities.*

I drag the crumpled leaflet from my pocket and glance at it once more. Not so far to go now. The street makes a junction up ahead which will take me there. I stuff the paper back in my pocket and blunder on through the crowds and the traffic.

It's a big old building, solidly built, with a tier of steps in front and a heavy, ornate portico. There are little metal bollards set out, and ropes slung between them, making a kind of funnel up to the main doors which I can imagine filling with a crowd of people earlier in the day. I can almost see Anna joining the queue, her shoulder bag by her side, waiting patiently to go in. It's the bag with her thesis notes in, I remember; that's why she won't trust it to the hold when we board our plane. Years of work. Except it isn't, not any more; and I doubt Anna's opened it to check since we've arrived. It's something else, now; something from another time that's surfaced here, without either of us guessing.

Except I did guess, I tell myself. *I worked it out. There's still time.*

There are two *carabinieri* standing at the top of the steps; it's a slight jolt to see them with their machine-pistols in this quiet street. Then I remember what Anna has told me about the speaker: some kind of politically sensitive character, extreme right-wing. A second later, I'm glad of their presence. Someone wants to hurt Anna, and they may be near here; may even be watching. Somewhere out there in the city is a woman with red streaks in her hair. I hurry up the steps through the funnel of ropes, and as I reach the top the two men step forward.

"This building is closed now," one of them says.

The words tumble over one another in my hurry to get them out, and it takes a time before the two men start to understand what I'm saying: about the bomb in Anna's bag, and the way we were there at the jazz club only a few minutes before it was destroyed. I see scepticism turn to uncertainty in their faces as I plough on through what I've realized—that Anna's in danger; that the coincidences have all added up at last to something I can understand and can't ignore. She's inside there, and she's in danger. Everyone is. I search their faces frantically for some lessening of the implacable authority that says I can't come inside, and when I see it, relief surges inside me like a wave breaking.

One of them stays on guard at the top of the steps, and the other ushers me inside. He looks at me with a mixture of wariness and curiosity. I know I've stumbled over the account I've given him, that I should have had it much clearer in my head by the time I reach the building; it's never occurred to me to plan what I'm going to say. But it's all right: I'm past the first boundary.

There's a uniformed official at one side of the lobby to take tickets and so on, but the officer who's brought me inside goes straight past him to an office in the corner. He stands in the doorway while I go inside. There is another man here: a senior officer, from his uniform and the pistol at his belt. They talk hurriedly, low, and the senior man stands. He's carrying a flattish plastic baton.

"Raise your arms."

It's a metal detector, I realize; they sweep it round me carefully.

"Nothing."

"You say there's a bomb in this building?" the senior man says.

"Yes."

"You're sure of this?"

I don't hesitate for a second. I say, "Yes."

"It's in a bag?"

"A shoulder bag. Carried by a young woman—she's wearing—"

"You could point her out?"

"Yes."

"Very well. We'll take you to the side gallery, and you can try to point her out. Don't make it obvious; just tell us who she is. Let's go."

We come out into the open space of the lobby, all three of us, and I'm turning to the senior officer. I want to say something about the woman he should be watching for—the one I've seen before—when a voice stops me.

"No, I listened for a while, but it's not my kind of thing. I'd rather be out in the sunshine than listening to crap, you know? Bye now."

The official behind the ticket desk laughs. "Goodbye, *signorina*. Enjoy the sunshine."

It's Anna—here. I shout out, "Wait! Anna!"

She swings round, her eyes wide. I see her mouth drop open in astonishment. "Alex!"

The officer by my side sees her too. "Stop there," he calls.

Anna looks from him to me, a kind of total incredulity in her eyes. I can't understand what it is that has surprised—appalled—her so much. "Alex," she says again.

"Anna, where's the bag?" I shout. I'm starting towards her, but for some reason the officer is holding my arm pulling me back. Behind Anna, out in the sunlight on the front steps of the building, the guard we left there is turning, starting to move inside, drawn by the shouts and commotion. "Where's the bag?"

It's not on her shoulder any longer. Her gaze flickers between me and the two armed *carabinieri* flanking me. "Jesus, Alex," she says; it's almost a whisper, but I hear it perfectly across thirty feet of space.

She turns, then, and must see the guard coming in behind her from the bright steps of the building. She flinches, turning back. The man at my left has taken a pace or two forward, and I can see from the corner of my eye that he looks puzzled, unsure of what exactly is happening. Anna's face is a mask of disbelief. For some reason I can't fathom, there is pain there, as though she's just realized something that hurts her almost as much as it surprises her. She's looking right at me and the two officers, and I can read it in her eyes as clearly as if I were holding her face, only inches from my own.

It's the strangest thing, what happens next; so strange I am hardly able to make sense of it. Anna turns once more, her body whipping round, the hem of her jacket flared out by the motion, towards the man on the steps—now half in and half out of shadow. And there's some kind of sound—a flat sound, like the sound a pebble makes when it misses the can you're aiming at and smacks into a rock instead. The man on the steps—almost inside the building now—is suddenly reeling backwards, his arms flailing out from his body, and the sunlight catches him again as he goes. He looks for a second as if he is dancing.

And then Anna is turning back, only now—and this makes no sense to me—her jacket has come open at the front, flapping loosely, and there's something in her hand: small and not properly visible because of how she's holding it. Around me there is sudden confusion. The senior officer is scrabbling madly at the holster on his belt, and at the same time throwing himself sideways away from me; and the other man is, for some reason, lifting the muzzle of his machine-pistol, pointing it towards the light, towards Anna. Something clutches me inside: fear, I suppose. I don't understand what they're doing. They've misunderstood what's happening; there's going to be some kind of hideous mistake. I draw in a breath to shout—*No!*—but the sound never gets past my lips.

There's another of those strange, flat *crack* sounds. But before I even hear it I'm staggering backwards, all the breath of my shout punched out of me. For a while—I don't know how long, but it's long enough to fall to my knees and then pitch sideways on the floor—I don't feel anything at all but that strange, dull punch: and then there's pain in my knees from where I've fallen on them, sharp and nauseating. And still it's only that—just the pain in my knees—even though I know now that I've been shot, that Anna's somehow shot me.

I can hear the machine-pistol firing now, a long, tearing sound like fabric being ripped.

I stare at her, across the marble floor of the lobby—*God*, I'm thinking, *they've hurt her, they've hurt her*—and I'm trying to get into my eyes the message that I understand, that I know she didn't mean it. She's sitting down now, her legs splayed out in front of her, and I know she's hurt. I can see it. I can see where the bullets have hit her. There are tears in my eyes suddenly, and she swims and blurs in them, shimmering for a moment the way she does when she dives below the surface, when she's racing with Jamie. I wonder if she knows about that time I let her win. Probably she doesn't. I won't tell her. I'll never tell her that.

The blurriness clears. I'm still staring at her, and although I know I can't speak yet—something to do with not having enough air, I think—I'm still trying to get her to know that I understand. It's like the games Jamie and I play sometimes, where we try to read each other's thoughts. But I've never tried it with Anna. I should have. We should have practised. It's too difficult, now; all I can see in her face is puzzlement. She has both hands holding the gun, but the little black shape that is the barrel is weaving to and fro in the air, unsteady. Her arms are tired, of course. We've been like this for hours. She needs to put it down, get some rest, but I know Anna, know how strong she is, how she never gives up.

There are sounds, too. The clattering, fast-breathing sound of the man trying to fit a second clip into his machine-pistol. It's taking him for ever; I can hear the rattling of metal on metal as his hands tremble. I try to smile at Anna, to show her how much I love her. She can't get the gun steady; it's drifting from side to side. She can't get it clear on the man with the automatic. We should have practised, worked on it, lain with our heads touching and tried to speak our thoughts through our minds. We need it now.

Anna's gun lurches to one side, and weaves to and fro. There's no shot clear for her. I know it's too late now.

Her mouth is slightly open, and her eyes are fixed on me. It makes me want to cry, the way she keeps looking at me even though she must know what's coming. The gun in her hands traces small, almost ethereal patterns in the air as it moves. She's so tired. I remember what she said, about the sunshine; she's so close to it. It's only a few feet away from where she's sitting. I wish she'd drop the gun and go outside. But she looks too tired to walk, anyway; and there's the blood all across her blouse, slick down the front of her belly. Even so, I wish it wasn't here, in this cavernous, gloomy place. It reminds me too much of somewhere else. She ought to be outside.

They're shooting her again, and although I try to keep them clear, my eyes are filling up with tears. The place where I'm shot might be hurting now; I'm not sure. Then I can see her again. She's let the gun down at last, and her head's rested back against the wall. She looks so beautiful, with her dark hair against the pale plaster there. She's still looking at me. There's sunlight on the floor just outside her reach, but she doesn't pay any attention to it; just to me. I try to tell her how much I love her, across the huge distance of the floor, but I don't know if I manage it. Maybe I do. Maybe she hears me, somewhere in her head. Maybe she even knows already.

It's very dark in here. I can see the dim shapes of the two *carabinieri* moving towards her, and I want to tell them to take her outside, to let her be in the sun for a while. But it may be too late for that. I think she's dead. Her face looks calm and earnest and the puzzlement and pain are all gone from it.

I sit on the floor for years looking at her, and gradually, in that time, the understanding comes, moving like a glacier across the landscape of the past, eroding, changing, reforming what was there before.

I think of Signor Ferucci in the bright sunlight, staring at Anna, smiling; and an invitation that he doesn't extend to Jamie or me.

It's so simple. It's so easy to be wrong, like I have been. I have been wrong all my life; about everything.

I think of Anna pulling my face close to hers across the table, whispering to me while the jazz is playing in the packed club; and I remember wondering how it is that she's changed her mind so suddenly—but not wondering that much, because I am too caught up in love of her and want of her. And in our wake, the explosion which we never even hear.

By a river-bank, she is angry and hurt when I call these people cowards; and I remember thinking that I don't really understand her, and thinking that it doesn't matter.

I understand her now. The airport. The different bags—almost the same, and yet not quite. The stickers of Anna's cities shifting in the instant of time it takes to switch the one bag for the other; and Anna shifting in the same moment, no longer the victim I thought she was.

So simple, I think to myself. And, *Oh God. What have I done?*

I brought them to her. I didn't mean to—I didn't even know—but I brought them. I killed her.

I killed them both. Oh God, I killed them both. I betrayed them both.

Somewhere behind me, doors are opening, and people are spilling out into the lobby. Very far away, I can hear them screaming. There's a great chaos of movement and fear and panic all around me, and it almost makes me smile to see that Anna and I are the only ones who stay calm. Even when the running shapes of the people from the lecture hall cut across my field of vision, I can still see her. I wish they'd all go, get out of here, and leave us alone, but they don't. They just keep running past me, scattering out into the sunshine where Anna should be. When they touch the light they seem to vanish, like confetti blown into a candle flame, or dandelion seeds in the wind.

Some of them escape past where Anna and I are sitting; but only some. Then the building shudders with the blast, and all the screaming and shouting is silenced for a moment in the vast pressure of the explosion from inside the hall.

I want to touch her hair. I want to hold her, and tell her it's all right, that I understand everything now and it doesn't matter in the least. I know what she was—who she was. It doesn't matter. It wouldn't have made a difference.

I think of her, in her belltower, writing her book, and waiting for the valley to fill up with hermits all singing, and drawing, and watching each other. I would have been there with her, if she'd have let me.

24

The background of the scene is dark: rocks and cliffs in shadow, and the dark strand of the beach, and the dark of water lit only with the tracery of light from the moon and stars. A curving promontory sheltering slower, calmer water. Three rocks off to one side. Wave-crests and shadows.

Standing on the curve of land is a boy. His body, naked, is pale in the moonlight, and braced to dive: hands up, legs bent a little at the knee, curving forward over the water. His head is down, and his feet grip the edge of the rock. The light off the water reflects the wave-patterns onto his face and ribs and onto the underside of his arms, and throw a soft shadow into the hollow of his belly. The backs of his calves are taut; the whole body stretched, containing the motion of the dive that hasn't yet come. Around his figure the night air seems to tremble slightly, as if a heat-haze radiates from him, and the ripples in the air continue this implicit motion through time, both back, to when he was standing relaxed, hands at his side and body turned more away towards the land, and forward, to when the tension will be released in a controlled arc of movement down to and into and through the mesh of ribboned light below.

His eyes are hidden from view by the upsweep of his arms, but his mouth is slightly open, the lips apart for a second with the last breath before the dive.

Behind him is the dark mass of the land, the suggestion of a shingle beach, rocks. The details are smudged, out of focus, made hazy and dull by the clean lines of the foreground. Just discernible is the point where the water meets the stones; and, beyond that, a shape paler than the surrounding shadow of the beach that might be a second figure, watching the diver.

It is night. By candlelight I look at the photographs ranged along the walls, the uneven lines of images set against the new image that rests in their midst, spreading across the wall to connect with them. I am seeing the paintings properly now; seeing them clearly for the first time. I can catch in them the first glimpse of what they are.

It's the eyes. It's just below the surface of these superficially different faces. I've painted young men and old women, and couples, and middle-aged people; and I've scattered them through a hundred different countries and situations, a thousand possibilities. All along, I've thought each painting I began was new. None of them has been; I can see that now. They're all the same painting. It's the eyes that make the faces, and no matter what the figures in these images seem to look like on the surface, the eyes are always Anna's, and Jamie's.

Every picture I have painted has been of them, and I've never realized—never broken far enough below the surface—until now. I must have been asleep, dreaming, for thirty years, not to have known; no wonder they seem so little like *my* paintings. I haven't even known what they are until now.

I walk from image to image, slowly, staring into them, seeing below the contours of the faces which are only the surface of these people. In my mind, Anna's eyes look straight at me across the marble floor of some old, echoing building, fixed on me; and I try to pass her a message through that impossible distance. From picture to picture it's the same. All along, I can trace her eyes in the figures: her eyes, and Jamie's.

We never saw the hermit again, after he left the valley; at least, Jamie and I didn't. What Anna saw, afterwards, I can only guess at. But I was wrong to think that not seeing him again meant he wasn't there.

He was always there; the stamp of that summer set the mould for all the years that were to follow. I should have seen that, but I didn't.

The candle takes me by faces of old men and young men, and women also old and young; and in every one of them I see the same glimmer of understanding and recognition. They're all the same people, under the surface of their clothes and skin and features. The room seems to be waveringly full, by candlelight, of Jamie and Anna; as though somehow, magically, they are still here.

The line rings the room, and it starts and ends with the newly finished painting of the boy diving; the night scene with the moonlight on the water and the reflection on his body. I hold the candle up to it, and the water seems to shimmer and move with the flame. I can almost hear the slap and wash of it against the rocks there.

And I think, *It depends where you start.* There's something in that—something to do with how to order these images, how to make sense of them. And this picture is the starting place: I can feel that. When the dial has no hands, you can start where and when you like; all times are the same.

I reach out and touch my hand to the wall, but there's only the cool, smooth feel of its surface against my fingers, unyielding, implacable.

"Tonight, then. Don't forget," Jamie says.

"I won't," I say.

He grins. "I'll see you at twelve."

The valley at night is full of the sounds I know well. I slip out of my bedroom window and feel my way carefully but confidently over the tiles of the kitchen roof. Down in the garden, the night cicadas shrill away and pay me no attention. I drop to the grass beside the verandah, and pad silently along in the shadow of the house to the front drive. The moon is low in the sky now, but it will come higher as the night goes on.

Jamie meets me at the gate.

"Hey," he says.

"Hey yourself."

The road is still warm from the day's heat; I can feel waves of warmth coming up from it as we walk. Below us, nestling in the curve of the land, the few scattered lights of the town make patterns like a lattice of stars; a lone constellation that's fallen from its place in the sky and come to rest here. It's very still, and very warm; much warmer than you'd think for this late in the summer. The storms haven't come yet this year; they'll come once Jamie is gone, in England, and I'll watch the hurling rain on my own.

But we're not thinking of that: it's promised. This is the last night Jamie will be here, and we're going to the beach. It's a secret. The night-times have always been ours, and this last one is special. We both know it.

When we round the last bulge of land and the cove opens up before us, the sea is like ink under the sky. The sounds of the water are quiet but clear; I can hear the waves slap gently against the rocks, only just moving here in the shelter of the spur. The cliffs reach up all around, shutting out the sky all round one side, while out across the sea there is no horizon any more; just the black of the sky and the black of the sea joining somewhere.

Jamie stands for a moment looking out. "It's beautiful at night," he says.

"Yeah."

"The water'll be warm, too. You want to go in?"

"Yeah," I say. "Let's."

A couple of yards from the water is a long, flat rock, inclined just a little up the grade of the beach. Jamie stops by it, kicks off his shoes, pulling off shirt and jeans. In a moment he's naked, and he stands there just looking at the water before picking his way through the stones to where the spur cuts out into the sea. I sit down to get my shoes off. I can see him tread lightly along the sharp and uneven surface of the rock, placing his feet in the right places, minding where the edges of the rock might cut you, until he's far enough out to dive. I've got my clothes off too, now. He glances back at me, and I wave. He waves back, and I catch the white gleam of his teeth as he grins. Then he has his arms over his head, and his body tenses for a second, and then falls like a knife into the oily darkness of the water. There's a sudden quick foaming of bubbles from the dive, and then everything's still until he breaks the surface, far out in the water.

"It's great!" I hear him call. "Come on!"

I follow his route out along the spur, though more slowly; we've never done this at night before, and I haven't Jamie's easy certainty about where to put my feet. I'm clumsier at diving than he is, but I'm past that point where all I can manage is to curl myself into a ball and throw myself in. I can at least keep my feet together, and get my hands in before the rest of me. I throw myself forward, and the water clutches me as I plunge down. Jamie's ducked under the surface at the same moment, and when I open my eyes underwater he's there—some distance off, but kicking towards me, his hair drifting and streaming around his face. I try to keep below, but I can't, and I trail up to the surface. We both emerge, grinning, shaking our heads like dogs to clear the water from our hair and ears.

"Not bad," he says. "It is warm, isn't it?"

"Yeah."

"I'm going to see if I can get all the way down to the bottom," he says. "You coming?"

"You bet."

"On three. One, two, three—"

We both gulp great lungfuls of air, and upend ourselves, kicking down through the storm of bubbles into the clear water below. The sea is changed, in the moonlight; where once there were great dancing slabs of light and colour, now everything is dark, shot through with moving lines of silver. When I look at Jamie, his body is ringed and wrapped in a lace of pallid light, shifting and moving across his shoulder and back. I can see his muscles working under the skin as he swims downwards, until at last he manages to anchor himself with one hand to a stone on the seabed. I'm trying to do the same, but no matter how hard I thrash my legs I can only hold position, a little above and to one side of him. He turns his head towards me, and shakes it to float the hair out of his eyes, and bubbles filter up from the corner of his mouth. For a moment, he looks like some creature of the sea—like one of the mermen in fairy stories. He looks like he could live down here for ever.

I fall away upwards, and a second or two later he slips past me, having pushed himself off from the rock. I catch a glimpse of his feet kicking off above me before I break through into the air again. Jamie is gasping and laughing on the surface.

"Great! *Ottimo!*"

He sweeps his arms out sideways and floats for a moment on his back, looking up.

"Hey. You should do this. It's the weirdest thing."

I let my body relax and do what he says. The water comes up over my ears, and the sounds of the waves dull down to an echoing murmur. Above me, the sky looks as if it's floating, too: the stars all feel somehow detached from their places, as if they've sprung free for a moment. I feel that, if I were to flick a drop of water up with my hand, I could make ripples spread out across the heavens, and watch the constellations tremble and shimmer.

"Wow!" I hear myself say, but the word, coming through the water, is strange and unfamiliar.

"Yeah," Jamie replies, and his voice is the same: changed, and strange.

We lie on the slowly moving surface of the sea, and the salt water buoys us up and holds us there. As long as you stay relaxed, you can float. My arms and legs are completely limp, spread out from me. I think of myself as a starfish, just lying there: a starfish watching the stars. The fingers of my right hand brush against something, and in a moment I recognize it as Jamie's hand, and I take hold of it; we won't drift apart that way. He gives my hand a quick squeeze before he lets his arm go relaxed again, and for a long time we lie like that, with the water lapping over us and round us, warm and comforting.

"Shooting star," says Jamie's strange new sea-voice, through the water to my ears, and I see it in the sky in the same instant.

"I see it," my sea-voice replies.

We're laced with silver. The moon climbs gradually higher in the sky, but there's no high haze or thin cloud, and the stars stay as sharp and diamond-clear as ever.

In the end it's Jamie who moves first. He lets go my hand and twists in the water, and I let myself sink down until only my head's showing, like before. My ears are out in the air, now, and when he speaks, his voice is back to normal.

"We've drifted," he says. "Look."

He's right; the gently lapping waves have carried us out towards the end of the spur. Beyond that is the open sea.

"It was good, though."

"Yeah, wasn't it?"

We start the swim back, a slow breaststroke. For some reason, neither of us suggests a race—not that I'd win, anyway, but in an afternoon we might have. Instead, though, we take our time, letting the land creep imperceptibly closer.

"I'm going to dive," Jamie says, when we're back in the centre of the little bay.

"I'll watch." I don't want to leave the comforting warmth of the water.

Going back to the beach, and then walking out along the spur, is the long way round. Jamie just swims over to where the bank of rock comes up out of the water, and grabs hold, and lodges one foot high in some crevice: a moment later he's pulled himself up out of the water, one lithe movement, and is standing there. From where I am, he's a kind of reverse silhouette against the night sky: light against black. He takes a second to compose himself, and then he puts his arms up, and jumps like his whole body was a spring—tension caught and then released in one swift moment. I can just see him shoot by me under the water, still ribbed and wrapped with silvery lines like strands of seaweed, and he breaks the surface some yards past me.

"That was a long one," I say.

"Yeah."

We swim and dive over and over, and the moon wears round in the sky. Neither of us knows or cares what time it is. The air is still warm, and there's no breeze, and the waves lap steadily and calmly in the little bay.

Finally we are tired and have had our fill of swimming and diving. We've been underwater, right down to the bottom, and we've lain on the surface and looked at the sky, and between the two we've splashed and swum and worn ourselves out with it. We head for the beach, swimming with slow, languid strokes that barely stir the surface.

The flat rock is big enough for two, and we sit on it, water streaming from us and running over and off the smooth stone. I'm expecting to shiver and be cold, but we've warmed ourselves with swimming, and the beach is still full of the warmth of the impossibly hot days of the summer, all that spent heat stored up in the rocks and cliffs and leaking slowly out now to keep us comfortable. The air here carries the scent of flowers from the cliffs—evening flowers now closed, and night-flowers, calling subtly to the big white moths that love them. We sit on the rock and wait for the air to dry our bodies.

"Alex?"

"Yeah?"

"I wish I wasn't going away."

We've promised not to talk about that; but because it's Jamie who's said it, I realize the promise doesn't count any more.

"Yeah," I say. "Me too."

"It's like—this—" he indicates the cove with his head, "all this is what's in me, you know? It's—who I am. I don't know what I'll do when I'm somewhere else."

I think I know what he means. "You'll be OK," I say. "It won't be so bad."

"Yes it will."

I have something to tell him, I remember. "Hey," I say.

"What?"

"I asked my parents if I could go to England too. Next year, I mean, when I'm old enough."

He looks at me, and there's a peculiar expression on his face.

"What did they say?"

"They were pleased, I think. My father was, anyway. They said I could, if I could do well enough at school, pass the exams, all that."

"Really?" It's like someone's lit a candle inside him: his face is glowing with a strange intensity. "You really think you might come too?"

"Yeah," I say. "I want to."

"That would be—" He hesitates. "That would be good."

"We could be together. I bet England wouldn't be so bad that way."

"No. I bet too."

"And it would only be a year before I came too."

He shakes his head slightly, as if in wonder. "That would be good," he says again, quietly.

"It was Anna's idea too," I say. "We were thinking about it, and I didn't want to tell you in case my parents said no."

"Oh, right," he says. "Yeah. But they said it was OK?" He doesn't sound like he quite believes it.

"Yeah. If I can do well enough."

"You can," he says, decisively. "You'll do fine."

I feel a glow in me, too, at his confidence. Nobody else believes so simply that I can do things, not even Anna.

Jamie says, "I—I'd just got used to the idea I wouldn't see you again. Except holidays, I mean."

"Oh. But you will."

"Yeah." He lies back on the rock, stretching himself, his arms behind his head. "Thanks, Alex."

"I was going to be lonely too," I point out.

"How quick do you think a year will go?"

"I don't know. Quite quick, if we keep writing to each other. Besides, it's not a whole year. It's just till Christmas."

"Yeah. That's true. You know it snows in England at Christmas? Well, sometimes."

"Wow. We could build snowmen. When I'm there."

"Yeah."

I lie down too, but on my side, so I can look at him. He's watching the sky, and his face is dreamy, as if full of the possibilities opened up by what I've said. I'm thrilled I've made him so happy.

Jamie says, "They'll all speak English, too. If we talk in Italian, no one will know what we're saying."

"Like a secret code," I say.

"Yeah. Imagine—we can talk about people right in front of them, and they won't know."

I am delighted at the idea. "That *would* be neat."

Jamie's quiet for a bit. Then he says, "Alex?"

"Mm?"

"You know what you want to be when you grow up?"

I think for a second. "No. Do you?"

"I don't know. I used to think I'd work on one of those big telescopes in New Mexico. Radio telescopes."

"The big dish ones?"

"Yeah. Looking out really far."

I imagine Jamie standing in the middle of a big circle of dish antennae, high up on a flat-topped mountain in New Mexico, staring at the sky. "Yeah," I say. "You'd be good at that."

"You think?"

"Of course. You're really good already. You know all the names and everything."

"Yeah. But now I'm not so sure. I don't really know what I want."

"Don't worry," I say. "You'll find something you like. You know you will."

There's a companionable silence for a time. Jamie's still staring at the stars, and I watch him as he does so: his face, intelligent and inquisitive and calm, with his dark hair still slick with seawater; his arms cradling his head; the faint shadows of the ribs down his side; the slight, flat hollow of his belly.

"Jamie?"

"Yeah?"

"It's different."

"What?"

I nod down at his body.

"Oh. Yeah."

It's been because of Anna, I suppose; Anna's insistence on swimming trunks and bathing costumes. Now that I think about it, I realize this is the first time for a year or more that I've seen Jamie completely naked. His body's got taller and slightly slimmer in that time, and I've noticed that I can see his muscles more clearly sometimes, but these are things I've seen from day to day. Now I can see that there have been other changes, too, which—because of Anna and the swimming trunks—I haven't noticed.

"It looks different," I say.

"Yeah. I know."

"And there's hair. Some," I add. There's not much, just a smudge.

Jamie props himself up on one elbow. "You don't mind, do you?"

I shake my head, surprised. It's a strange question to ask. "No. Course not." Jamie's still Jamie; how he looks doesn't make any difference. I'm just curious. I say, "How long've you had hair?"

"A while."

"Means you're growing up."

"I know."

"I wish I had hair."

"You will."

"What's it feel like?"

Jamie says, "Well—I don't know. Like hair."

"Can I touch it?" I say.

He hesitates for a moment. "If you want."

I reach over and touch my fingers briefly to the smudge. It's soft, softer than head hair. "It's nice," I say.

"You think?"

I touch again. "Yeah. It's—it's nice." There isn't a better word for it.

I'm still running my fingers to and from when something bumps gently against them.

"Hey," I say, grinning. Jamie sits up suddenly, drawing his legs up so I can't see. Even in the moonlight, I can tell he's blushing furiously.

"Shit," he says. "Sorry."

"It's OK."

"Sorry."

"It's OK," I say again. He turns his head away from me. "Hey, Jamie," I say. "It's all right."

"It does it all the time," he says, rather indistinctly, still looking away. "It's really—"

"It doesn't matter," I say.

"Shit. Sorry, Alex."

"What's it like?" I ask. I think of what has happened to me, looking at Anna and imagining touching her, and it reminds me of her voice, years before: *At least it wasn't—you know. Like that.* I know what happens sometimes to my body, and I've seen Jamie naked before; but never this. Besides, his body's changed, and I realize I'm curious.

Jamie looks back at me. He looks uncertain, like he's not sure whether to trust me or not.

"Go on," I say. "Show me." I can't believe he's so embarrassed.

Slowly he lets the leg nearest me down, until I can see. He says, "It keeps doing it."

"I hadn't noticed."

"Well—good."

"It's all right, though. I mean, it's not, like, weird or anything." I can't explain properly what I mean. The way Jamie's talking about it, you'd think it was something separate from him; but to me it still looks part of Jamie. I can feel he's worried about it, in some way, and I search for something to say that will make him feel better. "I think it looks nice."

"Do you?"

"Yeah."

There's a long silence. Then Jamie says—and his voice sounds slightly strange to me, though I can't tell quite why—"Do you want to touch it?"

I look at him, a little surprised. "OK." I reach out again and press my fingers lightly against it. "Hey. It's pretty hard."

"Mm," Jamie says. I'm going to take my hand away, but he puts his hand on mine and presses it back, so I leave it there instead.

I look at him, and he's looking back at me. There's still a lot of uncertainty in his eyes, as though he's really worried about something. I can guess that all the changes must be pretty strange for him; I try to imagine what I'd feel like, if they were happening to me. I know I'd want someone to reassure me that they were OK. I say, "It's—it's nice. I like it."

"You do?"

"Yeah." It's actually true. It feels very strange, touching Jamie here— I can't remember ever doing it before. And it's stranger still, the way it feels now, all hard to the touch. But at the same time that it feels strange, it also feels like a surprisingly tender thing to do, like Jamie's letting me touch something secret and part of him and special.

"Alex?"

"Yeah?"

His hand is back on mine, and I feel him shift my palm, where I'm touching him, slightly.

"Like this."

He rocks my hand back and forth a little, and I understand and do the same.

"That way?"

"Yeah," Jamie says. His voice is strange, like it was when we were in the sea and I was hearing it underwater. "Yeah. Like that."

I keep doing what he's showed me, and while I'm doing it, strange thoughts start to seep into my head. I think of how Jamie's body looks now, and remember what I've said: it means he's growing up. I've known what happens when you start growing up, known for a long time, but it's always struck me as something that's a long way off, something in the future, that'll come along one day and needn't worry me now. But suddenly it seems that, for Jamie, it's started to happen. And for Anna, too;

I think of the way she's looked, this summer; of her breasts and the new curves of her body, which used to be so much like Jamie's. They're both changing; both growing up. Just that smudge of hair between Jamie's legs means a whole world of difference between us.

And thinking of Anna, and Jamie, and how they've changed, brings a new thought. Jamie and I have talked about what happens between men and women when you're older, lots of times, and I know how the bodies fit together; I've imagined how you'd do it. But again, it's seemed an impossibly long way off from me. But now Jamie and Anna—I can see them, at once, in my head. They're old enough, now; they could do it. I think of Jamie, pressed up against Anna's body—all of him naked against her. I've only dared think as far as stretching out a hand and putting it on one of her breasts, but Jamie could—I know he could—be on top of her, like grown-ups do it. I can see them in my head, and see how good they would look together—how right. It hurts me right to the locked-away part of myself where I admit in secret that I love Anna, love her desperately; that I want it to be me there with her, not Jamie. And yet at the same time that it hurts me, it stirs something deep down in me. Thoughts of Anna and Jamie naked together whirl in my head.

Jamie's hand is on my shoulder, holding onto me tightly. I'm still moving my hand like he's shown me, and when I look at his face, I see he's still looking at me. His lips have parted slightly and I can feel his breath hot on my cheek. Then he clutches my shoulder tighter, almost hurting me.

"Alex—Alex—"

His whole body jerks as though he's been punched, and he gives a kind of gasp. I feel his fingers on my shoulder dig in hard for a second, and then very slowly relax. I'm scared for a moment, but then I see in his eyes that he's not hurt. He blinks, slowly, as if dazed. A few droplets of something hot have scattered across my belly. He shivers, and blinks again, and looks at me. In my hand, I can feel the hardness start to ebb away.

"That was weird," I say. I'm a little concerned still that I've hurt him in some way, but although he's out of breath, like he's run a race, I still can't see any pain in his face. After a second, he grins at me—a slightly shy, nervous grin. I say, "Is that what always happens?"

He nods, still breathless.

"Something came out," I say, still.

"Yeah."

"Is that what's supposed to happen?"

"I think so. Yeah," he says.

"Oh." His breathing's slowing a bit. "What's it feel like?" It must have felt like something very strong, from the way he was when it happened.

"It's—it's good," he says. "It's like—"

He looks down at me.

"Hey," he says. "You too."

He's right. The swirling images of Anna and him haven't worn off yet. I shrug, slightly embarrassed myself now. Compared to Jamie's, mine doesn't look like much.

"I could show you," he says. "How it feels, I mean." Then shyly, "If you want."

"Would it work for me?" I say, taken aback. It hasn't crossed my mind that I could do what Jamie does.

"I don't know. We could try."

I think for a moment. "OK," I say.

As Jamie touches me, I think of him with Anna, how their bodies would look if they were joined together; and I remember how it felt when she kissed me, among the lemon trees, that quick hot touch of her mouth against mine; and I think of how she grins, and of the smell of her hair, and sometimes even that it's her hand that's touching me down there. I'm looking up past Jamie's face at the stars when it happens, and it's like an earthquake—like an avalanche—like the whole sky lurches sideways and I'm falling away into it, and Jamie and Anna with me, our bodies tumbling and full of light and wonder.

We swim again afterwards, and the water feels cooler now against me, but still not so cool as to make you cold. Inside, a strange, deep warmth comes from what we've done, as though nothing is going to make me cold ever again. I can see it in Jamie, too: there's something bright and alive in his eyes, and the way he looks reminds me of Anna, of her aliveness. I watch him as if I've never seen him before, like this is the first time.

*   *   *

Our clothes are still scattered around the flat rock when the sky starts to lighten over the cliffs. We lie on the beach and crane our heads back to see it: far out, across the sea, the stars are still out, but the moon has been down for a long time now. The early dawn is full of colours: rose-petal pinks and eggshell blues and greens. It spreads slowly, silently through the sky, swallowing the stars; a gauze of light drawn gradually across the roof of the world.

Jamie stirs beside me. "It's beautiful," he says.

"Yeah."

"I used to watch it from the belltower," he says. "Back when—you know."

"Yeah. Me too."

"Really?"

"Sometimes."

We're quiet for a while. Then he says, "I didn't know you felt the same way."

"What about?" I know he doesn't mean the belltower any more, or the sunrise.

He says, "You know. About—you and me, and stuff."

I'm still not sure what he means. I say, "Like what?"

"Well—like what we did."

"Oh, that," I say. I haven't really thought about it. I say, "It was strange."

"Yeah. But . . . it was good, too."

"Well, yeah," I say.

He smiles at me: a wonderful smile that lights up his whole face. "I don't mind going away," he says. "Not now."

I'm glad. I say, "Good." I'm still going to miss him, I know, but I'm glad he feels better about it.

"I'll see you again at Christmas," he says. "And then later—"

"Later I'll come to England, too," I say.

"You really will? You promise?"

"I promise."

"I don't think I mind anything, now," he says. His voice is dreamy again, as if he's thinking of something in his head. I wonder what it is. Then he turns back to me. "Alex?"

"Yeah?"

"We should keep together," he says. "Always."

I nod. "We will."

He's quiet for a long time, while the light eases its way across the curve of the sky.

"Alex?"

"Mm?"

"You know what it feels like, when you—when you look at someone, and they make you feel all—I don't know. Like you were alive inside, in your tummy. And like you want to be with them for ever?"

I know exactly what he means. "Yeah," I say softly. I'm thinking of her with her hand on my face, the moment before she leans in to kiss me.

"And how you just want to—to hold them."

"Yeah."

"What do you think that is?"

I know what I think it is, but I can't bring myself to say it. I'm scared that saying the word will somehow diminish the feeling, will make what I have inside in some way less strong, less important. I say, "I don't know."

Jamie says, "I think maybe it's love." His voice is very low and quiet, and the way he says it makes it sound beautiful. What I feel inside doesn't diminish at all, and I feel a surge of gratitude to him for saying it for me. I wonder how he's understood what's in me so well.

I say, "Yeah. Me too."

"Really?"

"Yeah."

Jamie says, "I think I love you."

It makes no sense to me for a moment, and then I understand: it's a joke, a kind of weird, mad, joke. I clap my hand to my mouth and hoot with laughter. "Yeah!" I say, when I've got my breath back a bit. "You and me. We could get married. Neat." A fresh wave of giggles catches me, and it takes me a moment to recover. "That's good, Jamie," I say, grinning at him. "That's really good." I slap his arm, the way we do sometimes, to let him know I get it. But Jamie isn't laughing with me; there's a kind of weird expression on his face, like it might come apart suddenly. I say, "Hey. What is it?"

He doesn't say anything. He's just staring at me, and his mouth is open slightly, his eyes fixed on mine.

I don't feel like laughing any more. I say, "Hey, Jamie. What is it?" And when he's still silent, still just staring at me, I say—desperately— "It was a good joke. Really. What's—what's wrong?"

He sits up, hugging his knees to himself. "Nothing."

I reach out, uncertainly, and touch his back. "You're shivering."

"I'm cold," he says. His voice is shivering too.

"You should get dressed," I say. "You don't want to catch cold."

"No." But he doesn't move.

I look up at the sky. It's lightening more and more now; the day is going to be here soon. I start to cast about me for my clothes, and scrape together T-shirt and jeans and pants. As I pull them on, Jamie still sits there, shivering, hugging his knees, looking out at the water. I keep expecting him to start getting dressed too, but he doesn't; and in the end, when I sit back on the rock to do up my shoelaces, he's still naked. He looks strangely vulnerable, now that I'm dressed. I don't understand why. I've never thought of Jamie as vulnerable before.

"We should go," I say quietly.

"I know."

"Come on, then."

He shakes his head. "You go. I want to stay for a bit."

"Don't be silly."

"No. Really, Alex. You go."

"I'm not going back on my own," I say.

"Please."

I don't understand this. He sits there, rocking very slightly back and forth, heels drawn up, his back making a smooth curve up to his shoulders. His eyes are dark and focused on the faraway darkness of the sea.

I say, "Jamie? What is it?"

A long breath comes out of him, the ghost of a sigh. "Nothing."

"I'll wait for you, if you want," I say. My voice sounds small in the emptiness of the beach.

"You don't have to."

"I want to."

"Why?"

It's the strangest question. I frown. "So we can walk back together."

"Oh," he says.

He doesn't move for a long, long time; just looks out over the water. Then a breath escapes him—long and quiet, almost silent. He picks his T-shirt up from beside the flat rock, and towels his hair with it roughly to get the worst of the water out of it, and then pulls on his trousers and socks and shoes. The wet T-shirt he drapes over one shoulder.

"I'm ready."

Along the cliff path, I dart quick glances at him every so often. Something's happened, I think, but I don't really know what. Jamie seems to have hidden something away inside him, something which I feel I might almost have seen, if only I'd had longer to think about it. But it's gone again now.

I know it's my fault. I've done something, but I don't know what. I want to take it back—or at least say something—but I don't understand; I can't understand. It's impossible.

As we crest the last hill, and can look down on the lights of the town, he says, "You shouldn't come to England."

It takes me completely by surprise. I say, "Why not?"

"You don't have to. I have to, so I've got to. But you can stay here. You should stay. I would, if they'd let me."

"What, even if I was going?"

He nods, almost angrily. "Yes."

"Jamie—"

"I would. I wouldn't go to England just because you were going, not if—"

"Not if what?"

But he doesn't answer. Instead, after a long silence, he says, "What we did—on the beach. It was wrong. We shouldn't have done it."

"Why not?"

"We just shouldn't have, OK? It was a mistake. It was—it was wrong."

Hearing him say this is like a cold knife going into me. I say, "It didn't feel like it was wrong. It felt—nice."

"No it didn't," he says. "Maybe it did to you, but it didn't to me."

"Jamie—"

"Stop it. Don't talk to me."

"Why not? I don't understand. Why're you—"

But he doesn't hear me. I think maybe there are tears on his face, but I don't see them clearly; he starts to run, brushing past me hard, the T-shirt dropping from his shoulder. I grab it up from the ground and hurry after him, but he's running fast, his elbows jabbing back in short, vicious stabs, his legs eating up the distance eagerly. I can't match him. I run as best I can, but I keep tripping and stumbling over the uneven ground. I shout after him.

"Jamie!"

He doesn't turn; he doesn't even slow. It's like he doesn't hear me.

When my breath deserts me, I come staggering to a halt. He's half a mile away, it seems, still on the coast path into town, but quickly falling away from view. I hold his T-shirt in one hand as I stand, bent over, gasping for air. I have a stitch in one side. I stare after Jamie, but I've lost him now among the dark patches of scrub that line the way. He'll be home long before me.

Slowly, wearily, I start after him, just walking. Nothing makes sense. Anna cries when she takes the bus, as though something's ended; and I've felt in the air of the summer that things are changing. But I've always known that Jamie and I would understand each other. Now even that's been taken away.

I trudge onwards. It will be an hour or more before I'm home.

I wait all morning for him to come and see me. I know he will; his train is at one, and it's an hour at least into Salerno by car. I sit in my room, and wait.

When it's twelve, I go round to his house. Mrs. Anderson is downstairs.

"Where's Jamie?"

"Oh," she says. "You've missed him, Alex. He's gone to get the train. They took the car." She stops, and looks at me more closely. "Is everything all right?"

"Yes," I say.

"He said you two had said goodbye. That's right, isn't it?"

"Yes," I say, numbly. "We—we said it earlier."

"Oh, good." She still seems to be worried by something in my expression, because she smiles at me. "He'll be back before long," she says. "Christmas will be here before you know."

"I know," I say.

There's a silence. Then, surprisingly, she says, "You know, I'll miss him, too."

My eyes are suddenly hot with tears. I turn, running out of the room, leaving her standing there helplessly.

As the final days of the summer pass away, I'm completely alone for the first time in six years. Jamie's not just up the road; I can't signal to him from my bedroom window any more. It's not even that he's gone to England; it's worse than that. Something between us is gone, too, and I can't even find what it is.

As the days pass, I find that something else is gone, too. When I let myself drift, and wait to fall away into times when Jamie was still with me, nothing happens any more. Sometimes there are vague, slight impressions; but it's like a door has closed. I can't be on the roof at night with him, or hunting lizards, or trying beer for the first time. It's all gone, closed off somehow. I panic, and try to force myself to break through whatever it is that's walled these things off from me, but it's no good. They've vanished. It's as though that moment when the sky shudders and spins and I feel myself tumbling into it has set things tumbling in my head as well, and the way into the past has been swept away, lost under an avalanche.

When I'm alone in bed at night, I try to remember how it all was. But just remembering isn't enough. It's not the same. I want things to be the way they were, and I can't get them back that way no matter how hard I try.

Christmas comes. All the trembling changes have come down on the valley, now; the bedrock has shifted and the terraces and old olive fields are all falling and dying. Jamie stays in England. His family have moved out there; for good, it seems. We are supposed to have to wait only one term, until Christmas comes and we are together again; but the months and then weeks and days go by, and at the end of it—I've known it was coming, but it still pierces me like ice—there is nothing. No Jamie; no reunion. The house at the end of the row is empty, and they are looking for another family to fill it. Weeds grow in the driveway, and the windows are blank and dusty. From my bedroom, when I look, the house seems dead, as though it's never been alive. I can't even fall away and lose myself in how things used to be. Too many avalanches have settled over the valley for that.

I write to Jamie, just like I promised. My mother says letters from England will take a while to reach me, so I wait patiently, but they don't come. After a while, I stop writing. There's nothing to tell in any case.

Slowly, I take my fingers from the wall. The ends of them are white and numb from pressing against it so long, and my arm is stiff, tired. The boy in the painting is poised, caught in the moment on the edge of the boundary between one place and another.

Jamie gets to Italy, in the end. He does what he says: makes a stake in the London clubs and bars, and buys a ticket out there. I have a post-card, somewhere, from Rome: just a scribbled note. *Offer still stands. Knew this was where I was supposed to be. Love to Anna. Jamie.*

When they tell me he's dead, I don't believe it to begin with. He's too good a swimmer, and the water there isn't fast or dangerous. It's as if they've made up some ridiculous story out of shreds, a patchwork. *No,* I want to say; *that's where we used to swim when we were kids. He wouldn't go there now.* But he does. He goes back to see the valley, to see the old places, just like he said we should. Maybe he gets tired of waiting for me to join him, and just decides to do it alone. I don't know; there's nothing to tell me. And somehow, in the still, calm water of the little cove, it happens.

I'm right about the water: it's not deceptive or dangerous there. It's not that, they tell me. He drowns because he hits his head on something—a rock—and it stuns him; he drowns because he's uncon-scious. It's an accident. It could have been caused by an unexpected wave, if he was close in to the cliffs or the spur there; it could have swept him in hard against the stone in a moment, if he hadn't been watching for it. It could have been anything like that.

I ask if it could have been that he dived, if that could have caused it. They aren't sure. Maybe, if the water was very shallow, or the place he dived from was very high. Maybe. But probably a wave, when he was close in against the cliff.

I betrayed them both. I never meant to, but I did it all the same.

My eyes are full of the paintings that ring the room. They seem to swell up, now, as if the little uniform squares of the photographs are too small to hold them any more. They swell and grow until they burst out of their squares and are as real and as big as when I first made them. They wheel and tumble round me, shifting to and fro, and the faces in them are blurred and gathered until there are really only two. Two, and sometimes a third, at a distance, watching.

It's then that I realize what they are, what I've done. As they settle back into their neat little frames, I understand at last why I've painted these things, and why they can still be mine, even though—in one way—they never have been. And I understand also how they should be hung, how the gallery should be arranged. It's good. I think to myself how it would be, and feel myself smile.

I'm tired. My head throbs with tiredness and my body is numb with it, but I can't leave them like this, not now that I know. Now that I understand.

I start to gather the pictures down from the walls for the last time. I can do this now. The house is finished, and everything is back the way it once was, and at last I have understood it all.

I think I dream of them. There are faint voices that drift away from me as the night comes to an end, murmuring something soft while I sleep, and then fading.

I wake slowly. There is sunlight, warm across my face, and somewhere close by the sound of a bird singing. When I open my eyes, though, the first thing I see is a dark sky, strewn with silver, the tiny stars glittering high above me. There is a moment, halfway between sleeping and waking, when I'm not even sure how old I am, what time this is; and then it passes. I stretch, and remember, and sit up in the bed that I've moved back into this room. The shutters are wide and the room glows with sunshine, and the stars glitter and twinkle. It's perfect.

I go downstairs. Everything is done, at last. The house is finished; the ceiling is finished; and round the walls of the downstairs rooms are the pictures which finally make sense to me. Everything is done at last.

I go out onto the verandah and stare at the side of the valley, where the grey rocks are warming up. Down at the end of the garden, amid the tangle of plants and bushes, is the tree into which I used to scramble to get over the wall. Back there, I would find lizards, and lose myself for hours in worlds which, in turn, became lost to me—and which have now come back again. The trees of the garden murmur very gently in a slight breeze, and the air is warm and scented with pine and rock and great breaths of lavender and rosemary. I could close my eyes, I know, and be there when my mother first planted it: be there to see it start all over again.

Instead, I go back into the tranquil silence of the house.

I can see now why I felt that these pictures were in some way not mine. The eyes in the faces should have told me. I wander among them, following the new progression I've laid out, the sequence which finally makes sense of them. In London, in the gallery, they will be laid out all wrong—laid out according to the chronology of my life, the order in which they were painted, from my earliest work through to my most recent. It's such an easy mistake to make, to think that the paintings are to do with *my* life, that that's their framework. It's so easy a mistake that I've made it myself. As a child, I painted Altesa, and Jamie, and Anna; and as an adult, I told myself that all that was over, finished, hollow. My work swept on to new themes and new ideas, and I never saw what was really happening.

It's taken thirty years to get under the skin of these paintings—thirty years, and one image that has been a starting point, a beginning, a key.

In the sitting room, half covering the wall opposite the garden, is the image of the boy diving. It is locked down on plaster; it will never make it to the London gallery where now there are people walking through the quiet rooms and halls and studying a collection that makes no sense. I have painted it too late; but at least I have painted it. It has come so late because remembering has been so hard. It would be wrong in London anyway. Its place is here. It's the beginning of things, after all. It's the starting point.

It's the only painting of a child. I've never painted children because I've never thought I needed to; but it has to start somewhere, and so it starts with the dive. With being balanced on the brink of things; and with breaking from one world into another; with change, and where it leads. This is where it starts.

Then, further around the room, the faces are older, become young men and young women. The studies of people on the edge of adulthood. The woman at prayer in a church, looking up at the figure of

Christ. The young man in the city street, looking upwards among the crowds and the night-time traffic, his face caught with the neon lights of the shop signs so that it is red and blue and gold. A couple with their arms around each other in a rainstorm, the rain breaking their outlines into star-like facets. City scenes and street scenes and young people.

Further on, they're older. A woman writing in a book, her face intent on the words she's setting down, with a window behind her like an arch through which sunlight comes and falls on the pages. A man working late, and through the glass of his office window the city lights and—above them—the stars. A woman with a child in her arms, reading him stories. The faces change, ageing, altering, but the eyes are the same eyes in each.

Three friends at a table in some dark place, their faces animated with laughter and conversation and memory, of things shared and re-membered. A man in a boat on a lake, touching the water with one hand. Older now: a woman, with her hair tied back from her face, mak-ing a mark with charcoal on the mottled plaster of a wall. A man crouched down low, among earth and plants, with a stone held in his hands and a look of wonder in his face as he turns it this way and that. And older still: a white-haired woman bathing, the water running down the tired creases of her body, but her eyes as bright and alive as the sun-light that comes streaming into the bathroom through the open win-dow. A building, low and shabby and comfortable—a homestead—and lemon trees around, with a verandah out at the front and three old peo-ple in the shade there watching the fields and hills while two children play in the dust.

It's the best I can do for them. It's taken thirty years, and all that time I've thought that it was my own life I was leading. But it's done now, and now that I can see it, I don't begrudge any of it. I don't regret it. Something was owed, and I've done the best I can.

The house is finished. The painting is finished. As I walk through the empty rooms, they're filled with light and colour. The walls are bright and freshly painted, and the morning sun comes in through the windows and makes big rectangles of warmth on the floors. Lena's kitchen is white and scrubbed and clean, and the verandah glows in the sun with white, and the ceiling of stars is back the way it should be, and all around the walls are these images, these faces: Jamie and Anna.

*   *   *

I look around at what I've done, and everything is as it was when I was a child. I've taken my hands and I've remade the past, and while I've done so, the past has somehow caught me up as well: flooded into me and through me, until at last I have been able to see it clearly. Now it is over. Thirty years are gone, and I understand.

There will be buses in the town, if I go and wait in the square; but I won't do that. I'll walk. There is a little village inland where I can catch a lift, and besides, there is one last thing to be done.

I leave my bag. I've worn out the few changes of clothes I brought; there's nothing worth packing. I get dressed in the most presentable shirt and trousers I can manage, and stuff wallet and passport into a pocket. I leave the images ranged around the walls where they are; they belong here, after all. They won't last for ever, none of it will. The house will sell and what I have made here will be painted over; or it will fade with mould and damp and lose itself that way. Time will rub it out somehow. It doesn't matter: I don't need it any more. I leave it all, and close the door, stepping out into the clean bright sunshine.

Along the old farming tracks, lizards skitter away among the dry scrub of the verges, and blink at me with jewel-like eyes from the dry stones of the little walls. Along the bed of the empty river, red dust kicks up in little puffs as I walk. The sky is very blue, cupped in the twin arms of the hills.

The day's heat fades out under the stone pines. It's always cooler here. I stand on the springy cushion of fallen needles and stare at the chapel.

Things have changed since I was last here. The bushes and weeds have grown over far more of the churchyard, and one side of the building is green and tangled with creeper. Tiles have come loose from the roof and are broken on the ground all about, and a sapling is growing strongly in the shadow of the building, just by the corner, its trunk as thick as my wrist. The great double-doors at the near end are the same, but the side door has been patched across with a heavy piece of sheet steel, and twin zinc-plated padlocks hold a thick steel bar in place across it. There's no way into the chapel any more.

I clap my hands, and the noise is like a gunshot: there's a flutter, and pigeons whirl away out of the belltower. I smile to myself: so that, at least, hasn't changed.

I have to struggle to fight my way through the bushes that have come up at the side of the chapel, but at last I can crouch down and feel with my hand in the matted grass for the little grating that I know is there. I find it, and tug it loose; it comes away reluctantly.

The three rifle shells are dark, corroded with age and damp. Even the shiny, pointed bullets that cap them have dulled. Three rounds in the magazine, three spare in the case. If you can't do the job with three shots—with one—it's already too late. I hold them in my hand, and their weight is strange there, and cold.

It wouldn't have mattered, if she'd told me. It wouldn't have changed anything.

It's only a little way to the rusty iron fence. I grip the shells and close my eyes briefly. They're all that's left, now, of the oath we made never to tell. Then I throw them far out, over the grey-green bushes and swaying weeds of the bank, into the dry dust of the empty river. I stare after them for a while, and then turn back to the chapel. There's no way in any more, but I still have to see.

On one knee I get down and put my face in close against the wood of the big doors, finding the cracks I looked through last when I was eight.

The interior of the chapel is murky, as it always was; but there are bright shafts of light coming through the gloom, from the places where the tiles have come off, and there is the glow of the stained-glass window at the far end. Enough to see the dusty floor, and the old jumble of pews. Somewhere in the shadows, I suppose, the plaster Christ must still be lying, one hand outstretched towards the ceiling.

From somewhere in the half-light comes the sound of a girl's voice singing softly; the words both familiar and unfamiliar.

Aludj baba, aludjál;
Feljöt má a csillag.

I know them now. *Sleep, baby, sleep; the stars have risen in the sky.* A lullabye.

I stand up, and draw away from the building a little. The nearness of that voice has taken me by surprise, but I find there's no pain any more.

What do you call a clock without hands?

I don't know.

I look up. There, high above me, is the dandelion clock, watching me as always with its implacable blank gaze. I look at it straight, returning its stare unwavering, remembering how I thought once I might be able to force it into blinking first. I stare at it, and the clock stares back. As the minutes pass, my eyes start to water with the glare from the whiteness of the wall, but I don't look away. I don't blink. I stare and stare as if, this time, I might be able to make it happen. I stare and I don't look away.

The face of the clock is not a face any longer. Its smooth surface is a vast plain, impossibly huge, stretching out to the horizon in all directions. It is bigger than the chapel, bigger than the valley; it is all that there is. I am stranded at its centre, while over me the sky is black and sharply glittering. In the distance, almost too far away to see, there are the ghostly shapes of the numerals of the hours, like low mountains on the horizon. I turn, staring about me, and I can see them all—the whole sequence, from midday to midnight.

There are no hands here to guide the time, to drag it relentlessly from one moment to the next, past and present and future. There is no single line: only surface. I can choose any direction, walk from one hour to another, and the order can be anything I choose. All the points on the plain are the same, all as easy to explore as each other, all within my reach. I look about me in wonder, and as my gaze sweeps across the expanse that is the clock-plain, faint scraps of image and recollection seem to jump to life wherever I look.

I'm Jamie. Pleased to meet you.

There was a hermit, you see, who lived there.

Here. This is the Silver Surfer. You'll like him. And here's Spider-Man. You know him, of course.

They break through the surface of the pitted bronze, which is the colour of dark leather, almost black under the dark sky.

I think we could get up there. Wouldn't it be great to dive from?

Wait. He doesn't want us to go.

Look at the dust in the river. It looks like moon dust.

Everywhere I turn there are fragments of time, caught in the surface and held there, as if in amber. I can tell that all I have to do is walk among them, let them wash up over me. I haven't been able to do this for nearly forty years, but it has come back to me, and I know I can now.

I think he shot someone.

I'm going to be eleven tomorrow.

I think I love you.

And there is a kitten playing in dry grass; and over there, three children huddled around a fire in a deserted chapel; and there, a boy with a telescope; and a red light from the head of a dark valley. I can go anywhere.

There is a rustle like turning pages; and I see the words clear on paper, sheet after sheet of them, packed in tightly, and I know that I could read them now. On the first page, alone in the blank whiteness of the paper, is one phrase standing alone. *In csak fegyver vagyok.*

I am only the gun.

And I remember the hermit's voice in the darkness: words I don't understand as I hear them, which I have to wait forty years to hear clearly and truly in my head. *I'm only the method; I don't make the choices. I am the gun and someone else pulls the trigger.*

I blink. I can't help it.

Then the huge expanse of the plain is gone, and I'm back under the stone pines. The clock is back in its belltower. The valley is back all around me, hot with the smell of resin and shrill with cicadas. I wonder how long it has been.

There's a sound from the bushes away to one side of the churchyard: a cracking of twigs and swish of leaves. A second later, I can hear a voice: a child.

"And then they locked it up, and no-one's ever been inside again, ever."

Another voice. "What was he like, then?"

"Oh, you know how hermits are. With a beard, and teeth all like this."

"Why'd he go away?"

"*I* don't know. He just walked away into the hills."

"Maybe he'll come back."

"Well, he *might*, but I think—"

The voice stops dead. I can see them, now: two small girls, maybe eight years old, their bright T-shirts standing out sharply among the dusty greenery. I see their faces freeze—the one who's been talking still has her mouth open—and their eyes go wide. They've seen me, I realize.

I say, "Don't worry. I'm not the hermit."

"It's the *hermit!*" the second girl squeals, and with that they're off, crashing away through the bushes. I hear two more piercing squeals, and then a torrent of giggles, before they're out of earshot; and I find myself smiling to myself. I wonder who they'll think I really am, once they've calmed down. With imagination, I suppose I could become a new hermit for them. I shake my head, still grinning, as I wander among the piles of masonry and timber that are grown through with generations of weeds.

There is a past, and I can go there if I want. I know that now. Whatever shifted in the avalanche, and closed off the way, has shifted again in these past few weeks: from that first scent of rosemary in my mother's garden. If I want, I can fall away into the past the way I did as a child. The message from the great bronze plain is very clear. I can stay here, surround myself with it, sleep under a ceiling of stars and fill the empty house with the people I've loved: with their laughter, and sadness, and friendship, and trust. I can be here for ever. Every moment can be a new moment: a first look; a first word; a first kiss. I have been given all these things back, and I can have them over and over again, for all time. I can immerse myself completely in them. Jamie and Anna and Alex, always and always, and always in the times when there was no blame or betrayal or pain or change, when nobody died and nobody was hurt. Just the times when it was all right and good.

There is more. I've glimpsed the pages of the manuscript that Anna had with her in Florence. Then, the words were meaningless to me; but now, I could go back with the knowledge gained in the years since. I could read them now. *I am only the gun.* I could break into this empty chapel, and sit in the belltower, and read her words, and maybe understand her—actually understand her, the way I never did.

I shake my head, smile. It's too late for that. I already understand her.

Somehow, through the painting, and through the remembering, I have brought them back inside me. It was never Altesa that was hollow. I have done enough. I can do something else, now.

I have no idea what it will be.

In getting them back, I have lost something. I've filled my life with Jamie and Anna without realizing, and now that the realization has come and it's all over, I have nothing left to paint. There's nothing else that will fill that space. I will have to start all over again; and I'm fifty years old, and everything in me says it's too late to make new beginnings.

I should be scared. I'm not. If anything, what I feel is—exhilaration.

In the dry riverbed, the rifle shells will bake in the sun, and the soft red dust will blow over them, and the lizards will skitter past. And when the summer ends and the rains come down from the hills, the river will fill and they will be swept down the channel of the river and out into the sea. Everything will be gone.

Above me, the dandelion clock hangs, patient, waiting. Across its surface is the past, laid out like a landscape in which I could lose myself for ever; but there are other landscapes through which to make a way.

I turn, and walk away from the chapel up the valley, towards the road that leads into the hills.

I don't know where I'm going.

There are crickets in the bushes by the track, and the smell of thyme from the roadsides. The late spring sunshine is warm on my face as I walk. Above me, the pigeons are starting to fly back from the distant trees to which they've scattered.

The past is mine again, and I don't want it any more. I feel like laughing, or shouting, or singing.

Mad Alex, a faint voice grins, and I grin back.

I gave them what I could, and it's enough. I am whole. The valley is bright and warm as I walk away from it into the hills.

I feel alive.

GUY BURT won the W.H. Smith Young Writers Award when he was twelve. He wrote *The Hole*, his first novel, when he was eighteen, and his second novel, *Sophie*, soon thereafter. Burt attended Oxford University and taught for three years at Eton. He lives in Oxford.